MURDER IN THE LATIN QUARTER

BOOK 7 OF THE MAGGIE NEWBERRY MYSTERIES

SUSAN KIERNAN-LEWIS

SAN MARCO PRESS

Murder in the Latin Quarter. Book 7 of the Maggie Newberry Mysteries. Copyright © 2016 by Susan Kiernan-Lewis. All rights reserved.

Books by Susan Kiernan-Lewis

The Maggie Newberry Mysteries
Murder in the South of France
Murder à la Carte
Murder in Provence
Murder in Paris
Murder in Aix
Murder in Nice
Murder in the Latin Quarter
Murder in the Abbey
Murder in the Bistro
Murder in Cannes
Murder in Grenoble
Murder in the Vineyard
Murder in Arles
Murder in Marseille
Murder in St-Rémy
Murder à la Mode
Murder in Avignon
Murder in the Lavender
A Provençal Christmas: A Short Story
A Thanksgiving in Provence
Laurent's Kitchen

The Stranded in Provence Mysteries
Parlez-Vous Murder?
Crime and Croissants
Accent on Murder
A Bad Éclair Day
Croak, Monsieur!
Death du Jour

Murder Très Gauche
Wined and Died
A French Country Christmas

An American in Paris Mysteries
Déjà Dead
Death by Cliché
Dying to be French
Ménage à Murder

The Irish End Games
Free Falling
Going Gone
Heading Home
Blind Sided
Rising Tides
Cold Comfort
Never Never
Wit's End
Dead On
White Out
Black Out
End Game

The Mia Kazmaroff Mysteries
Reckless
Shameless
Breathless
Heartless
Clueless
Ruthless

Ella Out of Time

Swept Away
Carried Away
Stolen Away

The French Women's Diet

1

There's something about the way the air smells in Paris, Maggie thought, taking in a deep breath. *Not exactly lavender and fresh baked bread, but not far off either.* She immediately started coughing until her eyes watered.

"Quit breathing so deeply," her best friend Grace said. "Paris is having a garbage strike, for God's sake."

Maggie nodded and rearranged her six month old daughter in her arms. Little Mila Grace blinked her cornflower blue eyes at Maggie and gave her a toothless grin.

"Mommy's choking," Maggie said as she laughed and coughed again. "If I croak, you can tell your papa I died happy."

"Laurent wouldn't believe it," Grace said as she wiped the ice cream from her five-year-old daughter's face. They were sitting on a bench by the Seine. "He hates Paris, doesn't he?"

"Pretty much."

"It makes no sense." Grace wrinkled her nose. She was a stately blonde with a flawless complexion and perfect bow-shaped lips—a beauty in any language. "He was born here."

"That's part of the problem," Maggie said. "You know Laurent.

He's got so many secrets, God knows what horrors he's hiding about his life here when he was a kid."

"He really doesn't talk to you about his childhood?"

"Not a syllable. Really reinforces the whole *mystery guy* thing, let me tell you."

"Well, I'm glad you and the baby came up for the week," Grace said. "I can't wait for you to meet André."

Maggie was glad to see Grace embracing her new life. After two long years of indecision and heartbreak over the dissolution of her marriage, it was time to move on.

The spring was cooler than usual although every bit as wet. From where she sat with her back to the Seine, Maggie could see the line of immaculate upper class apartments in front of her like a carefully crafted barrier of style and heritage.

She had been only too happy to escape her country life in Provence for Paris—even if just for a week. A two and a half year old toddler and a six month old baby kept her busy all of the time back in St-Buvard. She smiled at how she'd accused Laurent of getting her pregnant just so she'd stop complaining about having nothing to do. God knows, between the grape harvest and her two little ones she couldn't *remember* a time when she had nothing to do. She'd jumped at the chance for a week in Paris with Grace—and her built-in childcare. Except for missing Jemmy, Maggie was very much enjoying the break.

"Dinner Thursday?" Grace said.

"Don't we pretty much have dinner every day?"

"Silly. I mean with André."

Maggie gazed down at the baby in her arms. Before she could respond, Grace said:

"No, Maggie. Just us. Darling Mila will be happy as two clams in a daiquiri with Beatrice and Zouzou."

"You just made that up about the clams and the daiquiri."

"I did."

"Well, it sounds disgusting. But I guess I can untether for the duration of a single meal." She looked at Mila. "Is that okay with you, puppy? If Mommy goes off with the grown ups?"

"Careful, darling," Grace said. "I don't have a cast iron stomach. Come on, let's get these two lambs back to the apartment. I feel a nap calling."

Maggie laughed and then dug out her vibrating cellphone.

"What time is it?" she asked. The screen showed a picture of her mother. With the time difference in Atlanta, Maggie always felt a tremor of fear if her folks called at an abnormally late hour.

"Two o'clock here," Grace said, "so nine in the morning in the US. Aren't you going to answer it?"

Maggie shook her head. "I'll call her back later."

Grace stood up and began scouting the sidewalk for a trash receptacle. "Something going on back home?" she asked.

"My mom wants me to bring the kids to Atlanta for the summer."

"Oh?" Grace waited for Maggie to climb to her feet and resettle Mila in her carrying sling. "Didn't they come over when Mila was born?"

"They did, yes."

"Does Laurent not want you to go?"

"That's just it. He says it'll be good for me to get away."

"Well, he's not wrong there, darling. You know how the provinces wear on you. I can't believe you're hesitating. When was the last time you were stateside?"

"Right after Jemmy was born. Almost three years now."

"So what's the problem?"

"I have a bad feeling about leaving."

"Oh, please. You mean like you're worried about the airplane falling out of the sky?"

Maggie took a long breath. "No, I'm afraid I won't want to come back."

∽

THE HOUSEKEEPER STOOD in the doorway of the kitchen and watched the old woman sitting in the living room. Was Madame breathing heavier than usual? Amelie felt a thin sheen of perspiration coat both her palms and she quickly wiped them against her apron. She could see Madame's eyes were closed even from here.

"Madame Normand?" Amelie said in a calm voice. "Are you all right?"

No answer.

A thrill of excitement needled between Amelie's shoulder blades.

"Madame?"

Amelie took two steps into the room. The thick carpeting underfoot eliminated any sound her heavy brogues made. The teacup was on the table with most of its contents drunk.

Amelie leaned across the old woman and carefully picked up the cup and saucer, her eyes never leaving Madame's face. Not a hint of a sound came from the old woman. Not a snore, not a purr.

Amelie crept back out of the room and down the hall to the kitchen. She noticed her hands trembled as she placed the cup and saucer in the sink and began to run water over them. As her hands worked to suds and rinse the china, she looked out the window over the sink. She could just see the spires of Notre-Dame from here but she felt the menace of its gargoyles as if they were perched on the apartment window ledge.

She knew this wasn't the same apartment. Of course not. Madame hadn't been wealthy then.

She dried the cup and saucer and carefully replaced it in the cabinet with the others. Then she took the vial from her apron pocket and poured its contents down the drain.

How soon before she could safely call for the ambulance? It would look bad to wait too long.

2

The minute Maggie and Grace opened the door, Grace's nanny Beatrice met them with arms held open to hug Zouzou and take the baby. A pretty girl in her mid-twenties, Beatrice had come to Paris from Le Havre on the western coast of France determined to be a professional au pair. Her fascination and love for little children beamed out of her.

"*Bonjour mes p'tits choux! Ça va?*" she gushed as she alternately kissed Mila and Zouzou's head. "Did *Maman* buy you ice cream?"

"*Mais oui!*" Zouzou said as she slipped her hand into Beatrice's. "And she said you'd read to us."

"But of course," Beatrice said with a laugh. She winked at Grace and Maggie and turned to disappear into the bedroom with the two children.

"Wow," Maggie said. "She really loves kids."

Maggie tried to remember her life before two children under the age of three dominated it. Did she really used to put her feet up and read a book? Or go to the bathroom or get dressed without an audience?

"Yes, and thank God for it," Grace said as she draped her raincoat on an armchair in the living room. "Drinkie, darling?"

"It's not even three o'clock."

Grace moved to the drinks cart by the fireplace. Her Left Bank apartment had been renovated in the late seventies preserving all the authentic and original details of a classic Parisian apartment, including carved moldings, curved doors, two working fireplaces, a series of gilt-framed mirrors, yards of glossy herringbone parquet throughout and—most amazing of all—built-in closets.

Grace's was the only apartment on her floor and with ongoing renovations being performed on the bottom two floors, she had the luxury of having the whole building to herself. While she was only renting, Grace was starting to talk more and more about making the owner an offer.

"So that's a no?" Grace said as she poured herself a whiskey and returned to the living room where she sat and kicked off her shoes.

Maggie had only been in Paris a day and already she knew something was off with Grace—and it wasn't just that she was in love.

"Heard from Windsor lately?" Maggie asked.

Grace made a face and took a long swallow of her drink.

"Turns out he doesn't know how to *spell* the word *amicable*," she said sourly.

"Really? Over what? Alimony?" Maggie knew Windsor well. He was generous to a fault and until his marriage had come crashing down on his head, devoted to Grace.

"Child custody if you can believe it," Grace said. She wore an original Valentino dress in deep green, its lines simple and streamlined on her slim body.

"Don't you have shared custody of Taylor and Zouzou?"

"Yes, but now he wants full custody. Bastard."

Maggie frowned. "That doesn't sound like Windsor."

"You don't know him as well as you think you do. It sounds exactly like him. And all because I suggested splitting Z and Taylor with him."

"What does that mean? Splitting them?"

"Well, I don't have Taylor, do I? She's in Indianapolis with her father and happy to stay there."

"So you asked for full custody of Zouzou and you offered to give up custody of Taylor?"

"And he's responded by trying to take Zouzou away from me!"

Maggie's head swam.

"I don't know, Grace. It might have sounded like you were trying to...abandon Taylor," she said carefully.

"That's absurd. Although, honestly, she refuses to come over here."

"She's only nine, Grace. Can't you go see her?"

"How can I, darling? You know how busy I am trying to get the business off the ground!"

Grace's online children's boutique had shown signs of promise at one point early on but Grace hadn't seemed too interested in it lately.

Not since she'd met André.

"Well, it's an online business," Maggie said reasonably. "Surely you can take your laptop and visit Taylor in the States this summer?"

"You sound like Windsor," Grace said, finishing off her drink. "My vendors are all in Paris and require face-to-face interaction. You know how business is done over here. I can't leave."

"And so Windsor wants full custody of both Taylor and Zouzou?"

"Can you imagine? He's hinting I'm not fit."

"That's ridiculous," Maggie said, leaning forward in agitation. "You're a wonderful mother!"

"Thank you, darling. Can we please talk about something else? How about we go out tomorrow morning and get you something to wear to dinner on Tuesday that's a little less provincial?"

. . .

THAT NIGHT AFTER DINNER, Maggie took Mila into the bedroom to Skype Laurent and little Jemmy. She had been looking forward to it all day. She was rarely separated from Jemmy and she missed him keenly.

"*Maman!*" he squealed as soon as the Skype screen opened up.

"Hello, sweetie. How is my big boy?"

"We are fine," Laurent said from behind Jemmy. The little boy squirmed on his father's lap, distracted. He didn't speak much yet but he was a lively, bright-eyed child who didn't miss a thing.

Laurent frowned. "Mila is sunburned, no?"

Maggie shifted the baby in her arms. "She is not sunburned, no," she said. "She got lots of fresh air today and a little bit of sun. You're one to talk, Laurent. I'll bet you rode the tractor today with Jemmy on your lap, didn't you?"

Laurent shrugged but a smile tugged at his lips as if in memory of the day. "*Peut-être,*" he said.

"Exactly. We sat near the Café de Flore this morning. Didn't you used to live near there as a kid?"

"*Non.*"

"Come on, Laurent. You can tell me your neighborhood, can't you? I want to take a selfie with me and Mila in front of it."

"Don't be *ridicule.*"

"What's ridiculous about wanting to see where you used to live?"

"There is nobody there now."

"That's not the point. Why do you think we have museums and statues and stuff? Because it's cool to go back to places and remember what happened there."

"I have no wish to remember."

"I can't believe Paris is your hometown and you never want to come here. Do you know how cool it is to be from Paris?"

"Tomorrow, put a hat on the baby, *si*?" Laurent said. "She is fair like you." He tossed Jemmy's hair. "Now, Monsieur Jemmy is like his papa, *non*? We were made for the Foreign Legion."

"He's not even three years old, Laurent," Maggie said. "He needs a hat too. In fact, it wouldn't hurt you to wear one." Mila squirmed and let out a fretful whimper.

"*Ma petite* is ready for bed," Laurent said. "We will let you go. Goodnight, *chérie*," he said, smiling fondly at them both.

"Night, Laurent. Sleep well, darling Jemmy," Maggie said. "Last separation until he's college age, okay? Hurts too much."

"*Je t'aime*, Maggie." He kissed his fingers and smiled.

"Love you too, Laurent," she said returning his smile.

There was a tap at the door and Beatrice stuck her head in.

"I have just put Zouzou to bed," she said. "Shall I take Mila too?"

"No," Maggie said. "I'll do it. Can you tell Grace to wait on me for that nightcap? Shouldn't take too long."

∽

MICHELLE NORMAND SAT at the café and drummed her fingers against the tabletop. The rain was coming down in a relentless deluge or she wouldn't be sitting here. She glanced at the interior of the café but the waiter was still engaged. As soon as he saw her he'd know she wasn't waiting to order. She hated that he'd know without even asking her, without even stepping out of the restaurant. And his face would tell her what his words didn't need to.

She wasn't welcome. She wouldn't be served even if she had money.

Michelle looked at the grey sheet of water pounding the cobblestones in front of her.

Was getting drenched better? Better than some stranger's disgust and revulsion?

She forced herself not to look in his direction again. She could see he was standing in the doorway now, watching her, waiting for her to look up so he could give her the sneer he'd prepared for her.

She wouldn't give him the satisfaction.

Let him come out here to throw me out.

She waited, the sounds of the rain drubbing in her brain and the shadow of the waiter's figure stark in her peripheral vision. And then he vanished, clearly not to be bothered with her.

It was days like this, moments like these, she thought, that her stepmother would pay for the most.

Because in the end it was not so much about the money...

But the sheer humiliation of it.

And that was a debt Delphine would pay for in blood.

3

The next morning Maggie was up before Grace. They'd talked long into the night and shared a bottle of wine although Maggie noticed that Grace drank most of it. While Grace seemed happy and effervescent all evening, something still didn't feel right with her. Was it the problems Grace was having with Windsor? Would he really try to get full custody of both children?

Maggie knew Laurent talked to Windsor now and then. Perhaps he knew more about what was going on. She made a mental note to ask him.

Beatrice walked into the room with a sleepy Zouzou in her arms.

"This little one has a runny nose," Beatrice said. "I think it best to keep her home today."

"Oh, I hope she's not sick," Maggie said. She instantly put her hand on Mila's forehead but the baby was cool, her face placid.

As Beatrice settled Zouzou in her chair at the kitchen table and turned to make her breakfast, Maggie's phone began to vibrate. Unless it was her mother again—unlikely at this hour—it could only be Laurent. She hadn't expected him to call so soon after last night. Her stomach clenched in anxiety.

"Hey," she said, answering. "What's wrong? Is Jemmy okay?"

"He is fine," Laurent said. "I need you to run a quick errand for me."

"An errand?" Maggie relaxed and spooned some stewed apples into Mila's open bow of a mouth.

"*Oui.* I have a phone call from a doctor not far from Grace's apartment. My great aunt is sick. Go check on her, yes? Five minutes, no more. Just to see she is well."

Maggie was speechless. *Laurent had a great aunt?* He'd never mentioned having any family. Except for his lowlife brother Gerard whom he hadn't heard from in five years, Maggie assumed there was none.

"Are you serious?" she said, the spoon poised in midair toward the baby's mouth.

"Not to make a big deal of this, *chérie*," Laurent said gruffly. "I don't have time to come up and do it myself."

"You never told me you had an aunt still alive," she said, putting the spoon down on the table.

"Her name is Delphine Normand. She lives at 16 rue du Bac in the Latin Quarter," he said. "Call me once you have seen her."

"Sure. No problem," Maggie said. "I'll go this morning."

"*Bon.* And *chérie*?"

"Yeah?"

"Just five minutes, *oui*?"

"Of course, Laurent. Trust me."

She heard him exhale a long sigh before signing off.

"Who was that?" Grace said as she came into the kitchen, her eyes were bleary and her hair uncharacteristically unkempt.

"You're not going to believe this," Maggie said "I'm about to meet someone who can confirm to me that Laurent had an actual childhood and wasn't hatched." She picked up the spoon and aimed it at the Mila's mouth. "Oh, we are going to have such fun today, aren't we, baby girl?"

～

"This is a very ritzy neighborhood, darling," Grace said as she and Maggie stood on the rue du Bac where it intersected rue de Lille. "Did you know Laurent came from money?"

Maggie jostled an unusually restless Mila in her sling as she peered up at the apartment building.

"He doesn't come from money," Maggie said. "His aunt must be rich through a marriage or something."

"I'd say Great Aunt Delphine isn't just well off—she's seriously loaded."

"So strange," Maggie murmured. "Laurent was on her next of kin contact list. The hospital called him late last night when she was ill. So she knows he's alive. And vice versa."

"Our Laurent is nothing if not a conundrum," Grace said, stopping to light a cigarette in the bright Paris morning.

"Well, not this time," Maggie said. "I'm squeezing the old dame for all her secrets. Laurent will be an open book by the time I'm finished with her."

"Remind me not to get old and feeble when you want something."

"You just can't appreciate how long I've wanted to know Laurent's story."

"Something tells me, darling, even after one of your famous interrogation sessions, that Laurent's secrets will still be intact."

"Yeah, well, we'll see about that. See you back at *mi-casa-su-casa*?"

"Let's try to master French before we branch out, why don't we?" Grace said, smiling and giving Maggie a small wave before leaving her on the sidewalk in front of the apartment building.

Grace was right. It was a really nice block. And that was

saying something for Paris, where all the wealthy residential blocks were gorgeous. This one, of course, was slightly different since it was in the Latin Quarter. Maybe the area didn't have its reputation for being bohemian back whenever this building was built? Maggie crossed the street and immediately saw the builder's plaque on the corner of the building. 1865.

Seriously cool before its time.

With its angled mansard roof, garret rooms, and dormer windows, the building was classic Haussmann—like any idealized version of Paris rooftops from *Madeleine* to *Rattatouie*. The building was fronted with the local cream-colored Lutetian limestone that gave the whole street a light, elegant presentation which continued on to the next building and the next, each with balconies and cornices perfectly aligned.

Maggie glanced at the GPS map on her cellphone. This was definitely the place. Not fifteen minutes from Notre Dame and five from the Université Paris-Sorbonne. Maggie felt a squeeze of sadness at the thought. Her sister Elise had attended the École des Beaux-Arts ten years ago.

A massive pair of towering walnut double doors were tucked into an ornate shelf of cut stone in the building she now faced off rue du Bac. Maggie looked to see if there was a directory to show the names of who lived inside but wasn't surprised not to find one. She gave Mila a quick kiss on the head and pushed open the doors to reveal a large green courtyard within. The windows and balconies of the apartments that looked down onto the little garden were full of the usual geraniums and climbing roses and while the building looked understated and sedate on the outside, inside it was clear that the wealthy of the Left Bank lived here.

Maggie followed the brick walkway through the courtyard to another set of doors, wondering how a ninety-two year old woman easily came and went across the bumpy brick walkway. Maybe she didn't have trouble walking? Most people Maggie knew back in the States were on walkers by the time they hit eighty but perhaps a lifetime of perambulating Paris had kept Aunt Delphine limber and sure footed.

Laurent said his aunt had become ill yesterday and her housekeeper had called an ambulance for her. He didn't believe it was a particularly close call—but at Delphine's age anything out of the ordinary was cause for alarm. She had a home health nurse but it had been the woman's night off. By the time the hospital had presumptively called Delphine's next of kin a friend of the family had come to drive her back to her apartment.

Even so. The call had been made and Laurent clearly felt he needed to respond in some way.

Was there bad blood between them? Maggie wondered. Knowing Laurent, it was a pretty safe bet that Aunt Delphine didn't even know Maggie existed—let alone her little great-grand nephew and niece. Perhaps this was a good opportunity to heal any family rifts? Laurent was a family man now. It was way *past* time to embrace the concept of family.

And that included his own.

4

The soldiers and their dogs swarmed the baggage claim for the Amsterdam carrier. Noel Lorraine carried his leather valise across the hectic setting and headed toward the taxi stands outside Charles DeGaulle Airport. He didn't really have time for this trip but his last conversation with his aunt had worried him. She'd sounded weaker than ever. Something in her voice had convinced him she was declining. In many ways it was what he'd been waiting for. He couldn't ignore it now.

Not with so much at stake. Could there be more at stake than one's own identity?

He waited in the taxi queue and scanned the skies over Paris.

Welcome to springtime in Paris, he thought dismally. Grey clouds ready to burst with rain any moment. He walked to the next taxi in line and climbed in. He was proud of his agility at his age. Seventy-one and still limber enough to carry his own luggage. Some of his friends were hobbling along on walkers at this age or at least used canes. But Noel had taken good care of himself. Always plenty of exercise and he watched his diet.

And of course thanks to the loving Fouquet sisters, money

had never been an issue.

"*Ou vas tu?*" the taxi driver asked.

"*Le Quartier latin,*" Noel said, leaning back into the seat.

This time he wouldn't take no for an answer. She wouldn't turn him away again. Not when time was running out for both of them. What did she possibly have to lose at this point?

He gripped the handle of his valise, his face falling into tight, tense lines.

She's dying anyway. This time, no matter what it takes.

Delphine will tell me the truth if I have to throttle it out of her.

∽

GRACE SETTLED into the leather couch of the corner brasserie. Even though it was not yet noon, she ordered a martini. Her hand rested on her cellphone. She'd just disconnected from André. He was late but hurrying toward her even now, striding down the rue Dante. She smiled at the image of him in her mind. His hair dark and wavy around his chiseled perfect cheekbones and eyes as blue as sapphires. She felt a delightful flutter in her stomach and her fingers tightened around the phone as if it was the closest connection she had to him.

Was there anything more exquisite than anticipation? She looked at the door to the restaurant. He would appear framed in that door at any moment. She would watch him scan the room with expectation—looking for her, hungering for her. She wouldn't move a muscle; no wave or eyebrow rise would indicate where she was.

Let him find me as a wolf finds its mate. Let him sense me and be drawn to me.

Her drink came and she downed it in one long swallow.

Her skin tingled as she resumed her focus on the door. Was it the alcohol or the anticipation? The sensual tingling, the anticipation...

Her phone rang and she snatched her hand away as if it burned her.

Her heart seemed to hiccup in her chest.

No. He wasn't calling to cancel. She had just talked to him.

The screen on her phone showed a smiling photo of her ex-husband Windsor.

She let out a snort of impatience. *Need to make this quick. André will be here any moment.*

"Yes, Windsor," she said coolly into the phone. "Now what is it?"

"I was hoping we could do this the friendly way." Windsor's voice was soft and so familiar. For a minute, Grace couldn't believe that this voice she knew so well was connected to the monster who was trying to ruin her life.

"What do you want, Windsor? I'm in a meeting."

"You haven't responded to anything my lawyer has sent to you—"

"Nor will I."

"I don't know why you need to make this as bad as it can be!"

"Why are you calling?" she said, her eyes going to the door but now fearfully. She didn't want Windsor to ruin this moment for her. Damn him. He ruined everything.

"I'm giving you a heads up, Grace. Come home with Zouzou or lose her for good. I am not kidding you. You need to quit ignoring—"

Grace disconnected the phone and set it down on the table. She had to. André had just walked through the door and he was looking for her. He didn't see her yet. Maybe she was sitting too far back? She shifted in her seat thinking the movement would catch his eye but he turned and stepped deeper into the restaurant just when she moved.

With a small soundless moan of frustration she saw the waiter watching her. She nodded for him to bring her another drink.

THE FOYER beyond the second set of doors was dimly lit, with only one small vertical window allowing a muted glow of light from the outside. It had looked like rain all morning and the light was murky at best. Maggie could see the floor was a pale yellow marble and again she couldn't help but wonder how an elderly woman walked across it without falling. Glancing at a brass mailbox on the wall, she noted the name *Madame Normand* was in apartment nine.

The stairs—also marble—curved around and disappeared upward in a steep spiral. The elevator was small. Its protective grill looked like it hadn't been replaced since the last world war.

What is with the French? Maggie thought with annoyance as she stepped into the elevator. She pulled the wrought iron grill back with a screech, waking Mila and causing her to begin crying. *You live in a multi-million dollar Haussmann era building smack in the heart of the Latin Quarter and you can't afford to put in a new elevator? Is the plan to wait until you plunge to your death in the old one first?*

Maggie knew the vast majority of Paris elevators located in nineteenth century buildings were retrofitted to the available space, which meant the elevator was often crammed into the shaft in the middle of spiral staircases leading to the upper floors. Depending on the size of the staircase, this often meant extremely small elevators were only able to comfortably accommodate one person at a time.

And that person not the normal sized American.

After a lifetime in Atlanta of everything brand new and virtually never-failing, it made Maggie nervous to trust her life—and the life of her baby—to a Frenchman's often relaxed work ethic.

Laurent said she was prejudiced because she assumed only Americans could build an elevator that worked every time. But Maggie knew you didn't have to live in France very long to know that many French workmen preferred to drink their lunch and show up at their job site every other day.

She jabbed the elevator buttons and sent a prayer upward, hoping that would cover her for her less than generous thoughts about French workmen and their work habits.

The elevator lurched to a stop on the fifth floor and Maggie quickly disembarked. Mila still hadn't calmed down—not that Maggie could blame her—but she was hoping that her first contact with Laurent's only living relative wouldn't be to the accompaniment of a screaming baby. Even Maggie knew that was off to a bad start.

The hallway that led to Delphine's apartment was as dimly lit as the foyer. The carpet was worn and thin. The pattern in it was still discernible, however, and went beautifully with the towering ten foot walls in the hall. It was quiet too. Enough so that little Mila's whimpers sounded particularly loud to Maggie.

"Shush, Mila!" she whispered. "We're going to meet your Auntie Delphine. Let's have a sweet smile when we meet her, okay?"

Mila blinked at Maggie as if listening. She stopped crying.

Aunt Delphine's door—number nine—was at the end of the hall. They must be large apartments, Maggie thought. There was only one other door in the hallway. The stairs curved upward to more apartments on the higher floors.

She squinted down the hall and in the gloom saw something dark lumped on the floor at the foot of the stairs opposite the door to apartment nine, which was ajar.

Maggie knew the French were always having garbage strikes and got ready to hold her breath as she neared. But usually the bags of trash were outside in the courtyard or on the sidewalk, not in the hallway.

In two steps, she saw the dark lump was not garbage at all.

But a woman's body.

5

"Mademoiselle?" Maggie said in a hollow voice, her heart beginning to pound in her chest. The body didn't move but a noise on the stairs leading up to the next floor made Maggie start.

Was somebody up there? She looked back at the woman on the floor and knelt by her. Before she touched her, she saw the gaping wound across her throat, and the pounding in Maggie's chest turned into jackhammers.

And someone is waiting on the stairs.

Maggie stood and turned in the direction of the stairs but she glanced down at Mila.

No. Effing. Way.

The sound came again. This time closer—as if whoever was up there...was coming down.

The door to Delphine Normand's apartment was open. Without thinking, Maggie slipped inside the apartment and closed the door quietly behind her, her breathing coming in ragged pants. Mila was whimpering louder now. Maggie locked the door and stood by it, pressing the baby against it in her attempt to see through the security hole.

A dark shape—a man's shape—jumped from the stairs, bounded over the body and ran down the steps. It happened too fast for Maggie to glimpse his face. One minute he was there in a flash of shadow and the next the landing was empty.

Maggie turned, leaning against the door and patting Mila's back. She tried to get her heart rate to slow down by taking deep breaths. She glanced around the foyer.

The door had been open. Had the dead woman come from in here?

"Madame?" Maggie called timidly. "Madame Normand?"

Mila let out a long wail, making Maggie jump. She took a few steps into the apartment. A huge chandelier hung over an impressive foyer of Versailles-style parquet flooring.

Maggie stepped through the foyer to the salon. A floor to ceiling window facing in the direction of the river allowed a sick cast of grey light into the room. Louis XVI chairs abutted an antique leopard-print sofa with matching Chinese porcelain lamps on flanking walnut tables. Maggie found herself holding her breath as she entered the room.

Thickly carpeted with an ancient coral Isfahan rug, the room spoke gentility and grace. Except for the window every wall was covered in gilt-framed paintings of all sizes. Maggie knew little about art and she didn't recognize any of the artists but even she could see they were examples of impressionism, realism and art deco.

"Wow, baby girl," Maggie whispered. "Your great aunt Delphine has got some serious class." She did a slow one-eighty examining the room before ending up staring at the front door again.

"Along with a dead body on her welcome mat," she said, digging out her cellphone.

∼

DELPHINE CLUTCHED VICTOR'S arm as she approached the apartment building. Although at his age it was a toss up what was more stable, him or her luck without him on the broken pavement. Although she knew he preferred his walker when he was indoors, his vanity made him switch to the walking stick when they were out. Their favorite restaurant, *La Table d'Angelino*, was easy walking distance from her apartment and so when they turned off boulevard Saint-Germain they were able to see from two blocks away the clutch of police vehicles parked in front of her building on Rue du Bac.

Victor tensed immediately and put his hand on top of hers as if the motion could somehow protect her from whatever was coming.

Was it a break in? Delphine wondered. With so many police, perhaps it was terrorism? She took a step toward the building and realized that Victor was not moving. She looked at him.

"Let us wait until the police have resolved things," he said. "If it is a bomb or a hostage situation…" He pointed to the building. "You see they are keeping the crowd back."

Delphine did see and it annoyed her greatly. After lunch she was looking forward to a nice cup of tea and a nap. Her legs were tired from the walk and she had stupidly not dressed warmly enough for her outing.

"I will tell them I live there," she said to him, tugging him gently to continue walking.

"Will that matter if there is a bomb in the building?" Victor said, although he allowed her to nudge him forward. He was a handsome man for his eighty-three years, Delphine thought. He'd kept his hair and had not put on too much weight over the years. That was the key.

But he was fearful, as only the elderly can be. It was as if he was constantly cataloguing all the things that could fall on him, crush him, run over him—*and at our age that was just about every-*

thing. Delphine was nearly ten years older than Victor and she could tell him and anyone else with the sense to listen—terrorist bombs not withstanding, the things that could really hurt you lived inside your heart.

"I see Amelie," Delphine said, dropping her hand from Victor's arm to point to her housekeeper standing in the crowd. Delphine wasn't surprised to see her cowering in the back. She was a timid woman—especially with authority. Delphine had found the characteristic useful on more than one occasion.

"And they are not letting *her* in either," Victor said stubbornly. "Oh! They are bringing out a stretcher!"

Delphine and Victor watched as the gurney—with its covered form—was carried out of the front door of the apartment building to a waiting coroner's wagon.

"Perhaps one of the older ones?" Delphine murmured. Although at ninety-two she knew she definitely qualified for the label herself.

"Why would the police come in riot gear for a simple death in the building?" Victor asked as they joined the people who stood gaping at the front of the building. Delphine knew they could see nothing—unless whoever the poor soul was had died in the courtyard—which was not completely out of the question. A fall or jump from any of the facing courtyard balconies would easily result in a trip to the morgue.

"It must be something else," Delphine murmured. Her legs ached and she knew, as weary as she was becoming, that her hands would soon begin to tremble. She probably should not have gone to lunch with Victor so soon after her illness. She'd only just come home from the hospital that morning. But she hated weakness, especially in herself. And to have begged off a standing engagement when even the doctor said she was perfectly fine would have put her out of sorts for the rest of the day.

"Excuse me!" Victor said loudly over the heads of the crowd. One of the policemen looked up.

"Are you allowing residents to return to their homes?" Victor asked.

The policeman beckoned Victor forward and he and Delphine pushed their way through the crowd. Delphine saw Amelie, her head tucked, moving quickly behind them.

"Your name, Monsieur?" the policeman said.

"I am Victor Rousseau," Victor said in a firm voice. "And this lady lives here."

"I am Delphine Normand," Delphine said. "Apartment nine."

The policeman looked at his notes and then waved Delphine closer as he lifted the yellow crime tape that had been stretched across the front of the building entrance.

"And my housekeeper?" Delphine said, half turning toward Amelie. "She is to clean today."

The police nodded but put a hand on Victor's chest as he attempted to follow Delphine and Amelie.

"*Non*, Monsieur," the policeman said.

"What?" Victor said, outrage creeping into his voice. "I must accompany Madame Normand!"

"*Non*."

Delphine took Victor's hand. "It's all right, *chéri*," she said. "I'm going straight to bed any way. Thank you for a lovely lunch as usual."

"But, Delphine..." Victor said, his eyes on the policeman.

"I will be fine," Delphine said. "I will call you later." She turned and followed the policeman into the courtyard. Several more police stood talking in the courtyard. One peeled away and looked at her with a questioningly look.

"She lives here," the policeman said. "Where the body was discovered."

Delphine took in a harsh breath. Instantly she regretted

sending Victor away. The other policeman nodded and turned to Delphine and Amelie.

"We will ask you a few questions, Madame," he said sternly.

AN HOUR after making it as clear as she could that she had been gone all afternoon and could have no information to give them about why the poor woman, whoever she was, had come to be murdered outside her apartment, Delphine and Amelie were escorted upstairs to her apartment.

As they climbed the stairs, all Delphine could think of was the luxury of peeling off her shoes and sinking onto her couch. She would ask Amelie to make her a cup of tea before the woman even put her handbag down.

The hallway was full of people and Delphine could see her apartment door was open.

The nerve! How dare they just come inside?

If her legs hadn't been so shaky at this point, she would have pushed past the young policeman and strode into her apartment to demand an explanation for this invasion.

As it was, when she got to her front door, she saw there were more police inside, standing, their guns strapped to their belts, and amazingly, there was a young woman sitting on her couch talking into a cellphone.

A young woman with a baby!

"Yeah, okay, Laurent," the woman was saying in English. "I'll call you as soon as I talk to her. No, I don't know when exactly. Yes, I—oh, hold on, Laurent. I think she's here. I'll call you back."

Delphine walked into her apartment to where the woman sat on the couch. Her intention had been to demand the woman leave her apartment immediately—or at least remove herself from her furniture. But when she saw the baby's face, her legs betrayed her and she staggered to the couch and sat down heavily next to her.

"Oh, this must be so upsetting for you," the woman said. "I'm so sorry. Can I get you something, Madame Normand?"

Delphine looked at her and drew herself up as if she was in complete control of herself and wasn't about to collapse into an exhausted heap on the rug.

"And you are?" she said, her voice trembling.

6

"I'm your nephew's wife," Maggie said. "Laurent Dernier? We have a farm in the south?"

The old woman's eyes never left Mila's face. Maggie decided to take that as a good sign. A sour-faced middle aged woman had come in with Delphine and by the way she jerked her jacket off and deposited her purse on a chair Maggie got the impression she was more servant than friend.

Aunt Delphine looked done in. Her face was white and the veins vivid and pronounced under her eyes.

"They said I could make tea or coffee," Maggie said. "Would you like something?"

Delphine's eyes went from the baby to Maggie.

"You are?"

"Laurent's wife," Maggie repeated. "Laurent Dernier, your nephew." Maggie pulled out her phone and called Laurent.

"Yes, *chèrie*?" he answered.

"Talk to your aunt," Maggie said. "She's had a shock." She handed the phone to Delphine who took it.

"*Oui*?" she said.

Maggie got up with Mila on her hip and pushed her way into

the kitchen to put the kettle on. The middle aged woman who'd come in with Delphine was in the kitchen, her back rigid, energetically wiping down the already spotless counters.

When Maggie stepped back into the living room with a mug of tea, she saw that Delphine had put the phone down next to her on the couch. Maggie handed her the mug and then crossed the living room to turn on one of the Chinese porcelain jar lamps. Through the tall northeast-facing windows she could just see a glint of the Seine in the distance.

She sat back down with Mila on her lap. The baby kicked her feet and clapped her hands. Maggie thought she caught a hint of a smile as the old woman watched the child.

Delphine's color seemed to be a little better after her conversation with Laurent. Her face was more relaxed too. Maggie was sorry to miss the phone conversation but she guessed her French likely wouldn't have been good enough to understand it anyway.

"I can't imagine how horrible this must be for you," Maggie said. "Did you know the dead woman?"

Delphine made a pained face as if the tea had suddenly gone bad.

"She was my home health nurse," she said quietly. "Isla."

"It's really terrible. I'm so sorry for your loss."

Delphine narrowed her eyes at Maggie as if examining her for the first time.

"I am surprised my nephew married," she said.

Well, that's an odd thing to say, Maggie thought. She wasn't sure how to respond.

The unhappy woman from the kitchen came into the room, a dishtowel in her hands and spoke abruptly to Delphine. Again, she spoke as an employee might. Not as a friend.

Maggie was able to make out that she was telling Delphine the police were about to leave.

Delphine nodded and placed her mug on the coffee table.

She looked at Maggie and the expression on her face was clear—Laurent's wife or not—she expected Maggie to be on her way too.

Maggie thought about pretending not to understand but she had a feeling the old girl could be very straightforward when necessary.

She stood up and gathered her purse and Mila's little cardigan. She didn't want to start their relationship out on the wrong foot.

Bad enough they had to work around the whole dead body thing.

∼

Laurent gestured to Jemmy to pick up his toys in the living room. Instead the child threw a ball at their little poodle. The dog yelped—mostly in surprise, Laurent was sure. The ball was a soft one.

"What was that?" Maggie said on the phone line.

"Your son putting his toys away," Laurent said.

"Sounded like Petit-Four."

"In any case," Laurent said as he watched Jemmy from the kitchen, the boy's half-eaten dinner still on the counter, "you are on your way back to Grace's?"

"I am."

"You should take a taxi."

"It's not even six blocks. I like the walk. So what did your aunt say when you talked to her?"

Laurent sighed. He should have called Delphine rather than send Maggie. It would have been better for everyone if he had.

"She was glad to hear that meeting *ma femme* does not always result in a dead body on her doorstep although I told her it often does."

"Very funny. Was she astounded to hear from you?"

"Since you had *her* call *me*? No."

"Jeez, Laurent, did you two talk? At all?"

"I asked after her health and she assured me she was fine. Jemmy, stop that."

"What's he doing?"

"It doesn't matter. Promise me you are not thinking of investigating this woman's death."

"Of course not. The cops said it was a burglary gone wrong."

"How is the baby?"

"Still alive. Surprised?"

"Your mother called."

Jemmy ran back to Laurent, giggling for no apparent reason that Laurent could see and he pulled him into his lap.

"Don't tell me she's trying to talk you into making me come home for the summer," Maggie said. "She's relentless."

"It is a good idea," Laurent said, kissing Jemmy on the forehead.

"Won't you miss us?"

"That is a ridiculous question."

"Wow, you old sweet talker," Maggie said. "Hey, did I tell you the dead woman was your aunt's home health nurse?"

Laurent gave a grunt of frustration. "I would like to know why these things always happen when you are around."

"Delphine has to make an inventory of anything she thinks is missing."

"Are you not at Grace's yet? Next time you must take a taxi."

"Are you staying on the phone with me until I'm safely at Grace's place?"

"You are a lone woman in a major metropolitan city with a six month old baby. Why must I explain this to you?"

"It's not even dark yet. There are lots of people everywhere. I'm perfectly safe."

"That is what you always say just before I am calling the police or pulling you out of car trunks."

"Your aunt told me you were a very quiet boy."

"*Non*," Laurent said, settling Jemmy down on the chair by his dinner plate.

"*Non* you *weren't* a quiet boy?"

"*Non* you are not to interrogate a ninety-two year old woman to satisfy your own curiosities."

"Well, I suppose I could go through all her letters and photo albums but I thought this way was less invasive."

"You have no need to see my aunt again."

"That's where you're wrong, Laurent. We're going shopping tomorrow."

"I do not believe you."

"You don't need to," Maggie said cheerfully. "And after that she says she'll dig up every single photograph of you there is in existence. Baby pictures, grade school report cards. The works."

"I forbid you to do this, Maggie."

Maggie laughed. "Oh, darling, I love you so much! When will you learn that that's not a thing in marriage these days?"

"This is not funny, *chérie*," he said firmly.

"Maybe not. But it's absolutely necessary. Kiss my baby boy for me, and save one for yourself. I'm at Grace's safe and sound. Good night, Laurent."

"Maggie…"

But she'd hung up. Laurent tossed the cellphone on the counter and saw Jemmy was watching him with questioning eyes while holding a fork of Laurent's *boeuf en Daube* poised in midair.

"*Ça ne fait rien*," Laurent said to him, his face relaxing as he reassured his son. "All is well."

Jemmy attacked his plate while the little poodle sat in position by his chair ready for whatever came next.

∽

MAGGIE SLID the phone into her jacket pocket and gave the baby a kiss.

"Your papa doesn't need to know every detail of what we do. Remember that, Mila. On the other hand, *you* must never keep secrets from your *maman*, ever..." She kissed the baby again. "But you already know that."

It had been a long walk from Delphine's to Grace's and Maggie felt the exertion in her legs.

What a wild afternoon. Not just discovering the body of that poor woman but the actual meeting with Laurent's aunt too.

Maggie cringed at the memory. No, Great Aunt Delphine had *not* been pleased to clap eyes on Maggie. She looked tired and every minute her ninety-two years. *Laurent needn't worry about girl talk and bistro outings with his aunt, that was for sure.*

She looked up at the front of Grace's building. Maggie hadn't had a moment to think of Grace all day, let alone text her to see what her plans were.

She unlocked the front door and the aroma of cassoulet wafted out from the kitchen.

That can't be Grace. Maybe her boyfriend cooks?

"Hello, Madame Dernier," Beatrice sang out from the kitchen. Zouzou stuck her head out and smiled shyly at Maggie.

"Hey, Beatrice," Maggie said as she unwrapped Mila from the sling. Maggie was looking forward to a hot shower and a big glass of Merlot so she could debrief with Grace on the day's bizarre happenings.

"I will take her, yes?" Beatrice said, wiping her hands on a towel as she came out of the kitchen. "The cassoulet is baking."

"Are you sure?" Maggie asked. "She needs changing."

"But of course," Beatrice said as she took Mila and tweaked the baby on the cheek.

"Grace not here?" It was obvious she wasn't. Grace wasn't someone who could be in an apartment—even hiding in a closet or sound asleep—and not fill it up entirely with her presence.

"Madame Van Sant is out for the evening," Beatrice said over her shoulder as she walked down the hall with the baby in her arms and Zouzou trailing behind.

Maggie frowned. She pulled out her phone but she was sure she hadn't missed a call. No texts either.

She sat down on the couch and slipped her shoes off. A feeling of unease grew subtly between her shoulder blades.

What the hell was going on with Grace?

∼

DELPHINE HEARD the door click behind Amelie as she left for the day. Usually, she hated the sound of Amelie in her apartment, convinced the woman was nosier than she needed to be just to irritate an old woman helpless to escape the rudeness of others. But tonight she was sorry to see her go.

It wasn't just that Delphine had gotten used to having someone with her at night—although that was certainly true. Isla was a dear girl and Delphine would miss her dearly.

But Delphine felt insecure tonight.

She moved into her bedroom and removed her shoes, placing them in the oversized painted armoire.

Was it really a burglary? Do people often cut the throats of those they steal from?

Delphine's attention was caught by her movement in the mirror over her makeup bench. An old woman stared back at her. A hunched over old woman who hadn't put on makeup for a decade.

Was she no longer safe here? A chill shot down her neck and she involuntarily pulled her cardigan tighter around her although she was meant to be undressing.

Had she ever been safe?

The police told her to make a list of anything stolen. She could understand how, when they saw her apartment, that theft might be the first thing they thought of. She would look around tomorrow after she was rested.

But she knew she would discover nothing missing.

She'd known that from the moment she'd entered the apartment.

From the moment when, in a glance, she'd seen that *it* was still safe.

Delphine sat on the side of her bed and unrolled her hose until they sat like fat doughnuts around each ankle. She'd been mad to go to lunch today. She was beyond exhausted now. And with Isla gone, all alone.

She took her diamond earrings off with a shaking hand and placed them in the dish by her bedside.

Laurent's wife and baby had distracted her from feeling the full brunt of what had happened. She was so astonished to see the woman—right in her own living room—that much of the horror of the day had been muted.

And she had been dreadful to her. American, true, but even so, friendly and willing to endure the insults of a nasty old woman.

And then the baby.

Delphine smiled in memory and touched her lips. The child had the Dernier lips, to be sure. But the eyes—they showed she was a Fouquet through and through. The minute Delphine saw her, looking so much like little Georgette as an infant, that Delphine's legs had given way beneath her.

So few babies had been born in this family over the years. And after the sisters, no girls at all. Well done, Laurent. Your grandmother would have adored her.

Delphine unbuttoned her sweater. The chill she'd felt earlier had turned into a damp film of icy perspiration. Her eyes settled on the locked drawer in her lingerie chest.

The drawer where she kept the key.

Perhaps the murder was a coincidence?

Perhaps someone in the apartment building *was* doing something criminal...and poor Isla just happened to see. But why would Isla be in the hallway? What reason would she have?

The police said the man entered the apartment without breaking the lock. They said the man thought the apartment was empty. When the man encountered poor Isla, she ran.

As far as the hallway.

Delphine stood and released the belt at her waist. With a tug, her silk dress slipped from her bony hips and pooled at her feet. She kicked it toward the armoire. Amelie would deal with it tomorrow. A thought crept unbidden into her head. It occurred to her that it was too bad it had been Isla in the apartment today instead of Amelie.

Delphine's cheeks burned at the thought. Amelie was angry and unhappy. It was Delphine's just lot in life to endure the censure in the poor woman's face every day until Delphine finally left this earth. Delphine knew she should be grateful for the opportunity.

But she wasn't. No real amends could be made by enduring Amelie's rancor. It helped no one. Least of all Amelie. Delphine wished the wretch would just go away.

As she stood to walk to the bathroom her thoughts returned to poor Isla and how much she would miss her.

And how unfair some things were.

7

Maggie flipped the collar up on her jacket. The brisk breeze off the Seine seemed to target her as she pushed Mila's stroller up the rue du Bac, the Quai Voltaire at her back. The sun had made a showing but the wind cancelled out any real benefits of it.

Maggie didn't know what to make of the fact that not only had Grace not responded to any of Maggie's texts all evening but she'd only tersely responded to Beatrice's. Just enough to assure the sitter she was alive.

Boy, this André guy must be something special, Maggie thought with annoyance. If it weren't for the fact that Maggie felt like she had something important to do today—try to make a good second impression on Aunt Delphine—she'd probably spend the morning obsessing over what was going on with Grace.

A pigeon launched up from a nearby bench on the sidewalk and startled Maggie. Mila, her eyes wide, laughed and clapped her hands. It was quiet for a Tuesday, Maggie thought. The boulevard was dotted with trees on this stretch heading into the residential section of the Latin Quarter. She knew if she kept walking she'd hit the popular bookstore Gilbert Jeune. Jemmy was at just the right age to enjoy all their colored markers and *cahiers*. Maggie made a mental note to run by there after her visit with Delphine.

She walked up the rue du Bac, marveling that Delphine lived so close to the Musée d'Orsay and imagining that she and Mila might spend an afternoon there with her sometime.

"Who am I kidding?" she said to Mila. "Your daddy's people are just like him. Total Sphinxes, every one of them."

The weather was fine—for a change not raining—and within moments, Maggie was standing in front of the old and beautifully imposing apartment building. This part of the street had picked up in noise level—between all the tourists and the increased traffic. Maggie was surprised that Delphine's apartment inside had been so quiet

She crossed the interior courtyard and pushed open the double doors that led into the marble foyer. Frowning at the tiny elevator, she decided it was probably just large enough to hold her and the stroller. It would have to. Dragging a stroller up four flights wasn't an option.

She centered the stroller in the elevator, straddled it, then pushed the floor button. She winced at the sound of the creaking gears as the cables haltingly pulled the elevator upwards.

Next time bring the sling, she thought, holding her breath until the elevator stopped with a lurch on the fifth floor. She threw back the wrought iron grill and pushed the stroller into the hallway.

A part of Maggie knew she probably should have called first. But in her experience, giving people advance notice usually didn't work out in her favor. She knocked on the apartment door, then caught Mila's eye and smiled, hoping the baby's good mood would last for as long as it took Delphine to send them away again.

The door opened and the same sour-faced woman who'd been tidying up yesterday stood there frowning.

"*Oui*?" she said.

Tempted to say she was selling Girl Scout cookies—*I mean, honestly, what does she think I want?*—Maggie kept her smile firmly in place.

"Is Madame Normand at home?" she asked sweetly.

"*Non*," the woman said and began to shut the door.

"Amelie?" a voice called from the living room. "Who is it?"

Amelie sighed and looked at Maggie.

"I am her niece by marriage," Maggie said. "Come to pay a visit if she's up to it."

"Have them come in!" Delphine called.

Amelie let out a snort of disgust and turned away, leaving Maggie to push the stroller into the apartment and shut the door behind her.

Delphine was sitting on the couch in the living room. A large decorative white marble fireplace was behind the couch flanked by twin ancient sconces.

"*Bonjour*, Madame Normand," Maggie said, her face flushed with hopeful expectation.

"You are my niece by marriage, are you not?" Delphine said, a small smile playing on her lips. Her eyes were on the stroller. "So you must call me Delphine. And who is this?"

Maggie pushed the stroller into the living room and lifted Mila out.

"This is Mila Grace," Maggie said, settling the baby on her knee. Mila instantly grinned at Delphine. Drool dribbled down her plump cheeks.

"She is beautiful," Delphine whispered, reaching out a long bony hand to touch the sleeve of Mila's pink cardigan. Delphine seemed entranced by the baby—which Maggie was only too willing to believe since *she* often spent many minutes herself watching Mila with awe.

"Amazing. This is Laurent's child," Delphine said, her eyes

moist. She looked at Maggie. "And you are his wife. So, he is not in prison."

Wow. Way to come to the point.

"Nope," Maggie said cheerfully. "Knock on wood."

Delphine turned to call toward the kitchen. "Amelie! Tea for two." She glanced back at Mila and smiled. "And cookies!"

∼

MICHELLE SQUINTED at her disposable phone and punched in the number. She stood at the edge of the platform at the train station at Paris Nord. Most of the beggars had something to offer. One fat man who'd surely missed very few meals sat with two sleeping dachshunds in his lap.

Another old woman played the violin. The dachshund man was doing better even though all he was doing was sitting and holding his dogs. Michelle had heard that the beggars kept pets with them because it ensured they could not be taken to jail.

At least the old woman was trying to give some kind of service for the money she begged.

Would it come to that? If it did what could Michelle offer? As it was, people tended to detour around her even as she walked down the sidewalk. She wasn't blessed with a face that made people want to throw money at it—not in charity, not in lust.

She'd heard cats did well. Most tourists weren't accustomed to seeing cats in the Metro. She'd have to drug them. That wouldn't be a problem. If she overdosed them, she could always get another damn cat. On the other hand drugs were expensive.

The phone rang and Delphine answered in a stronger voice than Michelle had heard in months. For a moment, she thought she'd gotten the wrong number.

"Delphine?" she said.

"Oh, Michelle, leave me alone," Delphine said with exasperation. "I have no money for you! We are not even related any longer!"

"You took my father's money, Delphine," Michelle said, feeling the vein in her forehead begin to throb. "Money that you know he intended for me!"

"It is *my* money, Michelle, whatever your father intended. You must accept this."

Michelle sputtered. "I know your secret, Delphine! You confided in my father and he told me. I will tell the world."

The silence that stretched between them shot hope into Michelle's chest.

She'd gotten to her!

"I don't want to be ugly about this," Michelle said as she watched the poor woman playing her violin as people passed her by to throw coins in the dog man's plastic bowl. "But there are still people to be hurt by the truth and you should know that better than anyone."

"Leave me alone, you horrid creature," Delphine said, her voice shaking now and weak.

She hung up and Michelle stared at the phone. Her hands were tingling and she felt a lightness in her arms.

It worked, Michelle thought with satisfaction. *Delphine understands now what is at stake.*

Michelle looked out at the busy swirl of people rushing by her in the train station. She turned to climb the stairs to the streets, swinging her arms as she walked.

It appeared she wouldn't need to find a cat just yet after all.

8

Maggie tucked Mila's blanket up to her chin as the baby slept. She could hear Delphine in the other room on the phone. The door was closed but she heard her voice rise and fall. Maggie frowned. She hoped everything was okay. Perhaps the phone call was with the relatives of the murdered home health nurse?

She and Delphine had carefully not mentioned the death—although they had talked of many things. Amazingly, Delphine had encouraged Maggie to stay for lunch and they had spent a pleasant morning talking.

So far Maggie had learned precisely nothing about Laurent.

Exotic artifacts from around the world graced every tabletop in the main living room giving the apartment a warm homey feel. Nearly every blank space of wall was covered with oil paintings.

South-facing French windows opened to a standing balcony with wrought iron railings that overlooked a green park across the street. Maggie didn't know what park it was or how long it had been there. Everything about the décor of Delphine's apartment said elegance but it also said history.

Paris is old. You don't need to walk down two streets to be reminded of that, Maggie thought wryly. The Latin Quarter especially felt steeped in the past. History had happened here. *You felt it in your bones when you walked down the cobblestone streets. Or when you sat in a beautiful Parisian salon like this one.*

When Delphine went to her bedroom to take the phone call Maggie texted Laurent to tell him she was with his aunt. He hadn't responded yet but that didn't mean anything. When Laurent was out in the vineyards, he often didn't bring his phone with him. Plus, he misplaced it more than she would've expected from someone as careful as Laurent.

She suspected it had to do with him not wanting to always be on a tether. Except now that he had children, she might encourage him to rethink that particular habit.

Delphine returned to the room and instantly Maggie saw she was upset. Her face was white and there was a noticeable tremor in her hands.

"Delphine?" Maggie said, standing up. "Are you all right?"

Delphine staggered to the couch where she sat down heavily. "I am well," she said unconvincingly.

Before Maggie could say more, Amelie came into the room. She had a raincoat on and her handbag. "I'm leaving now," she said, her eyes on the sleeping baby as if annoyed it was still there.

"Fine, Amelie," Delphine said.

Maggie watched Amelie leave, heard the sound of the door shut loudly behind her, and then it struck her: *Delphine doesn't want to be alone.*

"When will you be able to hire another home nurse?" Maggie asked.

Delphine looked at her with surprise as if startled that Maggie could read her mind so easily.

"The agency will be sending me candidates by the end of the week."

"How would you feel if Mila and I stayed with you until then?"

She had no idea the words were even in her head before she heard them come tumbling out of her mouth. She must have looked as surprised as Delphine.

"Are...are you serious?" Delphine asked, her eyes holding the hope and need that Maggie thought she had detected in her earlier.

"I am happy to stay if you think I can be of help."

Delphine put her hand to her mouth and closed her eyes and when she opened them, she smiled tremulously at the sight of Mila asleep in her stroller.

"I would be so happy if you would...Maggie."

Maggie couldn't help but wonder who it was on the phone that had upset Delphine so much. She was tempted to ask but held back. She was moving in with Laurent's aunt! *Take things slow. Don't rush it.*

As she stood to find the bathroom, Maggie noticed several framed family photographs on the piano in the corner of the room. Unable to harness her curiosity, she went to them.

"Is this some of Laurent's family?" she asked.

Delphine joined her at the piano.

"I'm afraid I have no photos of Laurent's parents. Many things were happening at the time and we lost touch."

How do you lose touch when you all live in the same city? Maggie wondered.

"My elder sister Jacqueline had two boys," Delphine said. "Your husband's father, Robert, and young Nicolas."

Maggie knew Nicolas was the uncle from whom Laurent inherited Domaine St-Buvard. She had no idea what happened to Robert or Laurent's mother Suzanne. She reached out to touch the silver frame of a young man.

"He's handsome," she said hopefully.

"Yes," Delphine said, taking the frame from Maggie and looking at it with a sad smile on her lips. "This is Noel. He is my younger sister's son. Raised by foster parents in Switzerland."

Oh? Oh! Family scandal time. Maggie looked closer at the photo and could see the man had Delphine's mouth so clearly Georgette must have passed on the family similarities. But unlike Delphine, Noel had a sharp, almost hawk-like nose that spoiled his otherwise handsome looks. He was dark haired with an easy smile. Maggie especially liked his eyes.

They were Laurent's eyes.

Delphine put the frame back on the piano.

"It was an unfortunate time," she said with a sigh. "Georgette was silly and impetuous as younger sisters often are. The father was only sixteen—and Georgette not even that."

"Well," Maggie said, not sure what to say to someone of Delphine's generation who tended to take these sorts of things hard. "These things happen."

Delphine smiled sadly. "Yes, they do," she said.

An hour later, after Mila had awakened, Maggie stood at the door to leave. She would need to get a few things from Grace's—most of them Mila's—before returning. She planned on picking up dinner on her way back. There were many bistros and restaurants along the way that offered take out service.

She was relieved to see that Delphine seemed to have recovered from her bad phone conversation and Maggie felt confident that she could help her by staying with her. As it was, Delphine was nothing less than fascinated with Mila. Maggie intended to take about a thousand selfies with Mila and Delphine so that, as the years passed, Mila would know she came from this amazing great grand aunt.

As Delphine walked Maggie to the door and waved at little Mila, Maggie mentioned the topic they'd carefully avoided all day.

"I know you must be so upset about what happened to Isla," Maggie said.

Delphine's smile faded from her face and she glanced in the direction of her bedroom as if remembering the phone conversation.

"I spoke with her parents," she said, looking away.

"That must have been terrible for you."

"They were bereft," Delphine said, looking down at her hands and then up at Maggie's face. Tears gathered in Delphine's eyes. "I cannot imagine the pain of losing a child."

9

The sun was dipping behind the Musée de Cluny as Maggie pushed her stroller down the Boulevard Saint-Germain. She hung a left on the Boulevard Saint-Michel at the McDonald's restaurant. She knew her new-found friendship with Delphine would probably take a quick nosedive if she were to bring dinner back from there. She remembered there was a decent Thai restaurant a block from Grace's that did takeout.

"Well! Fancy meeting you here."

She turned to see Grace striding toward her from the direction of her apartment.

"Hey," Maggie said. "You didn't need to send a posse out. Haven't you been getting my texts?"

"Sorry, darling. I left my cell at André's. Did you have an interesting day? Beatrice told me about the poor dead woman at your aunt's. I couldn't believe it."

"I was hoping to tell you all about it over a glass of wine," Maggie said with a frown.

"Oh, worst timing ever, darling! I promised André I'd meet him and a few of his friends. They're children's clothing buyers," she added hastily. "You know how it is. There is no nine to five for startups."

Maggie couldn't believe what she was hearing. Grace was totally bullshitting her. She'd eat her shoe if Grace was meeting anyone except André. She bit her lip from saying something she'd regret.

"I'm moving out for a few days," she said tersely.

Grace stopped walking. She was well past Maggie and heading in the direction of the Sorbonne when she turned around.

"Oh, Maggie, no! I know I've been a little unavailable lately—"

"It's not that," Maggie said. "Laurent's aunt needs some live-in help until she can replace her nurse."

Grace frowned. "In that case, I'm sure Beatrice would be happy to take Mila while you're gone."

"But *I* wouldn't be happy," Maggie said with impatience. "Listen, I'll catch up with you later, okay? I need to get back before it's too late. And keep your phone on you, will you?"

"I promise, darling," Grace said with a wide smile.

"Oh!" Maggie said, turning back again. "Delphine mentioned she's having a birthday party at her house in a couple of days. She said I could invite you if you wanted to come."

"Can André come?"

"I suppose so. But *I* haven't even met him yet."

"I know, darling! I hate that. How about tomorrow evening, six o'clock at Les Deux Magots? Can you make it? *Sans* the little darling?" Grace waggled her fingers in the direction of the stroller.

Maggie's phone began to ring.

"Tomorrow night!" Grace called before turning and hurrying down the sidewalk.

Maggie felt a stiffness develop in her jaw and she fought back a creeping bad mood.

"Hello?" she said into her phone without looking at the screen first.

"Where are you?" Laurent asked.

Maggie turned and wedged the phone between her shoulder and her chin to put both hands back on the stroller handle and begin walking again.

"About four minutes from Grace's apartment. How's Jemmy?"

"He is fine. Your phone was off today?"

"Okay, Laurent, no, it wasn't off. I had it on vibrate. I was at your aunt's today."

"I knew it!"

"Yes, and it's a good thing, too. She's very upset about the murder that took place practically in her living room and she has nobody to come stay with her while she—"

Laurent interrupted her with a loud Gallic snort.

"There are agencies for such things," he said. "And care facilities."

"What is your problem?" Maggie said in frustration. "She's your *aunt*. She's a sweet little old lady who has no family left and she's all alone in a very scary situation. Did she lock you in closets when you were little or something?"

"I rarely saw the woman."

"Well, what is the deal? You're nicer to people who cut and wrap your fish than you are to your own aunt!"

"I just do not want you to be a bother to her. I know how you are, Maggie."

"Okay, that is BS. She *wants* someone to bother with her."

"Are you at Grace's yet?"

"I'm just about to go in. But she's out again for the night."

"*Incroyable!*"

"What can I say? She's in love."

Maggie allowed a moment of silence between them as she stood outside Grace's apartment. The cathedral Notre-Dame was majestic in the gloom, lit up with the careful spot lighting that seemed to highlight all of Paris's architectural masterpieces. A city as beautiful as this one needed to be dramatically illuminated even after the sun went down.

"I am sorry, *chérie*," Laurent said with a sigh. "Your men are missing you."

Maggie picked up Mila from the stroller, holding her on her hip. Her heart swelled with longing for Laurent. She could imagine him, probably sitting in the courtyard in the back of their *mas*.

"Your girls miss you, too," she said softly. "But I really want to do this, Laurent. Our kids don't just have *my* family—they come from your family too and I want them to know that."

"They are too young. Delphine will be long—"

"I know that," Maggie said as she shoved the stroller into the foyer of Grace's apartment building and parked it against the mailboxes. "But for the few days I'm with Delphine I thought I might interview her. It would be so cool for Jemmy and Mila to have these stories later when they're older."

"*Peut-être*," Laurent said.

Maggie heard the sounds of a young boy on the other line. "Is that my Jemmy?"

"*Maman?*" The little voice piped up and filled Maggie with delight. Mila heard her brother too and began kicking her legs in excitement.

~

THE TALL, slope-shouldered man stood behind the postcard carousel and watched her as she talked on the phone. She was so focused on her conversation she didn't even look up a single time. He could probably stand much closer to her—even hear her conversation—and she wouldn't notice him.

But it didn't pay to take too many risks. He'd learned that the hard way.

He watched her as if mesmerized. She had a baby with her. The way she hesitated on her walk to the apartment made him believe this wasn't her address. She was either renting or visiting a friend.

Who was she talking to? She'd thrown her head back and laughed at least once. Surely she had not a care in this world. By the looks of her, she was still well off financially.

The memories of his last meeting with her created a roiling fester of fury that took all his power to tamp down.

It was because of her that he'd had to leave France and hide. He'd hidden in pock-holed dumps that rats wouldn't live in—from Marrakesh to Bagdagh. He'd lived in terror and dread for every moment of four full years until he'd finally received word that the man who hunted him had died.

With crippling trepidation he'd returned to France but the axe had not fallen.

He watched Maggie Newberry push the buttons to release the building's security code and then disappear inside. He touched the thick ridge of a scar that jagged from his left eye to the tip of his chin—a reminder of his years on the run.

Because of her.

He turned and began coughing into his hands until he saw blood on his palms and the proprietor of the souvenir shop came out to wave him away. He staggered into the street, wiping the blood from his lips and looking at the building where she had entered.

He'd be back.

After everything she'd done to him. After everything she'd taken from him.

He would definitely be back.

10

Delphine stood at the window and looked down the narrow road as it spilled out into the small park. She suddenly caught sight of Maggie, walking through the park pushing the stroller.

Even from this distance Delphine could see how confidently Maggie moved. She noticed the dinner bag Maggie carried and hoped she thought to get wine. Being the wife of a *vigneron*, Delphine imagined *that* would be second nature by now.

Amazing. *Laurent a respectable vigneron.* It was an image that wouldn't fully form in her mind. A husband and father? And yet Maggie seemed an intelligent girl. Surely, she wouldn't have married a hoodlum. Delphine was trying to remember the last time she'd seen Laurent when the phone rang. She hesitated.

Twice last week there had been a late evening call and a hang up. She moved to the living room and picked up the telephone receiver.

"Yes?"

"Well, you sound good," Victor said into the line. "But I am shocked you are not in bed. Do the police have any clues at all?"

Delphine sat on the couch. "I am fine, Victor. The police believe it was a burglary."

"Was anything stolen?"

"Not that I can see. Poor Isla must have interrupted him before he could take anything."

"And so he killed her? Does that make sense?"

"I know very little of these things, Victor," Delphine said, her good mood beginning to deflate. "I just know what the police told me."

"Are you sure you're up for the party?

Delphine shifted the phone to her other shoulder. "Yes, I am looking forward to it. Very much. Stop worrying."

"I don't like you alone there. Would you like for me to sleep in your guest room until you find another nurse?"

"I have a friend staying with me."

Victor dropped the phone on his end and Delphine nearly laughed out loud.

"Friend? What friend?" he sputtered.

"It is the wife of my nephew."

"Noel Lorraine?"

"No, *chèri*, my *grand*-nephew Laurent Dernier. He has a vineyard near Aix and an American wife. Can you imagine?"

"How did that happen?"

"The wife? Or my meeting her?"

"Both, I suppose."

"The hospital called my nephew when I became ill this week."

"I am not listed as your emergency contact?"

"Of course not, Victor. And since Laurent's wife was in Paris visiting …"

"An American, you say?"

"Yes, but she's absolutely charming, and oh, Victor! She has my great grandniece with her!"

Victor laughed and she felt all the tension leave the conversation.

What was it about babies that just made everything better?

"A baby in the house," he said. "Yes, that is the best medicine of all. I must meet them."

"You will. She's coming to my birthday party. You'll meet her then."

"I'm relieved you have someone with you," Victor said, "if disappointed that it cannot be me."

~

SHE HAD MADE a good choice with the Thai food, Maggie thought proudly. Like most French people, Delphine was culinarily adventuresome and clapped her hands with delight as Maggie set out the cartons of Pad Thai, panang curry and jasmine rice on her antique dining room table. Mila, having eaten earlier, dozed sleepily in her carrier on the chair next to Maggie's.

"It is a feast," Delphine said, her eyes sparkling, as Maggie pulled the cork out of the wine she'd brought.

"I love takeout," Maggie said. "To me it's like having a picnic but Laurent calls it lazy."

Delphine took the glass of wine Maggie poured for her and frowned. "My nephew cooks?"

"Boy, does he ever." Maggie hesitated. "I guess you don't know him very well?"

Delphine arched an eyebrow. "I knew *of* him well enough at one time," she said.

Maggie was surprised. The Laurent that Delphine remembered was clearly not one she approved of.

"It was a gorgeous walk this afternoon along the Boulevard Saint-Germaine to your apartment," Maggie said, changing the subject. "Has your family always lived in this part of Paris?"

"In the Latin Quarter? Yes," Delphine said. "But not this neighborhood. I moved here with my husband Louis."

"Well, it's got serious cool factor. But I guess you know that."

Delphine looked at Maggie as if making up her mind about something. Her glance turned to Mila, asleep in her carrier, and a smile formed on her lips.

"The Latin Quarter of my childhood," she said, "was an artist's mecca, *comprends-tu*? Picasso, Man Ray, Hemingway, Gertrude Stein."

"It's still got a bohemian reputation."

Delphine snorted. "It is a tourist destination now. But at one time, it was like no other."

"What do you think changed it?"

Delphine gazed past Maggie's shoulder toward the foyer as if seeing something in her mind's eye.

"The war," she murmured. "The war changed everything."

"I can't imagine what it must have been like."

Mila whimpered in her sleep and Maggie put a calming hand on her until she settled again.

"I was only eighteen when the war broke out," Delphine said. "A young girl full of life and romantic ideas."

"Did you meet your husband during the war?"

Delphine shook her head. "Paris in war time was a city of women and old men."

Maggie tried to remember her history. *Where were all the Frenchmen during the war?*

As if reading her mind, Delphine addressed her bowl of noodles and said, "Most of our men were placed in POW camps after the armistice was signed with Germany."

"The armistice?"

"How is it you Americans refer to us even today? Surrender monkeys?"

Maggie took in a sharp breath and stifled a cough into her

napkin. "I...I mean, I've heard the term," she said, blushing, "but I can't imagine...I would never..."

"Yes, it is all very embarrassing. Even seventy years later," Delphine said tiredly. "But what the world doesn't know is that we French had no idea our government was making a deal with Germany! Our men fought bravely, valiantly in World War One. Did you know that?"

Maggie shook her head.

"And then the government just handed us over to Hitler in 1940. Not a shot fired! I am sure you knew *that*."

Maggie could see Delphine was reliving the shame of the memory.

The Nazi occupation of Paris.

"I guess it was pretty tough during that time," Maggie said.

Delphine nodded. "So much hardship. Always we were without the things that gave life joy. Wine. Cigarettes. Chocolate. Even our bread was made with substitutes that made it mealy and inedible."

Delphine reached for her glass of wine and contemplated it before drinking. "The Germans in Paris did not lack for anything, of course," she said.

"That must have been really terrible."

"And as the years went on and the war refused to end—the sudden executions and constant reprisals—it was horrific. Sometime you must ask my friend Victor Rousseau for his family's story. It wasn't just the Jews who suffered at the hands of the oppressors."

Maggie cleared the table and put the leftovers in Delphine's refrigerator. Her kitchen was as modern as Maggie's back in St-Buvard—which is to say, very. Laurent might scrimp on basic plumbing but he insisted on having the latest in kitchen appliances.

When Maggie returned to the living room, Delphine sat on the couch with her ankles crossed, her hands in her lap and her mind far away. On impulse, Maggie picked up Mila and brought her to Delphine.

Delphine's eyes lit up and she held out her arms.

"She is a beauty, your Mila," Delphine murmured as she took the baby onto her lap. "She looks like her great aunt Georgette."

Great, Maggie thought with a wry grin. *She takes after the family skank. Perfect.*

"Shall I make tea?" Maggie asked.

"That would be lovely," Delphine said, smiling, mesmerized by the sleeping baby.

Maggie found two mugs in the kitchen and filled them with tea bags and boiling water. She checked her phone but there was no message from Laurent. Jemmy would soon be in bed if he wasn't already. She hated to miss her goodnight call with him but she had a feeling Delphine had a story to tell and after two glasses of wine and a dozing baby in her lap, tonight might well be the night.

Maggie set Delphine's tea mug on the table next to her. In the space of the ten minutes it had taken to make the tea, she could see how much more confident Delphine had become with Mila—holding her and rearranging her cotton blanket by her chin.

"It's true there were many hardships," Delphine said, not looking at Maggie. "I will never forget those four years. Not until my dying day."

"It must've been awful seeing the Germans everywhere—in your shops and hanging out at your favorite cafés and restaurants."

"It was. But in some ways it was worse for them."

"How so?"

Delphine concentrated on Mila's breathing and she was quiet for a moment.

"We ignored them, you see. We treated them like they were ghosts. We pretended—the best we could—like they weren't there. I read later that many of the Germans developed psychological issues from their time in Paris during the occupation."

"Wow. Way to passively resist, y'all," Maggie said with a laugh. "You pre-Ghandi'd Ghandi."

"Now, if you read the history of that time you would think our disgust and shame made our treatment of the Germans easy, but it wasn't. Not at all."

Maggie had a feeling Delphine was about to get down to the meat of things. She held her tongue and waited.

"Can you imagine how these German victors appeared to the average French girl?"

Maggie shook her head.

"Think of it. Our men were gone—many of them had fled the city. Even the resistance fighters slunk off into the bushes and the shadows. The others were held prisoner in Germany or were hiding in barns in the country. By contrast..."

Oh, I think I know what's coming, Maggie thought with a start.

"The Germans were young and handsome. Goebbels is said to have sent only their most stunning examples of young German manhood. They walked erect, proudly, their faces open and optimistic—after all they were the victors." Delphine looked at Maggie and shrugged. "And winners are sexy, *n'est-ce pas?*"

"I just assumed the Germans were all arrogant and making you eat shoe leather and stuff while they saved the good stuff for themselves."

"Most of them were not at all like that. Their shortages in Germany rivaled ours in Paris."

But naturally, Maggie thought, *it just took a few bad apples exterminating whole villages to spoil the reputation of the whole basket.*

"I had three sisters and we had many girlfriends but there were no boys anywhere in Paris," Delphine continued. "We hated the Germans, of course. But...we were drawn to them, too."

"I thought collaboration was a big no-no," Maggie said.

"*Bien sûr*. But have you not learned this essential fact in life, Maggie?"

"Remind me."

Delphine looked up from Mila and her face held incredible sadness.

"Sometimes the thing you are forbidden to have is the very thing you must have."

THEY SAT in companionable silence for the rest of the evening—Delphine reading a novel and Maggie texting on her smartphone. Her mother sent her a text at one o'clock Atlanta time—seven p.m. Paris time:

<Is your cell phone broken?>

Maggie winced and texted her back.

<I am so sorry, Mom! Laurent had a crisis here in Paris he needed me to help with.>

<I am aware of that, Maggie, since I have spoken with Laurent.>

Maggie sighed in frustration. Clearly her mother wasn't going to give up on this summer visit thing.

<I can't talk right now> Maggie texted her. <I'm trying to get the baby down but I promise I'll call you soon. Love to Dad.>

She turned her phone off without waiting for her mother's reply. It wasn't like Elspeth Newberry to be so insistent. There must be something going on back home—likely it had to do with Maggie's brother Ben and his legal problems—or his wife's. But Maggie didn't know how to convince her mother that the summerlong visit just wasn't viable.

Why was she pushing it so hard?

Maggie saw that Mila—still in Delphine's arms—was waking up and Delphine was falling asleep. As it was Maggie's first night with Delphine, she wanted everything to go as smoothly as possible—and that did not include crying babies in the middle of the night. Feeding Mila now and then keeping her awake for a bit would help ensure a peaceful night for everyone.

"I'm afraid I'm keeping you up," Maggie said as she gently removed the baby from Delphine's lap. As the loss of warmth of Mila's body registered, Delphine's eyes widened.

Maggie patted Mila's back and then switched her to one hip and held a hand out to Delphine.

"Can I help you to your bedroom?" she asked.

Delphine gratefully took her hand and Maggie eased the older woman to her feet. The long day seemed to be having its effect on Delphine. Her face sagged with weariness—or perhaps from the conversation about the war? Maggie cursed herself for upsetting her.

Maybe Laurent is right. I can't open my mouth without traumatizing people.

"I have enjoyed our talk this evening," Delphine said, surprising Maggie. "It was good to talk of it. I never do. Though I think of it often."

"Well, it was a fascinating time in history," Maggie said. "And you lived it."

Delphine shuffled across the dining room and then turned. "Do you have all you need for tonight?" she asked.

"I do. Mila and I will be in the guest room right down the hall if you need me."

Maggie watched Delphine's face clear and she knew staying with her had been the right decision.

Even if she *had* done her best to give the old dear nightmares about invading Nazis in hobnail boots.

11

The next morning Maggie plugged in the coffee maker and pulled a plate of stale croissants out of the breadbox. She knew there was a decent looking *boulangerie* across the street but she was hesitant to leave Mila with Delphine long enough to run down and pick up rolls. Perhaps by tomorrow, Laurent's aunt would be comfortable enough to watch the baby for a few moments.

The housekeeper, Amelie, had arrived early so clearly there appeared to be no set time for the woman to show up. Delphine didn't seem concerned with the woman's odd hours but, combined with Amelie's sour mien, Maggie still thought it strange.

Delphine entered the kitchen with a vague look on her face until she saw Mila in her stroller eating a bun. Delphine's face cleared and her eyes sparkled.

"We need to get the little one *une chaise d'enfant*," she said.

Wow, Maggie thought. *Wait until I tell Laurent his aunt is so in love with Mila she wants to buy a high chair for her.*

"There are too many people in the kitchen," Amelie snarled,

her back to all of them as she wiped down the already perfectly clean counters.

Maggie's phone vibrated loudly against the kitchen table. She could see it was her mother.

"You must take it, Maggie?" Delphine asked, frowning at the phone. "Mademoiselle Mila will be fine with her Aunt Delphine, *si*?" Delphine leaned over and patted Mila's knee.

"Okay," Maggie said. "I won't be long."

Eight a.m. in Paris meant it was two in the morning in Atlanta. Maggie hit *Accept* and went into the living room.

"Mom?"

"Maggie, you know I wouldn't hound you if I weren't absolutely at the end of my rope. I need you to come home. Please. Next week would be fine."

"Mom—"

"*No*. I have been patient. I don't believe I am asking too much."

"You've got Dad there. Can't he—?"

"Maggie, no. I need you to come home with the children! Just say you will."

"Yes, fine. I'll come."

"With the children."

"Mom, you are acting a little nuts. I said I'd come. What is going on there?"

"Ben has moved back home."

"And why do you need me there too?"

"Because…if you come…if you are here…"

Maggie heard her mother take a long ragged breath as if she were attempting to collect herself.

"If you're here with the children, I believe your brother will make a stronger attempt to pull himself together."

"In what way is he not together? Is he drinking?"

"No, dear. He's not drinking."

"Well, what…?"

"He's weeping, Maggie. Nearly all the time. And if you come, you can talk to him."

"Mom, I'm not good at this. Ben needs professional help. He—"

"He is seeing someone, Maggie. And he has appropriate medicine that he's taking. He needs his family. He needs all of us."

Maggie heard a shriek of delight coming from the kitchen and she smiled in spite of the phone conversation. Amelie had left the kitchen at the same time that Maggie did, leaving just Delphine and Mila together.

"I'll come home, Mom," Maggie said.

"For the whole summer."

Maggie sighed. "For as long as I can."

"Thank you, darling," Elspeth Newberry said with a long sigh. "I knew your brother could count on you."

When Maggie walked back into the kitchen, Mila was on Delphine's lap gumming a sweet roll. Delphine looked ten years younger than when she'd walked into the kitchen that morning.

"That is your mother? You are looking unhappy."

"It's nothing. She wants me to come home."

"You do not want to see your mother?"

"It's not her. My brother has a nightmare he's attempting to unravel with my poor parents in the middle. She wants the distraction of me there."

Delphine smiled and looked at Mila. "Children are certainly distracting, are they not?"

"Yeah, they so are." Maggie sat down next to Delphine and noticed there was a small metal box on the kitchen table in front of her. "What's this?"

"Open it and see."

Maggie pushed open the lid. The hinges were rusty and the lid was stubborn but she finally pried it open. Inside was a stack of old black and white photos with white crenelated borders.

"After our talk last night, I began to think of the time during the war. Of my sisters. Of many things."

Maggie drew the stack of photos out of the box.

"I do not think of the past often," Delphine said. "It is not good, I think, to visit there too much."

Maggie cycled through the photographs, most of which were of the three sisters. In one they appeared to be in their teens and were seated around a café table with their hands held primly in their laps and their ankles crossed. Georgette was the pretty one, that was clear. She had wavy dark hair and large eyes and full lips. Perhaps because Maggie knew a little something about Georgette's story, she didn't appear all that bright to her. Her eyes looked vacant.

Jacqueline, on the other hand, was easy to pick out as the oldest. She looked as sharp as Georgette looked dull. She was also the least handsome of the three sisters, although not totally plain. Maggie examined her face closely for any trace of Laurent but found none. She tried to imagine how Jacqueline might look if she smiled.

It's the traditional lot of the older sister, Maggie thought. *Always trying to keep the others in line, to be a role model.*

That is unless the older sister was Elise Newberry.

Maggie shook off the memory of her sister and picked up a photo of Delphine—her hair dark and wavy around her shoulders, her eyes bright, missing nothing. She was standing on a beach with another girl. Their arms were wrapped around each other's waists. The other girl was blonde with an upturned nose. Although the photo was black and white, Maggie imagined the girl had blue eyes to go with her blonde hair.

"I forgot I had that picture," Delphine said hoarsely, reaching for it.

"Who is it?"

"Nobody. Just a friend." Delphine plucked the photo from

Maggie's hand, glanced briefly at the back of it and then tucked it away in a drawer in the kitchen table.

"I have told you how much our little Mila resembles her great grand aunt Georgette?" Delphine said almost too brightly.

"You have," Maggie said, noting the drawer where Delphine put the photo. "I'm surprised Laurent never mentioned it."

Delphine snorted. "Men do not notice these things."

In my experience, Maggie thought, *there is very little that gets past Laurent.* But she held her tongue.

"Georgette of course shamed the family not long after that photo was taken," Delphine said.

"By getting pregnant with Noel," Maggie said.

"*C'est ça.*"

"Was this during the war?"

"Just after."

"And Noel was given to a family in Switzerland but y'all stayed in touch."

Delphine smiled sadly at Maggie. "It was different in those days. Today, perhaps Georgette would have kept the baby."

"And all these years Noel has known that Georgette was his real mother?"

"Of course."

"What happened to Georgette?"

Delphine frowned. "Eventually she married. She had no more children. She lived in Paris with her husband Stefan. He died in a car accident in 1955. She died of breast cancer in 1968."

"Gosh. Pretty bleak."

Delphine knitted her brows as if she didn't understand Maggie's words.

"Were you not close? You and Georgette?" Maggie asked.

Delphine picked up the photo of the three sisters. "*Non,*" she said.

It was clear she didn't want to go any further down that road. Maggie pointed to the photo of Jacqueline.

"That's Laurent's grandmother, right?"

"*Oui.*"

"What was she like?"

Delphine shrugged. "She was on the board of many charitable organizations in Paris. Her husband was wealthy and widely respected. As his wife, she commanded a highly esteemed position in society."

"What was she like as a sister?"

"Rigid. Very strict."

"So you two weren't close."

"Do you have a sister, Maggie?"

"I did."

"And were you close?"

Maggie sucked in a breath. "I wanted to be."

"But you weren't."

"We were too different."

"It was the same with me and my sisters. We were too different."

Maggie studied Jacqueline Fouquet's face in the picture and again tried to imagine her smiling. She tried to imagine Jacqueline rolling her eyes or laughing. She tried to imagine her baking cookies or hugging a young boy to her bosom.

The image wouldn't gel.

"Did she see her grandsons much as they grew up?" Maggie asked. "I mean, they all lived in the same city. Were they in contact with each other?"

Delphine looked at her with surprise. "You did not know?"

"I can guarantee you, Delphine," Maggie said firmly, "I know next to nothing. Tell me."

Delphine placed the photo of the sisters back in the box.

"Laurent and Gerard were raised by their grandmother," she said.

12

Amelie watched the door close behind Delphine and the American. As soon as they were gone, it seemed as if the tension in the room began to dissipate. The old woman never looked at her any more. And the American treated her as most Americans treated their servants—as if she wasn't even there. Oh, she made the obvious attempts at being friendly. But Amelie felt only revulsion towards her.

Whatever the American thought she was doing with Madame, it wouldn't matter. It wouldn't help.

As Amelie's sainted mother had always said to her: *The road is long and curving but the end always comes.*

The road for Delphine Normand had been long—too long and much longer than she deserved.

But the end was finally coming.

That was one thing Amelie—invisible though she may be—knew better than anyone else.

∾

MAGGIE PUT Mila into her stroller and touched the hall light switch as Delphine carefully negotiated the landing outside her door. Maggie wasn't sure a walk in the park was a great idea but Delphine had been so excited at the prospect that Maggie hadn't had the heart to say no. It was a cool spring morning—but sunny—and they'd all bundled up for it.

As Maggie pushed the button for the elevator, regretting that she'd have to somehow maneuver the stroller *and* Delphine with her cane into it, she allowed a moment to digest the bombshell Delphine had dropped at breakfast.

Laurent was raised by his grandmother!

How could he not mention such a thing? Was he embarrassed that his parents didn't stay together? Is that the reason they didn't raise him? What happened to them? Why had Laurent never mentioned Jacqueline? Not once. The woman who raised him? Who tucked him in at night, read him stories, looked over his homework? How could he just erase her as if she'd never existed?

She glanced at Delphine as the older woman braced herself in a corner of the narrow elevator.

There was definitely a story there and Maggie intended to get to the bottom of it.

Outside the apartment building, Maggie pretended to straighten out Mila's stroller blanket to give Delphine a moment to catch her breath. Even walking across the lobby seemed to have tired her.

The apartment faced the busy rue du Bac and while Maggie waited she noticed dents and holes in the facade of the building.

They looked like bullet holes.

Maggie imagined they might be evidence of the street battles that had come to the Latin Quarter in the last days of the city's liberation in 1944. She had already seen plaques on several buildings in Grace's neighborhood that announced that some young person had died on that spot at the hand of retreating Germans. She shivered.

"Are you warm enough, *chérie*?" Delphine asked. Her cheeks

were tinged with pink and Maggie thought the air must have revived her because she looked much more restored.

"I'm good."

"We must cross here to get to the park."

Maggie put a hand on the stroller and another on Delphine's elbow as they maneuvered down the sidewalk to the nearest side street. It was cobblestoned and Mila squealed with delight as they bumped roughly over the stones. The noise from the Boulevard Saint-Germain was loud even from this distance.

They emerged from the alley and saw the entrance to the park before them. "It's beautiful," Maggie said.

"When I was young I would often come to this park from the old neighborhood with my friends."

They entered the park and Maggie looked around at the benches, the pigeons, the young women minding their toddlers as they played in the grass.

"What did you used to do here?"

Delphine laughed. "I am sure it would sound very old-fashioned to you."

"I like to imagine you at eighteen walking through this same park," Maggie said as she rearranged Mila in her stroller and re-tucked in her blanket. "In the States, nothing stays the same. My mom was raised in Atlanta same as I was but there's very little that's still there from her time."

"Perhaps that is the better way."

Maggie gave her a skeptical look. "Do you really think so?"

Delphine smiled. "*Non*. It helps, I think, to have some things stay the same." She waved an arm at the park. "That I would stroll this same park with my great-grand niece in 2016 and also have memories of sitting on that bench with Camille, gossiping and smoking cigarettes—" Delphine's face softened and tears gathered in her eyes.

"Was Camille your best friend?" Maggie asked.

Delphine gazed at the park as if she was seeing a different time unfold before her.

"She was," she said softly.

"That was the girl in the picture with you, wasn't it?" Maggie asked. "The one where you're standing with your arms around each other?"

Delphine nodded, still gazing outward. "*Oui.*"

"You looked close, like sisters."

Delphine wiped her eyes with the back of her hand before smiling at Mila. Whatever had just happened, the spell was broken.

"She was much better than that," Delphine said. "I *had* three sisters and we fought all the time. Georgette was forever stealing my clothes and using up what little makeup I had. Jacqueline was prim and stern—not someone you felt comfortable confiding in. No, Camille was the best of all imaginable friends. I don't know what I would have done without her."

"Where is she now?" Immediately Maggie bit her tongue for asking the question. There weren't many who made it to Delphine's age. At best, Camille was in a nursing home somewhere. At worst...

Delphine took in a long breath as if steeling herself to answer. "She was arrested," she said.

"Oh my gosh, that's terrible. Was she Jewish?"

"No, Maggie," Delphine said. She put a hand on the stroller handle as if to support herself. "She wasn't arrested by the Germans."

Maggie's knowledge of the war was sketchy but even she knew the wartime French government was considered nearly as bad as the Nazis.

"The Vichy?"

Delphine snorted as if even the mention of the name was cause for scorn.

"*Non, chérie*," she said. "Camille was arrested after Paris was liberated."

Maggie felt a needle of anxiety invade her chest. She could see the shame in Delphine's face as she recalled her dear friend. Arrest *after* Paris was liberated could only mean that Camille had committed a crime in the eyes of the Resistance.

"Did she collaborate with the Germans?" Maggie asked in a whisper.

"She was not a *collabo*," Delphine said fiercely. "She was *in love*. She passed no secrets. She betrayed no vow. She simply fell in love with the wrong man."

They walked in silence down the curving asphalt walkway. A knee-high wrought-iron fence separated them from the green pond that meandered through the park. A squad of ducks skimmed along the surface, then scooted under a low cement footbridge.

Maggie couldn't even imagine how awful that must have been—to have your best friend arrested for such a publicly loathed crime. Maggie glanced at Delphine out of the corner of her eye and tried to decipher her mood.

"Shall we sit?" Maggie asked as she parked the stroller in front of a bench. "It's so beautiful here."

They sat and Maggie pulled Mila from her stroller and settled her on her lap. The baby clapped her hands, her large blue eyes wide, as if trying to see everything at once.

"So much like little Georgette," Delphine said wistfully. She reached out a tentative hand to Mila and the little girl grabbed her finger. Delphine and Maggie both laughed.

"I can't believe how fast she's growing," Maggie said. "So much has happened so quickly. Half the time I can't even believe I'm a mom."

"And you say my nephew is a good husband to you?"

"He is," Maggie said, wondering if it was possible to change

Delphine's mind about Laurent. "It sounds like he's not the man you knew."

"He was always so much like his father. In so many ways."

"That's Robert, right? What happened to him? Laurent never talks of him."

Delphine shook her head. "That the son could be ashamed of the father is believable but only from fifteen years distance. Jacqueline always said Laurent was different. I admit I never saw it."

A small boy ran down the walkway in front of them pushing his empty stroller. A young woman walked close behind—*just like any harried mother in any mall in America*, Maggie thought with a smile.

"Sometimes when I fall asleep at night," Delphine said, still holding Mila's hand, "I can still hear the police sirens or the airplane engines so close overhead. Otherwise it was so quiet during the occupation. There were no cars, no radios, no people. The city was like a vacant movie set."

"It's hard to imagine," Maggie said.

"My family didn't evacuate as so many did. It was terrifying to be left behind. But Camille's family stayed too."

"Why didn't you leave?"

"My father owned a dress shop." Delphine shrugged. "He said he would rather die than leave it to the Germans. So we stayed."

"That's gutsy."

Delphine glanced at Maggie as if trying to determine her meaning. Maggie reached into her bag and drew out a cookie. She gave a piece of it to Mila.

"She will make a mess," Delphine said as Mila promptly smeared chocolate across her face and blouse.

"It'll wash," Maggie said.

"I suppose so."

A movement by one of the nearby sycamore trees caught Maggie's attention. She squinted and for a moment thought she saw someone peeking from behind the large trunk. It was an odd place for anyone to stand, far from the pathway and on the lawn with its multiple signs warning people not to stand on the grass. Mila squealed and Maggie looked to see that the baby was happily shredding a paper napkin. When Maggie looked back at the tree she saw noone.

"Are you still in touch with Camille?" Maggie asked as she began to clean Mila's sticky fingers with a fresh napkin.

Delphine noticeably stiffened and for a moment Maggie thought she wouldn't answer.

Finally, Delphine said, "I'm afraid Camille's crime was quite serious. Her lover was no ordinary German, you see. He was a member of the Gestapo."

Ouch, Maggie thought. *Even I know that's bad.*

A silence settled between them. Maggie could see the longing in Delphine's eyes as she remembered her friend. When Delphine bent to touch Mila's blanket, her hands shook. But a look of resolution came over her. Maggie imagined how strong Delphine would have to be to have lived the terrible tale she was now remembering.

"This little one must be kept warm," Delphine said, gently touching Mila's arm. "It is easy to catch a chill."

Maggie tucked the blanket up around the baby. Delphine tore her gaze away from the baby to look out at a small flock of pigeons on the lawn. The air had gotten cooler. The leaves trembled in the trees above them.

"I am not in touch with her, no," Delphine said, her voice unwavering but with tears gathered in her eyes.

"On the day of her arrest, Camille was dragged screaming from our apartment building and hanged in the public square."

13

After their trip to the park, Maggie and Delphine went by a small outdoor produce market where Maggie picked up fruit and vegetables for their dinner. They returned to the apartment in time for both Delphine and Mila to take long afternoon naps.

Maggie sat in Delphine's sunny salon and tried to read a book on her smart phone.

Her mind wouldn't focus.

It was impossible for Maggie to imagine the horror of seeing your best friend arrested and then executed. *Could you ever get over something like that? Poor Delphine. Seventy years isn't long enough to forget the horror of losing your best friend so violently—by people you thought were on your side...*

And here I was thinking poor Camille got her head shaved. Maggie flinched at the image of the Resistance dragging a teenage girl out of her home weeping and hysterical—to be *hanged*.

Delphine hadn't talked of Camille again after that and Maggie hadn't pushed it. It was clear from the way she'd hidden the photo earlier at breakfast that Delphine was still haunted by the experience. Well, anyone would be.

Maggie gazed out the salon windows—the same windows that had been there she reminded herself—when Nazi squads roamed the streets below or pounded up the stairs to wrench open the door and—

Mila whimpered in her sleep, breaking Maggie out of her thoughts. She put a comforting hand on the baby but Mila's eyes popped open fully awake. Maggie glanced at her wristwatch. It was just before dinnertime. She glanced toward the kitchen wondering what Delphine normally did in the evening when Maggie wasn't bringing takeout. The kitchen had looked pretty bare when Maggie was putting the fruit and veggies away after their shopping trip.

"Why don't we slip out and find a nice curry to go?" she said to Mila who was starting to fret noisily. "That way your Aunt Delphine can get a few extra minutes to nap without listening to you blubber—no offense, darling girl—and I can sort out dinner. Sound good?"

Maggie jotted down a note for Delphine and left it on the kitchen counter, then bundled Mila up in her stroller. As she was pushing the button on the elevator, her phone rang. It was Grace.

"Hey," Maggie said as she positioned the stroller in the elevator. "I was just heading out the door. Where are you?"

"Where I said I'd be at this time," Grace said. "Did you forget?"

Maggie hesitated. She *had* forgotten. She was to meet Grace and André tonight. It occurred to her that Delphine likely had no expectations beyond what Maggie had promised in her note—a meal some time tonight. She hoped if she were late getting back she wouldn't worry.

"I remembered," Maggie lied. "*Les Deux Magots*. I thought we said six?"

"We did. But if you can come now, we can girl talk a bit before André gets here. I'm dying to catch up."

. . .

As Maggie approached the café, she realized why she'd originally thought that meeting here had been a bad idea. A serious hotbed of tourist activity, *Les Deux Magots* was packed even on a Wednesday evening. She knew from past experience that a baby and a stroller would not be welcome in the dining room so she looked for an outdoor table.

"Darling!" Grace called, waving to her from one of the outdoor tables closest to the front door. "*Ici, chérie!*"

Maggie pushed past a queue of gawking tourists on the sidewalk taking pictures of the restaurant. She nodded at the waiter who glowered at Mila and turned abruptly on his heel and slipped back into the restaurant.

Grace stood up and kissed Maggie on both cheeks.

"I ordered you a glass of wine," Grace said, reseating herself. She wore a lilac linen shift with a simple pashmina draped around her shoulders. As usual, she looked effortlessly glamorous. Maggie already felt the dampness in her clothes from her sweaty walk up the rue du Bac. Worse, she was seriously regretting not changing Mila's diaper before heading out the door.

"Great," Maggie said, settling down at the café table. American and Japanese accents floated around her from the other tables. *No self-respecting Frenchman would be caught dead here.*

"Tell me everything," Grace said, lighting a cigarette and blowing the smoke away from the table. "Have you found all of Laurent's secrets yet?"

Maggie took a sip of her wine and felt herself relaxing. The weather was beautiful and the jovial mood of the surrounding diners felt infectious. For that matter, Grace herself was so cheerful that it was impossible not to get pulled into her good mood.

"I'm working on it," Maggie said. "For one thing, I discovered that both Laurent and Gerard were basically thugs as teenagers."

"That's hardly a surprise about Gerard," Grace said. "Could your aunt be misremembering Laurent?"

"I don't know. I think Laurent was pretty wild when he was younger."

"That's so hard to imagine. He's always so controlled."

"And get this—he was raised by his grandmother."

"Really?" Grace frowned and tapped the ash from her cigarette. As soon as the words were out of her mouth, Maggie regretted them. Questions of children and the people who might or might not raise them would understandably be an uncomfortable subject for Grace.

"What happened to his parents?"

"I don't know. And so far, Delphine isn't telling."

"How bizarre. So, what's her story? She's rich as Croesus, isn't she?"

"I haven't seen her income tax statement yet," Maggie said dryly. "But she does have an amazing collection of artwork. Some of the paintings hanging in her living room look like they belong in the d'Orsay."

"Oh! I wonder if André knows her," Grace said, fully engaged now that the conversation seemed to have stretched to her beau. "He runs a gallery in the Latin Quarter, you know. Off rue du Four."

"Is he coming to the party tomorrow night?"

"I haven't asked him yet. Will Laurent be there?"

Maggie made a face. "He said he's too busy."

"What is with Laurent and family? Is *Delphine* the Greek word for monster?"

"Not at all! She's very sweet. You'd love her. And she's had a fascinating life."

Grace ticked the items off her slim, beautifully manicured fingers. "Let's see. Rich. Lives in the Latin Quarter. Has paintings that could hang in the national gallery. I'd say she's had a fascinating life."

"That's true. But it's also been fascinating in a terrible way.

She told me today about how when she was a girl her best friend was executed by the Resistance."

"How awful. What did she do to cause that?"

"Fell in love with the enemy."

"Oh! I got tingles when you said that! Leave it to the French to have *amour* at the crux of it all."

"I know, but Delphine is still affected by it over seventy years later. She cried this morning when she told me about it. Like it had just happened."

Maggie noticed that Grace seemed distracted, her eyes watching the crowd outside the café. She dashed out the cigarette she'd only half smoked and lit up another one.

"Speaking of family," Grace said as she motioned for the waiter to bring more wine, "have you made your mind up about going home for the summer?"

Maggie fished out a bottle of formula for Mila from a pocket in the stroller.

"I told my mom I'd come."

"Why the hesitation? I thought you loved Atlanta."

"Two months is a long time. What if I get used to four-hundred channel cable TV and people understanding me when I speak? It took me ages to settle down over here."

Grace lifted her wine glass and observed Maggie over the rim.

"Is that the whole reason?"

Maggie handed the bottle to Mila who grasped it with both hands.

"My brother seems to be having a nervous breakdown or something."

"Well, that's hardly a surprise. But I'm so sorry, Maggie." Grace scanned the crowd again as she spoke. Suddenly her face cleared and she waved to someone on the sidewalk approaching the café. "There he is!"

A tall man with close-cropped blond hair and a mouth a little too large for his face, approached the table, his arms held out wide as Grace stood and slid into them. He was handsome, Maggie thought, as she'd expect in a guy for Grace. Maggie scooted her chair back to allow him room to maneuver between her and Grace. He held out his hand to her.

"*Bonjour*, Maggie," he said, his dark brown eyes glittering. She shook his hand and found herself wondering—with those dark eyes—if he was a natural blond.

"*Bonjour* to you, too," Maggie said. "I'm so glad to finally meet you."

The waiter showed up with a bottle of Côte du Rhone and an extra glass and then disappeared.

Amazing, Maggie thought, *how they act when they think you're not a tourist.*

André pushed his chair close to Grace's and slipped his arm around her shoulders in a possessive gesture that surprised Maggie. Grace nestled into him as if she'd been waiting to do it all day.

Maggie felt a prickle up the back of her neck and she worked to shoo the feeling away. She had a habit of making her mind up about people way too soon and she was almost always wrong.

The fact was—within thirty seconds of having met him, she knew she didn't like André.

That was a record even for her.

"So this is Zouzou, *hein*?" André said, leaning down to prod Mila with a large forefinger. Mila frowned and moved her bottle away as if concerned this stranger might take it from her.

Maggie looked at Grace. She and André had been dating for nearly two months. Was it possible he'd never met Zouzou? Grace appeared to be studiously working at not returning Maggie's glance.

"Of course not, *chérie*," Grace said. "This is Maggie's baby. Zouzou is at home."

"Oh, yes," André said, pouring his wine and clearly not caring one way or the other. He turned to Grace and the two kissed languidly for several seconds.

Maggie felt her annoyance build in her as she looked away, then took a sip of her wine and straightened out her napkin in her lap. Finally, she coughed.

"Oh! Sorry, darling," Grace said, still leaning into André like a simpering schoolgirl. "It's just been so long since we've seen each other."

Maggie knew that wasn't true but she repressed her irritation. It was mildly possible her annoyance had less to do with being ignored than it did with the fact that Grace was getting the opportunity to fall in love again.

"*Chérie*, Maggie was just telling me that her aunt has this amazing collection of paintings in her home and I was thinking you might know her."

André turned expectantly to Maggie. "Ah, yes?"

"Her name is Delphine Normand. Have you heard of her?"

André clapped his hands together, forcing Grace to sit up straight in her chair.

"But of course!" he said. "Madame Normand is known in all of Paris for her patronage of the arts. That is remarkable!" He turned to Grace with excitement. "Her late husband's excellent art collection was well known." He turned back to Maggie. "I would love to meet Madame Normand if that would be possible."

"Maggie has invited us to her aunt's birthday party tomorrow night, darling," Grace said.

"This is true?" André said to Maggie, his face open in an expression of pure joy. "I would be so happy to come to Madame Normand's apartment to celebrate her special day."

Well, then I guess that just works out great for everyone, Maggie thought, smiling to hide the fact that André now appeared to be the very picture of a classic opportunist.

"Maggie was telling me a fascinating story about her aunt," Grace said.

Maggie looked at Grace, aghast that Grace seemed to be on the verge of revealing their private conversation.

"Ah, *oui*?" André prompted.

"It seems that during the war Delphine had a best friend who was killed by the Resistance after the city was liberated in 1944. Can you imagine? That's correct, isn't it, Maggie?"

Maggie flushed with anger and looked away. Although she'd never specifically said Delphine's story was a secret, somehow it felt like cheap gossip to have it blurted out like that to a total stranger.

"But that is remarkable!" André said, motioning to the waiter to bring their menus. "I must be sure and ask Madame Normand all about it when I meet her tomorrow."

Maggie stood up abruptly. This was too much. And it was her fault. She had shared Delphine's most guarded, heartbreakingly personal secret and now the poor woman was going to be quizzed about it at her own birthday dinner.

"Maggie? Darling?"

"Sorry," Maggie said, pulling the stroller away from the table. "I can't stay. Mila needs to...I have to get back. Maybe another time."

"Oh, for heaven's sakes!" Grace said in annoyance. "Why did you bring the baby? I told you not to. This is unbelievable!"

Forcing herself not to respond, Maggie nodded goodbye to André. She maneuvered the stroller through the tight wedge of café chairs and tables to the street, fighting to hold her tongue or to turn and give Grace one last goodbye glare.

∼

MAGGIE'S MIND was calm by the time she pushed the button on the elevator in Delphine's lobby. It had taken a two block walk before she'd settled down enough to realize she was actually walking away from Delphine's street and had to turn around. The rotund owner of the little curry kiosk on the corner of Saint-Germain and rue du Bac typically did a brisk business in takeout, from *jambon* sandwiches and Nutella crepes to Tandoori chicken. Maggie tucked the bag of fragrant rice and curry into the back pocket of Mila's stroller and hurried down rue du Bac.

She could honestly say she'd never seen Grace behave as she had at the café. She was practically mewling and starry-eyed. Everyone and everything else had fallen away except André in Grace's eyes.

Maggie couldn't help but think how dangerous it was to give someone that kind of power over you.

It was dark now but the street lamps and the constant stream of people—mostly tourists—kept Maggie company. With the sun dropping, however, she'd had to peel off her sweatshirt to add it to Mila's blanket, and by the time she made it to Delphine's building Maggie was shaking with the cold.

As she wedged the stroller into the tiny elevator and groped for the floor button, she marveled at the fact that she'd never seen any of Delphine's neighbors since the day of the murder.

The elevator climbed laboriously to the fifth floor where Maggie raked open the antique accordion door. The elevator had been so noisy in its ascent that Maggie hadn't heard the commotion that assailed her now as she stepped off the elevator and into the hall.

A man was screaming.

Maggie stopped, her hands gripping the stroller handle as if it would snap off in her hands.

She saw him standing in Delphine's open door. He was dark headed and tall. When he turned and saw Maggie, his lips twisted into a snarl.

Maggie stared at him in disbelief.

It was Gerard Dernier.

14

Maggie's heart raced as she pulled the stroller behind her. It had been so long since she'd seen Gerard, she nearly didn't recognize him. The venom and revulsion etched in his face when he looked at her brought the memories back to her in a nauseating rush.

"What do you want here?" she asked, her voice firm.

"Maggie?" Delphine called shakily from inside the apartment. "Is that you?"

"Are you all right, Delphine?" Maggie called. "Why are you here?" she said to Gerard. She noticed his eyes had gone to her stroller and then back to her. He smelled of dried sweat and urine. His clothes were disheveled as if he'd slept in them and his eyes were half-lidded and groggy.

"I do not need to say to you why I visit my own aunt!" he said loudly.

Mila began to cry at the sound of his voice.

"How dare you come here and create a scene?" Maggie said, feeling her anger overpower her fear. "Get out right now! Go on, go!"

Delphine peered around the doorjamb of her apartment, her eyes were wide with fright, her face bone-white.

"Do you hear me?" Maggie said, raising her voice and wondering if she could count on the neighbors if she needed them. She pulled out her phone and waved it at him. "You have five seconds to get out before I call the cops."

Gerard looked at her as if he didn't understand. His eyes went to her phone and back again to Mila who was now howling, her cries reverberating off the tiled walls of the hallway.

"Three seconds!" Maggie shouted over Mila's wailing.

Gerard looked back at Delphine and then plunged into the hallway, pushing past Maggie.

"You remember what I said," he bellowed over his shoulder as he jabbed at the buttons. "You owe it to my mother, you ungrateful cow! You know you do!"

"*One* second!" Maggie shouted.

Gerard wheeled from the elevator door and stumbled down the staircase. Maggie listened to the sound of his feet pounding all the way down—rivaling the pounding of her heart. She turned and unbuckled Mila from her stroller and scooped her up, leaving the stroller in the hallway.

"Are you all right?" she asked Delphine breathlessly as she entered the apartment.

Delphine clutched the door but she nodded. Maggie listened until she thought she heard the heavy front door in the lobby slam shut.

"He's gone," she said.

"I am so sorry, Maggie," Delphine said as she released the door and let Maggie close it.

"You have nothing to be sorry for," Maggie said. She put a hand on Delphine's arm to propel her toward the living room. She jostled Mila, who was still whimpering but no longer crying. "Let me get Mila sorted out with a new diaper and I'll be right in, okay?"

Delphine went to the living room sofa and sat down wearily.

Maggie took Mila into her bedroom and changed her and put her sleeper pajamas on her. Although she had alternately been nursing and bottle feeding Mila up until her Paris trip, she realized she was relying more and more on giving her formula. Tonight would be no exception.

She went into the living room where Delphine was seated, staring at her hands in her lap.

"Take the baby?" Maggie asked, holding Mila out to her.

Delphine looked up, her face brightening, and she nodded. She took the child.

"I'll get her bottle made up and fetch our dinner from the hallway," Maggie said. "And then you can tell me all about it."

She felt her phone vibrating in the pocket of her jeans and pulled it out to glance at the screen. It was Laurent. Maggie hesitated for a second and then pushed the button to send the call to voicemail.

∽

AN HOUR LATER, Mila was asleep on the sofa next to Delphine. Maggie had created a picnic of Indian food on the coffee table and opened a bottle of Pinot Noir.

If there was ever a time for a drink...

"How long had you been giving him money?" she asked.

Delphine shook her head. "Forever," she said.

"Why? There'll never be an end to it."

"Oh, I know."

"I can't believe how he was shouting at you like that. Does he come here much?"

"No, not often. And never like that. Shouting and angry. I feel so bad."

Maggie noticed Delphine had eaten little of her dinner.

"Well, you shouldn't. Gerard is a low-life scum ball at the best of times. But to come here and bully you..." Maggie shook her head and tried not to remember the Gerard she'd known years ago in Atlanta. The one who'd hurt her sister and lost their child one sultry night in the south of France.

"You know him?" Delphine asked, looking up from her hands for the first time since Mila fell asleep.

"Unfortunately, yes," Maggie said. "He was...once with my sister. They had a child together."

Delphine sucked in a quick breath and Maggie put a hand out to steady her. She probably shouldn't have told her that. The Nicole who lived in Atlanta as Elise's daughter was no blood relation to anyone they knew. If Maggie told Delphine the truth, that the real Nicole died before she was four years old...well, there was no point in that.

"There is a child?"

"Yes," Maggie said, reluctantly. "A girl. She lives in Atlanta with my parents."

"What is her name?" Delphine spoke dreamily as if she could somehow envision the child.

"Nicole. Margaret Nicole."

Delphine looked at Maggie. "Named after you?"

"So it would seem."

"And your sister? Why does the little girl not live with her?"

"Elise died," Maggie said, her face flushing at the thought of Elise...and of Gerard and all that he'd done to her before she died.

"I am sorry."

"Can you tell me what happened to Gerard? Was he like that as a child? Or did something happen to turn him like that?"

Delphine folded her unused napkin in her lap and reached for her wine. "I do not know."

"Why didn't he and Laurent live with their parents?"

Delphine shrugged. "Money, I believe."

Maggie struggled to keep her face impassive. *No mother just hands over her children, I don't care how broke she is.*

"Jacqueline and Marc had two sons," Delphine said.

Maggie nodded. "Robert and Nicolas."

"*Oui.* Nicolas never married but Robert found his Suzanne."

That was Laurent's mother. Maggie felt her excitement grow.

"What was she like?"

"I didn't know her well. I'm sorry."

"What happened to her and Robert?"

"What ever happens? Robert drank too much. He couldn't keep a job. He depended on Jacqueline and Marc for support. The more he drank, the more he needed them, the more he resented them."

That's an old story, Maggie thought. *But it rings true.*

"Laurent never talks of his father. Or his mother."

"Suzanne died of cancer when he was seven years old."

"Oh." Maggie's heart squeezed at the thought of Laurent at seven and motherless. She put a hand to her mouth and felt a lump develop in her throat.

"Gerard was barely four years old. Robert couldn't care for them," Delphine said. "Jacqueline was forced to take them both."

"I see."

"They were both wild horrible boys. Years later, as poor Jacqueline lay dying, she knew that Gerard was in prison and that Laurent was swindling rich tourists in the south of France. A liar for a living."

"He's not like that now."

"But he was like that then. He and Gerard broke her heart."

Maggie silently cleared away the dinner cartons. She checked her phone but Laurent hadn't tried to call again. She poured the last of the wine into their glasses and sat back down with Delphine.

"Victor came by while you were gone," Delphine said.

"Oh. I'm sorry I didn't get a chance to meet him."

"He is still so upset about Isla's death, he's insisting on putting new locks on the door and a video camera in the hallway."

"Sounds like he cares for you very much."

Delphine laughed without mirth. "People like Victor, if they can't have what they want try to control other areas. It helps assuage the helplessness."

"I can see that."

"My sister had regrets," Delphine said suddenly. "As we all do. She was angry with Laurent and Gerard, but she blamed herself."

"I don't know anyone without regrets," Maggie said.

"Do you believe that some wrong things can never be put right again?"

"I guess so."

"When I told you about Camille," Delphine said as she reached for her wine, "I neglected to mention something."

Maggie's heart ached to see how sad Delphine looked. She hated to think she was the one to remind Delphine of that terrible time.

"What was that?" Maggie asked.

"Camille had a daughter." Delphine looked at Maggie. "Six years old when her mother died."

"What happened to her?"

"I...I heard she was adopted by a family here in Paris."

"What about Camille's family?"

Delphine shook her head. "They were so ashamed. They wanted nothing to do with the child."

"Jeez. That's unbelievable."

"I heard a rumor once that the family moved south with her. But nothing after that."

Maggie reached out and took Delphine's hand. The old woman looked surprised at Maggie's gesture. Then the lines in her face softened and she smiled.

"I know it's hard to believe by looking at me now but when I was young, I was beautiful."

"I believe it. I saw the pictures."

Delphine gazed out the darkened window in the salon. "It will seem ludicrous to you, I know, but in my mind, I am still that young girl—slim and coquettish."

Mila whimpered and turned on her side. Delphine put a hand on the baby's back and a smile came over her face and spread to her eyes. Delphine's eyes lifted to the window again as if seeing a visage there of another time when she was a young girl waiting for life to happen.

"When the Germans came," she said, "so proud and confident, how could anyone blame a young girl for falling in love?"

"That must have been an unpopular point of view," Maggie said.

Delphine's eyes widened as if snapping out of a dream and in a flash, she glanced behind Maggie toward the hallway before looking away again.

"I was just a girl. I did not voice my thoughts."

"Did you know Camille was carrying on with the German?"

Delphine finished off her wine and stood up, her hand on her back as if to ease a sore muscle.

"I must go to bed now, *chérie*," she said. "Gerard's visit has exhausted me."

"Of course. Can I help you?" Maggie stood up with Mila. The baby slept soundly in her arms.

Delphine touched the peach soft cheek of the child and smiled.

"I cannot tell you how much you have already helped me."

∼

AFTER MAGGIE PUT Mila down in the makeshift crib in the guest room and tidied up the kitchen, she stood in the living room and listened to the creaking sounds of the old building. It was too dark outside to see the trees or even the ribbon of river that was visible by day from the window.

She texted Laurent. <Sorry I missed your call. All is well here. Talk to you tomorrow? Love you. Kiss Jemmy 4 me.>

She looked back out the window. *So there was a child.* Camille was gone but she'd left a child behind. A child who would be in her late seventies by now.

As Maggie looked out the window, she felt her conviction grow. There was a reason she was here with Delphine and now she knew what it was.

She needed to find Camille's daughter. She needed to find her and to help give Delphine the peace she'd been searching for all her life.

Another lost child, Maggie thought as she turned from the window to get ready for bed. *I always seem to be looking for lost little girls.* As she crossed the living room, her eyes went to the spot where Delphine had looked when she all but admitted to being attracted to the hated German invaders.

Maggie walked into the hallway and, peering into the shadows, saw what she had not seen before.

A small half door was built into the paneled wall. On its latch was a heavy padlock.

15

The next morning Maggie was awakened early by a small team of cleaners who'd arrived to prepare Delphine's apartment for the party that night. Maggie still could not get over the fact that Delphine felt well enough for a party—even a small gathering of fifteen—but Delphine wouldn't consider cancelling it.

Over the noise of the trio of women scrubbing, vacuuming and dusting, Maggie bundled Mila up in her stroller and gave Delphine a quick kiss.

"See you tonight," she said. "Are you sure you want to do this?"

"You sound like Victor," Delphine said with a laugh. "Yes, I'm sure. It is just one night."

"Get some rest if you can," Maggie said. "Is Amelie coming?"

"Yes, but not until later," Delphine said. "She will serve at the party."

Boy, that should be jolly. Maggie had an image of Amelie in an apron holding a tray of canapés daring anyone to enjoy themselves.

"Are you sure you must leave so soon?" Delphine asked. She looked suddenly vulnerable and frail.

"I'll be back long before the guests arrive," Maggie said. "But I want to get Mila settled." Maggie would spend the night at Grace's tonight so that Beatrice could watch both children. It was just one night.

"*Oui.* Of course."

"Is there anything I can pick up on my way back?"

"*Non*, Maggie. It is all done." Delphine smiled and made a shooing gesture with her hands.

"I'll be back soon," Maggie said as she pushed the stroller out into the hallway.

The walk back to Grace's took longer than usual. It began to sprinkle as soon as Maggie cleared the first overhang of the apartment building. Within steps, the morning drizzle turned into a downpour.

Maggie dashed under the nearest awning along the rue du Bac but she was already wet to the skin by then. Mila appeared to be enjoying the rain. She clapped her hands and squealed with delight as raindrops splattered up from the sidewalk onto her feet. Maggie grinned and reminded herself to slow down. She had all day to get back to Grace's and not much else to do in the meantime. She could afford to stand and watch the rain on one of the prettiest streets in the Latin Quarter.

What was behind that locked door in Delphine's foyer? Why was it hidden? Could Maggie find the key to the lock?

Was it a terrible breach of etiquette contemplating a way to break into your hostess's locked room?

Maggie shook her head in frustration. No, she couldn't go into that room without Delphine's permission. But why wasn't she able to get the thought out of her head that there were answers in there?

Answers about Laurent's family.

Answers about what happened to Camille's daughter.

From where she stood on the wet street, Maggie could see the grey stone bulwark that heralded the Seine straight ahead. Except for a few hardy souls with umbrellas people had fled the streets. It wasn't hard to imagine what this same street must have looked like seventy years ago during the occupation, Maggie thought.

Not much had changed. The Seine was still there. The stone bridge that crossed over it to the Tuileries was the same one built in 1735. The apartments that lined the street were the same gorgeous Haussmann style buildings that had stood here then.

Maggie thought of the bullet holes in Delphine's building. She marveled that this quiet, innocent looking street could have been the stage for such violence. All over Paris it must have been the same.

An elderly woman dressed in black and holding a gigantic umbrella hurried by with her collar turned up against the rain. She look determined to get where she was going, weather be damned, and Maggie again found herself glad not to be in a rush for a change.

It had been difficult to fall asleep last night with everything she'd learned about Laurent. It broke her heart to think of him as an unloved, motherless boy. And his grandmother definitely didn't sound like she was the cookies and hugs type. Probably explained Gerard being the way he was, too. At the thought of Gerard, Maggie winced. She knew she needed to tell Laurent that Gerard had been harassing Delphine.

But what could Laurent do but threaten his brother? Was he going to move in with his aunt to protect her?

Besides, Maggie was pretty sure she'd dealt with the problem. Gerard was cowed. He'd literally run down the stairs when Maggie told him to get out.

No, she'd handled it. She was sure she'd never need to even mention the incident to Laurent.

GRACE HUNG up the phone and turned in bed to look at André lying beside her. She knew he was awake. He'd heard her talking to Beatrice—as covertly as she could but still, hard to hide from two feet away.

She hated reminding him that she was someone's mother. And if the few comments he'd made to her about children were any indication, he hated being reminded. It wasn't that he didn't like children. Far from it. He was brilliant with children. But he wasn't ready for any of his own—he'd made that clear.

Yesterday she was appalled that Maggie had brought the baby with her to meet André. She'd so wanted him to love Maggie the way she did.

But as it happened it wasn't the baby who'd proven to be the problem.

She flushed with annoyance at the memory. Sometimes Maggie could be so stubborn. She never even gave André a chance!

"That was the *au pair, chérie*?" André murmured without opening his eyes.

"It's nothing," Grace said, as she snuggled up next to him.

He turned and looked at her, a lazy smile on his lips. "Good morning, *chérie*."

"Morning, darling man," she whispered.

"Have you heard from Maggie since last night?"

Grace paused. Was that a strange thing for him to ask? Or was it perfectly natural for him to want to know what her dearest friend thought of him?

"I haven't, no," she said, moving to sit on the side of the bed. She knew he would snake an arm around her waist and pull her back to bed. He hated for her to leave their warm bed...

"When will we get together again?" he asked through a yawn.

Grace stood and picked up her silk robe from the floor.

"I don't know, darling," she said, slipping on the robe but feeling the chill from the sparsely furnished room. André's apartment decor was classic Parisian, but cold both in temperature and style. Everything about the way he moved about in it—down to his hesitancy at times opening drawers, or operating the dishwasher, as if he wasn't quite sure where things were—screamed *temporary* but he said he'd lived here for years.

"Did you want to meet up again?" she asked.

"Don't you think so? Since she had to run off so soon?"

Grace watched him as he turned his back to her and pulled his pillow tight into his arms, obviously with no intention of getting up.

Or inviting her back to bed.

For some reason, as she watched him with his back to her after their night of love, she was reminded of the fact that he never received a phone call in her presence where he didn't slip out onto the balcony or the hallway or in some way remove himself to take it out of her hearing.

She had never really thought of it until now.

"Of course," she said lightly. "Great idea."

∽

Noel sat in a café across from the intersection of where Saint-Germain crossed rue du Bac and watched the traffic, both vehicular and pedestrian. It was a pretty spot for watching people.

How many years he'd come to this very café and sat at this same table. At first he drank lemonades and was too small to have his feet touch the ground. Later as the years unwound and he grew old he drank coffee and sometimes wine and wondered where the years had gone.

In the first twenty years of his many visits to Paris, it had always been Delphine who spent time with him, never Georgette

—and Delphine always came equipped with a multitude of excuses for why his biological mother wasn't available.

Is Delphine correct? Is it all just too late to matter at this point?

Of course she would say that. It wasn't her not knowing who her parents were or where she'd come from.

Noel finished the dregs of his espresso.

Only Delphine knew the truth. And the time for him to learn it from her was running out.

Had he really been in Paris two full days without yet calling on her? What was he afraid of?

He dropped two euros on the table.

Enough.

She will tell me what I need to know. All the questions will be answered, starting with *am I in your will for more than a token amount?*

She will be made to answer him. She will not take refuge in death. Not yet anyway.

His eyes followed the smooth contours of the Haussmann apartment buildings across the street that lined the rue du Bac, hiding the wealthy, the privileged, the entitled.

And of course, the biggest question of them all.

Are you my mother?

16

Delphine gazed around her apartment. The mantel was lined with fat pillar candles, all glowing and throwing warm wedges of golden light around the room. Bunches of the palest pink peonies were positioned throughout the living room in crystal vases on nearly every available tabletop. The candles and the flowers had been Maggie's doing. She'd returned to the apartment at midday with her arms full of flowers and a few ideas to make the evening even more special.

How is it I have found this delightful girl? How is it that she just dropped into my life? Can it be true that Laurent is worthy of her? Perhaps Maggie is hiding a secret of her own? Perhaps the reason she is alone in Paris with Mila is because the brute has abandoned her? Maggie is so brave. And the way she defends him after all he's done to her!

Delphine reminded herself to encourage Maggie to tell her the truth. She needn't be ashamed of having chosen the wrong man. She would survive that. Delphine would make sure of it.

"Do you have everything, Delphine?" Maggie asked as she sat down next to her on the sofa. The sounds of the caterers came from the kitchen. Maggie was dressed simply. A plain silk dress and flats. Not gauche by any means but not at all vogue.

"I am fine," Delphine said, lifting her glass of champagne to prove it. "They will be arriving shortly. Are you sure the little one will be all right?"

Maggie took a sip of her own champagne from a long crystal flute. "Beatrice is wonderful with her. She adores kids."

"That is helpful in a caretaker."

Maggie laughed. "It is, isn't it?"

The doorbell rang and immediately Amelie came out of the kitchen. She hesitated, staring at Delphine and Maggie on the couch.

"Don't just stand there, Amelie," Delphine said with impatience. She turned to Maggie as Amelie trudged toward the door. "I will bet you that our first guest is Monsieur Rousseau," she said.

"That's your beau, right?" Maggie said.

"Mm-mm. Well, he thinks so anyway," Delphine said, her eyes twinkling.

"Delphine! *Chérie!*"

Victor hobbled into the living room, his eyes bright. Delphine noticed he carried his walking stick tonight. He didn't always.

He came to Delphine and kissed her on both cheeks and then shook hands with Maggie.

"I have heard so much about you," he said to Maggie.

"And me you," Maggie said. "Sit down and I'll get you a drink."

"*Non*," Delphine said. "Amelie will do that. I want you and Victor to get to know each other."

Victor slipped his hand in Delphine's and squeezed it. Delphine could see how happy he was, how ready to relax and enjoy himself he was. It reminded her—always it reminded her—of the old days when life was a whirl of parties and champagne and so many handsome men wanting to hold her hand...and more.

How could anyone have imagined she'd give up even a single night like this?

∼

ONE THING WAS SURE. Victor was certifiably gaga about Delphine.

As Maggie watched the two of them holding hands and smiling over their private jokes, she realized it felt good to see two oldsters stare devotedly into each other's eyes.

Gives me hope for old age, Maggie thought, her thoughts drifting inevitably to Laurent. She'd had a brief phone call with him today but most of it had been spent with little Jemmy. She knew Laurent was busy. Getting the vineyard ready for harvest was a job in itself. Doing it with a two and a half year old boy underfoot was another thing altogether. She couldn't help but smile at the image. She had absolutely no doubt Jemmy was driving his dad to bed each night exhausted and brain dead.

Welcome to my world, Maggie thought with a smile.

As Amelie continued to answer the door, Maggie watched Delphine become stronger and more animated with every new arrival. *She knew better than I did*, Maggie thought. This night is energizing her, not sapping her. *Maybe she should throw parties once a month?*

Amelie had started passing trays of caviar and *foie gras* around the room by the time Grace and André made their entrance. Maggie was surprised they were so late. André had been so keen on coming, she thought it would mitigate any tendency on Grace's part for her usual fashionable tardiness.

Maggie was standing in the hallway talking to a middle-aged man who used to do business with Delphine's late husband when the doorbell rang.

"I'll get it," Maggie called to Amelie who rolled her eyes in answer and turned to storm into the kitchen for the scallop timbales and *gougères*.

Grace and André were kissing as Maggie opened the door. Instantly, Maggie was annoyed. Was this for show? Were they not expecting someone to answer the door?

"Are you coming in?" Maggie asked abruptly. "Or should I just leave the door ajar?"

"Maggie, darling!" Grace said. Her eyes were glassy and her lipstick had migrated from her mouth to her chin.

"*Bon soir*, Maggie," André said, leaning over and kissing her on both cheeks. "I am so excited to be meeting your aunt." He pushed past her into the apartment.

"Yeah, I can tell," Maggie muttered.

"Darling, which way is the loo?" Grace said as André beelined it for the living room where Delphine sat with Victor.

"Jeez, Grace. You're three sheets."

"Don't be offens...offensive," Grace slurred. "The bathroom, please?"

Maggie gestured down the hall and watched Grace stumble toward the guest bath.

Unbelievable! Maggie shook her head but before she could shut the front door, a man put his hand out to stop it from closing.

"Oh! I'm sorry," Maggie said. "I didn't know there was anyone else there."

"You must be Maggie," the man said. He was very tall and at least seventy. His hair was white and thick and he wore a grey bushy mustache under a hook nose which softened the effect. Maggie recognized him immediately from his photographs.

"Oh, my gosh. You're Uncle Noel," Maggie said with a laugh, holding out her hand. "I didn't know you were coming. Does Delphine know?"

"I just flew into Paris today," Noel said.

"She will be so delighted," Maggie said as she took his arm and headed for the living room with him.

Delphine and Victor were talking to André when Maggie and Noel entered. She could tell that André was a hit with them. Already, he spoke to Victor with his head close to his as if listening carefully to anything the elderly man had to say. Delphine turned when Maggie approached and her eyes lit up like Maggie had only seen when Mila was in the room.

"Noel! *Mon chou!*" Delphine said as Noel embraced and kissed her. "You made it."

"As you see," Noel said settling down beside Delphine. Maggie noticed that Victor was distracted from André's attentions with Noel's arrival and she found herself wondering if he knew the story behind Noel's birth.

Amelie set a large tray down on the coffee table in front of the group. Small stacks of china plates, linen napkins and silver forks were set next to a crystal bowl of golden *gougères*, the steam still wafting from them.

"More champagne, please, Amelie," Delphine said without looking at the woman.

Maggie stood up. "I'll do it," she said, giving Amelie a bright smile. She went into the kitchen to get a bottle of champagne and two more flutes. While she was there she stuck her head in the hallway to see if she could hear or see Grace. The bathroom was completely quiet.

If she's passed out in there, I swear...

"Maggie?"

She turned to see André in the hallway. He took the champagne bottle from her. "Your aunt sent me to help."

"What's going on with Grace?" Maggie asked.

André frowned. "Going on?"

"She's drunk."

He looked around as if just realizing he hadn't seen Grace in awhile. "Really?"

Maggie took the bottle back from him. "Why don't you go check on her? *Comprenez?*"

André grinned and wagged a finger at Maggie. "You don't like me, do you?"

"Don't be ridiculous."

"*Non, ce n'est pas ridicule,*" he said, his eyes languidly dropping to Maggie's breasts. "You don't like me."

Suddenly Maggie knew who André reminded her of and she also knew why Grace was attracted to him...*and why it couldn't last*. André was as close to being the French version of Connor MacKenzie as Maggie had ever seen. She couldn't believe she hadn't recognized it before.

Connor. The father of Zouzou. And the body in the cellar on Maggie's first Thanksgiving in Provence.

André leaned over before Maggie knew what he was doing and kissed her on the mouth. She jerked back and dropped the champagne bottle, her hand flying to her face. The bottle didn't break but gushed out in a foamy cascade onto the herringbone wood flooring. Two caterers in the kitchen cried out. One with a towel in her hands pushed past Maggie and immediately dropped to her knees to begin mopping up the mess.

André turned to walk toward the bathroom where Grace was. His laughter, genuine and warm, followed him down the hall.

∽

Most of the people had left by midnight. Delphine sat in the living room flanked by Victor and Noel all evening long. Maggie knew she was happy; Maggie could see that by her flushed face and by how many times she heard Delphine's deep-throated chuckle.

André had clearly discovered he had a problem with Grace since, moments after leaving Maggie in the kitchen, he carried Grace to the guest room where he left her for the rest of the evening. While he stood near Delphine in the living room, interjecting when he could, he very carefully did not catch Maggie's eye. Eventually, he went back to check on Grace and reappeared with her on his arm. She looked bedraggled, her hair a mess, her makeup rearranged down her face. Maggie had never seen Grace drunk. And she'd certainly never seen her passed-out, makeup-sloppy drunk.

Why had André kissed her? If she hadn't had an effing champagne bottle in her hand, she'd like to think she would have smacked him a good one. Maybe she should've hit him with the bottle? She certainly hadn't wanted the kiss—he smelled like cigarettes and licorice and he hadn't shaved. Had she been looking at him as she remembered Connor? She'd been fond of Connor. Perhaps André misread her cues?

Or perhaps he was just an ass-hat who didn't think twice about kissing his girlfriend's best friend.

Maggie watched André deliver his goodnights to Delphine and half carry Grace out the front door.

"I'm sorry your friend wasn't feeling well, Maggie," Delphine said.

"I wish you could know her as I do," Maggie said.

"She is in love," Noel said, shrugging. "It is not always our best moment."

Maggie laughed and felt some of the tension release in her shoulders. "You can say that again."

"Delphine tells me our boy Laurent is a different man," Noel said. "I would very much like to meet him again."

Delphine made a snorting noise and looked away. Maggie was surprised. She knew Delphine had a bad opinion of Laurent but she'd thought she was open to thinking he'd changed.

"I hope you will sometime," Maggie said. "He is the best man I know."

"Strong words," Delphine said, watching Maggie closely.

She doesn't believe me.

"Well, then, we will have to arrange it," Noel said. "It is important to remember family. There are so few of us left."

"Do you have to leave?" Delphine asked Noel. "I have a guest room, you know."

"I thought I was in the guest room tonight?" Victor said indignantly.

"Why did you think that?" Delphine said, clearly surprised.

"Because you shouldn't be alone," Victor said as his eyes went to Maggie. She realized that Delphine must have told Victor that she wasn't staying tonight.

"I will be fine," Delphine said.

Amelie came to the doorway of the kitchen and took off her apron. For a moment Maggie thought the woman would throw it down. Her face was tense and somber. *She's such an unpleasant woman*, Maggie thought. *And she clearly hates her job. What's the story behind that?*

Suddenly voices were raised in the kitchen.

"Get out of my way, you morons!" a woman shrieked.

Maggie started to stand but Victor put a hand out stopping her.

"It's that woman again," he said.

"Oh, no!" Delphine said. "How did she get in?"

Noel and Victor both stood up.

"This is unbelievable!" Noel said.

The elderly man who Maggie had been talking to earlier was just about to leave, with his coat over his arm. He came over to Noel and Victor. "Do you need help?" he asked.

"What's going on?" Maggie asked Delphine.

A heavyset woman pushed past Amelie and plunged into the living room.

"I see how you live! On my father's money! Enjoying your party, Mother?" The forty something woman had short hair that seemed to emphasize her long blunt jaw. Her face was twisted into a sneer as she stepped closer to confront Delphine.

"Get out, you wretched creature!" Delphine said. "Noel, call the police."

"No need, Delphine," Victor said. "We can handle this."

"Don't you touch me!" the woman shrieked, putting her fists up as Victor and the man with the overcoat advanced on her. "She is not going to live like nothing happened! I promised my father!"

"You are reprehensible, Michelle!" Noel called to her. "To spoil her birthday party like this. No wonder your father disowned you!"

"Noel, no," Delphine said. Her face was white and pinched with fatigue. "You'll just make it worse."

Noel joined Victor and the other man but before they could reach her, Michelle bolted for the door.

She wrenched it open and ran down the stairs screaming, "I'll make you pay! I'll make you all pay!"

17

Maggie awoke early the next morning. Grace's apartment was noisier than Delphine's—not just because of Zouzou and Mila who were both awake —but the booming clamor of the morning garbage trucks, the constantly honking taxis that lined the Quay St-Michel, and the babble of the Latin Quarter shopkeepers in the alleyway below Grace's apartment building.

Grace had spent the night at André's and when Maggie checked her phone, she saw that her two <*Are you okay*?> texts had been delivered but there was no response. She saw a text from Laurent that simply read <???> She smiled and swung her legs out of bed. The man just couldn't help being mysterious. Even texting her to see how things were ended up as an exercise in code deciphering.

Beatrice rapped on her bedroom door and then stuck her head in. "*Bonjour*, Madame Dernier!" She was carrying Mila on her hip. The baby had a piece of bread with jam in her fist with most of the jam on her face. "A walk in the park today, yes?"

Maggie hopped up and gave Mila a quick kiss. "Sounds great. Any idea when Grace will be back?"

"She did not say," Beatrice said, giving Mila a kiss too. "We are finishing our breakfast."

The sound of boxes falling came from the kitchen.

"Uh-oh!" Beatrice said. "*Petite* Zouzou is ready for her cereal." She turned and rushed down the hallway toward the kitchen.

Maggie sat on the edge of her bed, holding her cellphone in her hand. She'd gotten in late last night and—at Laurent's nagging and Victor's insistence—had taken a taxi back to Grace's. A shadow of doubt passed over her. She had never seen Grace as she was last night. And it wasn't just the alcohol or being in love or whatever it was. There was something fundamentally *off* about her. And Maggie couldn't figure out what direction it was coming from.

Should I call Windsor? Would Grace consider that the ultimate betrayal if I did?

As soon as the thought entered her head, she remembered André's kiss and she ran a hand over her face.

Would André tell Grace about that? It didn't seem likely. Should Maggie? Would Grace believe her when she said she'd done nothing to prompt it? *Had* she done nothing? Should she tell Grace that her boyfriend was a douche?

She stood up and went to look out her bedroom window. The spires of Notre Dame were clearly visible. It was early on a Saturday morning but already she could see the tourists lining up to get inside.

She was pretty sure Grace wouldn't believe her. That her new love had made a pass at her best friend? No, she wouldn't believe it and she'd be confused and furious with Maggie for suggesting it.

Maggie's phone vibrated. It was Laurent.

"You're up early," she said.

"I am a farmer," Laurent said. "But I could say the same for you."

"Kids don't let you sleep past six. Or aren't you discovering that with Jemmy?"

Laurent snorted. "Monsieur Jemmy is washed and fed and we are on our way to the market in Aix."

Maggie glanced at the wristwatch on her bedside table. "Wow. Really? Maybe you should take over the kids full time, Laurent. I'm just out of bed and someone else is feeding Mila."

"How was the party last night?"

"Oh, Laurent! Your uncle Noel showed up. You'd like him. He says he remembers you as a boy. And Delphine's stepdaughter made an appearance towards the end."

"*Oui?*"

"She tried to make a scene but Noel and your aunt's boyfriend tossed her out."

"My aunt has a boyfriend?"

"Well, as much as you can have at ninety. And, oh, Laurent, Grace came drunk."

"*Vraiment?*"

"Yes, *vraiment*. I couldn't believe it." A tingle of guilt washed over her. If she was going to mention the kiss to Laurent, now would be the time.

"Jemmy, put that down," Laurent said. "Wait in the car for me."

"I need to let you go," Maggie said, feeling the tingle grow more pronounced. "Call me later?"

"*Oui. Je t'aime*, Maggie."

"*Je t'aime*, you too, Laurent."

~

DELPHINE TOOK her time bathing and dressing. It was Amelie's morning off and Maggie and the baby wouldn't be back for hours. There was no reason to hurry.

The caterers had cleaned the kitchen and straightened the

living room before leaving last night. She'd been tempted to allow Victor to spend the night—Noel already had a hotel room —but in the end was glad to close the door on all the noise and the voices.

It had been a lovely evening, even with Michelle's interruption of it. But it had been a relief to be alone again.

That is Maggie's doing, Delphine realized with a surprise. *Before she came into my life, I could not spend a night alone without being terrified of my own dreams, my own memories.*

She looked at Mila's high chair and smiled. *Life has saved the best for me at the end*, she thought. She touched the plastic rim of the tray on the high chair and noticed a small doll in the chair. Her heart squeezed with pleasure at the sight.

The phone rang from the living room, making Delphine jump and breaking the perfect stillness of the apartment.

It was probably Amelie calling to beg for the rest of the day off. Delphine was disposed to give it to her. After all, Maggie and the baby would be back before lunchtime.

"*Allo?*" she said into the receiver.

"Do you know who this is?" the voice growled out, a gravelly, distorted robotic voice.

"What?" She put a hand to her throat.

"You have something I want, Madame Normand," the voice said. She couldn't determine the accent or even the gender of the voice.

"Who...who is this?"

"I want the secret you guard."

"I don't know what you're talking about!"

"It is a very old secret, Madame, but no less valuable for its age, eh?"

"What...what are you..."

"I will call again and you will give me what I ask for," the voice ground out. "Or I will hurt the ones nearest to you."

The caller hung up and Delphine fumbled for a chair and

collapsed into it, her heart beating in her chest like a trapped bird in a cage.

18

Maggie and Beatrice walked down the sidewalk with the Seine dark green to their right. Zouzou ran ahead but always turned to make sure Beatrice was watching her. And Beatrice always was. Maggie had opted for the back carrier today instead of the stroller. Mila peered out from around Maggie's head and kicked her feet with excitement as they walked.

It was a beautiful morning, although overcast with the ever present threat of spring showers. After a quick breakfast at Grace's of coffee and *pain au chocolat*, Maggie called Delphine to say she and Mila would be there sometime in the afternoon. Delphine encouraged her to take her time and that Amelie was due over shortly. It seemed to Maggie that Delphine sounded a little upset or breathless on the phone but it was hard to tell for sure. Perhaps she was just tired from the party last night.

The park where she and Beatrice were to meet Grace was off boulevard Saint-Germain. Maggie loved the park because although it was tucked into a copse off one of the busiest and most trafficked neighborhoods in the Latin Quarter, the park itself was a respite of calm and beauty. It backed up to the Jardin du musée de Cluny and was full of mothers watching their kids play on the climbing walls and swings. Inside the park were many wooden benches where office workers ate their lunch and tourists took a break from the stimulation of the world outside the park gates.

Along the way, Maggie stopped for chocolate at one of the ubiquitous chocolatiers in the Latin Quarter. She enjoyed wandering the narrow streets and quaint alleys as she and Beatrice wound their way to the park.

"I hope you know what a godsend you are to Grace," Maggie said to Beatrice as the girl stopped to wipe chocolate from Zouzou's face and to hold her hand so they could cross boulevard Saint-Germain.

Beatrice smiled but looked confused. "Godsend? What means...?"

"It means she couldn't do without you. Nor Zouzou either."

Maggie couldn't help but notice how attached Zouzou was to Beatrice. She never whined or asked about her absent mother. Although it was true Zouzou was normally a cheerful child—so unlike her older sister, Taylor—now that Maggie thought about it, it was a little strange that she didn't seem to be concerned about where her mother was.

But why would she? As long as she has Beatrice.

"I love Zouzou," Beatrice said as she put a hand on the child's head. "She is the dearest of girls."

"I can't thank you enough for all you've done for me in taking care of Mila, too."

"*Ça ne fait rien*," Beatrice said, blushing pink. "It is only my job. But it is a job I love."

Beatrice's phone rang and the girl glanced at the screen before pushing the button to send the call to voice mail.

"I must always keep it on," she explained to Maggie. "The parents of my little dear ones must know I will always respond if their child is with me. No matter what."

"Grace was lucky to have found you, that's all."

"Oh! Zouzou!" Beatrice said excitedly. "There is Maman! See? *Là-bas!*" Beatrice pointed across the street to the looming filigree double gates of the park. True enough, Grace was easily visible through the gates. She wore a bright chartreuse tunic that could literally be seen from a block away.

Beatrice kept a tight hand on Zouzou as they crossed the street but Maggie couldn't help noticing that there was no danger in Zouzou taking off and running to Grace. She seemed perfectly content to walk quietly by Beatrice's side.

The park was enclosed in an elaborate wrought iron fence with slides and climbing structures for the children. Large sycamore trees provided shade for the mothers and nannies smoking or eating their *jambon* sandwiches. An unbroken line of the classic Paris apartment buildings across the street faced the park.

As soon as they entered the park, Zouzou ran to the climbing wall, calling to Beatrice over her shoulder to come help her. Beatrice shrugged helplessly at Grace and hurriedly joined Zouzou as Maggie walked to where Grace was sitting.

"Well, you look like hell," Maggie said as she joined Grace at the bench. It wasn't true. Even hung-over, Grace looked luminescent and beautiful.

It was frankly annoying.

"Are you seriously wearing that child on your back, darling?" Grace said as she adjusted her sunglasses. "What next? Overalls and growing your own vegetables? You do know you're in Paris, right?"

"I'm surprised you were able to break away from André for a few minutes."

"He's at the gallery. Saturdays are big sales days for him," Grace said, lighting a cigarette and blowing a cloud of smoke over her shoulder.

"I'm sorry you missed the party last night," Maggie said,

pulling the baby carrier off her back and sitting down next to Grace. She settled Mila on her lap.

"If you're going to be mean to me," Grace said. "I won't stay."

"What's going on with you?" Maggie said with frustration. "I've never seen you blitzed like that."

"Really?" Grace shrugged. "I'm just enjoying myself for the first time in my life."

"That is a crock."

"Can we please talk about something other than your massive disappointment in me which, darling, someone might actually interpret as jealousy?"

"Are you kidding me?"

"Please?"

Maggie watched Beatrice and Zouzou as they negotiated the climbing wall. She couldn't help but notice that Grace hadn't even glanced in their direction.

"Well, you did miss some excitement last night," Maggie said. "Delphine's stepdaughter showed up uninvited and had to be escorted out on her ear."

"Mercy."

"Seems she slipped in with two of the caterers when they went out to empty the garbage."

"What did she want?"

"Delphine says Michelle thinks she should have gotten an inheritance when her father died."

"He left everything to Delphine?"

"Apparently."

Grace checked the screen of her phone. "Any news on the dead body you tripped over earlier in the week?"

"The cops said it was a home invasion gone wrong."

"So no suspects?"

"None that they've informed me of."

"Yes, well, don't hold your breath on that, darling."

"Oh, and get a load of this..." Maggie leaned toward Grace. "*Gerard* showed up the night before at Delphine's."

"What did he want?"

"Well, Delphine is his aunt, too, so he was trying to shake her down."

"What did Laurent say about Gerard showing up? I'll bet he flipped." When Maggie didn't respond, Grace tossed down her cigarette and ground it out with her shoe. "Oh, Maggie, you naughty girl. You haven't told him, have you?"

"I'm not sure what good it would do to have Laurent come charging up here, smoke pouring out of his ears," Maggie said with exasperation. "I mean, Gerard has a right to live in Paris."

"Maggie, when Laurent finds out you saw Gerard and didn't tell him, he will skin you alive."

"Why does he ever need to know about it?" She gave Grace a meaningful look.

"Don't look at *me*, daring. I would never spill your beans. But are you sure it's safe?"

"No worries. Gerard looked like he hadn't had a decent meal in a year. His hands were shaking and he could barely punch the button on the elevator."

"Still..."

"Trust me. Whatever threat Gerard was when he was putting my sister through hell, he isn't now. After our little talk, I'm sure he'll leave Delphine alone. Laurent doesn't need to know."

"Bad policy, darling. This much I know."

A squeal from the playground made both of them turn their heads. Zouzou was sitting on the ground, her face flushed. Beatrice knelt beside her and was speaking to her in a low voice.

"I think she's okay," Maggie said.

"Darling, is that a bag from *Un Dimanche a Paris?*" Grace asked.

Maggie looked at the small shopping bag full of designer chocolates she'd set down next to the baby carrier.

"It might be," she said.

"Oh, my God, Maggie Newberry Dernier. You are *never* going to lose that pregnancy weight."

"These aren't for me. They're for Mila." Maggie grinned, enjoying the bantering. This was the old Grace. The Grace she'd seen very little evidence of in the past week.

"Mila is six months old," Grace said, wagging a finger at Maggie.

"I'm saving them for her."

"So have you totally given up? I mean, do you just not *care* anymore?"

Maggie shrugged. "Not if it means I can't have chocolate."

"You *can* have chocolate, darling. Just not at every meal."

Maggie grinned good-naturedly and turned her attention back to Beatrice and Zouzou who were making their way over to them. Maggie was pretty sure Grace was waiting for her to say something about André—how much she liked him, how handsome he was—but Maggie couldn't do it. Not yet. She was terribly afraid if she tried to, something honest and unguarded would come tumbling out of her mouth.

"Hello, darling," Grace called to Zouzou. "Having fun?"

Zouzou looked up at Beatrice and tugged her hand. "*J'ai faim*," she said with a trace of a whine in her voice.

Maggie glanced at Grace but she didn't seem to notice that the child had ignored her. Now that Maggie thought of it, it struck her that she hadn't heard Zouzou speak English since she'd arrived. She and Laurent worked hard to make sure that Jemmy, and pretty soon Mila too, would both be bilingual. She was sure she'd had a discussion with Grace about it a few months back. And Grace felt the same way she did.

Did Grace not care any more?

"Oh! There he is!" Grace said, dropping a tube of lipstick into her purse and closing it with a loud click.

Maggie looked up to see André striding through the park gates toward them.

~

GERARD WATCHED her as she left the park. The hand holding the cigarette to his mouth shook. He let her get a block ahead, but always in sight. She was wearing a bright colored jacket and pausing often to look into the produce bins of the outdoor vendors. He watched her as she came to the crossroads, and stopped to survey the street, a smile playing on her lips.

What was she looking for?

She never thought to turn around. Never did she suspect he was there, behind her, always behind her.

Every step she took.

She had ruined his life at every corner. Turned his greatest love, his Elise, into a monster who preferred death to his caresses. Threw him to the wolves where his only hope for survival was to live like a roach scrabbling over filth—always looking over his shoulder for the man who hunted him.

Because of her.

She crossed the street, clearly heading toward his aunt's apartment.

And that was the worst insult of all. That she should come here to discredit him to the one person who didn't loathe him, who might possibly be persuaded to help him.

It was like she was just asking him to kill her

19

Maggie hesitated at the intersection of rue du Bac and Boulevard Saint-Germain. Delphine had said on the phone that Amelie would soon be with her. Maggie shifted the weight of Mila on her back. The weather was fine and Maggie had plenty of energy.

The fact was, in a surprisingly unguarded moment at breakfast yesterday Delphine had causally mentioned the name of the street where Laurent had grown up. It was a throwaway comment and Maggie had done everything in her power not to react. Laurent had always refused to even hint at the neighborhood where he'd lived as a boy.

Literally five minutes after Delphine had let the name of the street slip Maggie had typed *rue Bonaparte* into the GPS on her cellphone.

Now as she stood and stared at her phone screen she could see, amazingly, that the street was situated right off boulevard Saint-Germain across from Les Deux Magots, the restaurant where she'd met Grace and André. She immediately forced away the negative reaction that was triggered by the thought. She knew herself well enough to know she'd only make things worse by overanalyzing feelings when she had nothing but gut instinct to go on. And she probably owed Grace more than that.

She reversed her route until she was in front of the restaurant—an easy ten minutes from Delphine's apartment. Mila had gone very still in her backpack which Maggie assumed was because she'd nodded off.

She spotted the street sign for rue Bonaparte right off from Boulevard Saint-Germain, across from the famous Jean-Paul Sartre and Simone de Beauvoir restaurant. Maggie felt a burst of adrenaline.

Finally! She would see where Laurent came from! She would see the mean streets and witness the squalor and degradation that he'd had to overcome. The thought of it made her love him all the more.

I may never even tell him I saw it. Clearly he doesn't want me to see it. But he couldn't know how much more wonderful it makes his transformation from street urchin to prosperous vineyard owner. *Maybe it's a uniquely American concept—the whole rags to riches thing.*

The first block she walked down on rue Bonaparte was full of cafés, souvenir shops and upscale restaurants. Granted, she was still in the heart of the Latin Quarter. Perhaps what had been a slum in 1975 was now a polished up version of blue collar housing.

She passed a store that sold only cashmere hats and shawls. Next to it was a shop with an array of leather goods—belt, bags, shoes and wallets—that made her stop and press her nose up to the glass. If she hadn't been afraid it might wake Mila, she would have gone inside leading with her American Express card.

She continued down the street. A prickling on the back of her neck made her turn once to look behind her. A steady stream of people—office workers, shoppers, and tourists—appeared in a steady surge. Ahead, the street narrowed after a few hundred yards and the shops disappeared to reveal only apartment buildings on both sides of the road.

The buildings lined the road—their facades gleaming with the characteristic cream-colored limestone of the classic Parisian buildings. Their balconies, stark black against the light buildings, threaded across the fronts as if in a continuous line. The ornate cornices on each window were perfectly aligned.

Maggie frowned and looked down at her cellphone.

Can this be right?

Gazing back at the towering, majestic bone-white buildings that lined the road, Maggie came to the only conclusion she could faced with the evidence: *Laurent wasn't raised in a ghetto.*

He came from one of the wealthiest neighborhoods in the Latin Quarter.

~

THE ELEVATOR WAS NOT WORKING.

Amelie shouldered her heavy market bag and began the walk up the stairs to Madame's apartment.

It was bad enough she had to work like a common scullery maid and every single day face the woman who had ruined her life—and ruined her poor mother's life! When Amelie thought of her mother—old before her time, hunch-backed and bent from years of labor—she shook her head to chase away the image and the ensuing hatred that burned her like acid.

Amelie had known the name Delphine Normand from the day she could understand language. She'd known the name before she knew there was a devil or before she grasped the basic concept of evil. It was not just her mother who'd told her about Madame, but the neighbors, the village priest, her school mates, Amelie's own aunts and cousins—all of them sickened with shame to even look at her.

Yes, her mother had fallen. There was no father to help

shoulder the shame of Amelie's birth. But what did it matter? Could her mother have sunk any lower? It had always been just the two of them. She and Coeur. When her mother became too old to make enough money selling her body to the village men, she cleaned other people's homes, mended other people's laundry—anything to put food on the table.

Until the cancer took her.

A blessing, her aunt had called Coeur's death. She'd stood at the gravesite, refusing even to hold Amelie's hand, and said it like a judgment.

There was no doubt, the way she said it, that she believed Amelie's death could only be another *blessing* for the family.

It was then that Amelie—at fifteen years old—knew she could not leave this world without killing the one person responsible for her mother's tragedy.

Amelie stopped at the landing on the fourth floor and felt her breath come in long, noisy wheezes.

What should I do, ma mère? Do I wait for the right opportunity? Or do I make my own opportunity?

The poison in the tea had only sickened Madame because Amelie had been too fearful to make it stronger.

What do I have to be afraid of? Could prison be worse than the hell I am living?

But she knew she couldn't allow Madame to destroy her, too. There had to be a life for her after the old woman paid her debt.

Je promis, ma mère, Amelie thought, her eyes squeezed shut with determination. *I promise. I will make her pay for what she did to you and Grandmère.*

She looked up at the final flight of stairs leading to Delphine's apartment. She was sweating now and her heart was pounding too fast. The exertion was too much. She couldn't go much longer like this. If she didn't find a way to do it soon she would end up stabbing the bitch in her bed with her own steak knives.

And Amelie did not want to go to prison.

She trudged up the final steps until she stood in front of Madame's door. She hesitated before reaching for the doorknob. It sounded like weeping coming from inside. Amelie held her breath and listened. Madame was crying. Had something happened? As she stood, debating whether or not to go in or what the crying could mean for her, Amelie made a slow half turn as if to survey the empty hallway. It was then she noticed the grill door to the elevator was open. She took two steps toward it and stared with astonishment.

There was no elevator to step into.

She slowly turned her head back toward the apartment door.

Je promis, ma mère.

20

Maggie wiped the perspiration from her brow as she hit the second landing down from Delphine's apartment lobby.

Who would've guessed the stupid elevator would be stalled at one of the upper floors? Thank God she hadn't brought the stroller. She would have had to leave it in the lobby and carry Mila up five flights in her arms. She was also grateful she'd had the sense to switch from her flats to her tennis shoes. Although she'd taken flak for it from Grace, it made all the difference. Plus, there was the added benefit that she didn't sound like an army of cloggers coming up the stairwell of stone steps. Although not entirely silent due to her heavy breathing—*Mila was heavy!*—at least the neighbors would have nothing to complain about.

She took a quick rest on the last landing before powering through the remaining twenty stairs.

When she hit the top of the steps she saw Delphine and Amelie standing with their backs to her in front of the elevator with the door open.

Had the elevator stalled on Delphine's floor?

"I think the elevator's out of order," Maggie said breathlessly as she came up from behind them.

Amelie shrieked and jumped back from the open elevator door. It was then that Maggie saw that the elevator car was not there. The door opened directly onto an empty elevator shaft.

"Jeez! Be careful!" Maggie said as she shot a hand out to grab Delphine by the sleeve and pull her back. "God, Delphine. That's really dangerous. What were you thinking?" Maggie looked from Delphine to Amelie. Delphine looked confused. Her face was white and there was a distinct tremor racing up the arm that Maggie was holding.

"I am sorry, Madame," Amelie said. Maggie wasn't sure who she was speaking to but she stood with her hand over her mouth, her eyes wide and frightened.

How could Amelie have made such a stupid mistake? Was she really about to help Delphine onto the elevator without looking first?

"I didn't know you were going out this afternoon," Maggie said to Delphine who inched back toward her front door, wobbly stabbing the carpet with her cane as she went.

"I...I need to sit down," Delphine said.

"I'll make tea," Maggie said. She pushed Delphine's door open. "Are you coming or going, Amelie?"

Amelie flinched. "I am leaving," she said and then turned and fled down the stairs.

"That was a close one, Delphine." Maggie steered the elderly woman into the apartment. "Does it break down a lot?"

Delphine didn't answer but she didn't need to. In Maggie's experience, elevators in the older buildings in Paris were broken more than they worked. She never climbed onto one without major trepidation and full-on prayers for her safe arrival. Laurent said if she'd take the stairs instead she'd never have to worry about it.

She deposited Mila on the couch with Delphine and then went into the kitchen to make tea. When she returned, Mila was asleep in Delphine's arms and Delphine looked better. Maggie set the tray down on the coffee table.

"Where were you going? I didn't know you had an appointment."

"I...I didn't," Delphine said without looking at Maggie.

Maggie poured the tea then took Mila to put her down in the other room for her nap. When she returned, Delphine was sitting holding her teacup, but her thoughts were clearly a long way away.

The sun was bright on the multi-colored dhurrie rug in the living room. Maggie went to the floor length window to pull the blinds. As she did, she noticed a letter half written on the desk by the window. Before she could stop herself, she read *Cher Victor*. She could see that the rest of the note seemed to be thanking him for coming to her party and how much she enjoyed seeing him. Delphine's handwriting, although shaky from her age, exhibited distinctive flourishes and swirls. Maggie couldn't help but think how unfortunate it was that having a lovely hand was now a lost art in this age of texting and emails.

She stared out the window for a moment. She still couldn't believe that Laurent had not been raised in poverty. How could she have gotten that so wrong? He'd been raised with every imaginable opportunity and advantage—the same as Maggie.

But whether he'd been loved was another thing.

"I'm sorry, Maggie," Delphine said when Maggie rejoined her in the living room.

"What for?"

"I didn't mean to be rude. Amelie wanted me to go out..."

"You don't have to explain to me, Delphine," Maggie said, pouring her own tea. "I'm not your keeper."

"I am afraid the visits from Gerard and Michelle have... unnerved me."

"I'm not surprised. Did Michelle really think crashing your party was the way to get money from you?"

"Crashing?"

"Barging in."

Delphine sighed. "The girl has been difficult, always."

Maggie grinned at Delphine's reference to the forty-plus year old Michelle as "the girl."

"Louis—my husband—spoiled her relentlessly. *Ainsi*, she expected more when he died."

"Did he…was she not provided for in his will?" Maggie asked gently.

"No," Delphine said.

Maggie and Delphine sipped their tea in silence for a moment.

"Was it recent, his passing?" Maggie asked.

"Last year."

"I'm so sorry."

"I loved him very much," Delphine said matter of factly. "He was younger than me and that worked out well for both of us."

Whatever that means, Maggie thought.

"But of course there is always one who slipped away, *n'est-ce pas*?" Delphine said. Maggie had the distinct feeling that whomever Delphine was referring to was not Louis.

There was such a melancholy air to Delphine almost always—unless she was looking at Mila. Maggie knew she'd met Delphine under very trying times—what with the murder of Isla and then Maggie dredging up all her memories of Camille and the war. And yet, Maggie couldn't help but notice that at the same time the memories saddened Delphine, they also seemed to enliven her, even bringing her to life again, as if that time so many years ago had been a period of her life when she was really and truly alive.

"I never met anyone before Laurent who made me feel like that," Maggie ventured. "I had boyfriends—even some great ones." An image of Brownie came to mind and she smiled. "But nobody who I connected with like I did with him. For all our language barriers. Which reminds me. How did Laurent learn English?"

Delphine turned to study Maggie's face.

"There is much you do not know about your husband. You do not even know how it is he speaks your language so fluidly."

Maggie blushed hotly. "That is true, Delphine," she said. "But I do know a few things. I know Laurent always remembers to make my favorite dish when I've had a rough day. I know he will whisk both kids away to amuse them when he thinks I've had too much. I know he'd give his life for me—or either of our children. I know he'd never betray me with another woman. And I know all this in the best way you can know something. I know it in my heart and in my bones."

The two stared at each other for a moment. Maggie felt her lips trembling. She didn't know why she was getting so overwrought. Maybe because Laurent's only relative besides that low life Gerard couldn't see what the rest of the world saw when they met Laurent.

"So you can tell me he learned English in prison or in an Indian whorehouse," Maggie continued, her voice wobbly with emotion, "and it wouldn't matter to me. Because *however* he learned it, *however* his life was before he met me doesn't matter because it's what helped create the man he is today. And for that I'm grateful."

Delphine reached out to squeeze Maggie's hand. "I see I'm going to have to give my nephew another chance," she said.

"I'd appreciate it if you would," Maggie said, brushing away a tear. "Sorry I got all upset. I don't know what came over me."

"You are defending the man you love," Delphine said with a shrug. "I of all people know how this feels."

"Really? With whom?"

"I meant through my friend Camille," Delphine said. "I wish you could have known her, *chérie*. She was so beautiful. Her laugh sounded like bells on the breeze." Delphine smiled at the memory of it. She shook her head. "Oberleutnant Bauer and the French beauty," she murmured. "Could it have been true love do you think? I know she loved him. I know she never stopped loving him."

"That was his name? Bauer?"

Delphine withdrew her hand and sat up straight on the couch. She didn't answer.

"You know, Delphine, I think I can help you with what happened to Camille."

"Whatever do you mean? How can you do anything? It is over seventy years ago."

"I don't mean I can change what happened."

"*Chérie*, could you go to the kitchen for some bread to go with our tea? I'm afraid I forgot to have lunch today."

Knowing she was being asked to drop the subject, Maggie stood up. "Sure. Be right back."

Maggie checked on Mila who was still sleeping soundly, and then went to the kitchen to collect an assortment of cookies and croissants on a dish. Out the kitchen window she saw Notre-Dame in the distance. There was something claustrophobic about the Latin Quarter, she realized. It was only when you got up high and were able to see out beyond the Seine and the Île de la Cité that you sensed it.

She returned to the living room and set the dish of bakery goods down on the coffee table.

"Oh, that looks lovely. Thank you, *chérie*."

Maggie picked up a cookie and dunked it in her tea. "It was great meeting both Victor and Noel last night," she said.

Delphine's face cleared. "I am so glad Noel came," she said. "He is a true credit to the family. He is in politics in Switzerland, you know."

"I did not know that."

"*Oui*. He has a position for which he was elected. We are all very proud of him."

Maggie knew there was only Delphine, Gerard and Laurent left in the family and she was pretty sure the two brothers never thought of Noel let alone felt proud of him.

"And Victor is like having a husband without the downside," Maggie said.

Delphine laughed and covered her mouth, her eyes merry. "It is true," she said, nodding.

"How do you know him?"

"Through Jacqueline. He and I were better suited and so he became more my friend. Especially after Louis's death."

"I didn't want to bring down the party last night by asking him about his experience in the war," Maggie said. "Remember you said I could ask him about what happened to him?"

Delphine nodded. "His family was the target of a reprisal by the Nazis."

"By reprisal, you mean..."

Delphine grimaced. "When we French did something—killed a German soldier or blew up a truck depot—the Gestapo would murder dozens of innocent people in retaliation. Either they would execute French soldiers they already held prisoner or kill random people off the street. This time they massacred twenty people in a village just outside Paris, including Victor's parents and two sisters. Victor only survived because he was a small child napping and was missed."

"That's horrible."

Delphine shrugged. "It was the war."

"I can't imagine how any of you lived in that kind of environment."

"Where we lived was safer than the rest of Paris."

"How so?"

"You understand the whole of the Latin Quarter is bisected by two roads, *oui*?"

"Boulevard St-Germain and..." Maggie ventured.

"Boulevard St-Michel. Everything else is a maze of crooked

streets and narrow alleys—many too small to accommodate a vehicle."

Maggie knew about the confusing labyrinth of the area firsthand and had gotten lost more than a few times. Each twisting alleyway looked much like the other.

"It was easier here than the rest of Paris for hiding and fleeing the Germans," Delphine said. "There are so many places to lose yourself."

A soft moan came from Mila in the bedroom.

"She's waking up," Maggie said.

"It was bound to happen," Delphine said with a laugh.

"Can I ask you a quick question before I go get her?" Maggie asked.

Delphine smiled but her eyes were questioning. "*Bien sûr.*"

"I couldn't help but notice that you have a locked room in your foyer."

The smile dropped from Delphine's face and her eyes went involuntarily in the direction of the door.

"I was wondering what it was," Maggie said.

Delphine licked her lips, her eyes on the door. "It is nothing," she said. "A storage room only."

"Why is it padlocked?"

"Louis had some paintings from his collection stored there. I simply have not gotten around to going through all that is in there."

"I'd be happy to help you do that."

Delphine looked startled. Her eyes darted from the locked door to Maggie's face.

"Why ever would you want to?"

"If I were able to find out what happened to Camille's daughter, would you like that?"

Delphine didn't answer. She stretched out a hand to pick up her teacup. Her hand shook.

"But of course," she said finally.

"I might be able to discover something that will help ease your mind about what happened."

Delphine glanced at Maggie and then at the locked door but her shoulders sagged with resignation and even the sounds of an increasingly awake Mila didn't bring a smile to her lips.

"I seriously doubt that," she said bitterly.

21

The next morning, Mila was up early so Maggie was too. Delphine was still asleep so Maggie wrote her a quick note to say she'd be back shortly. It was a good morning to sit outside with a coffee. As Maggie was arranging Mila in her back carrier, the front door opened. Amelie stopped dramatically when she saw Maggie and the baby. Maggie considered asking Amelie where she thought she was taking Delphine yesterday but as usual the woman didn't make conversation easy. Maggie decided it wasn't important. No harm was done.

"*Bonjour*, Amelie," Maggie said cheerfully, not expecting an answer. "Madame Normand is still asleep."

Amelie grunted and pushed past Maggie to enter the kitchen.

"Yep," Maggie said under her breath as she slipped out the front door. "You have a good day, too."

What is with that woman? Did she just hate me on sight?

The elevator appeared to be working this morning but Maggie decided not to chance it and took her time descending the five floors to the lobby below. It wasn't raining for a change so she set out at a quick pace down the rue du Bac toward the boulevard Saint-Germain. There was a good bakery around the corner from Delphine's but Maggie was in the mood for a sit-down coffee. Her phone vibrated and she glanced at the screen.

It was Laurent.

<Call me when you have a moment.>

Maggie quickly typed in <K> and slid the phone back into her jacket pocket. It occurred to her that Laurent's urgent messages often sounded like no big deal. She pulled the phone out again, wondering if she should call him.

Another text came through. <Jemmy is fine.>

She breathed a sigh of relief and felt a wave of gratitude because Laurent knew her so well.

She tugged on the baby's foot. "Okay, Mila. Will it be *pain chocolat* again this morning or shall we branch out with a *crème pâtissière*?"

An hour later, Maggie sat at a café with Mila on her lap, an espresso in front of her and her iPad on the table. For being in such a touristy area, the café was light on patrons and for that Maggie was glad. It was slightly scuzzier than some of the other cafés on the famous street and the waiters seemed a tad more surly too. Maggie considered it a fair trade for a quiet morning.

She typed in the name *Bauer* in her iPad's search engine window and watched as hundreds of names showed up. She refined the search by typing in *WWII* and also *Gestapo* but only managed to reduce the number by a hundred or so.

"It can't be that complicated," Maggie muttered, tapping a spoon against her demitasse cup.

She typed in: *German officer Bauer during Paris occupation 1944.*

It was a long shot…

A man's name showed up in a chat room talking about the war and his father's involvement in it. Highlighted was a comment he made about his father's stories during the war in Paris with a Helmut Bauer.

Maggie felt her excitement grow. Now if she could just confirm with Delphine that Camille's guy's first name had been Helmut, she might really have something!

She picked up her phone and called Delphine's home number.

"*Oui?*" a woman barked into the receiver.

Great. Amelie.

"*Allo*, Amelie," Maggie said, hoping the hag didn't hang up on her. "Is my aunt available?"

A loud snorting broke onto the line followed by the sound of the phone dropping as Amelie went to fetch Delphine.

Mila kicked the table with her foot and reached for Maggie's spoon. To keep her quiet, Maggie handed it over. She looked on her tablet for the contact information for the person who had posted. His name was Rolf Schmidt. It looked like he'd made the comment two years ago.

"*Oui*, Maggie?" Delphine said into the receiver.

"Hey, Delphine. I hope I didn't drag you away from your breakfast."

"*Non, non.* Where are you?"

"Just running a few errands. Listen, I was wondering if you could tell me Herr Bauer's first name?"

Delphine sucked in a loud gasp and for a moment Maggie was afraid she was having a spell.

"Delphine? You okay?"

"Helmut," Delphine said softly as if attempting to hide the word from anyone who might be listening. "He was called Helmut."

Bingo! Maggie made a silent fist pump in the air.

"Okay, great. Listen, I'll bring home some sandwiches for lunch, okay? Is there anything else you need?"

"*Non*, Maggie. *Merci*."

Maggie was sorry if she'd upset Delphine but she was sure it was for a good cause. If Maggie could find Camille's daughter and help ease Delphine's mind about what happened to her, it would all be worth it.

She turned back to her iPad.

Schmidt had to be between fifty and seventy years old. That's old to be playing on the Internet, Maggie thought. With no comments in two years, maybe he died?

She clicked on his name and was sent to an active email address.

She typed: "*Dear Herr Schmidt, I hope you can help me. I am looking for information on a Helmut Bauer who was stationed in Paris during the German occupation. I understand your father knew him? Any information you can give me about Herr Bauer—what happened to him, or any descendants he might have—would be invaluable to me. Yours Sincerely, Margaret Dernier.*"

She hit *Send* and leaned back with satisfaction.

"Step One, baby girl," she said to Mila.

Maggie was proud of the fact that she'd confronted Delphine head on about the locked room last night instead of trying to break into it on her own—the very thought of which still gave her tremors of guilt. As soon as she talked Delphine into giving her the green light to look inside she just might uncover a lead to help ease Delphine's mind over the tragedy that had haunted her for over seventy years.

Another avenue of investigation that she had in her back pocket was checking out the village where Camille came from, an hour outside Paris. Delphine said Camille's family had refused to have anything to do with Camille's child but there might be someone left alive there who knew where she'd gone.

Maggie's phone rang and she checked the screen but didn't recognize the number.

"Hello?"

"Madame Dernier? It is Victor Rousseau. Delphine's friend?"

"Oh, yes, Monsieur Rousseau," Maggie said. "Of course I remember you."

"I got your number from Delphine. I hope you don't mind."

"Not at all. I'm glad you called. I didn't get a chance to talk with you much at the party."

"I was thinking the same thing. This is my usual luncheon time with Delphine but she doesn't feel up to it today. Would you care to meet me for lunch?"

Maggie laughed. "Sure, I'd love to. If you don't mind dealing with a six month old over the *foie gras*."

"*Pas de problème*," he said with a deep throated laugh. "I love babies!"

They arranged to meet at a small restaurant just a few blocks away. Meanwhile, Maggie waved to the waiter and ordered another coffee and a sweet roll for Mila. The waiter wasn't pleasant but he wasn't overtly rude either.

Feeling satisfied with her morning's work and delighted for the opportunity to grill Victor about Delphine, Maggie put in a call to Laurent.

"Where are you?" he asked when he picked up.

"Oh, you know," Maggie said. "At police headquarters in the missing children's department."

"Very *droll, chérie*. Your mother has called me."

"Again? I got that sorted out with her."

"She doesn't feel that you have. I booked your flights home."

"Damn it, Laurent!" Maggie said and then glanced at Mila who looked at her with a worried look. "I *told* her I'd come home. What's the hurry?"

"No, hurry," Laurent said calmly. "It's in two weeks."

"I can't leave in two weeks!"

"Why not?"

"I...you..." Maggie sputtered. "You know I don't like people arranging my life for me!"

"This is a new dislike of yours that I was not aware of."

"Stop it, Laurent. Stop sounding like you're in control of this. I'll go in my own time."

"*Non*. Your mother needs you home. Two weeks."

"Unbelievable!"

"Do you want to speak to your young man? He is right here. Jemmy?"

Maggie took in a long breath and tried to focus on how energized she'd been before Laurent and her mother collaborated to spoil her day.

"*Maman*?"

"Hey, baby boy," Maggie said, feeling the vexation drain from her.

That Laurent was a sly one, she thought as the tenseness in her shoulders softened at the sound of her son's voice.

Delphine definitely wasn't wrong about *that*.

∽

DELPHINE LISTENED to the phone ring with mounting annoyance.

Was that useless woman not even going to answer the phone?

She left her dressing table in her bedroom. "Amelie? Are you here?"

Delphine stepped into the living room and saw the note. <Gone to boulangerie.>

Her posture rigid with annoyance, Delphine snatched up the still ringing phone.

"*Allo*?" she said, her voice laced with dread and apprehension.

Before the caller even spoke, Delphine could hear the background rumble of traffic mixed with cars honking. Was he calling from somewhere in the city? Somewhere close?

"Are you ready, Madame?" the disembodied voice barked out, its mechanical delivery adding a disembodied and alien layer to the words. "Or do you think I am not serious?"

"I don't have anything. I don't know anything."

"Liar! Your secret from the war! If you think I will let it die with you, you are mad!"

"Please don't hurt my family. I will do anything you—"

"No, you are lying again. Always you are lying. But this time, no. This time, you will suffer the consequences. Because of your lies, Madame, tonight a loved one will die."

22

Delphine staggered to the kitchen and poured herself a glass of water. She steadied herself by the sink as she drank.

Who could they mean?

An image of Victor and Noel came to mind, replaced quickly by an image of Mila and then Maggie. Delphine sucked in a sharp breath of air.

They wouldn't really hurt them. It's just threats. Nasty, cowardly threats.

She poured a second glass of water and drank deeply again. Within moments she felt a little stronger. She looked at the phone in the living room as she recalled the terrible distorted voice.

Who could it be? Was it someone she knew?

A shiver of horror trembled through her whole body.

They know about the secret. Even if they don't know what it is. Somehow, whoever they are, they know.

How can I give them what they want as long as there is a Dernier alive to carry the name? How can I do that to my precious Mila or her brother?

Her eyes went to the storage room and a wave of hopelessness crashed over her.

~

THE BRASSERIE where Maggie was to meet Victor was down a quaint little alleyway not far from the famous St-Michel fountain. She still wasn't sure bringing Mila to a restaurant was the best idea but it beat backtracking to Delphine's apartment. Victor was waiting out front of *La Cuillère d'Or*, the tiniest restaurant Maggie had ever seen. Its front door was so narrow she was sure she'd have to enter sideways to get in. There were two tables outside but all the patrons seemed to be opting for indoor dining.

"*Bonjour*, Madame Dernier!" Victor said. They shook hands and he immediately exclaimed over the baby.

"Please call me Maggie," Maggie said. "I'm so glad you rang. Delphine talks about you all the time. I'm glad to get to know you better."

"And me, you, Maggie," he said, his eyes crinkling into a smile that nearly made them disappear into his face of wrinkles. "Come, come! Do you know *pot au feu*?"

He ushered her into the restaurant which was a narrow room with only five small wooden tables on each side wall. A woman in an apron and shoulder length dark hair, menus in hand, stepped up to meet them.

"*Deux*?" she asked and then before they could answer indicated that they should follow her to the back of the room.

Maggie sat across from Victor at a corner table jammed up against the back wall. She pulled Mila out of the carrier and set her beside her. Mila promptly grabbed a spoon and began banging it on the table.

"My husband makes *pot au feu*," Maggie said, taking the spoon from Mila and digging out a cloth toy for her instead.

"Ahhh, the nephew," Victor said, nodding. "So he cooks?"

"Does he ever. In fact, back in the States he was the chef for a country club in Atlanta."

The waitress took the open bottle of red wine on the table and poured Victor and Maggie each a glass. Victor handed the waitress the menus and spoke rapidly to her in French.

"May I hold her?" He nodded toward Mila and Maggie gratefully handed the baby over. Mila snuggled against Victor's tweed vest and yawned.

"Wow. You've got the touch," Maggie said. "If you can get her to fall asleep so we can eat, I'll have to adopt you."

"I love the little ones," Victor said fondly. "But, alas."

"No grandkiddies of your own?"

"It's generally preferred that one create actual children first," he said with a smile, "before moving on to grandchildren."

"Wow. We have the same rule in America."

Watching Victor's peaceful enjoyment of the baby made Maggie think there might be a place for a surrogate grandpa in their lives. Especially if Victor and Delphine were a couple as they seemed to be.

"How long have you known Delphine?" she asked.

"Oh, many years. She is my one, you see," Victor said, his eyes misting.

"Your one?"

"My purpose. My one."

"I think I see. Has she always been so…"

"Sad?"

"I guess I was going to say tortured."

"You are very observant, Maggie. *Oui*. As long as I am knowing her."

"Because of the war?"

"Partly." He sipped his wine and smiled at Mila as she fell asleep in his arms. He glanced at Maggie. "Try the wine. It is very good."

Maggie sipped her wine and felt a relaxing wave of peace

filter through her. She unbunched her shoulders and allowed herself the pleasure of being off the leash with Mila. Since she'd been away from Grace's and her live-in nanny, she'd had no break from childcare. It felt good to let Victor take over for a few precious moments.

"Delphine feels as if she has done something that needs forgiveness you see," he said. "But she can't forgive herself."

Maggie realized that Victor had nailed it precisely. The guilt she'd sensed in Delphine hadn't made sense up until now. Sorrow, yes, even regret, but not *culpability*.

An elderly man approached the table and spoke to Victor in a low voice. He held a menu in his hands. Maggie couldn't catch what he was saying but Victor nodded and said, "Of course. I would be honored." Victor pulled out a fountain pen and signed the back of the menu and then shook hands with the man.

"A fan?" Maggie asked when the older man left.

"In a way," Victor said. "You know of my personal tragedy during the war, yes?"

Maggie nodded.

"People remember the past. They remember the ones who survived, the ones who didn't. Do you know there is a fish shop in a village in Provence where some villagers refuse to shop because seventy years ago the family owners collaborated with the Germans?"

"Wow. Way to hold a grudge."

"My history gives me a special status, you see. It is one of the reasons I believe that only I can help Delphine forgive herself."

"You really love her."

"In any life, a great love comes. There is no doubt for me that love is Delphine. I just need to convince her that she is deserving."

"How long have you been at it?"

"Oh, I am not caring how long it takes. And perhaps she will never turn to me and say 'Victor, it is you. All along it is you.' But

I think in her heart she already knows and for me that is enough."

"I don't know what she'd do without you."

"She says the same thing about you!" They both laughed.

The waitress came and deposited two brimming bowls in front of them. The fragrance from the boiled beef mingled with the hearty vegetables swimming in the broth. Maggie cut into the beef and dredged a piece of French bread in the broth. It was redolent with cloves and pepper.

"Oh my God, this is amazing," she said after the first bite.

The waitress returned with a large plate of toast and a cellar of salt.

"Eat the marrow," Victor said. "Scoop it out and spread it on the toast. It's even better that way. Trust me." Maggie did and felt herself transported back to Laurent's kitchen. Her ecstasy over the dish was tempered by a sudden longing for her husband.

"How are you going to eat with one hand?" she asked, nodding at the sleeping baby in the crook of his left arm.

"I will treasure the handicap," he said, picking up a fork.

They ate in silence for a moment with only the sounds of Mila cooing happily in Victor's arms.

"You don't happen to know why Delphine and her nephews don't speak, do you?" Maggie asked.

"Gerard?"

"Well, I can understand her not wanting to talk to Gerard, but Laurent is a really good guy. He's practically a cornerstone of respectability in his wine co-op and the village where we live."

"But Delphine can only see the young man he was?"

"That's what I think."

"I'm sorry, *chérie*. She never speaks of them. Either of them."

"The whole family is just such a damn mystery, it's nice to talk to someone who also has to wade through all their defense mechanisms."

Victor laughed and reached for his glass of wine. "They're worth it," he said.

"Isn't it hard on you?" Maggie asked. "Being so close to Delphine and her ghosts from the war, considering what happened to you?"

"Not as much as you might think. I was a child during the war. I had no real experience with its horrors."

"Beyond losing your family to it."

"*Oui*," he said softly. "Beyond that."

"Do you know what it is that makes her so sad?"

"Delphine has said some things over the years but nothing to reveal the crux of why she cannot forgive herself. My purpose is to let her know that regardless of what she thinks she's done, it doesn't matter. She is loved. And she is forgiven."

"I think she feels she could have done something to save her friend Camille."

"The one executed as a *collabo*?" He shook his head. "There is no balm for that kind of wound. Not even time."

"I know, but I thought maybe if I was able to find out what happened to Camille's daughter...maybe Delphine could...get some closure on the whole thing."

"Americans," Victor said with a laugh. "Everything is a happy-ever-after Disney movie for you, yes? But, of course you may be right. We French think that sort of sentimentality is nonsense but half the time it is exactly right. Do you think you can find her?"

"I don't know," Maggie admitted. "And if I do, I'm not sure it will help."

Victor leaned out and touched Maggie's hand, his eyes glistening with emotion. "Just your trying has already helped beyond what you can even imagine."

~

AFTER LUNCH, Maggie waved goodbye to Victor. She hadn't found out any family secrets but she had gotten one step closer to understanding the family and that was something. She could see Victor's love for Delphine and could only imagine the kind of angst that wouldn't let Delphine enjoy it—or return it.

When she stepped off the elevator to Delphine's apartment Amelie was just leaving. Inside, Delphine was sitting in the living room. Her hands were clasped together in her lap, her eyes darting around the room.

"Hi, Delphine," Maggie said as she entered the apartment. "Everything okay?"

Delphine looked up at her as if she didn't know her at first but quickly shook herself out of her reverie.

"You are back."

"Let me change the baby," Maggie said moving down the hall to her room. "I'll be right in."

Why is it every time she left she had the feeling something bad had just happened? Had Gerard been back? Did Michelle make an unexpected visit? Maybe it was just sharing the same room with Amelie? Spending two hours with *her* would definitely have most people contemplating suicide ledges.

Maggie returned to the living room and put Mila on the floor after making sure any and all cords of expensive lamps were well out of reach. The transformation to Delphine upon seeing the baby was immediate. Her face cleared and a smile tugged at her lips. Before Maggie knew she was doing it, the elderly woman slipped from the couch to the carpet to sit next to the baby.

"Hello, *ma petite*," Delphine said to Mila. "Did you miss me a little?"

"I had lunch with Victor," Maggie said.

Delphine's eyes brightened. "I'm glad. I know he looks forward to our little lunches and I haven't felt up to it lately."

Mila crawled over to her and reached for Delphine's pearl bracelet.

"Have you eaten?" Maggie asked. "I picked up sandwiches on the way back."

Delphine looked up. "You may leave her with me, you know," she said. "Mademoiselle Mila and I will be just fine."

Maggie hesitated. The fact was she *was* a little restless. Until Delphine offered, she hadn't realized that a few hours on her own was exactly what she needed.

"Are you sure?" Maggie asked. "Now that you mention it, I'd love a little break. If you're sure."

Delphine pulled Mila onto her lap. She looked up at Maggie and whatever unhappiness or distress Maggie thought she'd seen when she first entered the apartment was gone.

"We are both very sure, *Maman*," Delphine said. "Go to a movie. Take a walk. Get your hair done."

Maggie laughed. "You sound just like Grace." She leaned down and kissed Mila on her head. "But a walk without my favorite appendage sounds great. I promise I won't be long."

"Take as long as you need, *chérie*. We will be fine here."

MAGGIE KNEW EXACTLY where she wanted to go. She would have gone there this morning but it was a longer walk than she could comfortably do carrying Mila. She'd worn her sneakers again and was glad she had. She started out at a brisk pace up rue du Bac until she reached and crossed the boulevard Saint-Germain and then continued on the Boulevard Raspail.

As she entered Montparnasse there seemed to be fewer tourists and more students than in the rest of the Latin Quarter. Maggie knew she wasn't far from the École des Beaux-Arts where her sister Elise had been a student all those many years ago. She forced herself not to look in the direction of the school. But banishing the painful memories of that time was much harder.

Elise had come to Paris as a young art student, hopeful and full of youthful exuberance. She'd left pregnant and addicted to heroin. The father of her child who was also her dealer, would later steal her child away and then abandon the girl. Both Elise and the child were now dead.

But the father, Gerard Dernier, still lived.

An image of Elise smiling up at her from the living room of Maggie's apartment in Atlanta—the last time Maggie ever saw her alive—flashed into Maggie's brain and she dug her fingernails into the palms of her hands to force the image away. Elise had brought her family nothing but pain.

And it seemed she wasn't finished yet.

Maggie stopped at the intersection of Boulevard Raspail and rue de Sevres. She vaguely knew the area—at least as much as most tourists do. She thought she remembered that the Luxembourg Gardens were nearby.

And so was the apartment building where Delphine and her sisters grew up.

Maggie glanced at the photo she'd taken that morning from the silver box while Delphine slept. It was a picture of Delphine and Jacqueline standing on the street in front of an apartment building. Delphine was smiling coquettishly. Jacqueline was scowling. On the back, someone had written *chez nous. 14 rue Canivet*.

Maggie wasn't sure what she expected to see from the building but she just knew that she needed to see it. She needed to see where the sisters had lived—where *Camille* had lived.

Maggie pulled out her smartphone and typed in the address, waiting for the data to download and direct her. Finally, her GPS pinpointed the building and she could see she wasn't far away. Following the screen directions, she turned a corner and was startled to see an enormous church in front of her. The sign read *Église Saint-Sulpice*. She shook her head in wonder.

Maggie was continually surprised that there were so many gorgeous churches in this city that most people had never even heard of. She hurried down the block, her eye on the screen of her phone as it led her past two more side streets. Like much of the Latin Quarter, this section was a maze of narrow cobblestone streets that appeared to have no logical connection to larger arteries. As she walked, it occurred to her that this neighborhood wasn't far from where her Uncle Stan had died—pushed from a seventh story window during a Paris Fashion Week party—three years earlier. Her chest ached at the thought of him.

Maybe Laurent is right about Paris, Maggie thought, suddenly feeling her energy and optimism seep away. *Maybe it really does hold more ghosts than it does delights.*

The street she was walking on was narrow and the pavement broken and ancient. Her calves ached and she felt the hard stones beneath her sneakers.

How in the world did Grace regularly walk around Paris in high heels? The thought of Grace didn't help Maggie's plummeting mood so she focused on her phone. The screen map indicated she should be right around the corner from Canivet.

Paris hadn't always been a memory dump of unhappiness. As a child, Maggie's mother had taken her and Elise shopping here on more than one occasion and always the experiences had been magical. She realized that if she wanted to mitigate her sad memories of Paris, she'd need to make some new wonderful ones.

I'll bring Jemmy and make sure he and Mila go to the d'Orsay and have happy memories of lunches and eating ice cream in the park and climbing the Eiffel Tower. We'll make their papa come to hold their hands and eat ice cream too. Maggie smiled at the image.

Drown out the bad memories with new, better ones.

She stopped at the corner and dialed Laurent's number. She was just moments from discovering the sisters' childhood home but she suddenly longed to hear Jemmy's voice. Especially after their less-than-satisfying call earlier, she felt an equally strong urge to hear Laurent's voice too.

There was no answer and eventually the call went to voice

mail. She didn't leave a message. Laurent was probably out in the fields with little Jemmy on his shoulders laughing and directing his papa, the sun on his face.

She turned the next corner and there it was: a long row of the classic creamy Haussmann apartments with looming windows—each tall enough to serve as doors if they hadn't been forty feet off the ground and each with the classic black wrought iron balconies perched in front of them. At the very top were the familiar mansard rooftops with their distinctive hatches.

Maggie gazed up at the dormer windows and imagined the hidden panels or secret attics that might have been used to hide Jewish families from the Nazis…

Or shameless French girls and their forbidden lovers.

She moved down the street, staring up at the building and wondering which apartment had been the Fouquet sisters' home. Which one had been Camille's? The cobblestones were older and rougher here and Maggie wondered whether a car could make it down the narrow avenue without scraping loose its undercarriage.

She walked the full block until the lane ended in a small square hemmed in by several cafés and shops—all topped with more apartments. There was an enormous sycamore tree in the center of the square and a small dry fountain anchored off the northern side. On the wall over it Maggie saw a large granite placard. She walked closer and read the words written in French.

On this spot the Gestapo gunned down five young people who spoke for France. August 21, 1944.

She rubbed the goose bumps off her arms. That was the beginning of the liberation of Paris. The war was nearly over and yet five young men and women…She looked around at the people sitting in the café or perusing the display bins in front of the cheese and produce shops. Life was so normal. Yet once this pretty square had been a place of death and injustice.

She glanced back at Delphine's apartment building and from

this angle could see that the main door to the building faced the square. She turned to see the gigantic sycamore tree growing in the middle of the square, its branches heavy and reaching heavenward.

A chill raced through her.

My God. This is where they hanged her.

23

Noel stood in Delphine's living room. He looked as if he were trying to decide whether or not to storm out or be civilized about it. For a moment, Delphine saw an image of him as a boy. The old man dissolved into the child and back again in the blink of an eye.

"I just don't know why you can't say the words," Noel said, his hands shoved into the pockets of his rain jacket. He glared at Delphine as she spooned stewed apricots into Mila's mouth.

He'd come by just minutes after Maggie had left—almost like he'd been watching—and for that Delphine was sorry. She knew he'd behave himself if others were around.

"I don't know what words you want me to say, *chérie*," Delphine said wearily. *Please just go. I am so tired of this game of yours.*

"I know you're my mother! Why not admit it?" He took two steps toward the kitchen but perhaps the sight of the baby in her high chair stopped him. He turned in frustration and retraced his steps back to the foyer as if preparing to leave. But again he didn't.

"What difference does any of that make now?" Delphine said,

feeling a pinch of ire at having to play this part over and over again. Could she not just have one afternoon where she wasn't fighting the same old battles? "You're an old man, for God's sakes. Want me to tuck you in at night?"

He slapped his hands against his sides in frustration, startling the baby. Mila burst into tears. Delphine patted the baby on the shoulder and tried to soothe her.

"Now see what you've done!" she said to him. "Just leave, Noel. I'm sick to death of you!"

"I just want to know," he said, his voice cracking pathetically. "My God, can you not understand that?" Then he finally, mercifully, turned and let himself out the door.

It took Delphine fifteen minutes to calm the baby after that. She was sorry she'd said what she had to Noel. But he'd upset Mila and there was no excuse for that.

She settled on the couch with the baby in her lap. Mila was such a compliant child and so cheerful too. Delphine wished she might live long enough to see the girl she would become—the amazing woman she would some day be. She cupped Mila's head and stared into her beautiful blue eyes.

So like Georgette but so much more.

The baby yawned and cuddled into the crook of Delphine's arms. Delphine felt the satisfying weight of the child finally release and grow heavy in her arms. She nuzzled Mila's head and relished the sweet baby smell of her. As the baby slept, she seemed to take Delphine's worries with her wherever it was she had gone. For one brief moment there seemed to open up a vista of peace in her mind where there was nothing to fear.

And then Delphine glanced across the salon to where the telephone sat. It perched like the most malevolent of Notre-Dame's gargoyles—waiting to end her peace and carry her to the depths of hell itself.

He wouldn't really hurt Maggie would he? Or the baby? Surely, those were just threats...

She wrenched her eyes from the silently waiting telephone to settle on the baby again

...and felt her fears ease once more.

~

MAGGIE SAT for a peaceful hour with a glass of wine in the café. The rain had held off and she could feel the weather getting warmer by the day. She tried to imagine what it must have been like to have lived in Delphine and Camille's building during that terrible time. Today only the sounds of people chatting and the muted clinking of coffee cups from inside the café filled the air. There were no air raid sirens now or screams of terror...

Her phone pinged and, thinking it might be Laurent, Maggie pulled it out to see she'd received an email from Herr Schmidt. With her pulse racing, Maggie scanned the message. He wrote that he believed the Bauer family had settled in Heidelberg. He had contact information of a relative! A wave of pleasure filled Maggie when she realized she was getting closer to solving the mystery of what had happened to Camille's daughter—and to easing Delphine's mind. She quickly responded to the email and threw down a few euros before jumping up to hurry back to Delphine's apartment.

The timing could not be more perfect! She was going to be able to give Delphine peace about this terrible time in her life—and still manage to get back to St-Buvard before the weekend as she'd promised Laurent.

As Maggie walked down the rue du Canivet, her thoughts unfocused but infused with a feeling of wellbeing, her phone vibrated briefly. She pulled it out and saw it displayed a *Low Battery* message. No problem. She was confident she could find the way back to Delphine's without the help of a GPS.

At the cross street, she paused and frowned. She was positive she'd come this way but it didn't look familiar. Shrugging, she chose a direction and hurried down the street until she could take the next first turn she came to.

After three more turns she stopped in frustration and looked around her. There was no way she'd come this way. Worse, she seemed to have left all the activity of people and traffic behind. The street she was on was typical of the Latin Quarter—claustrophobically narrow, with the apartment windows closed tight against light and noise. There were no cars. No people.

A vein of unease throbbed between her shoulders and she began walking again. Surely she would come to a place she recognized? Perhaps the street up ahead would reveal a bustling intersection? And people who could direct her?

But the next intersection was a dead end with shuttered businesses.

Maggie turned to look back the way she'd come. Her heart was thudding in her throat now. Without her noticing it, the warm day had dissolved into an overcast one and the street was cast in shadow. A sensation crawled across her skin like ants let loose over spoiled food. She rubbed her arms and felt a thin sheen of sweat on her hands.

The minute she stopped to take a deep breath to calm herself was the minute she realized she was being followed.

24

Maggie didn't stop to confirm it or ask why. If there really was someone following her, She knew she needed to lose him. *Now*.

Opting for decisiveness over analysis, she moved six steps back the way she'd come until she found a narrow alley she hadn't noticed when she'd passed before. She darted into it now. And ran.

Somewhere in the back of her mind she could hear the footsteps behind her—all pretense at stealth abandoned. She kept her hands on both sides of the rough stone walls to steady herself so she wouldn't fall on the lumpy cobblestones which hadn't been replaced in centuries. In front of her she saw only darkness but she had no other choice. She had to go forward. She'd committed to it and now she needed to follow through and pray for the best.

Looking up, she saw fire escapes hanging above her like iron aerial sculptures. Her left hand came to a gap in the wall and she realized she'd run past yet another narrow turn in the alley. Instinct made her swivel around and plunge down the new alley.

Whoever was following her would be able to look down the

alley and immediately see if she'd taken it. He'd see her clearly...unless...

She came to another alley on her left and turned again.

Now she was running in the opposite direction of the one she'd taken when she had originally entered the lane. But unless her assailant had kept her in view through every twist and turn—and he couldn't have—he wouldn't know she'd turned off.

He'd look and see nobody in the alley—and hopefully—he'd go on to the next turnoff before realizing she'd taken the first one.

Her heart pounded in her ears until she couldn't hear the sounds of her pursuer over her own breath and heartbeat. She froze, trying to swallow the noise of her panting as the terror ricocheted around her brain. She tried to listen but her panic consumed all her senses.

If he catches me here he can do whatever he likes to me. Nobody would ever know.

In desperation, she looked up again and saw the lowest rung of the iron handle on one of the hanging fire escape platforms.

If he looks down this alley...

She jumped for the iron handle and grabbed it. Using her sneakers to walk up the side of the rough stone wall, she pulled herself up to the platform and lay flat, feeling dirt and flakes of rust embed into her cheek as she turned her head to listen.

She heard him. Over the pounding of her heart, she heard him.

He wasn't running. He was walking. Purposefully. Deliberately. He was looking down each alley. Maggie felt sweat form on her palms. The sound of footsteps was coming nearer. He'd be at her alley within seconds. She willed herself to be as still as possible so nothing would catch his eye.

She held her breath just as he appeared in the alley. He was tall. A knit hat was jammed on his head and he had a hand to his mouth as if trying to think. It made it impossible to see his face clearly. He hesitated at the opening but didn't stop. He glanced down the alley.

He didn't look up.

And then he was gone.

As she lay there, too afraid to move but with relief pushing through every pore, it struck Maggie that she'd escaped using the maze of alleys in the Latin Quarter—just like so many had done during the Paris occupation.

Only instead of Nazi goons...who was after her?

Her knees began to tremble.

∼

GERARD HURRIED the last two blocks up the street to his apartment building. He'd ruined his feet in the Middle East by going barefoot too many times over terrain both cold and hard. He'd lost a toe to frostbite in the desert. It was a fascinating story that he had no one to tell. There was no one to care if he'd died in the desert or a hundred times over in the souks and the tents that had been his temporary refuge for four long years.

He slowed and concentrated on making the final steps to the front door of the apartment that his aunt paid for. He grimaced when he thought of Delphine.

The sooner she died, the better for everyone.

A homeless woman sat on the front stoop of his building. Gerard made a detour around her, but she stood up and touched his sleeve as he tried to enter the building.

"Monsieur..." she said.

"Piss off," he snarled, snatching his sleeve from her. "I'll call the flics!"

"I have a proposition for you, Monsieur," the woman said as she hurried into the building beside him.

"I'd rather screw a diseased pig," he said. "Get out before I call the landlord."

"I am not a prostitute, you bastard," the woman screeched. "I have money you are entitled to through your aunt Delphine Normand."

Gerard turned to look at her. She was in rags but heavyset so somehow she was getting enough to eat. Her hair hung in dark greasy strands to her shoulders. He made a grimace of distaste.

"Who are you?"

"My name is Michelle Normand," she said, approaching him. "May we talk in your apartment? What I have to say is of a delicate nature."

Gerard nearly laughed at the thought that this creature was delicate in any sense. But he would hear her out. She must be related to Delphine's dead husband in some way.

Inside his apartment, he tossed his key on the kitchen counter and turned to her.

"What money do you have that belongs to me?" he asked.

"Your inheritance from your aunt."

"What does that have to do with you?"

"I stand between you and inheriting the money your aunt wants to leave to you."

"What are you talking about?" He narrowed his eyes. If this stupid bitch thought she could blackmail him, she was as crazy as she looked.

"What if I told you that with a single phone call I could ensure that nobody with the name Dernier could ever lift his head without shame again?"

He barked out a laugh. "Like I give a shit about that."

"My father told me your aunt has hidden Nazi treasure from the war! He said he lived in fear every day of his marriage that it would be discovered. I will make sure that it is!"

"Your father must have been as crazy as you are."

"It's the truth! When I go to the police with what I know, your aunt will be impoverished! *And* she will go to prison!"

"And you are offering what exactly," Gerard said sarcastically, "to ensure this doesn't happen?"

"Tell your aunt to put me back in the will. I only ask for what's mine. Just what my father wanted me to have."

"So in return for carving into *my* piece of the pie you promise not to report these charges against my aunt?"

"Yes, Monsieur. I swear it. Delphine may keep her secret for perpetuity."

"Get out," Gerard said. He shoved her toward the door and she tripped, flailing with her arms to stay upright.

"Don't you understand me? I can ruin her! You'll get nothing!"

"And if I kill you?"

She stared at him with large uncomprehending eyes. "What?"

"*Kill* you," Gerard said, leaning over her, one arm slammed into the wall above her head where she cowered. "If I choke the life out of you…oh, not here when so many people have seen you walk into my apartment…but later? When you are in your bed thinking you are safe? If I slip out of the shadows and wrap my hands around your throat?"

Michelle pawed at the doorknob behind her, her eyes never leaving his. "You…you…"

"Then I won't have to share my inheritance with you or worry that you might attempt to reduce my share to…how is it you put it?…nothing?"

She got the door open and Gerard pushed her out, watching her stumble to her knees before he slammed the door on her. He heard her howling from the stairwell.

"I will bury you all! I will bury every useless one of you!"

25

Maggie didn't know how long she waited but the rain had started and the shadow in the alleyway had deepened. She was cold when she finally sat up and took the measure of what had happened to her.

She'd escaped. She was okay. There wasn't a sound, not a ghost of a whisper of a noise to tell her that someone was still hunting her.

She dropped softly onto the ancient cobblestones in the alley and carefully, silently retraced her steps back to the main lane where she'd first entered. If her pursuer assumed she'd fled all the way to the end of the alley—and since he didn't see her turn around why wouldn't he?—surely she didn't need to worry about being intercepted.

But at this point, Maggie was prepared to worry about just about everything.

Who was he? What did he want with her? Was it random? Was she being targeted? Could it possibly have something to do with Isla's murder?

Maggie ran to the first lane she'd entered and saw what she'd missed before—a bare glimmer of a blinking light three long blocks away that heralded a traffic intersection. She focused on the light and ran toward it without stopping. After the first block, she began to see people again. As she reached the traffic intersection she saw the back of the *Èglise Saint-Sulpice* and knew where she was.

Thirty minutes later she was taking the stairs in Delphine's apartment two at a time to arrive wheezing and damp with sweat at her front door. It was already late afternoon. In the time it took Maggie to jog all the way back to Delphine's, she had convinced herself that the incident had been all her own doing. She'd allowed herself to get lost in unfamiliar territory and then isolated—two obvious warning flags for any mugger worth his salt. It was ridiculous to think she had been somehow targeted. She'd just forgotten her surroundings and nearly paid a high price for it.

Just because this isn't inner city Detroit doesn't mean it's crime free. Paris is a major metropolitan city.

"Maggie?" Delphine called from the kitchen. "You have enjoyed your outing?"

Maggie came into the kitchen to see Mila sitting in a high chair with a spoon in one fist and a face full of pudding.

"Hey, you got a high chair," Maggie said breathlessly, coming over to Mila and giving her a kiss.

"Victor brought it today," Delphine said smiling.

Maggie tried to imagine old Victor struggling with the high chair down the busy streets of the Latin Quarter and up the stairwell. There was no way that chair would fit in the tiny elevator.

"You have been jogging?" Delphine asked.

"Kind of. I went to Montparnasse to see where you used to live."

"I understand that neighborhood is quite pretty today."

"It was beautiful. I think you have to be rich to live there, though." The last thing Maggie intended to do was tell Delphine about how she'd stupidly nearly allowed herself to get mugged.

"Your slacks are ripped!" Delphine said.

Maggie rubbed at the knee. "Yeah, I fell not looking where I was going. No biggie."

THAT NIGHT after Mila was put to bed, Maggie put together a meal of takeout leftovers with a bottle of Côte du Rhone. Maggie couldn't remember the last time she'd seen Delphine so relaxed.

Ah, the magic of Mila, Maggie thought fondly.

"So you are determined to write my biography, eh?" Delphine said with a smile as she sat at the dining table, their finished meal before them.

"Well, yours or Laurent's," Maggie said. "Learning about your past helps me learn about his past. And as you know, I don't know squat about his past."

"I have been thinking about that. And I have a gift for you," Delphine said. She slid an envelope across the table. Inside was a key.

"This is to the storage room in the foyer?"

Delphine nodded. "It is time," she said solemnly. "I have felt for so long that I was protecting these...items for the boys."

"By *the boys*, you mean...?"

"Laurent and Gerard. It is their birthright."

What the hell is in there? Maggie wondered with bewilderment.

"For years I felt I was keeping them safe, keeping all of us safe. But perhaps I was doing just the opposite."

Maggie waited for Delphine to explain but she just took a long sip of her wine. She looked over Maggie's shoulder in the direction of the locked door.

"I trust you, Maggie," she said. "You are family."

"Thank you, Delphine. I promise not to treat that trust lightly."

Delphine shrugged. "You cannot change the past. I know that. It's time."

Would it be rude to jump up and go unlock the door right now? Maggie thought wryly as she slipped the key into her slacks pocket.

"Finish your dinner, *chérie*," Delphine said as if she could read Maggie's mind. "It is a long walk from the old neighborhood. You must be tired."

You have no idea, Maggie thought, dutifully eating the last of her Thai chicken.

"It was interesting to see where you all lived as teenagers," Maggie said. "I'm always trying to find out more about Laurent's family."

"It's true I know very little about Laurent's parents," Delphine said. "But I can tell you that his grandparents were very much in love."

"I'm glad," Maggie said. "Great dynasties should start with great love stories."

"My father however was not happy with my sister's choice. Marc Dernier was a rogue, you see."

"You mean like...a thief?"

"No, no. I mean he had a dangerous kind of style."

"Sounds like Jacqueline had a thing for bad boys."

"My sister was very strong-willed. She would need a strong-minded man to be happy."

"Why didn't your dad like him?"

Delphine shrugged. "Fathers have different ideals for the men of their daughters. If Papa had not relented in the end and blessed the union, Jacqueline would have defied him."

"What did Marc do for a living?"

"He was a leader during the war. Afterward, he was in business. I am not sure what kind."

So mysterious. Is it possible Delphine really doesn't know?

"Marc and Jacqueline had two sons. Nicolas, the younger son, did well for himself although he never married. He moved south and grew his grapes and never returned to Paris."

Jeez, way to stay close family.

"And Laurent's father, Robert?"

"A disappointment."

Maggie could see that Delphine was tired. She'd babysat all afternoon and had obviously been thinking about family a good part of it too—something Maggie knew was emotionally draining for her.

Maggie had had a big day herself and not time enough to process much of it. Her response to Herr Schmidt—delivered hastily via her smartphone before its battery died—had prompted a reply with the name and email of Helmut Bauer's grandson. Maggie was vibrating with eagerness to send an email to him to see if they could meet.

After she said goodnight to Delphine and cleaned up the kitchen it was still relatively early. Laurent would probably call in another hour or so depending on what time he got Jemmy to bed. Maggie moved to the far corner of the living room, forcing herself not to go to the storage door and wrench it open to reveal all of its secrets. Not yet.

She put a call into Grace who answered on the first ring. Unusual for her.

"Hello?" Grace said breathlessly.

"You know it's me, right?" Maggie said. "I mean it should say so right on your phone screen."

Grace sighed. "I didn't look before I answered. Hello, Maggie."

Clearly, she'd been hoping it was someone else.

"Are you home for a change?" Maggie asked.

"I am. Is that why you're calling? To check on my whereabouts? You're starting to sound like Windsor."

"Sorry," Maggie said. "No, I'm calling because I have great news. Remember how I was telling you about Delphine's best friend during the war? The one who was arrested for consorting with a Nazi?"

"Of course."

"I think I've found a way to track down her daughter—"

"For what possible purpose?"

Maggie hesitated. "To give Delphine the peace of mind she's been missing all these years."

Grace made an impatient sound. "What if you discover something awful? After being tarred and feathered, what if Camille became a prostitute or ran for public office? Then what will you do?"

"Camille wasn't tarred and feathered, Grace." Maggie said with irritation. "Do you even listen to me? She was *hanged*. Besides, I'm not looking for Camille. I'm looking for her daughter."

"Fine. Whatever. But if Camille's daughter ended up having a terrible life of poverty and shame because of what happened to her mother, my question is the same: what will you do? Tell Delphine the truth? Or lie to her to give her the peace you think she craves?"

"God, Grace, you are so negative! How about I find out the truth first?"

A silence extended between them and Maggie tried to remember a single other time when Grace hadn't been fully ready to jump in and tackle a mystery with her.

"In any case," Maggie said, "I did a little online research and I found a guy who knows the name of the grandson of the guy Camille was having the affair with. He lives in Heidelberg. So I was thinking, maybe you and I could pack up the kids and take a day trip to Germany. What do you say? It'll be fun."

"Are you serious? What in the world would you say to him? '*Sorry you lost the war. Sorry your dirt bag grandfather had an affair with a Frenchwoman who was then executed. How's the rest of your life been?*'"

"I intend to phrase it differently."

"It's absurd to think this guy would know anything about the daughter of his grandfather's girlfriend! From seventy years ago? He probably didn't even know his grandfather's girlfriend *had* a daughter."

Maggie had to admit the way Grace put it, it sounded pretty weak.

"Maybe I should just call him?" she ventured.

"Yes, darling. Call him instead. Great idea. Especially since it's so much easier to hang up on you than close the door in your face."

"Are you trying to talk me out of it?"

"I'm not trying to do anything except say that even if I wanted to go, I can't leave town right now."

"Don't tell me it's because of your online business, Grace, because that dog won't hunt."

"Much as I love all your southern slang, darling, the truth is I promised André I'd be his plus one at a big gallery event tomorrow evening."

"I'll have you back in time. It takes three hours to get to Heidelberg."

"That is an egregious lie, Maggie Newberry Dernier. It is five hours one way if it's a minute. The answer is no."

"Fine. I'll go alone. Are you sure you don't want me to take Zouzou to give you a break for the day?" she said sarcastically. Instantly, she regretted the barb.

"Thank you, darling," Grace said coolly. "But I have that handled. Have a nice trip."

AFTER HANGING UP WITH GRACE, Maggie did a couple laps around the living room to work off her frustration. Grace wasn't interested in her friends, her family, or her own children! André wasn't a boyfriend. He was an obsession. And everybody knows obsessions are unhealthy. She glanced at the locked door of the storage room.

Mila moaned and Maggie turned away from the door and went to check on her. Once Mila settled down, Maggie poured herself another glass of wine and sat down at the dining room table with her laptop.

She typed out an email introduction to herself to the contact name that Herr Schmidt had given her. The Gestapo officer's grandson's name was Dieter Bauer. Maggie knew absolutely nothing about him and a quick Google search turned up nothing. In her email she explained that she was a friend of a friend of his grandfather's—*only a tiny lie*—and that she was hoping to find out what happened to his grandfather and any other information he might have about his grandfather's life during the occupation of Paris in 1944. She ended by saying she would be happy to meet him in Heidelberg if that was convenient for him.

Maggie finished off her wine and was about to close her laptop and give Laurent a call when her eye fell on Delphine's wine glass on the table which reminded Maggie of their dinner conversation. Delphine said she didn't know what Laurent's grandfather did after the war but that he'd been in a leadership position during the war.

Maggie opened up a new browser window and typed in the name *Marc Dernier WWII France*. The list of topics that resulted surprised her. She clicked on the one that said *France's hero* and a picture of Marc Dernier materialized on her screen.

Instantly she saw Laurent in the man's face and she felt her heart beat faster. This was Laurent's grandfather. *This was who he came from.* His eyes were dark like Laurent's and just as impossible to read. He had Laurent's full lips and thick brown hair. Maggie stared at the picture for a long time, trying to see if he were a kind man or tortured or complex or simple…or anything.

She finally gave up and scanned the two paragraphs of copy

under his picture and then reread them again slowly before sagging back in her chair with her mouth open in astonishment.

The name *Marc Dernier* was known by every French schoolchild in the sixties and seventies.

He was a decorated war hero for the French Resistance.

26

A *war hero!*

Why the hell didn't Delphine tell her that? Did she not like her brother-in-law? This was *major*. Did Laurent know? If so, why hadn't he told her?

Maggie quickly called Laurent.

"*Allo, chérie*," he answered, his voice warm and velvety in her ear.

"Did you know your grandfather was a war hero?"

He sighed and didn't answer for a moment. "That was a long time ago," he said finally.

"So was the Civil War, Laurent, but people still think it's a big deal. What was he like?"

"A drunk."

"God, Laurent. Do I have to go to Wikipedia? Because I'm pretty sure he has his own page."

"Whatever my grandfather did in the war doesn't matter. Not to his family or his children or his grandchildren and certainly not to his wife. Whatever he did, and whoever he was in 1944, he was a bitter drunkard in 1992 when he died alone and loved by no one."

"Whoa."

"*Chérie*, I am getting another call. It is the co-op and I must take it. I will call you back."

"Be sure you do. We're not finished with this."

Maggie hung up. It was only a little after eleven. Too early to go to bed and now she was too keyed up to even think about sleeping.

Laurent's grandfather was a national hero!

Why didn't Delphine mention it? What was going on? Had Marc Dernier really been an alcoholic? Maggie looked over the rim of her laptop. The door to the storage room seemed to glow in the dim shadow of the foyer, beckoning her.

Answers. She needed answers. And that door hid one big room full of them. She walked to the foyer and paused in the hall to listen. Both bedrooms were quiet. She slipped the key out of her pocket and unlocked the padlock. It sprang free and she carefully laid it on the floor and pulled open the door.

The smell was musty but not unpleasantly so. It smelled of paint and old books with a faint whiff of Chanel 5 perfume.

The room was small, roughly four feet by six. It had no windows but Maggie found a light switch, and walked in. The space was lined with floor to ceiling bookshelves on all three walls she faced. On the shelves were a crowd of baskets, books, boxes, file folders, paintings, African tribal masks—everything that would make a beautiful Paris apartment look like a junk shop if even a portion of it had been on display.

Delphine had said most of this stuff had belonged to her late husband. Two large oil paintings framed in gilt wooden frames leaned against the bookshelves. She didn't recognize the artists but the work didn't look amateur. She assumed the paintings were here because there was no available wall space in the apartment.

Her fingers tingled with anticipation. Where to start? Several of the shelves were dusty, indicating that no one had touched them for a long time—months, maybe even years. If anything, Delphine could probably use help in organizing this mess, Maggie thought. There seemed to be no logical order to how things were arranged on the shelves.

She pulled a box down and lifted the lid. Inside were hundreds of seashells, some still with sand clinging to them.

The junk and the valuable, Maggie thought. And the only way to tell the difference was by sifting through all of it piece by piece. She put the box back and pulled down a photo album. She settled on the floor and opened it up on her lap, excitement thrumming through her.

Most of the photos in the album had been removed. Maggie flipped through the whole book to the end wondering who had taken the photos and why. The few photos that remained were landscapes or seascapes with no people in them. They were also out of focus. When she put the album back on the shelf, a loose photo fell to the floor.

She picked it up and stared. Long moments passed and it wasn't until a tear rolled down her face and splashed on the wrist holding the photo that she realized she was crying. It was a photo of a woman, seated on a chaise, her dark hair wavy and to her shoulders, sunglasses on her head, her smile sweet and open. Beside her stood two small boys, one taller than the other. Maggie touched the face of the tall boy. It was Laurent. His face was hidden under a thick thatch of hair and a serious expression, his eyes almost challenging the photographer.

It was Laurent with his mother and brother. Suzanne was lovely—fragile looking but beautiful. She had a hand on each boy's shoulder. She looked like she cherished her boys. And both of them looked like they didn't trust whomever was taking their picture.

Oh, Laurent....

Maggie turned the photo over but there was nothing written on the back—not even a date. If what Delphine said was true, Suzanne probably died not long after this photo was taken. Laurent looked to be six or seven years old. Just a little fellow. Maggie glanced at Gerard and was shocked to see that he was actually very cute at four. In fact, he reminded her a little of Jemmy. He too was watching the photographer warily, and he had one hand on his older brother's arm as if for comfort.

Sometimes life just sucks, Maggie thought as she laid the photo aside. She wasn't sure if she would show Laurent the picture right away but some day he'd want it. And Maggie wanted Jemmy and Mila to see a picture of their beautiful French grandmother when they were older.

Her shoulders began to ache and she realized even with all the excitement of finally getting into the storage closet that she was tired. It had been a busy day—not to mention emotionally draining for its moments of sheer terror. She got to her feet and noticed a box with a label that said *cheques*. One last box before calling it a night she told herself. After all, she had all day tomorrow to go through the room.

As the label said, the box contained stacks of cancelled checks rubber-banded together. Maggie pulled a few of them free. The dates ranged from three years ago to last year. They were all signed by Delphine Normand. Maggie flipped through the stack until her eye caught a familiar name. In the memo section of the check, Gerard's name was written but the checks were made out to a company. The Balfourt Corporation.

Frowning, Maggie pulled other checks made out to the same company. In some cases, Gerard's name had been added to the memo line and in others the word *rent* was added.

Was Delphine paying Gerard's rent? Maggie placed one of the checks next to the photo. She'd look the company up on the Internet.

Digging further in the box, she found an envelope with more cancelled checks inside. Maggie flipped the envelope over. There was a return address on the envelope with Gerard's name. *Maybe*, Maggie thought, *this is the location of the apartment Delphine is paying rent on.* Maggie emptied the envelope and added it to her pile.

Well, Delphine did say she'd been giving him money. Maggie forced herself not to look at the photo of the little innocent boy standing next to his big brother.

It was sickening to look at this picture and to know how Gerard's story turned out.

As she stood, she massaged the small of her back. She was too out of shape to be climbing over fire escapes, running from would-be muggers and then shifting boxes around a dusty storage room. As she bent to pick up the photo with the checks and envelope, she noticed the label on a file folder on the shelf.

The label read—*Delphine Normand Last Will and Testament.* Maggie hesitated and then slowly put her hand out to touch the file.

This is probably not what Delphine had in mind when she said I could snoop around in here, she told herself as she stared at the file. *Anything I want to know about Laurent or Delphine's friend Camille is probably not in that file.*

But her hands were already pulling it off the shelf.

This is wrong. You know it is.

With mounting excitement, Maggie took the document out of the folder. Blocking out the voice that shrieked at her to put the file back, she shakily turned to the first page.

I Delphine Fouquet Normand, being of sound mind and...

Maggie flipped to the next page and stopped. Even though she was staring at the words—with no chance of misinterpretation—she couldn't believe what she was reading.

Delphine was naming *four* beneficiaries. Each to share

equally in the estate of Delphine Normand, *estimated at 4.5 million euros*. Maggie swallowed.

Laurent Dernier.

Gerard Dernier.

Noel Lorraine.

Amelie Taver.

27

The next day was cloudless and warm. Maggie pushed Mila's stroller down Place de la Madeleine toward the big department store Le Printemps. Delphine walked beside her. She'd been so excited all morning about the outing that Maggie swore she'd heard her giggle twice.

They'd taken a taxi to Fauchon—mostly as a point of reference but also because it had been years since Delphine had walked around the famous food shop. Maggie wasn't sure Delphine didn't enjoy filling her shopping bag with chocolate truffles and caviar more than the anticipation of visiting the grand department store.

Maggie slowed her pace to accommodate Delphine as they made their way from the Place de la Madeleine toward Boulevard Haussmann. Along the way, they passed all the major designer boutiques that Maggie had never had the interest or the money to shop at but where she was pretty sure Grace was known on a first-name basis.

"Not getting too tired, are you?" Maggie asked Delphine as they waited for the light to change so they could cross the street.

"It has been so long since I have been shopping!" Delphine

exclaimed, her cheeks pink with excitement, her eyes trying to take everything in at once. Maggie wanted to ask if Isla never took her out beyond doctor's appointments but decided not to risk dampening the mood of the day.

She'd been tempted to invite Beatrice and Zouzou along, but had decided against it in the end. Grace would take it as a veiled reprimand, and it was highly possible that Delphine's tolerance of small children only extended to those she was directly related to. Maggie wouldn't blame her for not wanting to spend the day with a high-energy five year old.

As they walked, Maggie couldn't help revisiting her astonishing discovery of the night before. That Gerard was in the will meant he definitely stood to benefit if something happened to Delphine. In Maggie's mind, that simple fact made the so-called home invasion that the police had painted of Isla's death feel like something very different.

What if Isla recognized who it was that had broken into Delphine's apartment? What if she could name Gerard? Maggie had no doubt Gerard would kill to protect himself.

But Gerard's guilt and all around low worth aside, Maggie had to admit it made sense for him to be included in the will. And of course, Laurent.

Even Noel fit—especially if he was really Delphine's son but even if he was only her nephew.

It was all quite logical except for one thing.

And that one thing could only be made sense of if you accepted a basic unthinkable tenet first.

Delphine owed Amelie a debt.

Why else would Delphine give Amelie a fourth of her fortune?

A few thousand euros Maggie could understand, but an equal share of her estate? Did Amelie know she was to inherit? It would be over a million euros. If Delphine wanted to make her housekeeper's life easier, why not do it before she died? And why an equal share? It didn't make sense.

Unless…

"Your phone is ringing, *chérie*," Delphine said as she put her hands on the stroller. "I will push Mademoiselle Mila while you answer it."

Maggie was startled to realize they'd already walked to the front of the gigantic department store while her mind had been elsewhere. The sidewalks were busy with lunchtime crowds and the usual scrum of tourists who had the money to shop this close to Place Vendome. She glanced at her phone screen and instantly her mouth became dry.

It was from Dieter Bauer. Quickly Maggie opened the email and scanned its contents.

"It is bad news, *chérie*?" Delphine said as she waited for Maggie. "Should we go home?"

Maggie looked at her and grinned. "No, it's good news. Great news, in fact. And no way we're cutting our shopping day short." She quickly typed out a response on her phone and then put it away.

Dieter Bauer had written to say he was in Paris for business and would be available to meet Maggie this evening at a café in Le Marais.

Everything was coming together perfectly.

She turned to face the façade of the looming department store and felt flush with her success and the promise of things to come.

"Shall we, ladies?" she said as they promenaded across the street to enter the famous store's gilt-edged double doors.

∽

MICHELLE STOOD at the corner and watched the crowds of tourists pour from the Metro tunnel. They all, to a man, looked around upon emerging from the trains with the same startled expression that seemed to say "uh oh, we're not in Paris any more."

And it wasn't the Paris they wanted. It wasn't the Paris they'd paid for with their travel agents and Internet credit cards.

She'd even seen one or two turn around and go back underground to find the Latin Quarter or Eiffel Tower or *grands magasins* that they'd paid for.

Not this dump of a crossroads.

The flea market was worth it to the rest of them, she noted. As if they needed any piece of useless garbage they'd find here. No, it was all worth it to be able to go back home and say, "Oh, that? I picked it up at the Paris flea market."

She wondered if the story would be as good if it came with a bash on the head and a stolen wallet.

A man sidled up to her. "You have my money?" His hands were tucked under his arms. He didn't look directly at her. She'd never seen him before. She didn't need to.

She held out her hand with the forty euros in it. He snorted and turned his back on her.

"Stupid bitch!" he snarled.

Michelle flushed but he turned and grabbed the money from her and shoved something hard into her chest, then disappeared into the crowd of tourists. She watched him go before looking at the small tissue-thin envelope he'd shoved at her.

Michelle felt her excitement build as she fingered the key inside the envelope. It had taken every euro she had to purchase it—a universal key—but it was her first step toward finally getting what was due her. Soon she wouldn't have to count her euros or ever come to this dump herself again.

Time to make things happen.

28

The early evening light did beautiful things to almost any street in Paris, Maggie thought. Was it possible Paris was specifically designed to look good in any light? The day had been an invigorating one for both Delphine and Maggie. Delphine insisted on buying Mila several new wardrobes—most of which the baby would outgrow before the month was over—and Maggie enjoyed every second of the older woman's happiness.

Maybe the apartment was toxic? Was there another explanation for how much stronger and more vibrant Delphine seemed to be once she was away from it? Even their walks to the nearby park put a special shade of pink in her cheeks. But once back inside the building, she seemed to sag into the woodwork and the two hundred year old wallpaper as if the effort to live was just too much.

Maggie took the Metro for her evening appointment. If it had been earlier in the day, she would have walked but they hadn't gotten back from their day of shopping until just before five o'clock and her appointment was for half past six. The Metro was full of commuters and exhausted shoppers and there was no place to sit. Maggie didn't mind. Le Marais was a straight shot with no transfers from the St-Michel Metro station where she'd gotten on. She hadn't had time to charge up her phone when she got back from shopping but figured she had just enough juice to use its GPS to find the café. From the map, it looked like it was in a relatively populated section of the arrondissement.

Was it strange that Dieter responded to her so quickly? Or even at all? Had he really been in Paris on business or had he make a special trip to see her? Maggie shook her head at how nonsensical that sounded. No wonder Grace thought she was losing her grip.

It's just a coincidence that he's in town and a really lucky one for me because if I thought proposing the Heidelberg trip to Grace was dicey, explaining it to Laurent would have been seriously problematic.

She got off at her stop and ran up the stone stairs to emerge in the midst of the Le Marais. She remembered reading somewhere that this section of Paris had been a largely Jewish neighborhood before WWII. A *wealthy* Jewish area and so had been taken over almost immediately by the Nazis as their preferred private residences. As she strode down the rue de Rivoli, glancing around her, she thought it didn't look very wealthy any more so much as it looked trendy. Which meant tourists.

Good. The more tourists there are, Maggie thought, *the fewer rusty fire escapes I'll find myself clinging to before the night is over.* Her phone indicated that the café where Dieter wanted to meet was just a few blocks away on the main drag. Maggie picked up her pace.

She waited at the rue de Moussy for the pedestrian green light before she could cross and it suddenly struck her that the name of the street was familiar. She glanced down the street and saw that it was shabby and dark, unlike so many of the other streets branching off from the rue de Rivoli. The street sign read *rue de l'Arbre Sec*. It was an odd name and Maggie suddenly remembered where she knew it from: it was where Gerard's apartment was located. She'd looked up the name of the Balfourt Corporation where Delphine had written the rent checks to and sure enough it was a real estate rental company.

So this is where Gerard lives? Well, that's convenient.

If Gerard *had* had something to do with Isla's death, the police would never know. Why would they even think to question him? Or ask where he was during the time of the burglary? Delphine probably didn't even mention Gerard to them.

But one thing Maggie knew without a doubt was that there was usually an unbroken line between Gerard and anybody else's misery. *Isla died on Delphine's doorstep.* Gerard—low life and general opportunist—regularly visited Delphine to shake her down for money. *This*, Maggie thought grimly, *is a slam dunk in anybody's book.*

The thought came to her like a slap across the face: She needed to confront him.

As volatile as Gerard was, he wasn't a skilled liar. Maggie knew that from past personal experience with him. And especially if she were to take him by surprise—*and ask the right questions*—there was no doubt in her mind she'd be able to tell straightaway if he was telling the truth. After all, she'd *seen* the murderer that day! The man who'd run down the stairs, leaping over poor Isla's body in his escape—could Gerard have done that?

Absolutely. With the adrenalin boost of having just slit someone's throat? Even drugged out and broken, Gerard could have mustered the energy. He definitely could have been the man she saw in the hall that day.

An image developed in her mind of her confrontation with him.

I demand you tell me the truth, Gerard. Did you kill Isla? She could just see his panicked look as he tried to deny it. *Me? No! I swear it! I wasn't there that day.* But Maggie would be ready for him: *How did you know it happened in the daytime?* And then, realizing lying was no use, Gerard would collapse into a puddle of confession.

The light changed and Maggie hurried ahead.

Yep. She'd talk with him this very night.

The café was directly in front of her and for reasons she couldn't explain, she was able to spot Dieter immediately. He was tall, his face creased into an unattractive frown, his hair blond and cut short. His cold blue eyes were scanning the crowd for her.

She lifted a hand and he nodded to her. No smile.

Maggie joined him at the table and he stood long enough to shake hands with her. He was drinking a beer.

"Thank you so much for meeting me," Maggie said. "What luck you happened to be in Paris."

If she was hoping to catch him in a bald-faced lie, she was disappointed. He reseated himself and the waiter appeared.

"*Bonsoir.* A glass of Pinot Grigio, please," Maggie said. The waiter turned and disappeared.

"I do not know what you want to know," Dieter said. He studiously did not look at Maggie. There was something odd about his face. Something familiar too but also something... wrong. She tried not to stare.

"I am looking for someone your grandfather may have known. She would have been a six-year old girl in 1944," Maggie said.

Dieter snorted but still didn't look at her. "You are looking for a seventy-five year old woman," he said.

Okay, so we know you have decent math skills, Maggie thought, forcing herself not to get annoyed. This was her only chance and she needed to remember that and be grateful for it. He might have no information that could help her but he might have the one thing that was the key to finding Camille's daughter.

Getting pissy would not be helpful.

"My sources tell me your grandfather had a liaison in 1944 with a woman named Camille Victoire."

"His French whore."

Maggie sucked in a breath. She wasn't sure what she'd expected from Dieter but this wasn't it. Before she could react, the waiter appeared and set Maggie's glass of wine down in front of her with the bill. Dieter picked up the little slip of paper and then peeled off a ten-euro note and tossed it on the table.

Is the meeting over? Maggie thought dumbfounded. *Am I being dismissed?*

"I was hoping you might remember hearing your grandfather talk about—"

"My grandfather died decades before I was born," Dieter said abruptly.

"Oh. Well, okay, maybe your *father* remembered hearing—"

"My father was not close to my grandfather. I'm sure you can understand why." He gave Maggie a meaningful look.

That must mean the family is embarrassed about Helmut Bauer's role during the war—which makes total sense. Maggie tried to imagine how awkward this must be for Dieter. But she could only tiptoe around the facts so much before she got exactly nowhere in her search for the truth.

"Do you think your father would be willing to talk to me?"

"I doubt it. He died twenty years ago. And my mother is gone too so there is no sense in your attempting to contact any more of my family."

"I see." Maggie's skin began to vibrate. Dieter wasn't here to give her answers. He was here to make sure she didn't bother him again. A shiver of disappointment descended on her.

"I'm sorry I cannot be of more help to you," Dieter said as he stood up.

Maggie didn't answer since his words were clearly false. She looked at him and realized when their eyes met that he was very uncomfortable. It wasn't the first time that she'd noted how the American habit of staring or coming right to the point seemed to unsettle—even disarm—most Europeans.

"Look, I didn't know my grandfather but I do have a...diary of his," he blurted.

Maggie blinked. *A diary?* She held her tongue and hoped her impassive stare would do the job she needed it to.

"I don't know where it is exactly. Perhaps I have thrown it away."

Maggie reached into her purse and pulled out her phone. "May I send you my mailing address in case you find it?" she asked bluntly.

He hesitated. "I will probably not find it."

She forced herself not to speak.

"If I find it, I'll send it to you. But please do not contact me again." He turned to leave when an idea came to Maggie.

"Herr Bauer? *Dieter*?" she called out. He cringed as he turned around, a look of dread on his face mixed with the horror of having his name shouted out in a public café.

"I was wondering if you come to Paris often on business," Maggie asked.

"*Ja*," he said with bewilderment.

"Would you remember if you were in town on the tenth of this month?"

"*Ja*," he said. "I was." Then he turned and plunged into the swarm of tourists and commuters in the street.

Maggie drank down half her wine as she watched Dieter disappear.

April 10 was the day Isla was killed.

Not sure what the information meant, Maggie glanced at the time on her phone and added three euros to what Dieter had left on the table. It was getting late but Gerard's apartment was right on the way home. It wouldn't take two minutes to find his place. As she stood up, her phone rang. It was Delphine.

"Hey, Delphine. Everything okay?"

"Are you coming home now?"

Maggie hesitated. Delphine's voice was trembling. Maggie thought she could hear Mila crying in the background.

Gerard would have to wait until morning.

∼

DIETER STOOD HIDDEN by the large kiosk at the end of the street. His heart was hammering in his chest as he watched the American continue to sit at their café table.

It was worse than he'd expected, almost as bad as he'd imagined. An American? Of all people. He ran a hand over his face and bit the inside of his cheek to distract himself from the nausea roiling in his stomach.

Hadn't he always known this day would come? Hadn't it always been hanging over him from the very beginning?

His stomach lurched with revulsion, his eyes never leaving the image of the attractive young woman sitting at the table—like a jilted lover, vulnerable and bereft.

Would she just leave it alone? Would she try to contact him again?

Something heavy and distasteful settled in his stomach.

Was there something he could do to make sure she didn't?

29

Maggie emerged from the Saint-Germain-des-Prés Metro station and hurried down the busy boulevard toward Delphine's street. It was dark but not late. Even so, she felt eyes on her as she made the turn onto rue du Bac. In fact, for the entire Metro trip she'd been uneasy. First, because there had been something distinctly off about Dieter—and it wasn't just his evasive, hostile nature with her. There was something off about his *face*.

Second, could he possibly be telling the truth about the diary? What kind of Gestapo thug kept a diary? And why, after Dieter had done everything he possibly could to tell her to piss off, had he told her about it?

The discouragement wafted over her like a dense blanket. She was no further along in her investigation into finding Camille's daughter than she had been before she met him. Unless there really was a diary—a big if—and Dieter actually took the time to send it to her—likewise, she wouldn't hold her breath—tonight had to go neatly and without delay into the Total Waste of Time Column.

She glanced down at the phone in her hand but it had gone

dead. It hadn't taken her long to get back to the Latin Quarter from Le Marais. Rush hour was over and the Metro had not been crowded for a Monday evening.

She hurried to the front of Delphine's building in time to slip through the double doors. Workmen were just packing up their tools after having installed a security buzzer on the side of the outer wall. Maggie was frankly surprised it had taken Delphine's apartment management so long to do it. Most apartment buildings in Paris had security keypads.

She moved through the small courtyard and then the interior doors to the lobby of Delphine's building. She was tired but not so tired she couldn't manage to walk the five flights up rather than risk another episode on the dodgy elevator.

She arrived at Delphine's front door panting and perspiring.

"Maggie! *Chérie!*" Delphine said as she opened the door. "It took you so long!"

Maggie's eyes went past Delphine toward the sound of her daughter's wails in the kitchen. She closed the door behind her and went to Mila who immediately stretched out her arms to Maggie.

This is my fault, Maggie thought as she picked Mila up. The baby was wet and if the carnage of baby food all over the high chair tray was any indication, hungry, too.

"I am so sorry, Delphine," Maggie said over Mila's slowly subsiding whimpers. "I shouldn't have been gone so long."

"No, it is me," Delphine said. "I couldn't make la Mademoiselle happy no matter what I did. She wanted her *maman.*"

"Let me change her and I'll be back in a flash." Maggie gave Delphine an encouraging smile and disappeared into the bedroom to clean and change Mila.

Fifteen minutes later, she sat with Delphine in the kitchen. Mila was calmer but still fussing.

There was no doubt in Maggie's mind that Mila was reacting to Delphine's affect which was jittery and tense.

What had happened? Had Gerard come back? Or Michelle?

"Did anyone come by while I was gone?" she asked carefully.

"*Non, non,*" Delphine said, sipping a glass of wine and watching the baby with fretful eyes.

Maggie so wanted to reassure Delphine. *Babies are just like this. It doesn't mean anything.*

"Victor's workmen came to install the new security bell on the front door," Delphine said.

"I saw them," Maggie said. "Do you have the new code?"

"*Oui.* It is on the dining room table."

"Anything else?"

"Noel called when I was trying to feed the *bébé,*" Delphine said, her eyes misting over. "I am afraid he was upset."

"Why?"

Delphine waved her hand as if to dismiss the subject. "It is an old argument. I do not know why I let it bother me today."

Maggie knew that Noel was to inherit. Did his phone call today have to do with money?

"Is there anything I can do?" Maggie asked. "I'm sure he hated upsetting you."

"*Je sais,*" Delphine said with a sigh. "He...is convinced I am his mother."

Whoa. Way to come right out with it.

"Really? What makes him think that?"

"It doesn't matter. It is what he wants to believe and he is not interested in hearing me."

If it's true, what possible reason could there be for keeping it secret now? Maggie wondered. *He'll find out when he sees he's inherited a fourth of her fortune. Why can't Delphine just put his mind at rest— and her own too while she's at it?*

But she kept her thoughts to herself. She hated seeing Delphine so unhappy but there were times when even *she* was wise enough to know when to keep her mouth shut.

"I fear I must retire early tonight," Delphine said.

"Of course. I'm just so sorry that Mila added to your stress this evening...and after such a lovely day of shopping."

Delphine laid a hand on Mila's head and smiled.

"Nothing could spoil our day," she said. "And tomorrow, both Mademoiselle Mila and I will both be our old selves again."

Delphine surprised Maggie by kissing her on the cheek before wishing her goodnight and going to her bedroom. Maggie finished feeding Mila who did not show any signs of being sleepy. Maggie took the baby into her bedroom where her phone was charging and checked for messages.

There was a text from Laurent that instructed her to text him back that she was alive. Maggie grinned ruefully and took a picture of Mila and sent it to him with the text <so far so good>. She noticed she'd also received a phone call from a number she didn't recognize. Because she hadn't answered it, it had gone to voice mail.

She settled on the bed with Mila in her arms and listened to the message.

"Bonjour Madame Dernier. My name is Michelle Normand. I would be grateful if you would call me back at this number so that we may meet. It is of the utmost importance. Merci."

Maggie played the message back again to try to pick up on anything in the woman's voice that made her sound unbalanced. Maggie only detected urgency.

How did she get my number? Or my name?

It had been a long day. From walking all over the main shopping district of Paris to tramping up and down Le Marais and racing back to the Latin Quarter with a panicked image in her head of Delphine and Mila—if not dead, then both extremely unhappy. She'd been promising herself all evening that she'd go back into the storage closet but Mila was only now just beginning to settle down, and Maggie realized she herself was pretty fried for tonight.

The closet would be there tomorrow.

As soon as Mila finally dropped off, Maggie put her in her baby bed and padded into the bathroom where she washed off her makeup and brushed her teeth. She returned to the bedroom, stripped off her clothes and climbed into bed with a groan. As she fell asleep she couldn't even remember if she'd heard back from Laurent after she sent her text.

Hours later, in the middle of the night, Maggie found herself being pulled out of her dreams. A noise, monotonous and insistent was buzzing in her head until she finally awoke. She sat up in the dark, disoriented and tried to place the noise.

It was the muffled ringing of a landline telephone.

Maggie put a hand on Mila to see that the baby still slept, then swung her feet out of bed and grabbed her robe from the floor. By the time she stepped into the hallway, the phone had stopped ringing. It had clearly come from Delphine's bedroom. Maggie paused in the hall and held her breath.

Who would call at this hour?

Suddenly she heard Delphine cry out.

Maggie dashed to her bedroom door and jerked it open. The bedside lamp illuminated the room. Delphine sat on her bed, the phone cradled to her chest. Her hair hung in a tangled disarray to her shoulders.

"Delphine?" Maggie said breathlessly. "What is it?"

Delphine turned to Maggie, her face a mask of horror and disbelief. She looked every minute her ninety-two years. Her shoulders sagged under her thick flannel nightgown.

"Delphine?" Maggie said coming around to her side of the bed. "What's happened?"

"It's Gerard," Delphine said with a shaking voice. "He's...he's dead."

30

There was no way anyone was going back to sleep.

Two detectives arrived within the hour and by then both Delphine and Maggie were dressed and working on their second pot of coffee. The two men were incredibly respectful of Delphine, if slightly suspicious of Maggie and her role in the household. *Or that could just be the whole being American thing*, Maggie thought as one of the men narrowed his eyes at her.

Gerard's body had been found by his landlord. His front door was left open and one of the neighbor's dogs had wandered in to look for food. The landlord found Gerard with his throat slit.

As soon as the words about Gerard's death were out of Delphine's mouth, Maggie knew this had something to do with Isla's murder.

How could it not? How many deaths happened right next to each other? How could it possibly be a coincidence?

As she made a third pot of coffee—wondering if it was really a good idea for anyone even French people at this point—it struck her that she was going to have to call Laurent as soon as it was officially morning. As light streamed through the kitchen window and the first sounds of Mila crying came through the apartment, she realized it was time.

What in the world could she say to him?

She went to fetch Mila and brought her into the living room. Maggie's French was just good enough to understand that the cops were consoling Delphine and alluding to the fact that it appeared that Monsieur Dernier's risky lifestyle had finally caught up with him.

Maggie served them the coffee with Mila on her hip. She watched Delphine closely to make sure she was bearing up and she tried to understand as much as she could of their conversation.

"When did you last hear from your nephew?" one of the detectives asked.

Delphine looked at the detective as if she didn't understand him. Her eyes turned to Maggie, beseeching.

"Thursday," Maggie said to the detective. "He came here last Thursday evening."

Both detectives looked at Maggie as if—instead of giving helpful information—they weren't entirely convinced she wasn't somehow involved.

"I am sorry, Madame," one of the detectives said to Delphine, deliberately turning from Maggie as if she hadn't spoken. "It is a terrible thing." He peeled off a business card and handed it to her. "If you think of anything else."

With one last negatively appraising look at Maggie, the detectives let themselves out of the apartment. Maggie went into the kitchen and found some teething crackers for Mila who began happily gnawing on them.

Did this mean Gerard *didn't* kill Isla? Did the same person who killed Isla also kill Gerard? And what does it have to do with Delphine?

When she returned to the living room, Maggie promptly settled Mila on the couch next to Delphine. Mila always calmed

Delphine. And this morning was no different. Maggie could see a tremor in Delpine's hand as she touched Mila's shoulder gingerly.

"You and the baby are in danger," Delphine said.

Maggie felt her heart begin to race. "Can you tell me why you think that, Delphine?"

Delphine looked at her and shook her head.

"I knew it would follow me to the grave," she said. "But I prayed it would leave my loved ones alone."

"What do you mean, Delphine? *What* would leave your loved ones alone?"

"The war, of course," Delphine said, looking away from Maggie and her eyes resting again on Mila. "I always knew it would find me."

Maggie sighed in frustration. "The war was a long time ago," she said.

"*Non, chérie,*" Delphine said, her eyes welling with tears. "It was yesterday."

∼

MAGGIE PREPARED a breakfast of scrambled eggs, bacon, and toast with jam. In her mind, cheese grits were an essential component of comfort food—and Laurent always made sure they had plenty in stock—but she had to give Delphine her best Southern healing without it.

After breakfast, Delphine went to her bedroom to lay down. Maggie had delayed calling Laurent for as long as she could. She also knew she'd have to tell him she'd seen Gerard last week—while doing everything in her power to downplay it—and she'd face the music on that. Although she knew from experience that Laurent's fury sounded absolutely nothing like music.

Before she could settle Mila in her bed for her morning nap, the landline in the living room rang. Maggie snatched it up before it could ring in Delphine's bedroom.

"*Allo?*" she said. She wasn't great at speaking or understanding French over the phone. She hoped this wasn't the police.

"Madame Dernier?"

Maggie recognized Michelle's voice immediately.

"This isn't a good time," Maggie said.

"We need to meet, Madame," Michelle said.

"Today is a bad day." Maggie hung up and waited, half expecting the phone to ring again. Before she could make the decision about whether or not to leave the phone off the hook, she saw that her phone was vibrating with a picture of her husband on the screen.

"Hey, you," Maggie said.

"What is wrong?"

"Wow. That is some serious radar even for you," Maggie said with a weak laugh.

"Is Mila—?"

"We're both fine, Laurent," Maggie said, sagging onto the couch and beginning to feel the exhaustion of not getting a full night's sleep. "But I do have some bad news. It's Gerard."

"Bad news how?"

"We just had a visit from two police detectives who informed your aunt that Gerard was killed last night."

There was a pause. "Why did they come to my aunt?"

"Well, she had been paying his rent for the last several months."

"How did he die?"

Maggie tried to imagine how Laurent was processing this. She tried to imagine his face and what he must be thinking. He hadn't been in touch with Gerard for years but still...Gerard was his brother.

"The cops said he'd had his throat cut," Maggie said softly.

"You saw him this visit, didn't you?" he asked abruptly.

How in the hell could he tell that?

Maggie sighed. "He came to your aunt's house last week."

"Last *week*?"

"Yes, I'm sorry, Laurent. I didn't want to worry you."

"*D'accord*. I will try that line next time I don't want you to know something."

Ouch. Maggie's stomach clenched. He was right. And Grace was right. She should have told him.

"I'm sorry, Laurent. There's no excuse. I screwed up."

He grunted and she could only imagine how furious he was with her right now. There'd been a few times in the past when his anger had gone volcanic, but he'd never been *nonverbal*.

"Your aunt doesn't want a memorial service," Maggie said, hoping to distract him. "I think she's afraid of who might come. There's nothing for you to do up here and I know how busy you are down there."

"When are you coming home?"

"Laurent, I've barely been here a full week yet. My visit was supposed to be for—"

"I'm no longer comfortable with you up there."

"Well, that's weird because you seem very comfortable with me going to Atlanta all summer."

"It is not the same thing."

"Look, Delphine has a few nurses coming in tomorrow for interviews and Mila and I will be on a train heading back to St-Buvard by Thursday. How's that? Two more days."

"I will come up there."

Voices in the room with Laurent came filtering to Maggie over the phone.

"Are the people from the co-op there with you now?"

"It doesn't matter."

"Yes it does, Laurent. Please don't go all eighteen hundreds on me when you know you need to be there to make sure our livelihood is running smoothly."

He didn't respond. There was every reason to believe—even as mad as he was—that he was at least half listening to her logic.

"I'm *fine*, Laurent. Gerard's visit to your aunt last week was about thirty seconds long. He didn't even come into the apartment."

There was a heavy sigh on his side and Maggie imagined how torn he must be. For a certifiable control freak like Laurent, letting Maggie run wild in Paris while two murders happened around her must be excruciating beyond her comprehension.

"Two more days," he said finally.

"I'll be home before you know it. Kiss Jemmy for me. And Laurent? I'm so sorry about Gerard."

Maggie went into the bedroom to check on Mila and then laid down on her bed. The weariness began to vibrate through her body. She hated conversations with Laurent where things were held back but she knew it would only worry him and he had his hands full running the vineyard.

It wasn't just that Gerard had threatened Delphine that Maggie had held back or that she had met with the descendant of a Gestapo thug. The thing that really worried Maggie was that she didn't feel she could tell him the very important fact that she had been in the room when Delphine called the police to report Gerard's murder.

Which meant it hadn't been the police who called her in the middle of the night to tell her about Gerard's death.

So who did?

31

The day was a quiet one and for that Maggie was grateful. Delphine woke up a little after two in the afternoon and Maggie put together a late lunch of cold cuts. Just before they sat down, the phone rang. Maggie hesitated to answer it, fearing it might be Michelle again—and she still hadn't sorted out in her mind what she was going to do about that—but Delphine picked it up and spoke tartly into the receiver in quick French to whoever was on the other end.

"Everything okay?" Maggie asked as Delphine came back to the dining table.

"That was Noel. He is downstairs and needing the code to enter. I told him to go get bread and come back."

It made sense that Noel would come—especially if he was in town—but Maggie worried about the after effects of the conversation he'd had with Delphine yesterday morning. Would he table his personal agenda long enough to comfort his aunt?

It suddenly occurred to Maggie that with Gerard out of the picture, Noel would inherit a much larger share of Delphine's fortune.

Noel showed up along with Amelie whom he'd met in the

foyer on the way up. Maggie tried to imagine anything more uncomfortable than sharing an elevator with Amelie even for the ninety seconds it took to ascend to the fifth floor. But if she had any doubts about Noel's behavior, she was quickly relieved. He took Delphine into his arms as soon as he stepped across the threshold.

The two stayed that way, rigid but connected. *Like mother and son?* Maggie couldn't help but wonder. Clearly that's how Noel felt, the way he held Delphine in his arms was the picture of a protective, loving son. When they finally broke apart, Noel gave Maggie a rueful smile.

She knew this wasn't really a sad day. Nobody loved Gerard nor had done so in many years. But Delphine was shaken by his death. And for her sake, Noel and Maggie had drawn the ranks in close.

Amelie went immediately to the kitchen and began to noisily straighten what was already a spotless kitchen.

"I'm so glad you came," Maggie said to Noel as he kissed her on both cheeks. The three sat down at the table.

"It is a terrible thing," Noel said as he handed the baguette to Maggie. "Not that we weren't always expecting something like this…" He shrugged.

"I just saw him. Did I tell you?" Delphine said, her hand still on Noel's sleeve. "He came last week to demand money."

"Such a charming relative," Noel said, causing Delphine to frown. "Yes, yes. Today of all days, we will not speak the truth. I am sorry his loss has upset you so much, *chérie*. And will we meet your husband now, Maggie?"

"I talked to Laurent while you were sleeping, Delphine," Maggie said. "He said he'd call you later."

Delphine nodded and Maggie addressed Noel.

"Delphine said there won't be a service. Naturally Laurent would come up if Delphine needed him but…"

Noel shook his head. "No, no. He is a busy man, of course. I remember Uncle Nicolas, eh? Always the vineyard was his mistress. And Laurent was not close to his brother?"

"Not at all." Maggie glanced at Delphine again as if to underscore her words. *They're nothing alike.* But Delphine was gazing at Noel.

"I thought while I was here today," Noel said, "that I would retrieve my mother's table linens. Are they still in her *trousseau, chérie*?"

Delphine removed her hand from Noel's sleeve and Maggie had the impression that some message had just passed between them. She hoped Noel wasn't going to upset Delphine.

"I will have Amelie fetch them for you before you leave," Delphine said.

Noel turned to Maggie. "Do you know my mother—my birth mother, Georgette—never once called or visited me in Switzerland? But Delphine did several times, didn't you, *chérie*?"

Delphine ate her lunch and ignored him.

"I wouldn't even know my mother's handwriting," Noel continued. "Isn't that odd? But every birthday and Christmas I would receive a present and a card from my dearest of aunts." He patted Delphine's hand as it lay on the table. "Who was like a mother to me."

"Georgette loved you," Delphine said almost sullenly.

"But of course," Noel said. "It was merely the communication of that emotion she was no good at."

Amelie came into the room and thumped down a crock of paté that had been in the refrigerator. She turned without a word and disappeared back into the kitchen.

Noel began to slather a piece of bread with the paté. The thought struck Maggie as she watched him blithely pop the morsel into his mouth and roll his eyes in exaggerated rapture: *does he know that Amelie is in the will too?*

"You are very quiet, Maggie," Noel said, reaching for the bottle of wine on the table.

Maggie smiled apologetically. Something felt wrong about sitting here eating lunch and not caring about Gerard—laying in a morgue somewhere about to be bundled away like a sack of garbage no one had any use for. Even if that was the case—and there was no doubt Gerard was an irredeemable swine—surely there should be at least a moment set aside for a thought of the loss of his life, however wasted a life it was.

Is that why Delphine is so quiet? Is she wondering if she could have done anything differently? Is she remembering Gerard as a little boy?

Or is she thinking about the person who called her to tell her of Gerard's death?

Does Delphine know who killed Gerard?

Noel poured his wine and then topped up his aunt's glass. *Noel is downright jolly*, Maggie thought with surprise. Does he know that Gerard's death made him a much richer man? Is he really here to give comfort to Delphine? Or to bring pressure on her to officially accept him as her son?

"*Le bébé* is falling asleep in her *chaise haute, chérie*," Noel said happily. Maggie could see that Mila had indeed nodded off in her high chair. As soon as she saw her, Maggie got an idea.

She released the high chair straps and picked the baby up.

"I'm going to put her down for another nap," she said, knowing it would likely mean Mila wouldn't go down this evening until midnight or later. "And then I thought I'd go take a little walk. Would that be all right?"

Delphine put a hand out to touch Mila's foot as Maggie passed her toward the bedroom.

"Of course, *chérie*," she said. "Noel and I will be fine."

"Better than fine," Noel said cheerfully.

Maggie settled Mila down, dimmed the bedroom lights and shut the door. When she returned to the dining room, Noel and Delphine had moved to the living room.

"I'll see you when I get back, Noel," Maggie said, hoping she wasn't leaving Delphine in a weakened state against yet another vulturous relative.

"Looking forward to it," Noel said pleasantly as he seated himself opposite Delphine.

"Enjoy your walk, *chérie*," Delphine said, the weariness and sadness evident in her voice.

"Will do," Maggie said before she changed her mind to stay and try to protect Delphine against Noel's campaign, whatever it was.

On the other hand, is that really my place? Especially if Delphine really is his mother?

She went out the front door and down the stairs.

She'd have to hurry if she wanted to make it to Gerard's apartment and back before Mila awakened and Delphine began to worry.

∽

AMELIE CRINGED when the front door slammed and she felt a burst of fury pulse through her.

Where did all these people come from? And when would they leave?

She gripped the coffee tray tightly in an attempt to force the tremor in her hands to stop.

All of these visitors weren't weakening the old woman. In some way they seemed to be energizing her. The damnable child was the worst! She actually seemed to be making Madame Normand grow stronger.

When would they leave?

I must be patient. And I must be brave.

To have come so close! To have thrown away her chance because of her cowardice. It was beyond galling.

She had been moments away—seconds away! Her hand outstretched...so very nearly there...when the American woman showed up and ruined everything.

It would have so obviously an accident. No one could have blamed her!

Amelie's mother had always told her: *In life you must use the opportunity when it comes. No need to create one. They always come.*

And it *had* come…with the broken elevator.

But she had hesitated.

Why?

Did she not want the old witch dead more than she wanted her own happiness? Was there anything she craved more than that?

So why had she hesitated?

She heard the sounds of Delphine and her nephew talking in the living room and felt the bitter bile rise in her throat.

I am waiting, Mother, for the opportunity to show itself. I am trying to be patient.

"Amelie! Where is our coffee?" Delphine called out from the living room.

Amelie gripped the tray as if it would snap apart in her hands.

Her opportunity would come.

It came once.

It would come again.

And this time she would not hesitate.

32

The Metro was crowded for this time of day but Maggie was too anxious to sit anyway. Her mind was reeling as she stood by the door, waiting for her stop.

Gerard and Isla's deaths were connected. They had to be. Two murders within a week of each other? Both connected to Delphine? It was too much of a coincidence.

If Delphine didn't know who killed Gerard, she clearly knew someone who did.

Did Gerard and Isla know each other? What was their connection? Was Delphine the intersection point?

Does that mean *Delphine's* life is in danger?

Was this all connected to the will? Except Isla wasn't in the will.

Maggie wasn't sure what she'd find at Gerard's apartment—or even if she'd be allowed in. She just knew that the cops were wrapping this murder up with a bow: degenerate ex-con gets killed by the degenerate class of people he hung with. She could see how they'd jump to that convenient conclusion. Anyone would be tempted to.

When she'd passed his street the day before she thought the neighborhood Gerard lived in hadn't looked very safe.

And honestly most people who met Gerard ended up wanting to slit his throat.

But still... two murders within six days and both connected to Delphine?

Her Metro stop came just as she saw she was getting a phone call. She hated talking while she walked—it definitely took her attention away from what she was doing and where she was going—but she had a strict time line today so she accepted the call and hurried up the steps to the Le Marais neighborhood in the fourth arrondissement.

"Darling, you sound out of breath. Did you find a Pilates gym near you?"

"Ha, ha, very funny, Grace," Maggie said. "But listen I'm glad you called."

Maggie crossed the street and zagged in between slower ambulating tourists and shoppers. "You're not going to believe this. Gerard was murdered last night."

"No! That's terrible. Or is it?"

"I'm on my way to his apartment right now to see what the police missed."

"Oh, Maggie, is that wise?"

"They're calling his death attributal to his risky lifestyle."

"Honestly, darling, that actually sounds pretty logical."

"Two murders in less than a week and both connected to Laurent's aunt? I don't buy it."

"Really, Maggie, you're overthinking it."

"I can't believe you're saying that," Maggie said in frustration. Was she really the only one who saw the connection?

"In any case, I'm calling, darling, because André was doing a little research on your Nazi lover. He was very impressed with your quest to try to find Camille's orphaned child."

"Grace, I can't believe you're sharing with him the stuff I tell you. This is personal and I'll ask you not to—"

"*Allo*, Maggie?" André's voice came over the line and Maggie slowed to a stop and stood at the corner of rue du Rivoli and Gerard's street, the rue de l'Arbre Sec.

"Yes, hello, André," Maggie said, briskly.

"How have you been, *chérie*?"

"Don't call me that. What is it you want?"

André laughed warmly. "I have found some information that I thought would be of interest to your research."

Maggie bit her tongue to keep from telling him she had no interest in hearing what he had to say. Her anger at Grace bubbled to the top and it was all she could do to remain civil.

"Well, let's hear it," she said tersely.

"Did your friend Herr Bauer happen to tell you his father died a few years ago, *oui*?"

"How is that important?"

"My research shows his father committed suicide."

"Well, that's tragic but I'm not sure how helpful it is," Maggie said sarcastically, enjoying the pleasure of dismissing his Intel.

"Yes, but his grandmother—the wife of Helmut Bauer—*also* committed suicide…did you know that? Within weeks of the war being over. Yes? More helpful?"

Maggie's stomach turned. "That's hardly surprising," she said uncertainly. "She was married to a murdering dirt bag. After his team lost the war, he probably was an even bigger jerk to live with."

"Ahhhh!" André said. "But now I see you have not uncovered the biggest surprise of all about your Helmut Bauer."

Wanting very much to tell André in no uncertain terms that the man was hardly *her* Helmut Bauer and bristling over his attempt to one-up her—but also wanting to hear what he had to say, Maggie took a long, steadying breath and held her tongue.

The pedestrian traffic had picked up on this block as people headed toward the café district not far away.

"It appears that Helmut Bauer shamed his entire family," André said, "not just because of what he did *during* the war but also after the war."

After the war? Maggie shut out the image of the people rushing past her and turned her attention fully back to what André was saying.

"Will you kindly spit it out?" she said in frustration. "What happened after the war?"

"He was hanged at Nuremberg."

33

Maggie stared unseeing down the street of busy people, cars and taxis moving past her.

Hanged at Nuremberg!

Only the worst of the worst were executed for war crimes at Nuremberg. In fact, only twelve in total. And it looked like one of them was Camille's lover.

No wonder Dieter didn't want her to contact him again. No wonder he didn't want to talk to her.

What a travesty his grandfather was—not just to hundreds of innocent French people—and one poor love-starved French girl—but to his own family for generations to come.

What did this mean? Did it matter in Maggie's search for Camille's daughter? Or did it only matter that certain people knew how devastatingly shameful it was to be connected to Bauer?

Did Delphine know about this?

If she did, why hadn't she led with that when she told Camille's story?

She must not know.

And Maggie wasn't going to tell her. The war was too painful to Delphine as it was. The last thing Maggie wanted to do was remind her of it all over again.

But one thing that this information did was give Maggie more to go on when she was doing her own Internet research. She opened up a browser on her phone and typed in: *Bauer Nuremberg.*

Immediately a photo came up of Oberleutnant Helmut Bauer. It was the first photo Maggie had seen of him. There didn't seem to be a lot more information than she already had but when she had time later tonight she'd follow the assorted hyperlinks to read about the crimes for which he was executed.

She studied the photo of Bauer. It was slightly out of focus and he had his Gestapo service cap pulled down low over his face. She could see his mouth and part of his nose but the rest was in shadow.

Be great if I could see his eyes, she thought and then shivered. *Or maybe not.*

Remembering her time constraint, she slid her phone into her jacket pocket and turned down the rue de l'Arbre Sec toward Gerard's apartment building. She expected to see, if not cop cars out front then at least yellow crime scene tape marking the area. But there was nothing. She had the address and went straight to the building. It was old—and not classic Haussmann kind of old, but ratty ready to be ripped down kind of old.

And that's saying something in Paris.

She went to the front door. There were no security keypads, no concierge, no foyer. Just a filthy landing inside the front door with dog feces piled in one corner and a metal plaque of mailboxes on one wall. The elevator had a *hors service* sign on it— which was just as well. She would seriously have considered scaling the outer wall of the building with a hook before she'd take a chance on the elevator. She headed up the steps.

She wasn't at all sure what she was looking for and she was entirely open to believing that this trip was a total waste of time.

On the other hand, if someone else dropped dead within the next few days, she might be glad she bothered.

At the landing on the third floor, she saw some evidence that a crime had been committed. Yellow crime scene tape crisscrossed the doorjamb of Gerard's apartment which was one of four apartments on the floor. Maggie went to the door and tried the door but it was locked.

Oh, well. It was worth a try.

She stood outside for a moment thinking and then went to the next door on the floor and knocked. She waited for two minutes but heard no sound inside. She went to the next door and knocked.

A young woman dressed in sweatpants and a ripped t-shirt answered the door. She held a cigarette between her lips. Her eyes went first to Maggie's clothes, then to her face.

"*Bonjour, Mademoiselle*," Maggie said. "I was wondering if you knew anything about what happened last night with Monsieur Dernier." She pointed in the direction of Gerard's apartment.

The girl's eyes followed Maggie's gesture and she shrugged.

"He is dead," she said in guttural French. Her accent was a patois, but that was hardly a surprise. There were a lot of refugees and immigrants in this impoverished area. Still, her dialect didn't sound like a foreign accent to Maggie's ear. She was native French, just not Parisian.

"I know," Maggie said. "I was wondering if you knew Monsieur Dernier."

"He was a pig."

Oh, so you did know him.

"But his name was not Dernier," the girl said. "It was Dubois."

Maggie nodded. Gerard had used that alias when she first met him. It was the reason why years ago she hadn't realized he was Laurent's brother until very late in the game.

"Is there an onsite landlord I could talk to?" Maggie asked as the girl began to close her door.

"Downstairs," the girl said as she shut the door.

Maggie went downstairs. There were three apartments on the ground floor and one with a handwritten plaque on the door that read *gardien*. Maggie knocked on the door and a man answered. He reeked of garlic and he too had a cigarette sticking out of his mouth.

"*Oui?*" he said, looking Maggie up and down.

"I need to get into Monsieur Dubois's apartment," Maggie said.

He made a snorting sound and blew out a puff of smoke. "Impossible. The police have sealed it."

Maggie was almost positive the police *sealing* involved putting tape on the door and walking away. She opened her wallet and took out the only bill in it and held it in front of him.

"Fifty euros," she said. "It's all I have. Is it enough?"

The man looked around the foyer as if worried he was being set up and then snatched the note from her fingers.

"I will get the key," he said.

Five minutes later, Maggie stood in Gerard's living room. If she had ever thought it would be impossible to feel sorry for the man she credited with turning her sister into a drug addict and losing her little niece, she was proved wrong today.

The apartment was bare. A mattress was on the floor—stained with Gerard's blood. There was no furniture, no books, no clothes, no dishes, nothing to show that someone had used this place as his home.

Maggie had no tools, no way to check for fingerprints—and no access to any kind of database even if she had. She wasn't even sure what it was she'd been hoping to see. It was just a sad little apartment in a bad section of town where a sad little man bled out his last with no one to care.

An image of the little boy standing next to Laurent flashed into Maggie's head. The little boy with his hand on the arm of his big brother, leaning into the arms of his beautiful mother. The little boy who looked so much like Jemmy that it broke Maggie's heart to think of it.

Maggie pushed thoughts of Gerard away—thoughts of him as Nicole's father, as the man Elise had fallen in love with, as the little brother who Laurent had once tried to protect. Her eyes burned with unshed tears.

The *gardien* stood outside in the hallway. "Quickly," he said, jingling the keys.

There was nothing here. Maggie could see that. Gerard had left nothing of himself behind except the bloodstain. There was no answer to anything here. No clues that painted a picture of what had happened.

Gerard was obviously killed on the bed. Perhaps as he slept? So, maybe by someone he knew?

"Madame..." the *gardien* said impatiently.

Fifty euros sure doesn't buy much time, Maggie thought as she left the apartment. The landlord locked and retaped the door and then disappeared down the stairs. Maggie began to follow him when she saw that the young girl's apartment door was ajar. As Maggie passed, the girl opened the door wider.

"He is a relative?" the girl asked.

"He was," Maggie said, finally claiming Gerard and feeling better for having done so.

"He had a visitor yesterday," the girl said.

Maggie turned to face her. She didn't speak but gave the girl time to continue without prompting.

"A woman. They screamed at each other. She said she'd make him pay."

"Did you tell the cops this?"

The girl gave Maggie a look of disdain for such a stupid question.

"Did you get a look at her?"

The girl shrugged. "*Peut-être*," she said.

Maggie dug out the hidden ten euro note in her wallet and handed it over.

"Fat. Ugly. Brown hair. Dressed like a beggar."

Could that have been Michelle?

"Did she have a big jaw and short brown hair?" Maggie asked, trying to tamp down her excitement.

"*Oui*, and bad teeth. She said *I will hurt your whole family.*"

MAGGIE WALKED outside the apartment building and glanced at her phone. The threat of rain had darkened the sky and it was getting late. Delphine hadn't called so either Mila hadn't awakened from her nap yet—*I'm so going to be up all night with her*—or she was awake and all was well. Maggie stood in front of the building and watched a few people pass down the street in front of her. Many pushed bikes or walked but all watched her distrustfully.

She'd found out exactly nothing in looking through Gerard's apartment except that he'd been killed where he slept. She'd looked at the lock on the door but it hadn't shown evidence of being forced.

Had Gerard let his killer in? And was that killer Michelle?

Why?

Maggie ran a tired hand over her face. So many questions and absolutely nothing that even hinted at a possible answer. She turned in the direction of rue du Rivoli and then on impulse turned around the other way. While it wasn't the most direct way back to the Metro, if she were someone who'd just killed a man, she might not choose the most direct and *visible* way out. The landlord and the girl upstairs had seen nobody on the night of Gerard's killing. But then, an apartment building like this wasn't exactly your best bet for block parties and get-togethers. Maggie was pretty sure most people kept their doors closed and minded their own business.

If it hadn't been for Michelle screaming as she left Gerard's apartment yesterday, nobody would even have known about her visit. Maggie walked the length of the apartment building and was surprised to see a narrow alleyway between the end of Gerard's building and the start of the next one.

Maggie looked at the walls but there were no windows on the side of either building. But she could see it was a thoroughfare the length of one full city block. She opened up her phone and pulled up a map. The street a block south of rue de l'Arbre Sec was rue du Louvre. Although it didn't show on her map, this alley connected with it.

If the killer had taken this alley to rue du Louvre, he'd be able to slip easily back onto rue du Rivoli well away from the scene of the crime with no one the wiser.

Without realizing she was doing it, Maggie stepped into the alley.

34

The light seemed to extinguish the moment Maggie entered the alley. A rat was startled from its food thirty feet ahead of her and scurried for its bolt hole in the side of Gerard's apartment building.

Maggie's stomach lurched. She forced herself not to run. The whole point was to take the same conduit the killer had. And that meant looking and seeing what the killer had seen.

Smells seemed to pour off both buildings and pool into the space between them, roiling up from the wet stone floor beneath her feet. She held her breath. There were no windows, no fire escapes, no pipes or ledges. No point in looking up. She alternated between focusing on her endpoint—rue du Louvre straight ahead—and the ground.

It was quiet. The two buildings had cut off all sound at the same time they dimmed the lights. Maggie put a hand on Gerard's building. Cold, rock hard. No vibrations. Nothing to indicate there was life inside.

This was a total waste of time.

And it was seriously creepy besides.

Halfway down the alley she stopped and listened. A horn

honked in the distance but she couldn't tell if it was ahead of her or behind.

This was stupid.

There were a few puddles on the ground from the rain earlier that morning. Maggie stepped over the piece of trash marking the spot where the rat had been and then turned around to examine it more closely. She bent down and saw it was a crumpled cigarette packet. Her heart began to beat fast.

Had the killer dropped this?

She tried to think if she'd smelled cigarettes on Michelle. Unfortunately she hadn't gotten close enough to tell. She rooted in her jacket pocket for a tissue—less to preserve any fingerprints than to protect herself from whatever disease the rat might be carrying—and picked up the cigarette packet.

The cellophane outer covering was wet. On one side of the packet was a bent matchbook with no matches. On the other side a slip of paper had been slid under the cellophane.

Forgetting her worry about the rat, Maggie withdrew the slip of paper with trembling fingers.

Five words were written in turquoise ink protected from the rain by the cellophane.

She blinked, her tissue falling forgotten to the ground.

Written on the slip of paper were the words, *Dernier, 43 de l'arbre sec.*

The killer *had* come this way.

Why else would Gerard's name and address be written down? It *wasn't* someone who knew him. It was someone who was following instructions.

It was a hit.

She stood and walked steadily to the end of the alley. When she emerged, the busy street seemed awash with color and light.

But if the person didn't know Gerard personally, how did he get inside Gerard's apartment? Maggie realized she only assumed Gerard had been attacked on the mattress. He could very well have answered the door and then struggled with his killer—ending up on the mattress where he was slain.

The police would know, she thought grimly. *But they aren't talking.*

As she walked in the direction of the Metro station—wondering if she dared bring her newfound evidence to the police—something that had been in the back of her mind since she found the cigarette packet came roaring to the foreground. She stopped, forcing a man behind her on his phone to bump into her and growl his annoyance.

She pulled the cigarette pack out of her pocket and turned it over to look at the spent matchbook.

Bistrot Danielle. 235 rue du Four.

Her mind swam as she realized how she knew that address.

It was located next to André's gallery.

35

Maggie sat on the train and stared at the note with Gerard's address on it. She felt overly warm and there was a constant fluttering in her stomach. *Is it a coincidence about the bistro being next door to André's gallery? Isn't it true that everything in the Latin Quarter is close to everything else?*

But right next door?

Maggie glanced at the schematic map of train stops over the doorway. Two more stops before her station at Saint-Germain-des-Prés.

Did André know Gerard?

Did André smoke? She fast-tracked back to the kiss André had forced on her the night of Delphine's party.

Yes, she'd tasted tobacco.

She fumbled in her pocket for her phone and texted Grace.

<Tell André thanks for the info and sorry I was abrupt before. Can I speak to him?>

<He's busy right now>

<That's cool. What's his #?>

Maggie waited for an answer but either Grace put the phone down and walked away or she was deliberately not answering.

Was Grace jealous of Maggie? Had André said something to her?

Maggie clenched her jaw. When her stop came she hurried off the subway car and wound her way through the long underground tunnel and up the steps to her street. It had started to rain and she was only wearing a light jacket. Her long hair immediately began to wilt as it soaked up the water. She felt a cold sluice of rain go down her collar.

So do I think Grace's boyfriend had something to do with Gerard's death? And if I do, does that mean he had something to do with Isla's death too?

Motive? She shook her head in frustration.

Opportunity? Well, *that* she could probably find out from Grace. *If* Grace felt like being helpful.

Now that Maggie thought of it, wasn't it terribly coincidental that André knew of Delphine?

Her phone vibrated and thinking it was Grace, Maggie ducked under the first restaurant awning she came to and looked at the screen.

It was a text message from Michelle.

<Well?>

All other questions aside, one thing Maggie knew for sure was that Michelle had seen Gerard the day he died.

That's opportunity.

And she could take a wild and probably very accurate guess as to motive.

Maggie texted, <When & where?>

∽

MAGGIE ARRIVED at Delphine's apartment just as Amelie was leaving. The housekeeper stood in the foyer, her coat on, her purse on her arm, and scowling as Maggie entered.

"You are late," Amelie snapped.

Maggie peered past the housekeeper to see Mila sitting in her high chair next to Delphine. Both seemed cheerful enough. Mila cried out, "*Maman!*"

Amelie pushed past Maggie to leave through the still open door which she slammed behind her. Maggie moved into the kitchen where Delphine was feeding Mila.

"Everything okay here?" Maggie asked. "Sorry I'm late."

"Ignore Amelie," Delphine said with a smile, but Maggie could see she was tired. "I asked her to watch the baby for one minute when I went to the bathroom. You would think I do not pay her enough."

Maggie thought of the will and the fact that Amelie would be a rich woman upon Delphine's death. She peeled off her wet jacket and hung it on a peg in the kitchen.

"There is a towel in the ante room," Delphine said, nodding to a small room off the kitchen. Maggie remembered that was where they'd stacked the cartons of champagne on the night of her birthday dinner.

The spot where André had kissed her.

"It's really coming down," Maggie said, giving Mila a quick kiss before reaching for a towel.

"The police called."

Maggie stopped drying her hair. "Yes?"

"They said they would dispose of Gerard's remains for us. The case is closed."

Maggie sat down at the kitchen table and watched Mila spread her dinner in thick globs of orange across her face.

"I see."

Maggie tried to imagine that a phone call to the police might reopen the case. But she'd been down this road before. The cops would take the cigarette pack and she'd never hear another thing about it.

"It is sad, of course," Delphine said. "And I have had too much sadness of late."

Maggie noticed the older woman's hand was shaking again. Maggie took the spoon from her.

"Was your visit with Noel okay?" She could see how Noel—as sweet as he generally seemed to be—might be a bit much on a day that was already emotionally draining.

"Of course I was glad he came. But I believe I will go to bed now."

"Have you eaten?"

"What I need now is rest." She stood and put a hand on Maggie's shoulder. "I am glad you are here, *chérie*. You are far more than I deserve."

"Well, that's not true at all. You deserve all your loving family around you during a time like this."

As soon as the words were out of Maggie's mouth, she realized that Delphine would think she meant Laurent.

Had she meant Laurent?

Shouldn't Laurent have come up? If not for Gerard, then for his aunt?

"I will settle for you and our little Mila," Delphine said as if reading Maggie's mind. Her smile was unwavering but wistful. "But I am changing my mind about my nephew. I can see his care for you in your face. He must not be the man I once knew."

"I can't wait for y'all to meet again."

"I too look forward to that," Delphine said, smiling sadly. "*Bonne nuit, chérie.*" She turned and shuffled slowly to her bedroom.

Maggie watched her go.

Why didn't I insist that Laurent come up? What was I thinking? Delphine needs him, regardless of what he thinks. Maggie resolved to call him as soon as she got the baby down.

After she finished feeding Mila, she held the child in her arms in her bedroom and hummed to her as Mila futilely resisted sleep. Maggie felt the weariness reach out to her too. The minute she knew Mila was asleep, she put her in her bed and then saw that her phone was vibrating.

It was Laurent.

"Hey, I was just going to call you," she said.

"To tell me when your train will get in to Aix?"

She let out a sigh of frustration.

"Laurent, no. Actually, I was going to try to talk you into coming to Paris."

"Not possible."

"You know this is a major family crisis up here, right? Your brother's dead and your only living relative is—"

"You are making this too dramatic," he said. "There is no church service. There is no one to mourn Gerard's passing."

"That's not the point, Laurent," Maggie said as she moved into the living room so as not to wake Mila. "Your *aunt* is the point."

"My aunt does not grieve for my brother."

Well, that was true enough and Maggie knew it. Trying to make this sound like a real family tragedy wasn't going to wash. Not with Laurent anyway.

"Whatever," she said with resignation, "I can't come back just yet. Delphine needs me."

"You are not a nurse!"

"She doesn't need a nurse! She needs family!"

A moment of silence blossomed between the two and Maggie felt a kernel of insecurity erupt in her stomach. She hated fighting with Laurent. Hated when they weren't on the same page. The fact that he couldn't see a reason for her to stay with his elderly aunt was upsetting on so many levels. Maggie knew for sure he wouldn't feel this way if it was Danielle or any of their other elderly neighbors.

What is it with him and Delphine?

"I know you will do as you wish regardless of my desires," he said coldly. "But trying to make me think that Gerard's death is a surprise to anyone is not believable."

"Laurent, the police aren't even investigating his death," Maggie said, "They've written it off the same way they wrote off the home health nurse's death and if you'd stop to think for *one minute*, you'd see that your frail ninety-two year old aunt stands right in the middle of all this! Do you really want me to leave her?"

"Are you finished? Because there is *no* connection between the two deaths as anyone can plainly see. Is it possible you are making everything worse instead of better?"

"I suppose anything is possible," Maggie said, shaking with indignation. "Perhaps you should come up here to make sure I'm not."

"I cannot leave the vineyard."

"Well, then I guess it sucks to be Delphine. You're too busy to be with her and I'm just making things worse."

"Maggie..."

"No, no, you're probably right but we'll never know so if you don't mind, kiss my son for me, and kindly go bugger off to your stupid grapes."

She hung up on him and immediately hated the fact that she did. She wasn't sure why she'd become so upset except she'd been expecting a little support from his direction—especially since she was getting precisely none these days from Grace—and what she got instead was a slap in the face.

Is Laurent right? Am I just upsetting her with talk about the war? Would it make things worse for her to know the truth about who killed Gerard and Isla?

She shook her head.

No way. There was no way the truth wouldn't help give Delphine closure.

And Camille. Finding out what had happened to Camille's daughter was the single best thing Maggie could do for Delphine.

Of that she had absolutely no doubt.

She shook off the fight with Laurent but checked her phone to see if he'd called her back. She knew he wouldn't though. She went into the bedroom to check on Mila and then tiptoed to Delphine's bedroom door. The sound of deep snores reached her where she stood.

Just thirty minutes ago Maggie had been so tired she could barely heft Mila into her crib, but now she felt agitated, wound up and alert.

She walked into the living room and her eye went straight to the storage closet. While she wasn't sure how she was going to use the clues she'd found surrounding Gerard's death, she knew there was more to discover about Laurent and Camille in that room. It might not put anyone in prison for the rest of their lives, she thought grimly, but it might still do *somebody* good.

She unlocked the padlock with the key she kept in her jeans pocket, pushed into the room, and turned on the light. She ran a finger over the spines of the dusty books on the shelf that was eye level to her. Most of them appeared to be philosophy or history books—probably belonging to Delphine's late husband—and all in French.

She pulled a box of files from a shelf and flipped through them quickly. Feeling like HIPAA was about to descend on her any moment, she opened up the box labeled "Children's Health Records." Maggie pulled out a file with Jacqueline's name on it. She scanned its contents. There was nothing exceptional about it. Her weight at birth was listed and the fact that she'd broken her arm at fourteen. Each of her annual health exams was listed until 1940. Maggie found Delphine's file next and flipped through it. It was similar to Jacqueline's. She'd had mumps at twelve and nothing much else.

Georgette's file was even thinner with just a few lines noting her weight at birth and the fact that she had been born with a benign condition called Turner Syndrome. Maggie knew most parents tended to start out with boundless energy and good intentions on everything having to do with their firstborns but intensity inevitably flagged with the children who followed. Maggie noted ruefully that she had a scrapbook two inches thick on Jemmy but had yet to start work on Mila's.

Putting the medical file aside, Maggie went through the rest of the folders in the box until her head began to ache and her back twinged from how she was sitting on the floor. She pulled her legs out in front of her and stretched out her back by leaning forward over her knees.

From this position she saw a small wooden toy under the bookcase. She reached in and drew it out. It was a wooden car with moving wheels. She turned it over in her hands. On the bottom was written in a childish scrawl, *Laurent Dernier.*

So he *had* existed as a child, she thought bemusedly as she turned the car in her hands. And somehow a loving aunt or grandmother had kept this toy instead of bunging it into the French equivalent of a Goodwill bin. Or it was just forgotten—like everything else about Laurent's childhood. It had gotten swept under a bookcase and lost as the boy became a man.

She hated fighting with Laurent. It usually never got this far. He was impossible to get a rise out of. Half the time he'd shrug off whatever disagreement they were having and Maggie was left having the fight with herself.

It was harder to do that on the telephone. The nuances of his responses to her—usually so subtle in person that they were hard to register—seemed to jump out of the phone. Had she overreacted? He wanted her back home; she wanted to stay. She wasn't willing to hear his argument and he wasn't buying hers.

She felt a thickness in the back of her throat. She hated that she'd hung up on him. *It was such a childish thing to do and he doesn't deserve it.* But it had been a stressful day in a lot of ways.

Not that that was any excuse. She picked up her phone. He wouldn't be asleep and he wouldn't play games and not answer either.

All she had to do was apologize.

But she knew him. He was less interested in her *mea culpas* than in her proving her contrition by doing what he asked—by packing up and getting on the next train south.

And that she was not ready to do.

She put the phone back down.

She set the little car by the door. Someday Jemmy might like to have the toy his father played with as a boy. When she took her seat again and tried to decide which box she'd go through next, she noticed a piece of molding on the wall behind one bookshelf.

Getting to her feet to take a closer look, she could see that the molding surrounding the panel was about three feet square. The panel looked like the sort of built-in door that usually went with a dumbwaiter or cupboard. By kneeling and reaching behind the bookshelf, Maggie could get her hand on the door. There was no latch but a hole at one end of the door. She reached a finger through the hole and was able to slide the panel an inch to the left.

Why put the bookcase in front of a door? Her heart began to pound with excitement.

What was in there?

She needed to get the heavy bookcase away from the wall. She pulled all of the boxes off the bookshelf except some smaller ones on the bottom shelf and then removed all of the books. This took about twenty minutes. Then, hugging the bookcase with both arms and shoving hard with her hip, she was able to move it several inches away from the wall.

There couldn't be anything valuable stored in there, she reasoned. *What sense does it make to shove a bookcase in front of a cupboard or whatever it is?*

Unless whatever was in there was something someone did not want to be discovered.

She stood up and wrapped her arms around the bookcase again and put her whole weight into shifting it. Every time she moved it a few inches, she'd stop briefly, massage the small of her back to make sure she hadn't done any permanent damage, and then put her shoulder and hip back into the job for another few inches. Finally, she had it shoved far enough from the wall.

She knelt in front of the panel. Had it been created when the apartment was built? Or had it been made afterward? Maggie ran her fingers across the surface of the panel, trying to imagine people hiding their jewels or children from the Nazis during the occupation. Is that what this was?

She stuck her finger through the hole in the panel and sucked in a quick breath, hesitating momentarily.

Was she really ready to see what was behind here? Maybe a skeleton? A festering rat's nest?

Without thinking more about it, Maggie pulled on the hole and pushed with her other hand. The panel slid away and onto the floor, leaving a gaping square of darkness. She started in surprise but nothing jumped out at her. No animal crept out, no skeleton rattled its bones at her.

She pointed her cellphone light into the recesses of the hidden alcove.

A face appeared and Maggie dropped her phone and jumped backwards. Finally her brain caught up with her panic. The face wasn't real.

She picked up her phone and directed the light inside the hole.

It was an unframed painting.

And it was absolutely beautiful.

Maggie reached into the recess and gingerly pulled the small canvas out into the light of the room.

In soft, evocative colors, the painting portrayed a ballerina, nude, brushing her hair, her face half shielded by her long hair.

Maggie felt her heart pound in double time.

Could this be real? Is that possible?

Maggie knew very little about art but even she knew a Degas when she saw it. She could not stop staring at the painting

Can this possibly be real?

Her eyes went to the corner of the canvas where the artist had signed his name: *Edgar Degas.*

Why would anyone hide a fake? A chill went across her skin.

But if it is real...

A thought wormed its way into Maggie's brain and she carefully put the canvas down, leaning it beside the opened panel. She picked up her phone, aware that her fingers were trembling.

She typed into the search engine window: *Degas girl brushing her hair.*

As she waited for the search results to appear, her mind was spinning.

It can't be real. It just can't be.

Then Maggie saw the words on her phone screen that she hadn't dared to form in her mind.

With her heart racing, she stared at them, re-reading them over and over again as if they might somehow disappear.

"Dancer brushing her hair" 1890, Edgar Degas. Believed stolen by the Nazis in 1940. Never recovered.

36

Maggie stared at the painting, her mouth open in mute shock. *What is it doing here? What is Delphine doing with it? Does Delphine know it's here?* She rubbed her arms as if she'd felt a sudden chill.

This painting was stolen by the Nazis over seventy years ago. The fact that it's not hanging in her living room means Delphine knows she's not supposed to have it.

Why does she have it? Why does she have it hidden in a secret panel behind a bookcase in a locked room?

Why hasn't it been returned? How did Delphine get it in the first place? Did Camille receive it from her German lover? Did she somehow give it to Delphine? Did Delphine find it among Camille's things?

Maggie double-checked the Internet site on her phone. There was no mistake. Carefully, with shaking fingers she set the painting back inside its hiding place and replaced the panel.

Her mind could not stop buzzing with questions. The biggest even beyond *How did it get here* was *Does Delphine know it is here?* This was always answered in her mind by...

How could she not?

What was it Delphine had said when she gave Maggie the key? That she had been protecting Laurent and Gerard's birthright? It hadn't made sense at the time but if Delphine meant the painting—*a stolen painting worth millions but impossible to sell*—as if it was somehow a way to protect them, then she was clearly not as sane as Maggie had believed.

Knowing she was in for a long sleepless night, Maggie picked up Laurent's wooden car, turned off the light and locked the storage room behind her.

She would ask Delphine about it tomorrow. And if at all possible she would try very hard not to fill in the answers for herself in the meantime.

Maggie went again to Delphine's bedroom door and listened to the elderly woman's snores before going to her own room and undressing. As she slipped under the covers, her phone vibrated dully against her bedside table.

It was a text message from Grace.

<Meet me in the Tuileries tomorrow noon. I have something for you.>

Maggie fell back into her pillows and fell almost instantly asleep to dream of Nazis and German storm troopers pounding without end up the spiral staircase to where she lay.

∼

THE NEXT MORNING Maggie dressed herself and Mila. She had a very difficult conversation ahead of her with Delphine but she couldn't see any way out of it. She had to know if Delphine knew about the painting and if she did...Maggie forced herself not to get ahead of things. Delphine would have an explanation, she was sure of it. When she brought Mila into the kitchen, Maggie was surprised to see that Delphine was not in the kitchen. Maggie went to her bedroom door and tapped lightly.

"Delphine?" she called. "Is everything all right?"

"Oh, *oui, chérie*," Delphine said in a weak voice. "I have days like this, I'm afraid, after a big outing."

"Is there anything I can get you?"

"*Non*, I just need to rest. I will be fine tonight."

Maggie didn't feel good about leaving Delphine but if she really was just going to sleep all day...

"Mila and I are headed to the park," she said. "I'll call when we're on our way back to see if I can pick up anything, okay?"

"That would be fine," Delphine said, her voice sounding even weaker.

"Feel better," Maggie said. She turned back to the kitchen.

The questions about the stolen Degas would have to wait.

She typed a quick text to Laurent: <*Sorry.*>

Knowing him, the only text he wanted to read was *I'm on my way home* but she felt better after having sent it. She noticed the message was delivered and read immediately. But he didn't answer.

Maggie quickly fed Mila her breakfast and then tucked her in the back carrier. She'd debated about the stroller but in the end, because their day appeared to be a long outdoorsy one traversing several parks, the carrier felt like a more sensible choice.

She had two hours before she was to meet Grace in the Tuileries which worked out perfect time-wise since she'd also arranged to meet Michelle in less than thirty minutes.

ARMED SOLDIERS WALKED NONCHALANTLY in front of the entrance to the Jardin du musée de Cluny, their fingers on the triggers of their military-style assault weapons. Massive sycamore trees sprouting new bright green leaves lined the boulevard Saint-Germain. The uniform cream-colored apartment buildings that faced the park and its massive black wrought iron gates were the perfect backdrop behind the trim and orderly sycamores. A rotating poster kiosk with its large onion-shaped dome reminded Maggie of the Paris of her childhood visits.

Maggie had gotten to the park before Michelle. She sat down on her usual bench with Mila at her feet. The baby was too little to play with the other children—all of whom were running about the playground squealing feverishly. The same group of parents and nannies sat on the other benches gossiping, smoking, eating and occasionally calling out to the children.

Maggie was determined not to think about the stolen painting until she could ask Delphine about it. She thought about telling Laurent but found herself hesitating and not just because of their fight the night before. Something was odd about Laurent in reference to Delphine. With everything that was going on with her he hadn't behaved particularly protective of his aunt.

Which was odd because if there was one thing Laurent was in spades it was protective. Seriously, deeply, annoyingly protective.

Oh, yes. There is a story there, Maggie thought.

She saw Michelle enter the park. Maggie watched with amazement as the woman tiptoed through the gates, looking around as though she'd never been on a playground in her life. She seemed to be regarding the children as if they might attack at any moment.

Maggie lifted a hand to indicate where she was sitting and as soon as Michelle spotted her and began to walk toward her, Maggie started to wonder if this had been a very good idea. At all.

Michelle reached her and her eyes went instantly to Mila seated on the ground playing in the grass.

What is with this woman? Maggie thought with annoyance. She touched Mila on the shoulder more to reassure herself than the child.

Michelle sat on the bench on the other side of Maggie. She wore baggy workman pants and a gray pullover sweater frayed at the cuffs. Her hair was pulled back in a greasy ponytail and her nails were bitten and dirty. Her eyes darted around the playground.

It suddenly occurred to Maggie that Delphine hadn't been hyperbolic when she said Michelle was crazy.

Michelle really *was* crazy.

Maggie's stomach lurched and she fought the temptation to pull Mila into her lap.

This woman had possibly killed Gerard and maybe Isla too. She was desperate.

And she was insane.

"I need your help," Michelle said, her eyes still on Mila. She spoke French with a strong nasal twang that Maggie was barely able to understand.

"What can I do for you?" Maggie said guardedly. Her body was tensed as if ready to snatch up Mila and bolt with a second's notice.

"You can tell your aunt to put me back in her will before things get ugly."

"Okay."

Michelle snapped her head to look at Maggie. "You think I lie?"

"Not at all. I'll tell her."

Michelle's eyes dropped to Maggie's clothes. Maggie was wearing jeans and a cashmere cardigan over a t-shirt. She supposed, to Michelle, she probably looked affluent.

"I know a secret that Madame Normand would not want the world to know," Michelle said, her lip curling over yellowed teeth.

When Maggie didn't respond, Michelle turned to face her fully on the bench.

"A child out of wedlock. Are you shocked?"

"Since this isn't 1905, not really. Unwed mothers are no big deal."

"How about collaborating with the Nazis during the war? A little bigger deal?"

Maggie felt her heart hammering in her chest but she kept her face impassive and merely shrugged.

"Nobody cares what happened during the war any more," she said.

"Oh no? *Madame Normand* cares. She cares very much to keep the family name from dipping into shame."

"What do you think you know?"

"Oh, no, Madame. I don't give my secrets away so easily."

"Because you don't know anything."

"I know Madame Normand had a child out of wedlock. She confessed it to my father the day he proposed to her."

"Again. This is 2016. Nobody cares."

"I know she committed a war crime in 1944."

"I don't believe it."

"You don't need to. My accusation will be enough. Formal state investigation will follow. She will live out the last years of her life—if not in prison then in complete disgrace."

"What is this about? Money?"

"I want what's mine. She stole my inheritance."

Maggie had had enough. She picked up Mila and slipped her back into the back carrier.

"Where are you…what…?" Michelle stood up, her eyes going from Mila to Maggie's face.

"You know, Michelle," Maggie said as she hoisted the carrier onto her back. "I think you should do whatever you think you need to. But just for the record? I bet if your dad had wanted to leave you money he would have. So if you come to Madame Normand's apartment again, I'll call the cops. *Comprenez-vous*?"

Maggie turned and strode toward the exit of the park, feeling way less confident than she hoped she appeared to Michelle.

At the sound of footsteps running up hard behind her, Maggie whirled around to see Michelle charging her. Her face was flushed and her teeth bared in a grimace but she veered around Maggie at the last minute and made for the gate.

With her heart fluttering in her chest, Maggie concentrated on controlling her breathing as she watched Michelle leave.

That woman fit all the criteria for both murders and yet the cops hadn't even questioned her.

Opportunity? Michelle was at Gerard's apartment the day he died.

Check.

Motive? He's in Delphine's will whereas she was left out.

Check.

Means? Both murders were done with a knife at close range.

Maggie watched the thickset Michelle stomp away, flexing her fists in fury as she went.

Check and double check.

37

From her position in an iron chair by the Tuileries fountain, Maggie could see the obelisk of the Place de la Concorde like a Saturn V rocket about to launch into orbit.

As usual, Grace was late.

Maggie shivered in her thin jacket and double-checked that Mila was warm in her boiled wool jacket and knit hat. The baby sat happily kicking her feet from Maggie's lap.

Maggie wasn't sure what to think. Her mind was swirling with possibilities and conjectures.

Laurent was mad at her and wanted her to come home and she'd still learned almost nothing about his early years. Grace was barely speaking to her—or to her own daughters it appeared.

Delphine was an unhappy woman tortured by something that happened more than seventy years ago and was an even bigger enigma than her nephew.

Was she involved with stolen Nazi treasure? Had she been an unwed mother? Was she Noel's mother?

And then there were the murders.

From what Maggie had heard, Isla was a sweet, hardworking

girl who'd known no one in Paris and who'd started working for Delphine only a month before she was killed.

Gerard was a degenerate lowlife killed in the apartment paid for by Delphine.

Michelle was a crazy person with daddy issues intent on blackmailing her stepmother for money—and who might very possibly have killed both Gerard and Isla.

Maggie reran the memory tape in her mind of the figure jumping over Isla's body. *Could it have been Michelle?* Was she tall enough to have been the mystery figure? Honestly, if Maggie's memory could be trusted, the figure seemed taller, more masculine. Was that just Maggie's assumption playing tricks on her memory?

Maggie ran a tired hand across her face.

Which of it was connected? None of it? Some of it?

Mila suddenly squealed and raised her hands. Maggie turned to the shadow that materialized into Grace over her shoulder.

"Hello, darling Mila!" Grace said, holding her arms out for the baby. Maggie lifted her up and watched as Grace nuzzled Mila and then turned to André who stood behind her. Maggie looked beyond him but it was just the two of them.

"You didn't bring Zouzou?" she asked.

"Isn't she precious?" Grace said to André and he instantly clucked Mila under her chin and made a kissing noise.

Maggie felt a flush of annoyance. First, because Grace hadn't brought Zouzou and second because she *had* brought André.

"*Bonjour*, Maggie," André said, leaning in to kiss her on the cheek. "*Ça va?*"

"Yes, thank you," Maggie said stiffly.

"Sorry we're late, darling," Grace said, shifting Mila to her hip. "Give her the package, *chéri*."

André pulled a thick letter out of his leather carryall and handed it to Maggie. It was still wrapped in its postal paper but one corner of it had been ripped free.

"It's the diary," Grace said. "Or at least we assume it is. It's from Heidelberg and you can see it's a diary through the tear."

Maggie took the package and hesitated. The last thing she wanted to do was open it in front of André. She wasn't sure precisely why but she didn't trust him. And the parcel looked like someone had already started opening it.

"Sorry for the rip," Grace said with a laugh. "André was so excited when it arrived, it was everything I could do to stop him from opening it."

I'll bet, Maggie thought, fingering the ripped section. Grace was right though. It was definitely the diary and her excitement about that threatened to overpower her annoyance. She pulled the rest of the wrapping off. A letter from Dieter rested on top of a small leather volume. In the letter, Dieter apologized for being rude when they met. *"My grandfather, as you can imagine, was a source of endless humiliation."* He wrote that if Maggie would simply dispose of the diary when she was finished that would be fine.

"What does he say?" Grace asked as she handed Mila back to Maggie.

"Says he's sorry for being an ass the other day and here's his grandfather's diary."

"Do you read German?" André asked as Maggie flipped through the handwritten book.

"No." She looked up at him. "Do you?"

He shook his head and she could see he was very interested in getting a look at the diary himself. For that reason alone she decided he wouldn't. On the other hand, she really needed to ask him some leading questions about Gerard to see if he acted guilty. She glanced at Grace who lit a cigarette and was frowning in the direction of the Place de la Concorde. There was no way Maggie could ask André questions without Grace catching on and ending up furious about it.

She glanced back at the diary and picked out the phrase "*meine Schaetzle C*" and in another place "*Liebling C.*"

"Well, it definitely looks like he's talking about Camille," Maggie says.

"Except I didn't think that part was the mystery," Grace said.

"You're right." Maggie shut the diary and slid it into the pouch on the side of Mila's carrier. "I'll just have to track down someone who reads German."

"You know," André said, "it occurred to me that any one of the nursing homes in the Latin Quarter should be teeming with people who lived in Paris during the war."

"That's a brilliant suggestion, André. Isn't it, Maggie?"

"Sure. Brilliant." Maggie hoped she didn't sound too sarcastic. Especially since, actually, it wasn't a half-bad idea.

Grace turned to André and put her hand on his arm.

"Darling *chéri*," she said. "Would you be *une ange* and get us a couple of ice creams? I'm dying for something sweet." She gave him a kiss and he hurried off to a nearby ice cream vendor.

Maggie wasn't fooled. Grace didn't fit into her perfect size four slacks by *ever* dying for something sweet.

Grace turned to Maggie. "What is your problem?" she said coldly.

"Where is Zouzou?"

"Are you serious? *That's* what this is about? Why take it out on André?"

"I didn't think I was."

"He only wants to help. You've made up your mind that you don't like him."

"And you've decided to share with him everything I tell you!"

"That is not true." But Maggie could tell she'd hit a nerve.

"And come to think of it, I'm not sure how it is André just *happened* to know Laurent's aunt," Maggie said. As soon as the words were out of her mouth, Maggie regretted them.

"Have you lost your mind? You *suspect* him of something?"

Grace stared at her, her eyes narrowing. Maggie tried to remember another time in their friendship when they'd ever looked at each other like this.

"No," Maggie said unconvincingly. "Of course not."

Except his gallery is right next door to where Gerard's killer hangs out. So there's that.

"This is what I get for trying to help you." Grace turned and marched over to where André had finished buying three ice cream cones. "Sorry, darling," she called to him. "Maggie can't stay so let's just go on."

André looked at Grace with surprise and then turned to follow her out of the gardens. He handed Grace one of the ice cream cones which she promptly dropped in a nearby trash receptacle.

Maggie watched her go, her fury and guilt mingling in a vortex of discouragement.

So I guess this isn't a good time to mention your boyfriend planted a juicy one on me last week?

∼

MAGGIE BOUGHT an ice cream and shared it with Mila. She put a call in to Delphine but there was no answer. That didn't worry her since she knew Delphine was trying to rest. She tried to remember if this was Amelie's day off. It occurred to her that she hadn't seen Amelie since the day after Gerard died.

That is another strange one, she thought. She still didn't know how Amelie fit into all this. Maybe she should just bring home a bottle of wine and ask Delphine flat out why she was giving a fourth of her estate to her housekeeper and why she had a stolen Degas in her broom closet.

Maggie wiped Mila's cheeks and realized she wasn't ready to go back just yet. It was a beautiful spring day in Paris. And she was determined not to let Grace spoil it for her. She glanced at her phone to see if she'd received any messages.

She hadn't.

With her phone out, she decided to take André up on his idea and check the area for nursing homes. It was probably a long shot but she had no other leads to follow up on. Within minutes she'd found a facility right in the heart of the Latin Quarter. In fact, it wasn't six blocks from Delphine's childhood home.

"Up for a nice walk Mila?" she said to the baby who giggled in reply. Maggie resettled the baby in her backpack and checked her GPS for walking directions for the nursing home. She had no idea how French old folks homes worked but one thing she was fairly sure of—a baby was almost always a welcome distraction.

Because she was coming at the neighborhood from the opposite side of the Latin Quarter from where Delphine now lived, Maggie paid careful attention to her GPS and was grateful that the route looked to be fairly populated, the streets busy with lunch time office workers and tourists. And her phone was fully charged. It took her an hour of walking with periodic rests to reach the street with the facility.

Maggie wasn't surprised to see massive stone archways off the narrow roadway heralding the home. Like most of the other apartments on the street, once she pushed past the twelve-foot high double wooden doors, she entered into a courtyard area. All of Paris, she mused, was like this massive frontispiece on the outside with the inside a mystery. Sometimes a manicured courtyard like this one, sometimes a foul-smelling back alley for the apartment dwellers to dump their garbage, and sometimes just a car park.

Across the courtyard was another set of doors with the plaque *Entrée* positioned across the top.

Maggie went inside and walked up to the reception desk.

"*Bonjour*," she said.

The woman behind the desk wasn't young but not ready for

residence status either. She surprised Maggie by looking up, glimpsing Mila in her backpack, and clapping her hands with delight.

"*Bonjour.* You are coming to entertain the guests?" The woman spoke in English.

How do they always know I'm not French? From just one word?

"Yes," Maggie said. She pulled Mila out of the carrier. "And this is Mademoiselle Mila."

"Our guests will be eager to meet Mademoiselle," the woman said. "Have you come before?"

"Uh, no, this is our first visit."

"You do not have a relative here, Madame?"

"I don't, no. Will that be a problem?"

The woman shrugged. "*Pas pour moi,*" she said, gesturing for Maggie to follow her down the long hall.

AN HOUR LATER, Maggie sat with a group of women—none younger than eighty years old. Mila sat happily on the lap of one of the younger women—she was eighty-two—and proceeded to sufficiently enchant everyone in the room. Maggie had been to nursing homes before when her grandfather had become too weak to be cared for at home. He hadn't lasted long and Maggie always wondered if he would have lived longer if he hadn't had to leave his own home. Even in one of the more expensive facilities in Atlanta, Maggie remembered the smell of urine underneath disinfectant most of all.

After some small talk where Maggie discovered that two of the women spoke English well enough to translate for her, she asked the group in French:

"Has this building always been a home for the elderly?" She was hoping to get some idea of who knew the neighborhood.

"It was a hospital many years ago," said Madame Remey, an old woman with white hair and lively blue eyes. Maggie tried to imagine what life was like in here for someone whose mind was still so quick.

"Are you all from this area?"

Most of them nodded.

"I'm related to the Fouquets," Maggie said. "Three sisters who lived on rue du Canivet? Do you know them?"

Madame Remey pointed to a severely humped-back woman who had a perennially worried look on her face.

"Madame Belgert lived in the same building as the Fouquet sisters, didn't you Marguerite?"

Madame Remey asked Maggie's question louder and directly at Madame Belgert as if the woman was hard of hearing.

"My husband is Delphine's grand nephew," Maggie said. "Little Mila is her great grand niece."

Madame Remey turned to Maggie. "I did not know them personally. But of course the whole street knew of them."

Maggie laughed. "Were they famous or something? How did you know *of* them?"

One of the white-haired old ladies was dressed in severe black. She pointed a finger at Maggie. Her face was serious, her eyes slightly crossed. "Everyone knew who they were," she intoned in guttural French.

Before Maggie could respond, another old woman with badly dyed auburn hair reached over and tapped Maggie on the knee.

"It's because of the hanging. Do you not know the story?"

Maggie nodded, stunned. "I do. I guess it makes sense that it would be famous."

How often are young girls strung up in the marketplace?

Maggie turned to the old woman with the dyed hair. "Did you know Camille Victoire?"

The woman grimaced. "I saw her die."

Maggie felt the excitement well up in her. She was finally going to get some of the missing details on what happened that day.

"Stop telling lies, Aideen!" Madame Remey said. "Everyone knows your family fled Paris when the *boche* came! You saw nothing."

Aideen flushed and crossed her arms in front of her. She frowned fiercely at Madame Remey but didn't respond.

Madame Remey turned to Maggie. "It was terrible, of course. But it was the war. Young people today wouldn't understand. They do every manner of thing without consequence."

"I was friends with Jacqueline Fouquet," Madame Belgert said softly. "After the war, her family moved out of the building. I never saw her again."

Maggie tried to gauge the mood of the little group. Nobody seemed upset about discussing the war or even recounting the grisly details of Camille's death. It had simply been too long ago. In some ways, it probably felt more like an old TV program they'd seen a hundred times rather than something they'd all lived through.

Aideen reached out to the woman who was holding Mila. "My turn!" she said gleefully. The two old women gingerly swapped the baby and Mila clapped her hands, prompting immediate squeals of delight from the women.

Maggie turned to Madame Remey. There had been certain parts of Camille's story that she hadn't felt comfortable asking Delphine about. In fact, after that first afternoon when Delphine told her the story, she'd not brought it up again.

"I wondered how it was that the Resistance knew where to find Camille," Maggie said. "Do you know?"

Madame Remey shrugged. "They asked the *gardienne*, of course."

Maggie knew that in the old days, especially in the larger more well to do apartment buildings, *gardiennes* were employed as professional gatekeepers. They typically lived in a bottom floor apartment of the building. Not unlike the one in Gerard's apartment, now that she thought of it.

"And the *gardienne* told the men where to find her?"

The old woman's eyes looked meaningfully at Maggie. "The *gardienne* was often in the pocket of the German bastards. But she was ready for when the tide shifted. She directed them to the German whore."

Madame Belgert chimed in: "Her name was Lizette. A mean old thing I can tell you. She saw everything."

Aideen piped up: "I heard that when Mademoiselle Fouquet answered the door—"

"Wait." Maggie put a hand to her head in confusion. "The *gardienne* directed the Resistance to the *Fouquet's* apartment?"

"Of course," Madame Remey said.

"Well, I thought you said she knew everything that was going on," Maggie said. "Was she confused?"

The old woman leaned back in her chair and regarded Maggie with a cocked eyebrow.

"That is precisely what Delphine Fouquet said to the men when they came to her door—'Are you confused?' she said to them. And then she explained that her sister Jacqueline was engaged to Marc Dernier, the Resistance hero. You know about that, yes?"

Maggie nodded but she felt an uncomfortable lurch in her stomach.

"What happened when she told them they were at the wrong apartment?" she asked.

Madame Belgert glanced over Maggie's shoulder at the sight of a tea cart being pushed into the room. She beckoned to the aide pushing it to come closer.

"As you might guess," Madame Remey said as she also waved to the woman with the cart.

Maggie clutched the arm of her chair and listened as the old woman's words tumbled relentlessly out.

"Delphine told them Camille Victoire's apartment was up one more floor," she said.

38

The aide poured tea and handed out cookies to all of the women in the group. Maggie watched in stunned silence as they laughed and fed Mila cookies and tweaked her cheeks.

She couldn't believe what she'd just heard.

"So you're saying *Delphine* told them where Camille was?" she asked, trying to keep her voice light. Her heart was pounding and she felt a light sheen of perspiration pop up on her forehead.

"Who else?" Madame Remey said, examining one of the cookies closely.

Maggie's stomach churned with nausea.

Delphine gave Camille up? Can this be true?

Aideen said with her mouth full of cookies, "That Camille was a sly one. No one had ever seen her with any Germans. But who better than her best friend would know the truth?"

"They took her out by her hair, screaming her innocence," Madame Remey said. "*Putain*! German whore."

"Okay, let's bring it down a notch, shall we?" Maggie said with irritation. "The war's been over for a good while now."

One of the women squawked out, "That slutty Fouquet girl was seen with a German or two."

A terrible question slithered into Maggie's head.

Why would Delphine send the Resistance to Camille's door?

Madame Remey said, "Camille Victoire betrayed her country by whoring around with the *boche*. She knew what she was doing. And then, of course, there was the child…"

Maggie snapped out of her daze. "Do you know what became of her?" she asked.

"I heard she was taken to Normandy to be raised by relatives," Madame Remey said.

"Her family didn't come from Normandy," Maggie said.

Madame Belgert pointed at Maggie with a cookie in her hand. "The child was the vile product of the Nazi and the whore."

"Well, the numbers don't add up for that to be true," Maggie said wearily. "If Camille and the German met in 1940—which would be the earliest they could possibly have hooked up—how could the child be six years old by the time of Camille's death in 1944?"

"It *is* true," the woman said stubbornly. "Everyone knows it to be true."

The women munched their cookies and grinned their toothless smiles at the baby.

"Well, if that was the rumor going around, I'll bet it made that kid's life a living hell," Maggie said. She couldn't help but think of Amelie, although she knew there was no way she was old enough to be Camille's missing daughter.

"I'd say *that* was a given as soon as they hanged her mother," Madame Belgert said solemnly.

~

MICHELLE WALKED to one of the empty shop fronts on rue Avaulée and stood with her back to its boarded up window while she dug out her disposable mobile phone. She already had two calls into the number and so just needed to hit *Redial* to make the call.

She felt for the universal key in her jacket pocket. It seemed to burn in her hand, tingling with possibility, as she waited for him to answer.

"*Allo?*" His voice was guarded but eager.

"I am ready to do this, Monsieur. Today."

"What do I need to do?"

"Just get her out of the apartment for one hour. I will do the rest. It is that easy. And at the end, you will have the answers you seek and I will have my due."

"What time?"

"The American is gone right now. Can you come immediately?"

He hesitated and then said, "Yes."

"*Bon.* It will all be over in the time it takes you to finish your first course. Both of our lives will have changed for the better. When can you be there?"

"Thirty minutes?"

"*Bon.* Our lives have begun to change already, Monsieur Lorraine."

~

ALL THE ATTENTION at the nursing home combined with an overabundance of sugar had worn even Mila out. Before she left Maggie rearranged the carrier straps so as to carry Mila in front where she immediately fell fast asleep.

Maggie walked slowly away from the nursing home. Stunned. Unseeing. Disbelieving.

It can't be.

The revelations from the women at the facility had blown out of the water just about every fact Delphine had told Maggie. If what they said was true, Delphine had lied about all of it. In fact, the only thing she hadn't lied about was what happened to Camille.

The first thing Maggie did when Madame Remey and the rest of them confirmed the lynching was to go on the Internet via her phone. She should have done it when Delphine told her about it but she'd had no reason to doubt her.

The Internet blurb was just a tiny part of a bigger story on the Resistance. Maggie's skin crawled remembering how the words looked on her phone screen.

Camille Victoire was executed in Paris by members of the Resistance for collaboration activities.

One thing that was true: Camille Victoire had been hanged on August 26, 1944.

And just about everything else Maggie thought she knew about the event was a lie.

She should have known Delphine wasn't telling the whole truth as soon as she discovered the Degas in the closet.

Delphine was the one who led the Resistance to Camille.

An urge gripped Maggie, nearly making her gasp. She must talk to Delphine. But immediately she was slammed with an image of Delphine's face—tortured, hopeful, always so sad.

Is that really what I want to do? How would forcing her to admit the truth help anyone?

Maggie was vaguely aware of passing a large cemetery on her right. She glanced around and realized she had been walking in the opposite direction to the way she had come. She didn't recognize any landmarks but the road she was on was one she knew: Avenue du General Leclerc. At least she wasn't lost this time.

Delphine had betrayed her friend. Her best friend. Maggie took in a long breath and the next thought came at her like a battering ram.

Had Camille been innocent?

Maggie flushed. Why else would Delphine have sent the executioners to Camille? Why else except to save herself? If

Delphine had been the one consorting with the German—and let's face it, she's got a stolen Degas—it would explain why she would direct the men to Camille *rather than just keep quiet.*

She saved herself. By betraying Camille.

No wonder Delphine was tormented. No wonder she didn't act very excited about finding Camille's daughter.

Maggie's stomach roiled at the thought. She swallowed back a sour taste in her mouth as she walked to the front of the cemetery. A plaque outside read *Cimetiere du Montparnasse.*

Jacqueline and Georgette must be buried here, Maggie realized. And their parents, Laurent's great grandparents.

She entered through the massive wrought iron gates until she came to a concrete bench. Like many Paris cemeteries, this one felt more like a park than a place of eternal rest. Mila was still asleep and Maggie sat on the bench with her arms wrapped around the baby. She missed Laurent and Jemmy so much it felt like a physical craving.

Laurent was right. I should have gone home. Maybe I never should have come.

Grace certainly didn't have time for her. And Maggie had done nothing to make Delphine's life better. Delphine was still estranged from Laurent—and Noel too. As hard as Noel was trying to get her to admit their real connection, Delphine continued to resist. If she *was* his mother surely there could be no harm in telling him. What was stopping her?

Maggie moved a curl away from Mila's sleeping face. As she sat, staring out at the obelisks and monuments studded across the landscape, her legs felt heavy and it was only the realization that the sky had darkened that made her finally get to her feet. It was a long walk back to Delphine's and she hadn't seen any taxi stands along the way.

Maybe the old ladies in the nursing home were wrong.

Maggie shifted the heavy sleeping baby in her arms and checked the straps to make sure they were securely buckled before dropping one of her arms, already aching, to her side. She walked out of the cemetery, barely aware of the fact that she hadn't seen a living soul since she'd entered.

What about the painting? Do I just wait until the will is read and let the executor return it to its rightful owner? And not say anything?

Would they check it for fingerprints?

And what about the question of why Amelie was in Delphine's will? Maggie had read the will through several times and there was nothing to reveal why Delphine was including her.

Maggie walked down a side road outside the cemetery toward what her phone GPS indicated was the direction of the Place Denfert-Rochereau. There was a Metro station there. As the light faded and the temperature dropped, she noticed that there were hardly any people on the street with her. She shivered and glanced over her shoulder. A shadow wobbled in the distance. Was it the breeze moving a tree limb? Just the light shifting?

Suddenly, a feeling of being watched came over her like ants crawling through her scalp. She must have reacted physically, because Mila woke with a start.

Maggie wrapped her arms around her but the tension in her grip startled Mila further. The baby began to cry. Maggie patted her on the back. Maggie looked down at the cobblestone road. She didn't dare run with the baby in her arms.

But there was no doubt now.

Someone was behind her.

39

The alleyway at first looked like no more than a simple chasm in the brickwork of the wall. But Maggie had seen enough of them to know it for what it was. Without thinking, she dashed down the alley, looking wildly for another corridor, or a door, a balcony...something.

She could hear him behind her, his foot tread heavy and thudding on the cobblestones. Mila squirmed in Maggie's chest holder and began wailing ensuring there would be no chance of hiding anywhere undetected.

Even if she were able to disappear before his very eyes, whoever was behind her would be able to find her easily by the sounds of her distraught child.

Maggie darted down another even narrower alleyway but as soon as she turned into it she could see it was a dead end. A brick wall loomed at the end of the alley. She ran towards it anyway. Her only hope was to find something on the ground—a weapon of some kind—that she could use to defend herself.

"Help me!" she screamed, scanning the walls of the alley for any hint of life or activity. But there were no windows, no balconies.

The man behind her snarled, "*Khalfak tamarnaan.*"

Maggie didn't know what it meant. It wasn't French. She tried to block out everything but the path before her. Her lungs burned as she ran, her mind was a fusion of desperation and terror.

Just before the brick wall, she spotted a door on her immediate right, half open and flanked by two sets of broken windows, the building itself was clearly abandoned. Maggie darted through the door, dodging around debris and broken furniture.

Once inside, she chanced a look behind her and saw him. His eyes were narrowed and small and focused on her.

In his hand was a knife.

He no longer attempted to match her speed. A thin smile was etched across his features.

He doesn't need to hurry. He knows I'm trapped.

Maggie clutched Mila tightly and bolted into an adjoining room. The first thing she saw was a set of descending stairs. Without thinking, she ran to them, knocking debris out of her way. Not knowing if it would even hold her, she plunged down the stairs taking the steps two at a time.

She could hear him moving relentlessly behind her across the room. The smell from the basement rose up to meet her. It was terrible, musty and foul. Before she hit the bottom step, she pulled out her phone and flipped on her phone's flashlight function to shine the beam in front of her.

The darkened room emptied into a long hallway.

With no other option, Maggie ran down the tunnel, Mila now screaming the whole way.

∽

NOEL SAT in the taxicab outside Delphine's apartment with his cellphone in his hands. And his hands were trembling.

Should he feel guilty?

But why? Hadn't it always been coming to this moment?

He looked up at Delphine's apartment window. The light in the living room was on just as he'd left it.

There was no more to do. Now he could finally walk away.

No, he refused to feel guilt. Whatever Delphine had felt for him—whoever she had been to him—that was gone now. None of it mattered now.

Dear God. Did I really just jeopardize everything I have? For what? Is this peace? Do I feel peace?

Insanity. That's what this was. I was temporarily insane. I was not myself. What better defense could there be?

I was not responsible for my actions.

He bowed his head in the back of the taxi and began to rock himself slowly back and forth.

∽

MAGGIE RAN, slipping once on the slick floor. She caught herself and plunged onward.

Why had she come down here? At least if he'd caught her on the street, Mila would eventually be found. But down here...

She shook the thought from her head. *Neither of us are dying down here!*

She heard him hit the last step on the stairs. He still wasn't running but he wasn't stopping either.

The hall going forward seemed to narrow. It sides were now clearly ancient stone like a medieval underground tunnel. Maggie hit a small puddle of water and the water splashing up against her legs startled her and spurred her to go faster.

One hand held the cellphone lighting the way ahead while the other hugged a still crying Mila or touched the narrowing tunnel walls of the tunnel, whose ceiling was dropping noticeably the further she went.

Her pursuer seemed to have slowed even more. He clearly felt there was no reason to hurry. Did that mean he knew for a fact there was no way out? Even so the distance between them gave Maggie hope and she quickened her pace to lengthen it further.

Mila's howls echoed off the stone walls until Maggie couldn't hear her own breathing or the pounding of her heart or the sounds of her steps splashing through the puddles. The cellphone light illuminated only four or five feet of tunnel ahead, never more than that. The sides of the tunnel were slick with mold.

She glanced down at her phone. The screen indicated *no service*. She wasn't surprised but she felt her hopes plunge even further at the sight.

Suddenly, Mila stopped crying. And when she did, Maggie realized they were completely shrouded in silence. There was no sound at all. Anywhere.

She turned and shone the light over her shoulder. There was no sound behind them. Just empty tunnel.

Mila sniffled.

Was he still back there? Waiting? Did he know there was no way out? Was he just waiting for her to come to him?

She stood still and held her breath, waiting to hear something. She looked in the direction she'd been running.

If it *was* a dead end she would eventually have to turn around and go back the way she'd come.

But if it wasn't…if there was even a breath of a chance that it led out…she had to see.

She patted Mila on the back and held her phone up to show the way forward. It was then that she saw the luminescent objects built into the walls on both sides.

She sucked in a breath and looked closer.

Bones. They were bones. Stacks and stacks of human bones. And skulls.

Millions of them.

Maggie dropped her phone. It fell face up illuminating the

wall in front of her and casting a ghostly distorted beam straight into to the darkness above where the ceiling must be.

The bones were stacked up as far as she could see on both sides of the tunnel.

Maggie bent over and snatched up the light, trying to force her breathing to slow.

Where is this place? Is this the basement to the cemetery?

A feeling of dread and foreboding crawled over her skin as she shined the light ahead—the beam bouncing now erratically with her shaking hand..

The silence was ominous and complete. Even Mila seemed touched by it. Her eyes were wide with fright.

Maggie took another step forward down the tunnel. Her whole body was shaking now. Keeping the light on the ground before her, she forced herself not to look at the walls of the gaping, mocking skulls.

We were alive once too. Your time will come.

Maggie swallowed. She realized that this tunnel must be part of the Paris catacombs. She remembered Laurent saying there were dozens of secret openings through basements and abandoned Metro tunnels. .

When was the last time someone walked here? When they stacked those bones? Hundred of years ago?

Her teeth began to chatter and she gripped Mila tightly.

Would the tunnel meet up with the main repository? She knew a part of the catacombs was open to the public. Her phone said it was seven o'clock. Was the tourist part of the catacombs closed by now? Was she even near to wherever the public part was? Dear God, would she end up trapped in here all night?

Forever?

She glanced again over her shoulder but still saw and heard nothing from behind her. Whoever had been following her had given up.

Does he know something I don't?

Khalfak tamarnaan. That's what he'd shouted at her. So whoever he was, he wasn't French or even European. The words sounded like a Middle Eastern dialect. Maybe Arabic?

Maggie strained to hear any noise at all. She heard a slight vibration or rumbling in the walls and her stomach muscles tightened.

Heaven help me, are we under the Metro?

She knew the catacombs wound under Paris for hundreds of miles. If she didn't find another opening, she and Mila would both die down here. She stopped and looked behind her.

She couldn't go back there. She couldn't take the chance that he was waiting for her to emerge. She had to go forward—wherever that led. She glanced down at Mila but thankfully the baby was too young to understand what she was seeing. The walls of skulls and bones were just shapes to her, unattached to the horror and repugnance that even a four year old would register.

Maggie slowed her pace to avoid slipping on the slick flooring. The puddles were more frequent now and Maggie chose to believe that was a good sign. It had to mean, she hoped, that rain had somehow gotten in. Surely that meant she wasn't that far below the surface? But she recalled the basement steps had gone on and on and she feared she was still deep underground.

Because she had a goal—*keep walking and pray*—her shaking seemed to have diminished. She patted Mila and murmured encouragingly to her—more to hear the optimism in her own voice than anything else—and put one foot in front of the other.

For the first hour, the tunnel stayed largely the same—dark and cold. If it narrowed as it snaked around a corner, it widened again and continued on that way for long stretches. It was mind-boggling to realize how many skeletons had been entombed here. The stacks of bones along both walls never stopped.

Once, she stopped and considered turning around. It felt like madness to go further down this tunnel of death, not knowing where it would lead.

But every time she imagined the man following her standing in the doorway of the abandoned building waiting for her and she knew she couldn't go back. As bad as it was when she entered the alley, this time it would be worse. It would be night now.

She walked on.

The hours passed as she walked. Mila fell back asleep which gave Maggie a strange kind of comfort, feeling her against her chest.

In the hours that she'd been in the catacombs, Maggie had worked hard not to panic, not to think of putting Mila in a situation where she would die cold and starving deep in the bowels of a giant graveyard.

She couldn't think of Laurent or Jemmy. Both images weakened her and she needed every ounce of her strength for whatever lay ahead. When she got out—when she and Mila were both rescued and this was all just a terrible memory—she would indulge in thinking of the two of them. But not now. Now she needed to be stronger than she'd ever been before.

As she walked, Maggie devised a back-up plan to bring Mila to the surface in one piece. If worse came to worse—after a day of walking and getting nowhere—Maggie would make her way back to the abandoned house where she'd entered the catacombs. Her pursuer might well be there waiting for her but Maggie had to believe—whatever he did to her—he wouldn't hurt the baby.

It wasn't much to hope for, but it was better than imagining Mila dying in this cold underworld of death.

She walked on until her knees gave way and she slowly lowered herself to the hard, wet ground. When she awoke, she had no idea how long she had slept but when she looked at her phone—now blinking its low battery warning—she saw she'd been asleep for an hour. She pulled herself to her feet, kissed her sleeping baby, and began to move forward again.

She walked for another hour before she realized that once her phone died she would have to walk back in complete darkness. It was just before midnight—and oh, Delphine must be hysterical with worry!—but the morning would bring no dawn light. There was no time down here—no morning, no evening. Just perennial darkness.

Maggie switched off the light to save the battery but also to see how bad it would be without it.

It was bad.

The darkness was so complete that Maggie knew she could turn herself around completely without realizing it. If she did that enough times and she did decide to go back to the house, she'd never make it. She would just walk in slow circles until she and Mila both died of starvation. She put a hand up and touched the damp wall of bones. She recoiled with disgust at the feel of a human skull.

But she quickly steeled herself and touched the bones again. She knew that without a light she would have to depend on touching the walls in order to escape this labyrinth.

Dear God, can this get any worse?

She walked another hour hoping her eyes would adjust to the total darkness, touching the bones of the dead with every step. Instead of feeling as if they were helping her, she couldn't escape the feeling that they were waiting to turn her and Mila into bones too. She knew that was crazy. But walking in the pitch dark surrounded by the remains of thousands of centuries-old Parisians felt a little crazy too.

Just when she thought she couldn't take the dark any longer and she reached for her phone to give herself a moment of light, she felt a faint vibration in the tunnel. Her hand froze on the phone. She took a silent step forward. And then another.

She realized she'd been sensing a low-grade thrumming in the walls ever since she started touching them. The sound had gotten noticeably louder. The more steps she took forward, the more distinct the sound became.

She was coming toward something.

She flipped on her light and pointed it down the tunnel. Still nothing. She took several quick steps forward and the noise was definitely louder. She switched off her light and used the wall of bones again to guide her forward until she realized the tunnel had gradually become less dark.

There was light coming from somewhere!

She hurried forward, waking Mila with her jogging. The baby cried out and lashed a fist out that struck Maggie in the face. Maggie barely noticed. There, up ahead, was a splotch of dim light on the stone tunnel floor. Her breath turned into quick pants as Maggie ran to the dim patch of light and then looked up.

There was clearly light above. She whipped out her phone light and directed at the ceiling. As she moved the beam back down the facade of macabre bones and skulls, she saw something that was not bones. There, embedded among the bones on the wall, were rusting iron bars.

Maggie reached over to touch it.

It was a ladder.

She looked up again. Somewhere, somehow, even though she couldn't see it, there was a light source up there. And there was a way to get to it. There was a planned, expected, way to get to it. Maggie was about to turn off her phone when its battery died and it winked off by itself.

She shoved the phone in her jacket pocket and found the first rung on the ladder three feet off the ground on the wall before her. Gripping the sides of the iron ladder with both hands, she pulled herself up to the first rung.

40

Maggie climbed slowly, awkwardly with Mila between her and the wall of bones. Twice her knee brushed the edges of sharp protruding pieces of bone. Both times her jeans ripped down to the skin.

This had to be a way out. *Why would they put a ladder here if it wasn't a conduit of some kind?*

The further Maggie climbed, stopping occasionally to hug the ladder and rest, praying her freezing fingers and shaking knees could make one more step and then one more, the louder the hum of the noise became until there was no doubt she was hearing street traffic.

She nearly cried when she realized she was getting closer to where people were. Even if it was the middle of the night there would be somebody who would hear her cries for help. If she could hear traffic, surely they would be able to hear her!

After what seemed like an hour of painstakingly crawling up the ladder, she could finally see where the source of the light—a street lamp up above. The opening she was looking for appeared to be a grilled manhole cover.

She didn't care if it was positioned in the middle of the

Champs-Élysées, she was coming out of that sewer hole. She'd rather take her chances on a hundred crazed French drivers than one more minute in this mass burial pit.

Slowly, she reached the top and grabbed the metal lattice work of the sewer cover. It shifted slightly but was too heavy to move more than that. She tried not to think of how high she was, holding on to an iron ladder with numb fingers and a kicking, actively awake six-month old baby strapped to her chest.

She was getting out of this pit if she had to lift the manhole cover with her head and spend the rest of her life in a wheel chair with a crooked spine as a result. It was either that or die trying, because she wasn't going to be able to hold on much longer.

"Mommy's going to make a big noise, okay, pudding?" she said hoarsely to Mila. "Don't be afraid, okay?"

Mila looked at her uncomprehendingly.

Hoping she wasn't condemning her child to a lifetime of mental therapy, Maggie waited until the sounds of traffic shifted to a lower ebb and then threw back her head and screamed as loudly as she could: "Help me! I'm in the sewer!"

Mila promptly burst into tears and it occurred to Maggie that the added noise of the wailing baby couldn't hurt.

Maggie screamed again, feeling all the fear and panic and anger course through her in one exhausting, cathartic release.

"Help meeeeeeeee!" she screamed to the street above.

As she sucked in another long breath for a third scream, terrified because she could now not feel her fingers on the ladder, a male voice yelled down to her.

"*Qui est là?*"

Looking up, she saw a face looking down at her. A beautiful, angelic face.

Mila sealed the deal by raising her screams another octave before Maggie could answer the man.

"*Nous sommes...perdus,*" Maggie said, her voice a tearful rasp.

Praying she didn't let go in a reflex of pure relief, she watched the man as he wrenched the manhole cover off, flinging decades of trash and leaves onto her upturned face. Before she could realize what was happening, strong hands grabbed her arms harshly but surely and pulled her free.

∼

HE GRIPPED the phone receiver so tightly he felt the plastic crack beneath his fingers. When the man finally answered, it was all he could do not scream.

"How is it you let a woman with an infant in her arms slip by you?"

"Bitch went into the catacombs!"

"So? You coward!"

"Americans carry guns. I am not getting paid to be shot."

"You're not getting paid at all if you can't catch a single woman and a baby!"

"Am I supposed to kill the baby too?"

The caller let out a snort of frustration. *The world is populated with morons and they all seem to be working for me.*

If only I could do this myself!

"Forget it," he said, attempting to regain some calm in his voice. "We'll go about this from a different angle. Perhaps one that even you can comprehend. Go to the old woman's apartment on rue du Bac. The American is constantly coming and going from there."

"I thought you did not want me seen in that neighborhood?"

"That was before I knew what an incompetent imbecile you were! *Go* to the rue du Bac! I don't care if it's the middle of the night or broad daylight! I don't care if the president himself is standing outside having a smoke! Go to the apartment on the rue du Bac and kill her!"

41

Maggie sat in the back of the taxi. She had a hundred euros in her wallet and gave it all to her good Samaritan. When he was pulling her to safety, she could have sworn he was the size of Thor, but it turned out he was a young homeless man in his early twenties. He escorted her to an all night taxi stand and she gave him her phone number. She wasn't through thanking him for saving her life.

She might never be through thanking him.

She fleetingly considered calling the police but knowing they would keep her answering questions the rest of the night at the police station and likely turn up a big fat nothing as far as her assailant, she decided against it.

After she gave the taxi driver Delphine's address—and confirmed that he took credit cards—she spent the twenty minute ride attempting to calm Mila with no success. The baby was wet and hungry and not nearly over the trauma of hearing her mother scream her head off at close range.

Come to think of it, I don't think I'm quite over it myself.

Once on rue du Bac, she over tipped the driver and looked down the darkened sidewalk before darting out the door to stand in front of the heavy double doors of Delphine's building. She plugged in the security code and hurried up the stairs, ignoring the elevator. As exhausted as she was, she'd had enough of small narrow places to last her a lifetime.

As soon as she had a moment to think of something other than their immediate survival, Maggie knew that this was not random. The guy had followed her with a knife. He hadn't wanted money. He'd wanted Maggie. And if she had to guess, he'd wanted her dead.

But why? What am I doing?

It can't be that I'm investigating Gerard's death. Nobody cares about Gerard. Was his murder an organized crime hit? Perhaps they thought, since Maggie went to his apartment that she knew something about whatever scheme or skullduggery Gerard was involved with?

But Gerard was alive when Maggie was followed the first time. So that didn't add up. Because there was no doubt in her mind that the two incidences were related.

Maybe it had nothing to do with Gerard?

But then why?

Her cell phone was still dead and she cringed to think of the series of texts and phone messages that Laurent must surely have left her. She hoped Delphine had gone on to bed and that they could deal with all this in the morning.

What could Maggie possibly tell her that wouldn't worry her?

I was delayed and couldn't call because my phone was dead?

All night?

Pretty weak.

Maggie slipped in the front door with Mila still whimpering and fretful and was surprised to see that the living room light was on. Imagining that Delphine had left it on for her, Maggie went straight to her bedroom where she stripped off Mila's clothes, washed her, powdered her, put a fresh diaper on her and put her in her pajamas before bringing her into the kitchen where Maggie made a bottle of formula as quietly as she could.

There was so much to think of—so much that she'd learned today—from the diary to the nursing home and everything that happened after—that Maggie was so weary she couldn't keep all her thoughts straight in her head.

She remembered in the moments before she realized she was being followed that she'd been thinking about confronting Delphine with what she'd learned at the nursing home. But now that she was back in Delphine's apartment, all her eagerness and determination to find out the truth seemed to have dissolved.

She plugged her phone into its charger in the kitchen and watched as all of Laurent's texts began to appear. She quickly texted him <Sorry. Mila and I are fine. Phone died. Call you in a.m?> She had barely set the phone back down before it dinged musically. <See that you do> he'd written. Maggie smiled. It was two o'clock in the morning. She felt his love like a bond that wrapped around both children and pulled her snugly into his strong arms.

And after a night like tonight, just thinking the words brought tears to her eyes. *Tomorrow*. She would be on a train heading home to him tomorrow. There was no reason to stay in Paris any longer and she needed to be with her family again. She needed to feel Laurent's arms around her. His strength and fortitude flowing from him to her. How long had it been since she'd held Jemmy? A week?

Never again.

Not until he goes off to college am I being separated from him for this long again.

She held the blessedly quiet baby in her arms and fed her the bottle. Noticing again the living room lamp was on she stepped into the living room to turn it off when she stopped abruptly.

There, seated hunched over in the largest creweled wing chair in the room was Delphine. Her head was cocked at an unnatural angle. Her eyes were closed.

42

"It's two in the morning, you selfish jerk," Grace said through the haze of sleep and an encroaching hangover.

"I've tried calling you at an hour that's convenient for you, Grace," Windsor said tightly. "It doesn't seem to matter so I thought I'd make it convenient for my attorney whose office I'm now calling from."

"More threats?" Grace said, pinching her cheeks to wake herself up. She pulled back the covers to slip out of bed so as not to disturb André but saw that he was not in the bed.

"I've got a court order for both kids. Maybe you'll hear this since you refuse to hear anything else."

"What are you talking about?" Grace stood up and walked to André's side of the bed as if expecting to find him on the floor hiding.

Did he leave in the middle of the night?

She and André had slept at her place for a change of scenery. It had been André's idea. He still hadn't met Zouzou and so she and André had brought takeout to the apartment. It had been a delightful evening. Not only did André get along wonderfully with Zouzou—dangling her on his knee and singing silly French songs to her—he'd even helped Beatrice clean up the dishes afterwards while Grace had given Zouzou her bath.

It had felt like a family again for the first time in a long time.

And now Windsor was talking about breaking all that up?

"It's called good faith, Grace. This is the last bone I'm throwing to you and trust me I'm only doing it because Taylor begged me to."

"Taylor?"

"Yes, you remember her? Your daughter? The deal goes like this. Bring Zouzou home immediately and I'll okay a shared custody arrangement. Make me come to Paris and get her and I swear you'll be lucky to see her once a month with supervision."

Why had André left? Had something happened?

Grace sagged to a sitting position on the bed and passed a hand across her face. She drew her hand back and saw it was smeared with mascara. She hadn't washed her face before falling into bed.

"Oh, and Grace?" Windsor said, "Not that I think you'd make the effort, but if you try to take my daughter and run I'll see that you go to prison. Ask me if you think I'm serious."

Before Grace could respond, he hung up. She sat for one moment with the phone in her hands, staring at it in disbelief before dropping it to the floor and burying her face in her hands. Her sobs came from deep inside her like a wild animal clawing to get out.

Beatrice tapped on the door and opened it to peer inside. Her eyes were wide with concern.

"Madame Van Sant?" she said breathlessly. "Is everything all right?"

∽

MAGGIE PROPPED Mila on the couch with her bottle and knelt by

Delphine. Her mind was a whirl. She noticed the telephone receiver was still in Delphine's lap.

Something about the way Delphine was positioned told Maggie as loudly as if the words were spoken aloud that she was not sleeping.

"Delphine?" Maggie said gently, reaching for her wrist. Delphine's face was bone white. The veins in her face were harshly visible beneath her thin, fragile skin. Her pulse was faint and thready.

Maggie put a hand to Delphine's face and the old woman's eyes fluttered open.

"*Chèrie*," she said in a whisper.

"I'm here, Delphine," Maggie said.

Delphine's eyes closed again. Maggie jumped up and ran to the kitchen snatching up her phone and dialing the Paris emergency number. She gave the address and then poured a glass of water and hurried back to the living room. Mila had fallen over on her back on the couch but was still drinking her bottle. Maggie went to Delphine and hung up the telephone next to the chair.

She set the glass of water down on the floor and took Delphine's hand.

Delphine tightened her fingers on Maggie's hand.

"It is just," she said in a small breathy voice. She sighed once, emitting a deep rattle in her chest as she expelled the breath.

And went still.

Maggie watched Delphine's face lose all tension. She watched the life and warmth leave her, leave this world.

"Delphine?" Maggie said hoarsely, but she knew she was gone.

This cannot be happening. I didn't get enough time with her. She never got to know Laurent again. A wellspring of sadness and tears brimmed up in Maggie's heart and she bowed her head over the old woman's hand. The world felt like it had slowed down and there was only this living room in the whole of Paris—and the sounds of Maggie's grief.

After a moment Maggie heard the bottle drop onto the carpet and she looked up to see Mila on the couch yawning.

"She's gone, sweetie," Maggie said as she picked up the baby and hugged her close. She sat on the couch facing Delphine and held the baby until she heard the first purrs of the child's snores in her arms.

Maggie sat there for a long time, watching Delphine's face in repose. Did she imagine that Delphine looked finally at peace?

She thought back to Delphine's last words: *it is just*. What was just? Dying?

An enigma to the end, Maggie thought sadly. *Just like the whole family*

She needed to call Laurent. She needed him here. With her. Now.

She carried the sleeping baby to the bedroom and settled her in her bed, then went to the kitchen and called Laurent. He answered on the first ring.

"Laurent, Delphine just died. I'm so sorry. I…" Maggie broke down. "I need you, Laurent. I need you up here."

Laurent's voice came to her deep and comforting. "I am coming, *chèrie*," he said. "I will be there before breakfast."

"And Jemmy too…"

"*Bien sûr*, Jemmy too.

"I've missed you so much, Laurent. I can't believe she's gone. I can't believe you didn't get a chance to see her one more time."

"*Anon, chèrie*," Laurent said, his voice soothing and warm. "I will meet you at my aunt's apartment in a few hours."

"No, meet me at Grace's. It hurts too much to be here."

They spoke a few minutes longer and then disconnected. It helped so much to talk to him, to hear his voice, so strong and assured. Maggie wiped her tears and took in a deep breath and let it out. She felt a little better.

She pulled her suitcase from behind the dresser in her bedroom and began to pack her and Mila's clothes. All of a sudden the sadness of this apartment—and of the poor tormented woman who'd lived and died here—was just too much to endure. Maggie wouldn't wait for morning. She would take a taxi back to Grace's as soon as the ambulance arrived.

She looked at her open suitcase and realized there were a few things of Delphine's that needed to come with her to Grace's. She might not get a chance later and for Jemmy and Mila's sake—and possibly even Laurent's—she needed to take them now before the estate locked things down.

Leaving Mila in the bedroom, she went to the storage room. She unlocked the door and stood for a moment looking around. Nothing had been touched since she'd been here last. She went to a small box of photos and letters that she'd set aside the day before and tucked them under her arm. Before she could do anything else, she heard the distinct sound of a key in the front door.

She froze. Her heart leaped to her throat. *Who has a key to Delphine's apartment?*

And who would use it at two in the morning?

She held her breath as she heard footsteps enter the apartment.

Mila!

Maggie made a move toward the door when she stopped—her hand still outstretched.

The doorknob to the storage room was turning.

43

Maggie looked wildly around the room for anything she could use as a weapon. Her mind raced and she felt a tightening in her chest. Suddenly she saw a yardstick propped up against the bookcase and she snatched it up and whirled around to face the door. The door began to inch open slowly. Maggie's palms were damp. She held the yardstick up high like a spear at eye level to whoever was coming through the door, and willed her heart to stop crashing in her chest like a drum.

Suddenly the door flung open. Startled, Maggie lunged at the figure in the door, stabbing at his face with her stick. She heard a grunt of pain as she connected. The man's hands flew to his face and he staggered back but he was still blocking the door.

Maggie needed to get to Mila in the bedroom. She dropped the stick and pushed him hard in the chest with both hands. He was off balance and started to fall but before she could dart past him, he grabbed her arm and pulled her to the floor with him.

Instantly, Maggie jabbed him in the throat with her elbow. She knew being on the floor was bad.

You don't get back up once you're down.

She grabbed his hair and wrenched with all her strength. He howled and released her as his hands flew to his head.

"Maggie, stop!" he gasped. "It's me, Noel!"

Maggie scrambled to her feet. Noel's nose was bleeding from where she'd hit him with the yardstick.

"What are you doing here?" Maggie yelled, her eye on the front door. If she could get it open, the neighbors would hear her screams. "Why didn't you knock?" She scanned the foyer to see if there was a vase or something she could use if she needed to.

Noel pulled a handkerchief from his coat pocket and held it to his face. When he covered up his big nose, Maggie was startled to realize how handsome he was.

"I didn't want to wake Delphine," he said in a muffled voice behind the handkerchief. "She'd invited me to stay the night—"

"That's a lie, Noel," Maggie said. "She only has one guest room and she knows I'm in it."

"All right, all right," he said, struggling to get to his feet. "But I knew she wouldn't mind. I was just going to sleep on her couch so I could talk to her first thing in the morning."

"If that's true then why were you trying to get into the storage closet?"

Noel looked at her with surprise. "I saw the light under the door. I could hear someone was in there."

Maggie took a long steadying breath. The ambulance would be here any minute. She had nothing to worry about from Noel. He was an old man.

"What was so important it couldn't wait until morning?" she asked.

"I thought Delphine might still be up."

"At two in the morning?"

"I saw you go in nearly an hour ago and when the salon light didn't go off—"

"You were watching from the street?"

Noel ran a hand across his face and his head drooped as if too heavy for his neck.

"I was with Delphine this evening. I tried to get her to come out with me. She wouldn't. One thing led to another…"

"And you began haranguing her again."

He looked at her and for a moment Maggie felt a twinge of pity for him.

"How did you get a key?" she asked.

"I didn't. The door was open. May we do this from the relative comfort of the living room, please? It's very uncomfortable down here on the floor."

"How was she when you left her?" she asked.

"Upset."

"But alive?"

Maggie studied his reaction which was swift and guileless. If he had goaded Delphine to the point where her heart failed, he was unaware of it.

"What are you saying?" His voice was a whisper.

Maggie's shoulders sagged and she stepped out of the way as he pulled himself to his feet. He took two steps into the foyer and saw Delphine slumped in the wing back chair. With a moan, he ran to her and dropped to his knees.

"No, no, no, no…." He clasped her hands and kissed them, the tears flooding his face. "I am such a fool," he whispered. "Mother, forgive me. Delphine, dearest aunt, forgive me." His shoulders shook with silent sobs. Maggie stood watching him as the minutes ticked by.

Eventually, he leaned back on his heels. His face was a grimace of anguish.

"The last thing she said to me was *please leave me in peace*," he choked out.

"Do you have any idea who she could have been talking to on the phone tonight?" Maggie asked gently.

Noel looked at her and shook his head. "I've been calling all evening to apologize but the line was busy."

"I'm so sorry, Noel," Maggie said.

He looked at Delphine through wet eyes. Maggie went to the kitchen and put the kettle on for tea. When she returned, he was sitting opposite Delphine with his hands looped together between his knees, the picture of woe.

"The front door wasn't open," Maggie said, placing a mug of tea in front of him. "It locks when it closes."

He nodded and sipped the tea. "Michelle Normand had a universal key created," he said dully. "I put it over the door ledge."

"*Michelle* has a key to Delphine's apartment," Maggie said. "Crazy ragbag Michelle who hates Delphine. You were plotting with *Michelle*? Against your aunt?"

"My *mother* you mean!" Noel said fiercely and then he sagged back into his gloom. "And it wasn't like that. But nothing else I'd ever done or said made a difference. Not me being a perfect son, not trying to make her proud of my accomplishments in office, not badgering her, not throwing tantrums or ultimatums. I'm not proud of it but time was running out! She had to tell me the truth!"

"Did it ever occur to you that she *was* telling you the truth?"

"No. She loved me. Georgette didn't."

"Maybe Georgette was embarrassed about the circumstances of your birth. Maybe Georgette just wasn't the maternal type. Did you ever think of that?"

"Delphine was my mother. I just needed her to say it."

"If whatever Michelle did tonight is the reason Delphine is dead, Noel, you're an accessory to murder."

"That's ridiculous! It's clearly a heart attack. And besides, we called it off. Michelle was never here." He put his face in his hands. "I just wanted her to claim me."

Maggie sipped her tea. The clock over the mantel said it was nearly three now. It looked like nobody was getting any sleep tonight.

"So what was your plan?"

"What?" he lifted his head to look at her.

"What were you and Michelle planning to do?"

He dragged a hand through his thick white hair and Maggie thought he looked even older than his seventy-two years.

"I was to get Delphine out of the apartment while Michelle looked around for the treasure Delphine told Michelle's father she had."

"Treasure?"

"Michelle seemed convinced Delphine had some kind of treasure—from the war."

The Degas!

"That's grand larceny, Noel."

"Michelle said Delphine wouldn't go to the police about it. But whatever it was Michelle believed it was something she *could* blackmail Delphine with."

"Gee, Noel, you're a son any mother would be proud to have."

"Do not judge me! You have no idea what my life has been! I was desperate."

"And how was this going to help you? Once you had your mother quaking in her boots about going to prison or destroying the family name, she would then admit you were her son?"

He shook his head. "I was crazy to think anything would change her mind."

"So what went wrong tonight?"

"Delphine wouldn't leave with me. Said she wanted to have supper with you and the baby. I rang Michelle and called it off."

"Bet she was thrilled with that."

"Look, you can hate me. Now that Delphine's gone—which was the very thing I worried about for years—I can see it doesn't matter. What I had with her—whatever name you want to put on it—*that's* what mattered. I'm a fool. And nobody can make me feel worse than I already do. "

"How awful that you had to go through all this to finally learn that," Maggie said standing up. "Go home, Noel. Go back to Switzerland."

He stood and walked to the front door like the old man he was. Only now he was beaten and heartbroken too. Maggie touched his hand at the door.

"The key, Noel," she said softly.

He dug in his pocket and handed her the key. "I loved her, you know."

"She knew that, Noel," Maggie said, patting him on the arm as he trudged through the door. "I'm sure she did."

He smiled bleakly and then turned to walk down the stairs. Maggie closed the door and moved back into the apartment to finish packing. A few minutes later she heard the medical personnel finally clanging their equipment and gurney in the narrow stairwell.

She walked over to Delphine and kissed her on the cheek.

"Goodbye, Delphine," she whispered. "I'll make sure Mila doesn't forget you, or Laurent either. And I promise I never will."

Then Maggie called for a taxi and went to open the door to greet the last guests Delphine would ever receive.

∼

MAGGIE WAS NEVER MORE grateful for Beatrice. She arrived at Grace's apartment just after five in the morning. Beatrice was already up making muffins and eagerly took an unusually cranky Mila out of Maggie's arms when Maggie stepped across the threshold.

"It is such a surprise that you are back!" Beatrice said. Maggie wasn't sure she wasn't talking more to Mila than her.

"Is Grace here?" she asked.

"She is still asleep," Beatrice said.

Well, at least Grace was home, Maggie thought. She dragged her bag to the guest room and took her shoes off and fell into bed too tired to care about anything.

She awoke hours later with the feeling of the sun shining through her bedroom window. A quick glance at the bedside clock revealed it was nearly noon. The bedroom door opened and Laurent came in with a steaming mug of coffee in one hand. As usual, his timing was uncanny.

Maggie held out her arms to him and after he set the coffee down, he gathered her close to him on the bed. He just held her for several moments. A familiar voice coming from the living room made Maggie lift her head.

"Jemmy," she said with a smile.

"I told him to allow his *maman* her morning coffee first," Laurent said. He kissed her mouth and pushed her bangs off her forehead. "A hard night for you, *chèrie*."

A flash of the catacombs came into Maggie's mind and she shivered. "You have no idea," she said.

"But you will tell me everything?"

"Eventually. Oh, Laurent, I'm so sorry you didn't get a chance to see Delphine before she died. She was a wonderful woman. I'm just so grateful I got to know her."

"*C'est juste*," he murmured as he held her and kissed her hair. "I am glad too. What did the medical *techniciens* say?"

Maggie sighed and disentangled herself from him long enough to reach for her coffee. It was aromatic with chicory and cinnamon and felt like something they might serve in Heaven.

"They said it looked like natural causes," Maggie said. Laurent nodded. His thick brown hair was longer than usual, she noted, as if he hadn't had time to get a haircut. As usual, his dark eyes were impossible to read.

"After I talked with you last night, Noel showed up." Maggie said.

Laurent's eyebrows shot up but he didn't say anything.

"Plus, some of Delphine's neighbors were milling about when the ambulance came and one lady said she saw Noel there yesterday in the early evening and she heard shouting. He told me as much but I didn't know they'd actually been yelling at each other."

"You think Noel had something to do with her death?"

"I don't know. My gut says no. When I found her she had the phone receiver in her lap like she'd been talking to someone."

"The police will be able to determine who it was she was speaking to."

"If they bother. I hope so."

There was a light tap at the door and Maggie pulled away from Laurent to see Jemmy standing in the doorway.

"There's my baby boy!" Maggie said, holding her arms out wide to him. Jemmy ran and threw himself into her arms. Maggie smothered his face with kisses. "Oh, I missed you so much! I'm never leaving again. Ever."

"*Bon*," Laurent said, wrapping his arms around both of them.

That afternoon after lunch Laurent carried a sleepy Jemmy off to take his nap—as effortlessly as if he were carrying a football. As he passed Maggie standing with Mila he reached for them both with his free arm and pulled them into a hug. The sensation of his strength and the sweet love of her family broke down her last defense and Maggie began to cry which woke both Jemmy and Mila. Beatrice took the children away as Maggie watched from Laurent's arms, grateful beyond words for the girl's expert care and attention.

Laurent lifted Maggie's chin and wiped away her tears.

"There is more to tell me, *oui*?" he asked firmly but gently.

Maggie nodded. He'd probably never let her out of the house again with either of the children even go to the grocery store once he heard about the Catacombs—and she could hardly blame him—but she couldn't keep it from him either.

They went downstairs and walked down the wide sidewalk, with Notre-Dame looming in the distance like a benign presence, until they came to the first café nearest the apartment. Laurent ordered them both sherry and toast spears with foie gras and Maggie told him everything that had happened, from Gerard's apartment to André's kiss to her night in the catacombs and ending with Delphine's last words.

"*Incroyable*," Laurent said, shaking his head.

"I wanted to give her peace. I wanted to ease her mind." Maggie said, finishing off her third sherry and feeling the exhaustion of everything that had happened in the last twenty-four hours pressing down on her.

"Turns out I didn't succeed on doing either."

44

Maggie wasn't surprised that Laurent's presence in the apartment should fill up every inch of it with noise and activity. Although taciturn himself, there was something about the man that naturally energized those around him. As soon as they got back from the café, he set to work in the kitchen making dinner. Maggie sat at the kitchen table with Jemmy on her lap until the toddler grew impatient with her attention.

Laurent stood at the stove stirring a pot of coq au vin. He held Mila in one arm and Beatrice and Zouzou stood beside him.

The cozy picture infused a burst of contentment in Maggie as she watched. Like most women, Beatrice was transfixed by Laurent. She gazed at him with adoring eyes and tripped over herself to be of service to him, handing him dishtowels, wooden spoons and spices before he asked for them.

The children too clustered about him, vying for his attention. Maggie sipped her wine and watched how they hung on him, chattering and laughing. She wondered how a boy with no happy memories of his own childhood could grow up to be a man who easily and naturally generated them for others. She watched Mila and Jemmy and felt a flush of gratitude—not just for herself that she had them, which she felt on a daily basis, but because she was able to give them Laurent for a father.

"*Papa! Papa! Moi!*" Little Jemmy called out while tugging on Laurent's pant leg.

"*Moi aussi, Papa!*" Zouzou said, pulling on his other leg.

Laurent handed the baby to Maggie and picked up Zouzou. He continued to stir the steaming pot.

"You have a papa, *oui, ma petite*?" he murmured to her in mostly English.

"*Tu, es mon papa!*" Zouzou crowed. Laurent turned to give Maggie a frown.

It was hardly surprising that Zouzou had forgotten Windsor. She hadn't seen him in eighteen months, nearly half her life. Maybe they should be grateful Grace hadn't brought her men home. At least Zouzou wasn't remembering André as her father —or whoever had come before André.

"Your father lives in America, yes, little one?" Laurent asked as he moved about the kitchen, taking lids off pots and checking on a casserole in the oven. He turned to Beatrice. "Do you speak English with her?"

Maggie felt sorry for Beatrice. The girl so wanted to please her new idol. But the ability to speak English had not been one of the requirements on Grace's checklist for an au pair. Beatrice spoke only French.

"*Monsieur?*" she said, her bottom lip trembling.

"*Ça ne fait rien,*" Laurent said. But Maggie recognized the look of determination on his face. He'd already settled on a course of action that probably included confronting Grace or phoning Windsor—or both.

Before they sat down to dinner, Maggie made another attempt to talk Grace out of her darkened bedroom—where she'd been all day—and join them. Maggie tapped on the door and opened it a crack.

"Grace, can you come out? Laurent is here."

"Darling, I'm sorry. I'll see everyone in the morning, all right?"

"Is she ill?" Laurent asked Beatrice when Maggie returned to the table. He sat with Mila in one arm and passed the bowls around the table with the other hand.

"Not really," Beatrice said eagerly, determined to reinstate herself in Laurent's good graces. "Perhaps hung over?"

"All day?" Laurent asked. "Jemmy, do not start eating until I say, yes?"

Jemmy nodded at his father but his eyes went back to his plate. Even Maggie had to force herself not to grab up her fork. It smelled and looked amazing and she realized she was starving. She gave a wink to Zouzou who giggled.

The meal was lively and fast as only one with two toddlers and a baby can be. Afterwards as Maggie and Beatrice bathed the children and put them to bed, Laurent cleaned the kitchen. Once the children were in bed and—after too many stories that only Laurent could read to them—finally asleep, Beatrice retired to her bedroom and Maggie and Laurent sat outside on the small balcony overlooking the back alley of specialty shops and bakeries below. While the street shops had been closed for hours, there were still many people walking to and from the area's popular restaurants and clubs.

"What is the matter with Grace?" Laurent asked.

"My guess? She's either in the process of getting dumped—and that's a new feeling for her—or she's managed to develop a drinking problem."

Laurent did not look surprised. He brought his cigarette to his lips and nodded reflectively. "And Windsor?"

"Last I heard he was making noise about getting custody of both kids."

"*Vraiment?*"

"Yes. Grace has been totally distracted by this André guy."

"The one who kissed you."

"Okay, Laurent, I hope that's not how you're going to define him going forward. For one thing, Grace doesn't know about it."

He shrugged. "She is not being a good mother."

"Well, she's made sure Zouzou is clothed and fed and loved by a very good caretaker."

Laurent gave her a baleful glance.

"But yeah, you're right. She's not being a good mother."

"I am surprised you haven't gotten to the bottom of this."

"I haven't had time. What with Delphine and all."

"Of course." A shadow passed over Laurent's face.

"Can I ask you something, Laurent?"

He raised an eyebrow and his full lips held the hint of a smile.

"Why didn't you tell me you came from a wealthy background?"

He let out a long sigh.

"I mean, were you ashamed of being too rich or something?"

"*Non*," he said, "of being given every opportunity by a woman who loved me and throwing it all away with both hands."

Oh. That.

"It pains me to think of all my grandmother sacrificed for me and for Gerard. And how we repaid her. She died thinking I was a thug."

"Oh, Laurent. I'm sure that's not true."

"I *was* a thug.

"I wish you could have seen Aunt Delphine again so she could've seen how you'd changed."

"To what end? To be in her good opinion? Did I deserve that?"

"Pretty hard on yourself, Laurent."

"*Au contraire.*" He held Maggie's hand and nodded in the direction of the room where Mila and Jemmy slept. "I have been rewarded for my bad choices beyond what I deserve."

THE NEXT MORNING, Maggie and Beatrice fed the children while Laurent was on the phone with the executor of Delphine's estate. Maggie had wanted an autopsy performed but Laurent had seen no point in it. It was clearly natural causes.

Grace still hadn't come out of her room.

Laurent came into the kitchen as Maggie was unbuckling Mila from her highchair.

"I am to meet the executor at Delphine's lawyer's office today," he said.

"Oh?" Maggie turned and looked at Laurent. "Oh!" She'd totally forgotten that Laurent was to inherit a third of a very big fortune. While she'd mentioned the will to him last night and the fact that he, Noel and Amelie were to inherit, everything else had pressed on her until she'd forgotten the fact. Now as she watched Laurent pick up his cigarettes and car keys and pat his pockets to make sure he hadn't forgotten anything, it occurred to her that their money problems in the vineyard were about to be over.

"Will Noel be there too?" she asked, trying to keep the bounce out of her step as she walked him to the apartment door.

"*Oui.* And Madame Tavers. I've set up a service for Delphine for the end of the week but I will need to return home and come back for that."

"I'm so ready to be home, too," Maggie said wistfully.

"Just a few more days, *chèrie*," Laurent said, kissing her at the door. "There is no point in you returning before then."

"Leave Jemmy with me."

"I have already promised him he may stay," Laurent said with a grin. "I won't be long today. Keep your phone on."

Maggie returned to the sunny kitchen where Beatrice was putting a jacket on Zouzou.

"I am taking them to the park, Madame," Beatrice said. "You will come?"

"You know, if you don't mind, Beatrice," Maggie said, "I have some work I'd like to do to get ready for Madame Normand's memorial service. Do you mind going alone?"

"Not at all."

Beatrice herded both older children out of the apartment and pushed Mila in her stroller while Maggie waved them off. Then Maggie came back inside and, after pausing at Grace's door to see if she could hear anything, went to her bedroom to finish unpacking. She brought the packet of old photos and letters that she'd taken from Delphine's apartment and put them on the kitchen table to sort through them.

She probably hadn't needed to be so secretive about bringing the photos back. Surely nobody but her was interested in them. But she knew how the French inheritance system could be and it was much better—in her experience—to apologize later than ask permission first. In fact, she was pretty sure that approach was basically invented for the French legal system.

She poured herself another cup of coffee and sat down with the photos and also Dieter's grandfather's diary. She flipped through it but again could find nothing that made sense to her. She'd stuck the photo of Delphine and Camille that had first prompted her questions between its pages. Delphine had put it in the kitchen drawer, and Maggie had later retrieved it. She looked at it now and turned it over. On the back was written a single word: *Toujours.*

That could mean forever or always. And both were very different meanings. She put the photo back inside the diary. *This might be a puzzle I work on during a cold winter night back home in St-Buvard,* she told herself as she dropped the diary into her tote bag.

She'd found the photographs in a cigar box on a shelf in the storage closet a few days earlier and had transferred them to the envelope the night Delphine died. From the looks of them she'd already determined that many of them had to be the missing photos from the album she'd found earlier.

Now she spread them out on the kitchen table and, enjoying

the fact that her own family was back together again, began to sort through them. Soon however the melancholy of losing Delphine began to seep into her mood. She'd only known Delphine a week but Maggie knew she'd grown to love her in that time. While in the long run the loss of her wouldn't dramatically affect Maggie's life, knowing her somehow already had.

Maggie looked at several pictures that all seemed to have been taken during the same session. There were photos of Delphine with her two sisters and a cloudy, damaged photo of the three sisters with two people who must have been their parents. Maggie squinted but the photo was too blurry. She knew she wouldn't find photos of Laurent in this batch. The photos were old. They were family photos from long before he was born. She found a photo of Noel as a teenager and his nose was the first thing one saw in the picture. There was a baby picture but with nothing written on the back, she couldn't tell who it was. She tried to see if the baby's features resembled Mila or Jemmy.

At this stage, most babies just look like big bald heads with no specific features, she thought. In any case, the photos would go into a photo album back at St-Buvard so that Jemmy and Mila could see what their paternal ancestors looked like. And maybe, just maybe, Laurent could think from time to time about who it was he came from too.

There was never any point in trying to deny who you were or where you came from, Maggie thought as she gathered up the photos and slipped them back in the envelope. Sooner or later it comes back to bite you on the...

Suddenly, a thought—ill-formed and amorphous—crept into her brain. Without realizing she was doing it, she pulled her phone out of her purse. The two things were probably not connected but something had suggested it to her—something unconscious and suppressed. She sent a text to Dieter.

<*Sorry to bother you. Wondering if you have a photo of your grandfather? All Internet shots fuzzy.*>

She got up to pour herself another cup of coffee and then walked again to Grace's door. Was she even alive? This can't be a hangover. Should I force her to come out?

She heard the unmistakable *ding* of her phone receiving a text and she hurried back to the table.

<No>

She sat down in frustration. He was willing to engage with her but not help her? What was his deal? Ignoring his response, she quickly wrote another text.

<All the photos I find of him on the Internet his face is in shadow or his hat is pulled down.>

She waited until she could see that Dieter was forming a reply.

<He was trying to hide a facial deformity. Plastic surgery not so easy in those days.>

Deformity? Maggie looked around the kitchen in bewilderment trying to imagine what Dieter could be talking about. Then she felt her hands go cold.

The truth came to her like a lightning bolt to the brain.

That's what was off about him! Dieter's nose was smaller than it should have been. His face was created for a larger nose. Dieter had had a nose job! She looked down at the phone in her hands, her thoughts racing faster than she could keep up with them.

<Your grandfather had a big nose?>

There was no response. Maggie didn't want to ask again. If she had to, she'd call him. Dieter probably knew that. Why was this exciting? Why was this important? What did this mean?

Her phone dinged again.

<I'm sending the only photo I have of him without a hat. Please to not contact again.>

Maggie waited while the photo downloaded.

She was about to see the face of Camille's lover, the man who had murdered thousands of innocent people and ruined so many lives.

The black and white photo uploaded. Maggie stared at it. Helmut had blond hair and a cruel gaze. His lips were full and he had high cheekbones. He would have been a strikingly handsome man if not for the protrusion of the bony hawk nose centered in the middle of his face.

The very same nose on Noel Lorraine.

45

Noel was the Gestapo officer's child.

Maggie stood up from the kitchen table. The revelation hit her like a train slamming into a brick wall.

Noel was Helmut's son. And since Noel couldn't be Camille's son—he was born six months after she was killed—it meant someone else had slept with the German.

Someone in addition to Camille?

Someone *instead* of Camille?

Maggie thought back to the women in the nursing home who had referred to "that slutty Fouquet girl" and the fact that they'd never seen Camille with a German.

It wasn't Camille with the German. It had never been.

Maggie put a hand to her mouth to stifle the moan.

Delphine.

Noel was right about Delphine being his mother. Does that mean he knows about his father? Noel holds political office in Switzerland. A scandal of this magnitude—that he was the son of a Gestapo officer convicted of war crimes at Nuremberg—would be bad. If Noel knew…if the world knew…

A terrible thought came to Maggie.

Had Noel discovered the truth and killed Delphine in a rage? Or to keep her secret forever sealed? No, that couldn't be right. Delphine wasn't murdered.

Maggie wrung her hands. She had to talk to Noel again. He was the last person besides Maggie to see Delphine alive. She glanced at her phone. He was probably with Laurent and Amelie talking to Delphine's attorney right now.

Unbelievable. And on top of everything else he was collecting a third of her estate.

Don't jump to conclusions, she thought. *Talk to him first. See if he knows about his father.*

Her phone chimed indicating another text and she snatched it up, thinking Dieter had more information for her.

It was from Laurent.

<*Delphine to be buried in Cimetiere du Montparnasse. Memorial mass scheduled for Friday at ten o'clock.*>

Maggie's mind was a whirlwind of thoughts and emotions. She knew Delphine had been tormented by what she did to her friend over seventy years ago. Many horrific things had happened in the war. But Delphine carried the knowledge with her that what had happened to Camille was *her fault.*

The door to the apartment opened and Maggie was surprised to see that Beatrice and the children were already back for lunch.

"It is a beautiful day," Beatrice said to Maggie. "And Monsieur Jemmy is a most clever boy. He can count to twenty. Did you know?"

Jemmy beamed and ran to Maggie. She knelt and wrapped her arms around him and buried her face in his neck.

"He gets smarter by the hour," Maggie said, her voice catching with emotion.

He giggled. "Tickles, Mommy!" he said, pulling away.

Maggie stood and kissed Mila in Beatrice's arms.

"Is Madame Van Sant still in bed?" Beatrice asked, nodding at Grace's door.

"Appears so. Beatrice, can I ask you watch the children a little longer today?"

"You are going out? Of course, I am happy to!"

"Great. I won't be long and I really appreciate it."

Before she went down this road, before she convicted Delphine without any real evidence, Maggie was going to find out the truth once and for all. If she had to go to her grave with the secret of what Delphine did, she would.

But she wouldn't let it tarnish the memory she had of Delphine if it wasn't true.

She grabbed up her tote and quickly texted Laurent to let him know she was running a few errands and would be back in time for dinner. He was planning on driving back to St-Buvard in the morning and she intended to have everything wrapped up in a nice big bow by then.

She hesitated at Grace's bedroom door but decided not to bother checking on her. She kissed Mila and Jemmy and gave a grateful look to Beatrice and then left the apartment.

∼

AMELIE STOOD in the square with her arms wrapped around her shoulders and her breath coming in short, labored pants.

So Madame was dead. Finally.

She took in a long breath and tried to expel it to see if she felt different. Nothing. The pain that sat in her heart like a malignant growth was there still.

Does the old bitch think it is over? That death has released her?

She looked at the ancient sycamore. In seventy years it had grown. Which branch was the one they'd thrown the rope over? Had her grandmother watched in terror and disbelief as they threw the rope into the branches of the tree?

Her phone vibrated in her purse but she didn't look at it.

Madame's attorney. It seems Madame Normand had left Amelie some money.

I am fifty-four years old. No husband, no children, no education. Her money might have helped before. I don't know. Would it have changed anything? Would I have taken the money and forgiven her the crime?

When I die, could I look into Coeur's eyes or Camille's? And explained to them how much the money was needed?

No. However I might have reacted, I don't need to worry. That temptation was never offered to me. And now?

Now to be thrown a few crumbs from a grateful employer? And never to admit the truth for the world to know?

Amelie wished she'd had the courage to tell Madame before she died. She was sorry for that.

But it's not too late. Not as long as there is a single person with Delphine Fouquet's blood running in her veins.

The baby will be enough. She will replace the one who provoked such shame and infamy.

Amelie had been too meek before now.

She would be meek no more.

46

I should have come here first.
      Maggie stepped from the train platform at Brétigny-sur-Orge. The little village was less than an hour outside Paris.
Instead of tracking down descendants of German lovers or thinking about going to Heidelberg—all along the answer was here and if I'd only doubted even a little of what Delphine told me about the story, I would have known to come here first.

This is where Camille Victoire came from.

The story of who Camille was and what happened to her daughter was here.

Why didn't I come here first?

Because Delphine said that Camille's daughter was taken to the south.

If I hadn't believed everything she told me, I would have come here first.

She glanced at her cell phone and checked the address of the Catholic church. It might be just a chapel or it might be something more grand, but there was always a church. And in Maggie's experience, the French Catholic clergy rivaled the Mormons for keeping records of their parishioners.

She was counting on it.

Brétigny-sur-Orge was a pretty village, especially in spring. The gardens that lined the walkway leading from the train station to the center of town were spilling with wood violets and cowslip. It was a perfect picture of tranquility and serenity. Maggie tried to imagine a child being raised here in disgrace. She tried to imagine what Camille's daughter's life must have been like so soon after the war.

As she stepped into the village Maggie could see the grey stone medieval church at the end of town. Maggie thought it had at least been there for generations and generations of villagers—for baptisms, communions, confirmations, weddings and funerals. Birth, life, death.

The village itself was only marginally more active than any typical day in St-Buvard. Maggie nodded at the grocer, a stout frowning woman who stood in front of her store with her hands on her hips openly observing Maggie as she passed. Most small villages in France tended to be, if not out and out unfriendly, then extremely wary.

Maggie made her way through the village toward the end of the street. She had worked very hard during the train ride not to think of Delphine. But her revelation about Noel's birth made that difficult. It explained why Delphine didn't want Noel to know she was his mother—because when he did there were just a few steps from that fact to the one that had her pregnant by an officer of the Gestapo.

Maggie shivered.

Enough! I'll accept what I have to when it's time and not a second before.

She reached the front steps of the village church. It was a classic example of Norman architecture. Grim and grey with massive thick walls and a main tower pointing heavenward. The large wooden front door was recessed under a rounded archway.

She didn't go through the front door but walked around to the back following a crumbling stone wall that defined the churchyard. Except for the grumpy grocer, she hadn't seen anyone since arriving at the village. It was just after two o'clock so it was possible everyone was either still eating lunch or napping. The village was close enough—just—to serve as a bedroom community to Paris. It didn't matter. The person she hoped to talk to—whether or not he would be able to help her—would be at the church and not in some office in Paris.

The cemetery behind the church was well-tended. Each of the plots was carefully weeded and several had fresh flowers placed by them. Unlike in the States, Maggie was surprised to see that there were actual planted flowers on some graves. Many of the tombstones looked ancient. She walked around until she found graves from the 1940's.

It's not that she needed proof that Camille had died. That was a fact of history. But she knew if she could find her grave, it would tell her much more.

I should have come here first.

A breeze picked up and she buttoned her jacket against the cold. The clouds looked heavy and full but Maggie was betting it wouldn't start pouring until she was back on the train to Paris. Her tote bag was heavy. She wondered if Laurent was out of his meeting yet with the lawyer. Was he back at the apartment?

She focused on the rear portion of the churchyard. This section was not kept up. Although many of the markers dated back to the twelve hundreds, some were more recent. Suddenly Maggie spotted a simple stone marker choked with weeds. It looked unloved and apart from the rest. When she stepped closer to it, past the brambles and the nettles, she could just make out the words carved on the stone: *Camille Victoire. Mort 1944.*

Maggie knelt by the grave. So Camille *was* buried in her village. Delphine had lied about that too. A wave of sadness crashed over Maggie. This woman was innocent. This woman had been betrayed by her best friend and died a gruesome and humiliating death. Tears stung Maggie's eyes. *Delphine, how could you?*

She scanned the surrounding gravestones until she found what she was now sure would be there. It was just behind Camille's grave with several plastic flowers jammed into the ground near it. The weeds were overgrown so whoever had taken the time to honor the grave hadn't done so in awhile.

She read the words carved into the stone.

Coeur Tavel.

Maggie was robbed of her breath as she recognized Amelie's last name. She squatted down and pushed the vines and overgrowth away from the marker.

Nee 1938 Mort 1978.

The birthdate matched up. The fact that she was buried next to Camille did too.

She'd found her. *Camille's daughter.*

She reached out and touched the stone.

"Dead at forty," Maggie said softly, shaking her head.

Suddenly she was aware of footsteps moving toward her. She twisted around but lost her balance and fell forward as a strong male voice boomed out close behind her.

"I've been watching you," he said.

47

The elderly priest stepped up from behind one of the taller gravestones. He was dressed all in black except for the dingy white collar that peeked out from below a long gray beard.

"Gosh, you startled me," Maggie said, her hand to her throat. "I'm sorry. I didn't mean to trespass."

"Can I help you, Madame?" He didn't sound unfriendly but like most French—especially out in the countryside—he wasn't particularly warm either.

Maggie had been hoping to track down someone from the church before she left anyway. She'd have preferred not to be caught skulking around the graveyard but she quickly pulled herself together. She reached into her tote bag and pulled out the German's diary and found the photo of Camille and Delphine. She handed it to the priest.

"I'm trying to find out what happened to Camille Victoire's daughter," she said.

The priest looked carefully at the photo and then handed it back to Maggie. "As you see," he said with a shrug.

"Right, yes, I do see that she's dead. But I was wondering if you knew the family? Or maybe the priest who had the job before you?"

He narrowed his eyes at Maggie and seemed to closely examine her clothing. She was wearing sneakers, jeans and a thin rain jacket. Her long dark hair was pulled back in a low-hanging ponytail. Maggie knew she didn't look like a criminal and there was no doubt he could tell she wasn't French.

He turned away and began walking toward the church.

"You'll have tea?" he called over his shoulder. "You English love your tea, yes?"

It didn't matter that he thought she was English. The fact was, he spoke English and was willing to answer her questions.

"Oh, yes, we do," Maggie said as she hurried to catch up with him.

THE VILLAGE RECTORY was small and except for the refrigerator and microwave, looked like it had served the same purpose for a few centuries. Maggie sat on the couch while the priest put a kettle on the stove and a cat ran to her and instantly rubbed up against her legs.

"I am Père Michel," he said. "In fact I knew both Coeur and her daughter."

"Amelie?"

The priest turned to look at her as if analyzing her. "You know Amelie?"

"She's the housekeeper for my husband's aunt in Paris."

The man nodded as if this was not a surprise to him. "She is doing well?"

"I guess so," Maggie said. "She's going to inherit a lot of money so she'll probably be doing a lot better real soon."

Should she not have said that? Maggie wasn't supposed to know what was in the will. But the priest didn't seem to register her words. She sat quietly forming her questions until he came back into the room with a tray of two mugs and a plate of thinly sliced bread.

"I am afraid I have no biscuits," he said. "I rarely have company."

"No worries," Maggie said, taking her tea mug. "Thank you for this."

"I have not kept up Madame Victoire's gravesite and for this I apologize. I am an old man."

"I guess she doesn't have any family left to do it?"

"Only Amelie."

"I was wondering if you could tell me what you know about Camille. Did you know her personally?"

He shook his head. "*Non.* I was not yet a priest then. But the rector before me, Père Joseph knew her family very well."

"I guess he was pretty shocked by what happened."

"He never believed it. Not for a moment."

"He didn't believe that Camille had been consorting with Germans?"

Delphine had said all the young German officers were *hot.* Even the good girls were swooning over them—especially when they knew they shouldn't be.

"He swore that she could not have done what she was accused of."

"Did he tell you why?"

"It was something Camille told him in the confessional."

Father Michel solemnly tapped his nose with a forefinger. Maggie wasn't familiar with the gesture but the message was clear: Camille had a secret that she'd revealed to her priest that made it impossible for her to have been with the German. Or perhaps any man?

"Camille was *gay*?" Maggie blurted out.

"I never met her myself," the priest said, a thin smile on his lips. "But Father Joseph was quite adamant about her innocence in this matter."

"Well, that would explain a few things," Maggie said with a sigh. "Did you know Coeur?"

"Of course. A good woman but troubled."

With every right to be.

"She was raised by Camille's parents until they passed and then taken on by a family who informally adopted her." The priest shrugged as if to indicate this might not have been a great thing. "Coeur changed her name from Victoire to Tavel, which was the name of her foster family. She never married and died of cancer before she was forty. She had one child, Amelie. Out of wedlock."

So there's that mystery solved. Delphine had surely known all along where Camille's daughter was. That's why Amelie is in the will.

It wasn't Camille who consorted with the German officer.

It was Delphine.

It had always been Delphine.

"I am sorry, Madame. Is this information not helpful to you?"

Maggie set her tea mug down. She was suddenly feeling very tired. "Oh, no, it's helpful. It's just...so tragic. Don't you think?"

He shrugged. "But of course," he said. As if all of life was tragic and some parts simply more so than others.

∼

FROM HER CORNER café table Amelie saw when the tall blonde woman left the apartment. She shifted in her café chair. It was too cold for anyone to sit outside and for that Amelie was glad. The waiter had demanded payment in advance for her coffee.

Amelie didn't care.

Amelie had watched Madame Dernier's husband leave first followed later by Madame Dernier. With the blonde woman gone, that just left the babysitter. And of course the children.

When you're no longer afraid of prison, Amelie thought, *all opportunities open to you.*

Killing the babysitter will be easy. And the other children too. Yes, why not.

But her true goal was Madame's little niece. The one who had sat in the apartment this entire last week charming Madame and taunting Amelie. Taunting her with all that she had—her loving parents, her expensive sweaters and shoes, her sheltered life—in the face of all that Amelie and her mother had lost.

Yes, her true goal will be that the baby breathe its last this very hour.

Amelie slipped her hand into her coat pocket to touch the razor sharpness of the knife. She sighed with pleasure at the sensation of the prick against her finger.

Then she stood up and walked to the apartment building.

48

Maggie sat in her train seat. She stared out the window, her mind numb with all that she'd learned.

Delphine had been carrying on with the Nazi. Delphine had led the Resistance to Camille's door. Delphine had had a child and passed it off as her younger sister's.

Maggie's brain spun. Did she really know the woman she'd lived with for the last week? Could Delphine have changed so much from the person she'd been back in 1944?

And then there was Amelie. There was no doubt that Delphine knew her housekeeper was the direct descendant of the woman she'd betrayed.

Camille's daughter.

Maggie thought of all the times she babbled on to Delphine about how she was working hard to find Camille's daughter and all along Delphine knew Coeur was dead and her daughter was washing dishes in Delphine's kitchen

Maggie looked out the window of the passing scenery of the countryside as the train sped toward Paris.

Amelie had sought out Delphine and taken the job in her house. For what possible purpose?

What purpose could there be? Except revenge?

Could Amelie have killed Isla? What about Gerard? He'd certainly have opened his door to Amelie, unconcerned that she was any kind of a threat to him.

But why attack the ones around Delphine? Why not go after the source?

Could it have been *Amelie* who followed Maggie into the catacombs? Or who leapt over the body of Isla in the stairwell? Maggie shook her head. She was positive that both of those had been men. She hesitated. But was that because she'd assumed it?

Everyone believed that Noel was the last one to see Delphine before Maggie found her but of course Amelie could come and go and nobody would think anything of it.

Had Amelie done something to Delphine?

Maggie pulled out her phone. Laurent *had* to change his mind and okay an autopsy, she thought. She started to text him as much but decided it was an argument best done in person. Instead she texted: <Coming home soon. See you then.>

Maggie had one more errand to run and it wouldn't do to have Laurent worry needlessly about her.

She had no idea in what section of Paris Amelie lived in but she was sure she could find something at Delphine's apartment with her address on it.

∼

THE WALL-LENGTH MIRRORS HANGING above the long mahogany bar made the brasserie appear twice the size that it was. The restaurant was a classic brasserie, traditionally decorated with marquetry and polished wall paneling against scarlet banquettes with solid, homey food. Laurent and Noel sat in a booth with gleaming copper pans of plump, garlicky escargots and a second bottle of Gigondas.

They had left the attorney's office after the contents of the will had been revealed to them.

Laurent had known before he walked into the office of Delphine's executor that he would walk out a rich man. Maggie had already told him he would inherit an equal share with Amelie Taver and Noel. Maggie had been right about the amount too. What he was mildly shocked about was the unmistakable impression that he'd also walked out of the attorney's office with an uncle he'd never really known before.

"I love this place," Noel said, ripping off a piece of bread to dredge up the oily garlic butter in his dish. "I used to come here with Delphine, you know. When I was a boy."

"I had no idea it had been around that long."

Laurent hadn't known what to expect in meeting Noel this morning. His memory of the man was hazy, almost nonexistent. Family rarely came to visit when he'd lived with his grandmother.

He couldn't imagine being taken to a restaurant such as this as a child.

"Why do you think the housekeeper didn't show?" Noel asked.

Laurent shrugged.

"Incredible that she should get a full third, don't you think? I have to say I was shocked."

When Laurent still didn't answer, Noel laughed.

"Man of few words, eh, Laurent? Although as I recall you were quiet as a boy too."

They ate in silence for a moment.

"I can't believe she's gone," Noel murmured almost to himself.

"You were close," Laurent said. It wasn't a question. He knew Maggie had her suspicions about the old fellow but even in the few minutes Laurent had spent in Noel's company he could not believe Noel capable of hurting his aunt.

"Close, yes. I was…I am…convinced that she was my mother,"

Noel said with a helpless shrug. "But more than that—and this I did not share with your wife—I came into more recent information that made me believe my father was a famous man whose identity Delphine had reason to go to great lengths to prevent me from learning."

Laurent frowned. "Who do you think your father was?" he asked.

"The story has always been that my father was a dimwitted boy who impregnated Georgette and was then conveniently killed during the liberation of Paris."

"And the true story? With the famous father?"

"Delphine's stepdaughter Michelle Normand said that Delphine once confessed that my real father was, well, your grandfather, Laurent."

Laurent poured himself another glass of wine. "Marc Dernier the Resistance hero had an affair with Georgette?" he said.

"Delphine," Noel said. "At least that's what Michelle said. And it made sense to me since, logically, when Georgette died—if she was truly my mother—there should have been no more reason to keep the secret of my birth. But since Delphine still wasn't admitting anything, it had to be because *she* was the one who'd betrayed her sister by sleeping with her brother-in-law."

"And you heard this from Delphine's bitter crazy stepdaughter?"

"Yes, I grant you the source isn't credible," Noel said with a sigh. "And I suppose I wanted to believe it. My constituents already know I am illegitimate. But with a hero father? That could not have hurt me at all." He glanced ruefully at his plate. "But alas, it was not to be. Turns out I truly am the illegitimate son of a dimwitted boy run over on his bicycle on the most important day in the history of Paris."

Laurent gave him a questioning glance.

"Delphine confirmed it," Noel said. "I hated myself for coming to her with the accusation. But if you could have seen the look on her face when I asked her...I'm sure she was telling me the truth." His shoulders slumped in dejection.

"I'm sorry, Noel."

Noel struggled back into his smile.

"Oh, well. We all have our life stories to tell, *n'est-ce pas*? I suppose some of us are more intent than others on rewriting them." He held his wine glass up in a toast to Laurent and after Laurent drank Noel kept his wine glass held up.

"To my aunt or my mother or whoever the hell she was," Noel said. "She was a good woman and loved me when there were no other volunteers."

They toasted. Before he knew the words were coming out of his mouth, Laurent lifted his glass again and said, "To Gerard."

Noel nodded and drank. "Poor bastard."

Laurent stared at the blood red color of his wine and realized it was a relief to speak Gerard's name without acrimony.

There was a time when I loved you, brother, he thought. Quickly, he shook himself out of the reflections.

"I hope you will come and visit us in St-Buvard," Laurent said.

"I would love that, but I am pretty sure Maggie doesn't like me," Noel said as he popped the last escargot in his mouth.

"It is not a requirement to like family," Laurent said with a shrug. "But she will welcome you."

"It's because I behaved badly with Delphine, you see."

"If I turned away everyone who behaved badly, I would be very alone—starting with my wife. Leave her to me."

They finished their meal and Laurent felt the first strains of familial connection since the brief days before his own mother died. This elderly, slightly vacuous man—whether his mother was Delphine or Georgette—was his uncle and Laurent found himself grateful to know him.

With Gerard and Delphine gone, it occurred to him that Noel was the only extended family he had left in the world.

An hour later as Noel was taking his leave, Laurent shook his uncle's hand and looked him in the eye.

"I could order a DNA test on Delphine's remains," he said.

Just the sound of the words felt like a betrayal to his aunt. But if Laurent had learned anything in this world it was that life was for the living. Delphine was gone. Noel was here.

Noel smiled sadly. "Thank you, *mon vieux*," he said. "And I love you for offering. I cannot believe I'm going to say this, but I think when it comes right down to it, I prefer my own version of who Delphine was to me." He shrugged. "True or not."

49

The light was totally gone from the sky. It would be another two months at least before it was light this late in the day. In St-Buvard, Maggie and Laurent could sit out on the back patio sipping wine and talking over the day until nine at night and still see enough light to watch the magpies divebomb the vineyard that surrounded them.

As the train neared the Montparnasse station in Paris, Maggie pulled the diary out of her bag and flipped through its pages. As she was about to put it away, she noticed the spine threads were coming loose. When she tried to press them back together, a tiny triangle of paper appeared. She gently tugged on it until she had pulled a folded, tissue-thin piece of paper out from behind the diary's leather cover.

She carefully unfolded the sheet and saw it was a letter written in French in an elaborate cursive hand. Her excitement mounted. *This was a letter written to Helmut from his French lover!*

Maggie scanned the letter. The date on the letter was February 1945. Camille had been dead for more than six months. As love letters went, it seemed pretty standard. Lots of *missing you* and confidence that justice would prevail. Since the letter had obviously been sent to Helmut while he awaited trial, that made sense although it probably wasn't terribly encouraging to a man who was as guilty as Helmut Bauer.

Justice *would* prevail and it would see him swing.

In the last line of the note, Maggie caught the word *enceinte*. Delphine was telling him she was pregnant.

Maggie sat back with the letter in her hands and stared at the passing scenery.

So that's that.

It proves it wasn't Camille.

Except...

Maggie picked up the diary and went to an entry where Helmut referred to his lover as "my dearest C." She squinted at the letter. *Was* it a C? Now she wasn't sure.

She turned back to the letter which was signed "your angel." She refolded the letter and put it between the pages of the diary. All Maggie had to do now was match the letter's looping cursive with a sample of Delphine's handwriting and the mystery would be solved.

As if she needed another nail in the coffin of Delphine's guilt.

Delphine was the collaborator and she'd thrown her best friend to the wolves to save herself. Maggie's stomach turned at the thought. She had grown to love the old woman. While it was many years ago, the crime felt no less horrific for the passage of time.

To have sentenced your best friend to death to save yourself?

She shivered. No wonder Delphine wept at night. Victor was right about that. She could never find forgiveness in this life for what she did.

Crap! Victor.

Maggie pulled her phone out. Would anyone have told him about Delphine's passing? She found his number on her phone and put the call through. Victor obviously hadn't set up his voice mail. The phone just rang.

She hated telling him this over the phone. Maybe he'd already tried to contact Delphine?

No, it was cowardly to hope he would find out on his own. Maggie knew she needed to keep trying to contact him.

∼

As Laurent watched Noel negotiate his way through the crowded restaurant to a waiting taxi outside, he had to admit the day had been a surprise. Amazingly, in a day that saw Laurent become a wealthy man, the biggest surprise of all was the peace he'd gotten by talking about Gerard with Noel.

I will have to tell Maggie that she was right after all. Or maybe not. He grinned as an image of his earnest and very American wife came to mind. He took out his phone to call her and saw her text. *<Coming home soon. See you then.>*

Where has she been today? he wondered. His eye was drawn to a flash of color in the front of the restaurant and he looked up to see Grace enter the restaurant with a man. Laurent frowned as he watched them take a table near the front window. The man was well dressed and effortless in his gestures toward Grace. He was nodding as Grace talked, but Laurent could see the man's eyes were darting around the restaurant.

Laurent felt a stab of annoyance that Grace had sequestered herself in her room for the last twelve hours and *now* instead of spending time with Zouzou she was out with a man.

A man who clearly did not care about her.

As Laurent signaled the waiter for the bill, he saw his phone vibrating with an incoming call. When he looked at the screen, it said *Unknown Caller*.

"*Oui?*" he answered.

"Monsieur Dernier? Laurent Dernier?" an officious voice asked.

"Who is this?" *And how did you get my number?*

"I am Sergeant Detective Benet," the caller said, "of the Paris Centrale Police Judiciare. I was told you requested a phone trace on the last phone calls made to your late aunt Delphine Normand?"

Laurent waved away the waiter who approached the table.

"Yes?" he said.

"We've found something you should know about."

∼

WHEN THE TRAIN pulled into the station, Maggie felt her energy seriously diminished. She'd started her trip this afternoon with such hope that she might find information that didn't point at Delphine. And honestly, if everybody was right and Maggie was wrong—not unheard of, she had to admit—then Delphine *did* just die of natural causes and whoever had a grudge against her did what most people in this world did with it—nursed it and made themselves miserable about it.

And never acted on it.

Even so, Maggie knew she had a rare window of freedom away from the children and she wouldn't waste it. She texted Beatrice that she would be another hour *at most* and then hurried from the train platform to the taxi stand outside.

She would slip into Delphine's apartment and grab something with Amelie's address on it—*surely it couldn't hurt to just talk to the woman.* Maggie already had plenty of samples of Delphine's handwriting on various notes and photographs back at Grace's.

Not that it mattered, she thought. *Not at this point. Just loose ends is all.*

The taxi ride from the station to Delphine's apartment took less than twenty minutes. Maggie watched the lights of nighttime Paris twinkle outside her window and wondered when she would come back again.

She'd promised her mother she'd spend the summer in

Atlanta and then with Grace spiraling out of control the idea of coming back for a visit just wasn't attractive. She made a face. As if Laurent would even allow it without a major throwdown.

She passed the Jardin du Luxembourg and felt a flush of commitment and resolve. Paris would always be here. It would wait for her.

And I'll be back with the children—and with Laurent too—so we can create our happy memories. Yes, it's time to go home but we'll be back.

The taxi pulled up to Delphine's apartment. Maggie asked the driver to wait and hurried inside. She was sure the security code hadn't been changed. Who would do it, she wondered, besides Laurent? On the other hand Noel and Amelie probably owned this apartment together with Laurent now.

She glanced up at the video cameras in the hall above Delphine's door. Had they ever been turned on? Was someone watching her? Looking closely, she couldn't see any telltale red light to indicate the cameras were taping.

Too bad, she thought as she inserted the key into Delphine's front door. *Would've helped answer a lot of questions about who was here yesterday.* She pulled open the door but it stopped halfway as if something was blocking it.

A sense of foreboding crawled up Maggie's spine, leaving her skin tingling.

Yesterday she had watched the medics load Delphine up before locking the apartment herself. She had definitely been the last one out.

Carefully, she pushed the door open and stepped into the foyer. Her hand hit the light switch on the wall and the foyer shot into brightness.

The first thing she saw was the pool of blood.

And then the body.

50

Grace hissed at André. "You slept with my au pair! Don't deny it!"

She and André sat in the front window of her neighborhood brasserie. It used to be *their* place. She remembered it was the first place they'd come all those months ago after they first made love. She shook the memory out of her head. He looked at her now with a sad smile on his lips. His eyes no longer held for her what she had seen in them just two days ago.

In just two days? How is that possible?

André sighed. "I do not find jealous women attractive, Grace."

Grace sputtered and then made an effort to calm herself. She actually felt a twinge of fear that she was appearing less attractive to him.

After everything I've done! After everything I've given up for him.

"Did you or did you not—" she started.

"Don't be absurd. I did not sleep with your au pair. You are embarrassing both of us to suggest it."

The tension she held in her shoulders relaxed. Was she insane? Had she well and truly lost it? Of *course* he hadn't slept with Beatrice. She could see that now. It was absurd to think it.

Beatrice was practically a child. And borderline simpleminded on top of that.

What is the matter with me?

"Why did you leave in the middle of the night?" If there was any coming back from this, she needed to distract him from how ludicrous her accusation had been. He had left in the middle of the night. That was surely strange behavior. She was entitled to some answers.

"I had another appointment. I am sure I mentioned it to you."

André was scanning the restaurant as if looking for someone. Now that Grace watched him, she could see he was looking everywhere except at her.

Was this just a spat? Would they come back from this?

An appointment in the middle of the night?

"Look, André," she said, forcing a tremulous smile to her lips, "I'm sorry if I made it sound like—"

"*Chèri!*" A young woman materialized beside André and kissed him on both cheeks. She was wearing an impossibly short miniskirt and a midriff-baring top showing off toned, taut skin. She glanced at Grace. "I thought you would be alone," she said with a pout.

"I told you to wait for me, *chèrie*," André said, his eyes glittering with amusement as he scolded the girl. "I told you I wouldn't be long."

Grace's mouth fell open in stark astonishment.

∞

LAURENT SAT in his booth with his cellphone on the table and his mind far away.

Is it just a coincidence? Surely the phone record the cops discovered could have no relevant connection to his aunt.

But knowing Maggie, she will want to know.

He picked up his phone and then, realizing it was too noisy in the restaurant to talk he wrote out a short text instead. Just as he was gathering his keys and wallet to leave, he heard Grace's voice shrill and piercing. He looked in her direction. In the time it took for him to talk to the police investigator and text a message to Maggie, it seemed Grace had been joined by another person at her table. A woman.

A very attractive young woman.

Without warning, Grace leaned across the table and slapped the girl's face. Other patrons near them moved their chairs away as silverware fell from the table. The girl stood up, her face red with outrage. In an instant, her painted talons outstretched, the girl launched herself at Grace.

Merde.

Laurent jumped to his feet.

~

MAGGIE CONTROLLED her breathing as she stared at the body. It was Michelle. She was lying on her back, her eyes open. Her throat had been cut.

Maggie's mind began to whirl. She knew she shouldn't step inside. She knew she should call the police. Her mind raced as she tried to imagine a new scenario where Michelle *dead* fit.

Could Amelie have done this? Why?

She rested her hand on the doorknob and then jerked it away. She shouldn't be here.

What was Michelle doing here? She must have made a copy of the key she gave to Noel. The key that was in Maggie's hand.

This is murder and there can't be any question about it, she thought. Even the police will see it for what it...as she tried to fit the pieces together, her eyes went around the foyer.

The door to the storage room was open.

Maggie's breath was coming in rasps now, her body tense and shaking. She knew she'd locked that door. Without thinking, she stepped into the foyer and stood in the doorway of the storage room.

The interior was trashed as if someone had gone through it in a violent temper. Her stomach cramped painfully. The hidden panel was open. The door lay flung against the far wall.

Someone had found the hiding place. Someone angry and desperate and deadly.

A feeling of growing panic swept her arms and chest.

It's not revenge. It's the painting...

Maggie backed out of the room, her breath coming in short, labored pants.

...the painting I hid in Grace's apartment.

Where the children are.

51

Maggie ran into the hallway, careful not to step in the blood. She pulled her phone out. She knew she should report Michelle's death to the police but first she had to warn Beatrice. The phone screen showed *no service*.

Had Beatrice responded to the text Maggie had sent from the train?

No. No messages except a text from Laurent. She glanced at the time. It was sent over ten minutes ago.

With mounting panic and without thinking what she was doing, Maggie stepped into the elevator. As she pushed the lobby button, her mind whirled with horror.

Who did this? André? Noel? Amelie? Dieter?

Who wants that painting? Who even knows about it?

Amelie couldn't possibly have worked in Delphine's apartment for nine months and known a stolen Degas was in the same apartment with her and not acted on it. Could she?

It has to be André. He owns an art gallery. But how would a famous stolen painting benefit him? And how would he even know it existed?

Noel had gone straight to the storage room the night

Delphine died. He said it was because he saw a light but what if it was because he wanted to get the painting he knew was there?

Dieter could easily have known about the painting. All it would take was one comment from his infamous grandpa to reveal he'd given an original Degas to his French girlfriend.

Maggie ran a hand over her face.

But isn't the painting worthless to anyone?

Not if they were an art connoisseur like André...Or someone who felt he was owed big time by the person who stole it. Maybe Noel thought a Degas was recompense for the life of lies he believed Delphine had consigned him?

The elevator moved slowly. Maggie cursed herself for not taking the stairs. She looked at Laurent's text. It was lengthy. Unusual for him.

<Cops traced the last call made to Delphine. A burner phone. 685-888.>

Maggie reached for the grab bar as the elevator jerkily descended. Something niggled in the back of her brain. *Why does that number sound familiar?*

There was more.

<They said the burner phone made several calls to a known Algerian hit man. Not sure what connection is w/Delphine>

Maggie felt her skin crawl. The man who chased her into the catacombs—the words he'd shouted at her sounded like Arabic.

They speak Arabic in Algeria.

A chill started in Maggie's stomach and the hand holding her phone began to shake.

As the elevator car lurched to the lobby floor, Maggie fell against the door, grappling with the bar to stay on her feet. She wrenched the grill back and bolted into the lobby. Her screen still showed *no service* but she didn't need an Internet connection for what she needed to do. She stepped into the interior courtyard. It was already late afternoon and the sky had darkened with impending bad weather. She felt the first drops of rain on her shoulders.

She'd seen that number somewhere. Her stomach soured and then roiled as she realized she had just tried to *call* that number. She held her breath and scrolled down her list of received calls.

There it was. 685-888.

She stared at the numerals, stunned. The world seemed to whirl around her in a cyclone of malevolence.

It was the call she'd received five days ago from Victor Rousseau.

52

In six long strides, Laurent was at the table but the girl was already on top of Grace, slapping and pulling her hair. Both women were screaming and knocking cutlery and glassware to the floor. Two waiters stood congenially watching the brawl, their arms crossed in front of them. The man at the table had stood up but was regarding the women with obvious bemusement.

Laurent pulled the young woman off Grace and shoved her into the man's arms.

"Control her!" he snarled at him.

Grace was on her feet now, a shallow scratch across one cheek, her lipstick smeared down her chin, her eyes wild. She turned to her male companion who stood with one arm draped loosely around the angry young woman.

"You bastard!" she said. "You lied to me."

"Is this your husband?" the man said, indicating Laurent with a nod of his head. "I thought you said he was out of the picture?"

Laurent turned to the man and saw his laughing eyes, his taunting look at Grace. Laurent grabbed the arm of the young woman and pulled her from the man.

"Hey!" she squawked. "What do you think—"

Then Laurent drew back a fist and slammed it into the man's face, watching him crumple to his knees, his laugh replaced by a stunned look. Blood gushed from his broken nose. The girl screamed again and looked around as if someone might be enlisted to come to her aid.

"I am not her husband," Laurent said to him before turning to Grace. "But he's a friend of mine."

Grace looked at the moaning man on his knees, now being comforted by the young woman, and then at Laurent with blazing eyes.

"How dare you!" Grace gasped. "You can't come in here and—"

"Get your bag," Laurent said, his voice hardening. "We're leaving."

"No, I am not leaving!" Grace said looking again at the man struggling to get to his feet. She made a move to go to him and Laurent grabbed her arm.

"*Oui*, you are," he said. "On your own feet or over my shoulder. Your choice."

"You...you..." Grace snatched up a glass of wine from the table and splashed it into Laurent's face.

"*Bon*." Laurent bent and tossed Grace over his shoulder. He turned to the waiters and nodded to indicate he'd be back to pay for any damages. Then he turned with Grace kicking and pounding on his back and exited the restaurant. As soon as they were on the street, Laurent dropped Grace to her feet. He was fully prepared for her to try to slap him but she didn't. Instead, she covered her face with both hands and burst into tears.

"What is the matter with me?" she said through her tears. "I am so sorry, Laurent. I have lost my damn mind."

"*Ça ne fait rien*," Laurent said, leading her away from the restaurant and the curious stares of people sitting at the outdoor tables.

"I have made such a terrible mess of everything," Grace said.

"Oh! My handbag—"

"I'll pick it up later. The wait staff will keep it safe."

Grace looked at him and then back at the restaurant, her eyes suddenly narrowing.

"Wait. You weren't following me, were you? Is that why you are here?"

Laurent sighed and wondered if he was going to have the patience to deal with Grace when she was like this. He wasn't entirely sure she was completely sober.

"Is that what you think?" he asked.

Her shoulders sagged. "Please, Laurent. I can't go home yet. Every time I look at Beatrice I feel I'm letting everyone down."

Laurent couldn't help but wonder why it was looking at *Beatrice* that made Grace that way and not little Zouzou.

"Please, Laurent?"

"*Bon,*" he said, taking her elbow and steering her back down the sidewalk. "There is a place I know near here that makes a very good omelet. We will eat first and then return home, yes?"

His phone began to vibrate and he saw it was an incoming call from Maggie.

"Thank you, Laurent," Grace said. "I don't deserve your friendship. But thank you." She began to sob quietly. Laurent patted her hand and continued down the sidewalk with her, his unanswered phone back in his pocket.

If it's important, she will leave a message...

∾

Victor was the killer?

That's impossible. He loved Delphine. It has to be a mistake. Victor has no reason to hurt Gerard or Isla...or Michelle. It doesn't make sense.

Maggie called Beatrice and listened to the call go to voicemail. She pinched her lips together. Suddenly, the memory of

Victor at the restaurant signing the menu came swooping back to her. He'd pulled out his pen and signed it with a laugh and a flourish.

Turquoise blue ink.

The same color of ink on the note she'd found in the alley behind Gerard's apartment.

The note dropped by Gerard's killer.

She jumped into the waiting taxi and gave the driver Grace's address. As he turned the vehicle around, Maggie called Beatrice again. No answer. A sick icy dread formed in her stomach.

She called the police. After endless ringing, it was finally answered by a bored dispatcher whose accent Maggie couldn't understand and who hung up on her. Seething with frustration, she called them back. She knew she needed to be careful what she said. If she sounded crazy they wouldn't come at all. As she waited for the police to answer, she stared out the taxi window at the Seine, dark and omnipresent, on her left.

Maggie couldn't believe it had only been a week since she'd walked down this street with Mila, not a care in the world. The taxi sped past the dark structures of Ponte des Arts and then Ponte Neuf.

Victor killed them all. And he was the last person to talk to Delphine. Whatever he'd said to her had prompted her heart failure.

Why? Why was he doing this? Think! Think!

Victor hired someone to kill three people. Was that who was following her? Had Victor sent his killer after Maggie too?

It had to be the painting. Whoever killed Michelle had ripped the storage room apart looking for it.

What would he do now? Now that he knew the painting was gone?

He probably knew it was Maggie who'd moved the painting so he knew it had to be where Maggie was staying with Grace off the Quai Saint-Michel.

The police dispatcher came back on the line and Maggie

spoke in painstakingly slow French. The dispatcher took Grace's address and hung up.

Maggie put a second call into Laurent and listened to it go to voicemail again. She cursed in frustration. Was his phone even on?

They stopped at a traffic light and a hoard of tourists moved sluggishly across the street. Maggie wondered if it wouldn't be faster to jump out and run the rest of the way.

Would she be in time? How far ahead of her was Victor? Would it be Victor there or his Algerian thug?

Gripping her phone tightly, she called Beatrice a third time. Even if Beatrice was giving one of the kids a bath Maggie knew she never went anywhere without her cellphone—or turned it off.

All three of Maggie's calls had gone straight to voice mail. A cold splinter of fear invaded Maggie's breast.

Beatrice *always* picked up.

The drive to Grace's apartment seemed to take forever. Maggie was so intent on getting to the apartment and seeing with her own eyes that everything was fine that she had the door to the taxi open before it had fully stopped. She threw a twenty euro bill at him—twice what the meter said—and raced into Grace's apartment building.

Surely Laurent was back by now. But why wasn't he answering his phone? Or Beatrice? It hadn't even occurred to Maggie to try calling Grace. Not stopping to deal with the elevator, Maggie immediately ran up the stairwell.

The sounds of her shoes hitting the stone steps echoed in her ears. Because the other apartments were all being renovated, there was nobody in the building but workmen.

And tonight there were no workmen.

Her breath came in agonizing pants from her sprint up the stairs. When she finally reached the third floor, the first thing she saw was the door to Grace's apartment.

It was open. Maggie froze, her heart in her throat.

The next thing she saw was Victor. He was standing between the open apartment door and the elevator.

And he was holding Mila.

53

Victor stepped out of the shadows. Maggie saw that Mila was asleep in his arms. He cupped her chin as if he might snap her neck at any moment.

"Victor, don't do this," Maggie said, her eyes on her baby. She started toward him.

"No, Madame," he said. "Come no closer."

Maggie's mouth went dry and she felt a throbbing sensation in her throat. She wanted to touch her baby so bad it was all she could do not to run over and snatch her from him. Victor looked like he was standing straighter than she'd seen him do before. There was no cane, there was no stoop to his shoulders.

"I notice you keep looking toward the apartment," he said. "The other children are fine. The sitter I'm afraid I had to kill."

Maggie sucked in a harsh breath. *Dear God. Beatrice.*

"The police are on their way," she said.

"Then we'd best hurry." He walked to the elevator and wrenched the metal grill door aside. The sound woke Mila and her face puckered into the beginnings of an unhappy wail. Maggie ran to him and he clutched Mila with both hands and swung her over the empty shaft.

"Not another step or I drop her!"

Maggie sucked in a gasp of pure hysteria. Mila struggled, flailing her arms, her cries echoing in the stone stairwell as she hung from his hands over the void.

"What do you want?" she said, her arms outstretched toward Mila as if she could will the baby to leap into them.

"You know what I want," Victor said, bringing Mila away from the shaft. He wiped his face with a free hand. "I want the treasure!" Sweat was dribbling down his forehead. "I know you found it. Delphine said as much last night on the phone."

Maggie couldn't take her eyes off Mila. She was squirming and Victor was not a young man.

"Delphine trusted you," Maggie said, feeling the panic crawling up her throat. She prayed the police were coming although she had no reason to really believe it. But surely *somebody* would be coming! She needed to stall him.

"She used me," Victor said. "She was well aware of the crime committed against me by her sister's husband. She never apologized for it. She never even acknowledged it."

"Are you talking about Marc Dernier? What did he do?"

Surely, the longer I keep him talking, the greater chance the police will show up? Or Laurent? Or somebody?

"I'm not surprised you don't know. The great Marc Dernier blew up a German truck depot outside of Paris. He was decorated for it."

Maggie realized she didn't know the specifics of why Marc Dernier was considered a Resistance hero. She had a feeling she was about to.

"De Gaulle called it *pivotal* in the turning point of the war. Ridiculous, of course. It was the Allies who turned the war. All Dernier did—and zealots like him—was to aggravate the Germans who held France in a death grip."

"You're talking about the massacre that killed your family? But the Nazis did that." Maggie tried not to look at Mila.

"Let me ask you, Madame—have you ever jabbed a stick at a rabid dog? Or attempted to poke a venomous viper? No? Probably because you can imagine the outcome if you had. Marc Dernier knew exactly what the outcome of his actions would be."

Maggie listened helplessly. Was her only option really just to wait for someone to come?

"The reprisal for what Dernier did," Victor continued, "was the murder of twenty-five people including my parents and two sisters."

Maggie prayed that Zouzou or Jemmy didn't come out of the apartment. Why didn't they? Were they really okay or had Victor hurt them?

"It was unspeakable," Maggie said, her voice shaking. "But it was over seventy years ago. And Marc Dernier has been dead for more than thirty years. Why now?"

Victor's color darkened. He shifted Mila in his arms as if she was growing heavy for him.

"What was I to do before now? Kill a national war hero? So I could live the rest of my life in prison?"

Maggie couldn't take her eyes off her baby. Mila was starting to settle down and for that Maggie felt a spasm of relief.

"So, I lived with it," Victor said. "But it was irony, don't you see? That in order to get Delphine to release the Nazi treasure she'd stolen I was to get justice on the man who wiped out my family. Finally."

"Nazi treasure?"

"Do not attempt to appear guileless, Madame Dernier," he said. "I know about the gold."

Does he mean the Degas? Does he not know it's a painting?

"She told me one evening after too much wine at dinner. She said she had a treasure in her possession worth more than all of her wealth. I thought long and hard about what to do about it. Finally I hired someone to find and steal it while Delphine was at lunch—with me as it happens—but it went bad and her nurse was killed."

Maggie's mind was swimming. Even an innocent move on Maggie's part might prompt him to drop Mila into the empty shaft.

"I decided to take the direct approach after that," Victor said. "I began calling her. Without revealing my identity."

"Threatening her," Maggie said.

"I told her, 'give me the treasure or your loved ones will die one by one.'"

"So you killed Gerard too? And attacked me in the catacombs?"

"Not me personally but yes. I needed Delphine to see I was serious. I thought if she could see how easily her worthless nephew could be taken from her, she would see how easy it would be for you to be killed or this little one." Obscenely, he patted Mila's back like a fond uncle.

Tears pricked Maggie's eyes and her hands ached to touch her baby.

"But you don't know what the treasure is?" she asked, still trying to keep him talking. She knew the minute he discovered the treasure was a painting he could neither sell nor display in his home, he would likely become even more unhinged.

"Do not attempt to distract me. Whatever it is, it's priceless," Victor said with annoyance. "The Nazis weren't known for stealing shit."

Maggie heard a police siren in the distance. She held her breath but the sound began to fade as it went further and further away.

"I was with her at the end, you know," she said.

"We all die," he said shrugging. "Stop stalling."

"She knew it was you," Maggie said. "That's what killed her."

He shifted uncomfortably. "I disguised my voice. She couldn't have known."

"But in the end she did."

"You're lying." He licked his lips and looked around nervously as if expecting Delphine to appear and confront him.

"Am I lying about what happened to Michelle? When you went to Delphine's apartment tonight, she was there first, wasn't she?"

"Enough!" Victor said. "I see what you're doing! You have thirty seconds to bring me the gold from inside the apartment where I know you hid it before I kill this child. And trust me, I don't care what happens to me after that."

"If you...if you—" Maggie's stomach lurched with helpless terror at the sight of her baby in his arms. She couldn't walk away. She couldn't leave her...

"I will not kill her unless I see you returning with empty hands, Madame. *Now, go.*"

Maggie edged toward the open door, her eyes on Mila. The baby reached for her as she passed and it was all Maggie could do not to touch her but Victor turned his body toward the open elevator shaft. All he needed to do was let go and Mila would plunge to her death. With one last look at her child in a madman's hands, Maggie turned and ran into the apartment.

She forced herself not to think of what might happen if the police or Laurent were to come back now. The only thing that stood between life and death for her baby was whatever panicked, mad plan Maggie could come up with before somebody showed up and forced Victor's hand.

She ran into the apartment and straight to the children's bedroom—she couldn't not. She heard snoring coming from both Jemmy and Zouzou and saw them in their beds. Had they been drugged? It didn't seem possible that they were really asleep. She saw the stiff form of a body lying between the beds and she forced herself not to look closer.

If Beatrice were still alive, Maggie could do nothing at the moment to help her.

Maggie turned, a prayer on her lips, and hurried to her bedroom. She pulled her valise off the shelf in the closet and, looking wildly around, tried to think what to do.

Should I get a knife from the kitchen? But he said he'd drop her if she came back empty-handed!

A shout from Victor sent an ice pick of fear up her spine until it exploded in her brain.

Stop thinking! Just do it!

She flung open the suitcase and scraped the tabletop contents of her dresser—books, perfume, a marble-based alarm clock—into the bag, latched it shut and ran back to the stairwell.

Victor still stood by the elevator shaft. He held Mila outstretched in his arms over the dark empty shaft.

Maggie's voice trembled. "If you drop her, you won't get the... treasure. Take the bag and *go*. The police are coming."

Except of course Victor couldn't take the bag and leave Maggie alive. And they both knew that.

"A little closer, if you please, Madame," Victor said, his eyes on the satchel in her arms.

"It's very heavy," Maggie said.

He now clutched Mila to his chest. "Then push it to me. Closer."

"First give me my baby."

"Not quite yet, Madame."

She didn't know how he would do it—how he thought he could kill her and still escape—but she could see in his eyes that he had a plan.

Even if she could somehow grab Mila away from him, she knew she couldn't escape. She couldn't leave Jem and Zouzou—and she couldn't lock herself in the apartment either. Victor stood between her and the door.

Maggie set the heavy suitcase down. She shoved it slowly to where he stood. His eyes were on the suitcase, clearly trying to imagine what wonders it might hold.

And then she kicked it hard and watched it skid into the open shaft.

Victor turned and watched it fall, a shriek of horror bursting from his lips.

At the same time Maggie lunged at him. She wrapped her arms around him. She felt Mila's soft body in her hands.

Her momentum took them all down the gaping shaft.

54

Maggie hit the side of the elevator shaft. Pain thundered through her as her knee hit a narrow workman's ledge that spanned the space. The impact jarred her and she flailed out with one arm to grab the chain elevator cable hanging by her head.

Praying it would hold her, and with Mila in her free arm she swung on the chain to the other side of the small shaft. Her right foot fought and found purchase on the ledge just above the second floor lintel.

The elevator shaft reverberated with Mila's screams—obliterating all other sound. Maggie's hands were slippery with her own blood and burning from holding the cable—the cable that kept her balanced on the ledge. Not daring to breathe, she looked down. Maggie's eyes finally made out the shape at the bottom of the shaft. Victor was sprawled on the top of the stalled car, the open valise beneath him.

"*Ici! Ici! Ils sont dans l'ascenseur!*" a man's voice shouted over the opening above. Maggie looked up and saw a policeman looking down.

She willed herself not to relax. Not yet. She kissed Mila's still wailing face and hugged her tight.

It was nearly over.

THIRTY MINUTES LATER, as the police were bringing Victor's broken and lifeless body out of the elevator shaft, Maggie sat in the apartment kitchen, all three children in her lap, and a cup of tea on the table in front of her. Beatrice—who had been attacked by Amelie hours earlier and shoved unconscious into a closet—was having the cut on her head cleaned and bandaged by an emergency medical technician.

Amelie's body was found between the children's beds where Victor, who hadn't realized the real sitter was alive and in the apartment, had left her after he killed her.

Amazingly, neither Jemmy or Zouzou had been drugged. They were simply sleeping deeply after an exhausting day of play with their beloved Beatrice.

Laurent burst into the kitchen, his eyes wild and astonished. He ran to Maggie and knelt by her, one arm encompassing her and the children.

"*Mon Dieu,*" he said. "What—?"

Maggie laid her head on his shoulder, the fear and the adrenalin finally melting away until all she felt was the safety of his arms around her.

"Later," she whispered. "I'll tell you everything. Later."

∼

THAT NIGHT after the police had cordoned off the floor and Grace's apartment, Laurent moved everyone except Beatrice into a furnished apartment rental two blocks away. Beatrice's parents drove up from Provins and took her home with them. Beatrice, who was happily stoned on painkillers by that time, kissed everyone goodbye and both Jemmy and Zouzou cried loudly for thirty minutes after she'd gone.

When Maggie revealed that there was yet another dead body at Delphine Normand's apartment, it became apparent that it was nothing short of a miracle combined with Laurent's power of persuasion that Maggie wasn't spending the evening in an interrogation room rather than relaxing in a fairly luxurious apartment rental. Nonetheless, she was resigned to spending the better part of the next day at the police station having her statement taken.

ONCE THEY'D ARRIVED at the rental apartment and after a quick trip to the grocer's, Laurent quickly fed the children and settled the two older ones down in the larger bedroom. He deposited a sleepy Mila into Maggie's arms where she sat in the living room with Grace. Then he went into the kitchen to put together dinner.

Maggie watched Mila lose her fight with sleep. The very thought that Mila had been in the clutches of that madman earlier today...that there was even a breath of a chance that Maggie could have lost her...made Maggie shudder. She held her baby tighter.

"I can't believe all that's happened," Grace said quietly.

Grace was sitting on the couch with Maggie, her feet tucked up under her and what appeared to be not a speck of make up on. Maggie noticed that Grace had been very quiet since she'd returned with Laurent, allowing him to make all the decisions—including speaking with the police and Beatrice's parents, finding a place to stay for the night, and finally bundling them all into a taxi for the move out of the apartment.

"I'm so sorry, Maggie," Grace said, her eyes on the baby in Maggie's arms.

Maggie still didn't know what had gone on with Grace today

or where she'd been. She was sure she'd hear all about it in due time.

The sound of Laurent moving pots and pans around in the kitchen filtered through the small apartment. At one point Maggie heard him go into the children's room where she heard their little voices before he came back out. A few moments later he brought two glasses of wine to her and Grace. The front of his shirt was wet and since Maggie knew they'd skipped bath time tonight, she could only assume it was the result of an energetic bout of toddler tooth brushing. She and Grace had heard giggling coming from the bedroom and she thanked God that the children didn't seem to have suffered any lasting damage from the terrible day.

I only hope Beatrice can someday shake it off, Maggie thought.

"I'm a mess," Grace said. "Did Laurent tell you?"

"No. He kind of saw I had my hands full with my own drama tonight."

"See? Can you believe I'm about to tell you what happened to me and André when you and the children were nearly killed today? What is the matter with me?"

"I don't know, Grace."

"Windsor is taking the kids. Both kids."

Thank God. Maggie's face flushed when the thought came to her. Was that a betrayal? It was only the truth.

"I've made such a mess of everything," Grace said. "Do you think I can fix it?"

"Sure. If you want to."

"You don't think I want to?"

"I don't know, Grace. Frankly, I don't know who you are any more."

Grace stared at her, her mouth open and then she burst into tears. Maggie shifted Mila to her other arm and put a hand on Grace's knee.

"Sweetie, I'm sorry," Maggie said. "I'm so sorry."

"No, you're right," Grace said through her tears. "I've made a mess of everything only please don't give up on me, Maggie."

"I would never, Grace."

The two were still sitting closely on the couch when Laurent came back in with three plates of steaming Indian curry.

"Do you want more wine?" Laurent asked.

"Do you have to ask?" Maggie said. "Get yourself a glass, too. I'm going to tell my story once and then I'm running back to St-Buvard to be the most perfectly boring housewife the country has ever seen."

Laurent snorted. "I will believe that when I see it," he said as he picked up the sleeping baby to transfer her to the bedroom he and Maggie would share tonight.

When he returned, Grace cleared her throat. Her porcelain-white face was blotchy and reddened from her tears.

"I want to thank you for your intervention today, dearest Laurent," she said. "And I do, most sincerely, but Maggie has warned me that tonight is not all about me."

"Too right," Maggie said, grinning at Grace and hoping her friend could take a little teasing. It was going to be a long time before she saw the old Grace again, if she ever did. And if Grace lost Zouzou and Taylor, Maggie was pretty sure she never would.

55

The aromas from the chicken curry seemed to swirl visibly in the small living room. The wine had already done part of its work and Maggie felt relaxed and, with Laurent sitting by her on the couch, his knee touching hers, safe at last.

She couldn't help but wish Delphine could be here too.

"I'm surprised you got the police to come," Grace said, sipping her wine. "I'm told they're notoriously slow when it comes to emergency calls by tourists with American accents."

"I just called and told them I was being held hostage by three members of ISIS. Honestly, if Victor *hadn't* been waiting for me at the apartment it could have been really embarrassing. But I thought it was worth the risk."

"You always have all the luck, darling," Grace said with a weak smile as she picked at her plate. "Not a band of terrorists. Just one lone sociopath with a seventy year old grudge."

"We are ready to hear how it is you and Mila were found hanging from a chain in a broken elevator shaft," Laurent said gruffly.

Maggie's hands were lightly bandaged and her left knee throbbed from where she'd hit the side of the elevator shaft.

"Gosh, Laurent," she said. "It sounds so much more interesting when you put it like that."

He gave her a baleful look.

"The first thing I want to know," Grace said, "is why? What was Victor's motivation? I thought he loved Delphine."

"Maybe at one time," Maggie said. "People forgot that he was a lot younger than her."

"He didn't look it. I thought they were roughly the same age."

"That's what he wanted people to think. But he wasn't so much wanting to hurt Delphine as use her to get the treasure he thought he was owed."

"Talk about reparations," Grace said, shaking her head.

"Victor blamed Marc Dernier for causing the reprisal that killed his family," Maggie said. "But Dernier was untouchable because he was a national war hero. Plus I don't think Victor even really had a plan until the night Delphine let it slip that she was in possession of a treasure stolen during the war. Somehow Victor got the idea it was Nazi gold. And that it should be his as recompense."

"And was there really a treasure?" Grace asked.

"Of course not," Maggie said, not meeting Grace's eyes. "Victor was crazy."

"So how did it all go down today, if you'll pardon the expression?" Grace asked.

"I could see the only thing that mattered to him was the treasure. So I used that. When he saw it going down the elevator shaft, I had a split second to jump him and grab Mila. And I did." She smiled at Laurent who did not smile back.

"Unfortunately, it got a bit sloppy there at the end," she admitted, "what with me and Mila going over the edge too."

"When did you know for sure it was Victor?" Grace asked.

"Honestly even after I got Laurent's text about the burner

phone I still couldn't believe it. I actually thought for a moment that maybe Victor found the phone in the street and just decided to use it.

"It wasn't until I thought about the hit man whose number the cops found that I realized I had a clue in my possession. It was a note that Gerard's killer had dropped."

Maggie reached for her handbag and pulled out an envelope with the cigarette packet in it.

"That's called withholding evidence, you know," Grace said with an arched eyebrow.

"The police already have what they need to convict," Laurent said, but he glowered at Maggie. The hit man whose number was on the burner phone had been taken into custody earlier in the day. Maggie was confident that forensic evidence would place the man at both crime scenes and he would be charged with the murders of Gerard and Isla.

"Anyway," Maggie said showing the note to Grace and Laurent, "do you see how the words are written in fountain pen ink?"

"Pretty elegant touch for a contract killer," Grace said.

"That's because the killer didn't write it," Maggie said. "*Victor* did when he wrote down Gerard's address for the hit. I'd seen this ink color once before and suddenly I remembered where. Victor signed a menu for someone at the restaurant using his fountain pen with the same turquoise color."

"Clever you, darling," Grace said. Her color was pale and Maggie could see she was trying hard to hold it together.

"It is fortunate for us," Laurent said, "that Rousseau forgot and used the burner phone to call Maggie for the luncheon date."

"Yeah," Maggie said, "except by the time I figured out it was Victor, he was holding Mila over an open elevator shaft."

"What about poor Amelie?" Grace asked. "Why was she in my apartment?"

"I totally misread that situation," Maggie said with a sigh. "I knew Amelie was unhappy and maybe even wanted a piece of Delphine because of what had happened to her mother—"

"*Quoi*?" Laurent asked. "Who is her mother?"

"Didn't I tell you? Amelie is the daughter of Camille's daughter."

"So you found her," Grace said. "Well done, darling."

"Twenty years too late to do her any good. But yeah, I found her."

"So Amelie was in Paris looking for revenge because of what happened to her grandmother?" Laurent asked.

"We'll never know for sure," Maggie said. "But what we *do* know is that she followed me to your apartment, Grace, attacked Beatrice and clearly meant to hurt the kids somehow." Maggie rubbed her arms as if she felt a sudden chill. "I knew how angry she was with Delphine. I even wondered at one point if she could have killed Gerard, but I never really believed she was capable of something like this."

"How did the cops know that Victor's burner phone was used to call a contract killer?" Grace asked.

Laurent answered. "They ran the number through their database of known criminal contacts and got a hit with the number of this man in Algiers."

"So they couldn't see what other calls the burner phone made?" Grace asked.

"No," Laurent said, giving Maggie a dark look. "It is the reason why Maggie is not sitting in a police station tonight explaining how it is she received a phone call from a suspected murderer."

"You can hardly be pissed at *me*, Laurent," Maggie said with astonishment.

"And yet somehow I am," he said.

"Oh, go easy on her, Laurent," Grace said standing up, her plate untouched. "One thing I've learned today is that in the end we only have each other. And a little tenderness goes a very long way."

MAGGIE WATCHED Grace disappear into the children's bedroom where she would sleep for the night.

"She's really in a bad way. I wish I knew how to help her."

"She'll be fine. I spoke with Windsor. He only wants what's best for the girls. In her heart, so does Grace."

Maggie picked up her wine glass and leaned back into the couch feeling the exhaustion of the day settle into her bones.

"You have a little more to tell me, I think, *oui*?" Laurent said.

Maggie sighed. "I do. When it all came together, Laurent, it came together like a steam engine being hit by a tsunami."

Laurent stacked the dishes on the coffee table and poured more wine in each of their glasses.

"Go on," he said.

"You know I was trying to find Camille's daughter, right? I had this idea that it would give Delphine peace if I found her. Well, while I was trying to find out where she was, I discovered a real jaw dropper."

"Jaw...? I am not knowing this term."

"I found out that Noel was the love child of the Nazi everyone thought was carrying on with Camille."

Laurent frowned.

"Helmut Bauer has Noel's exact, identical nose. And it's a family trait because I met Bauer's grandson and he had the same nose—only he'd had it surgically altered." She watched a faint flush of annoyance flash across Laurent's cheeks. She probably shouldn't keep reminding him that she'd tracked down the German's grandson.

"Anyway, so that meant Noel's father wasn't the dimwitted teenager that got run over during the liberation of Paris," she said.

"You are sure about this?"

"Only a DNA test could be more sure. I'll show you the pictures. Noel is the spitting image of his goose-stepping daddy."

"Noel was hoping his father was my grandfather," Laurent said.

"Really?"

He shrugged. "He was hoping. He has reluctantly accepted Delphine's story about the boy on the bike."

"That just leaves the question of who his mother is. I knew it couldn't be Camille because she was executed eight months before Noel was born."

"Noel never thought it was Camille."

"And it couldn't be Georgette either."

Laurent frowned. "Why not?"

Maggie got up and went to the bedroom where she found the folder she was looking for in her suitcase. She brought it back to the living room.

"Delphine had medical files on all the sisters as children. I found it in the storage room."

"You have been busy."

"Georgette's file revealed that she was born with something called Turner Syndrome. I didn't think anything of it at the time because the note in the file said it was benign. I looked it up on the train ride back from Brétigny-sur-Orge. Women born with it are infertile."

"So Noel's mother is Delphine." Laurent shrugged. "He always suspected as much."

"And he's wrong. Delphine wasn't his mother either."

"Are you sure?"

Maggie pulled out the letter she'd found in the German's diary.

"I found this letter that his mother wrote to his father when Bauer was in prison. I thought he was awaiting trial but I'll tell you about that later. Anyway, the first thing I did when you were talking to the cops this afternoon was compare the letter with

Delphine's handwriting. It doesn't match. Delphine wasn't the German's lover. So she can't be Noel's mother."

"So we are back to square one."

"Maybe not." Maggie pulled out the diary that Dieter had sent her and handed it to Laurent. "In his diary, Helmut referred to his French lover by the initial cursive letter *C*. I know now it didn't stand for *Camille* but I don't know anyone else whose name starts with the letter C."

Laurent took the diary, his eyes dark and intractable. "It is not a 'C,'" he said quietly.

Maggie watched Laurent's face carefully. "It's hard for my American eye to decipher the European cursive," she said.

"It is the letter 'J,'" he said. He held his hand out for the letter and Maggie gave it to him. He glanced at it and handed it and the diary back, his eyes finally meeting hers. He nodded briefly in recognition of the handwriting.

Not Camille or Delphine.

But *Jacqueline*.

Laurent's grandmother.

Delphine betrayed her best friend—not to save herself—but to save her sister.

∼

MAGGIE WASHED her face and changed into her nightgown. She expected to fall dead asleep from her day but found herself surprisingly wound up, even after two bottles of wine. When Laurent came to bed, he slipped under the covers and drew her close to him. They were both exhausted but so grateful for each other and the safety of their family. Within the strong frame of her husband's arms and body against hers, Maggie fell quickly asleep.

Sometime in the middle of the night she awoke and realized the space beside her was vacant. She sat up and rubbed her eyes.

"Go back to sleep, *chèrie*," Laurent said, his voice soft and distant. He stood by the window and stared out into the Paris night. She knew he could see Notre-Dame from there.

"Talk to me, Laurent," she said.

He laughed quietly. "So American," he murmured.

Maggie got out of bed and went to him, putting her arm around his waist and pulling him to face her.

"Talk to me," she said.

He looked away again. "How could she have loved something so evil?"

Maggie took a long breath. *The inner lives of our parents, our grandparents. Do we ever truly know them?*

"There must have been another part of him that she saw," she said.

He looked at her with incredulity in his eyes. "Knowing what he'd done? How is it possible?"

"Turns out he may not have been all that evil."

"He was hung at Nuremberg! How could he not have been anything less than a monster?"

"When I was on the train coming back from Camille's village, I had some time on my hands so I decided to dig a little deeper into Helmut Bauer's story."

"*Pourquoi?*"

"Because every time I researched the Nuremberg trials online I saw that it was only concerned with top level Nazis and Gestapo—which Bauer definitely wasn't. Plus I couldn't find Bauer's name listed as one of the ones executed. There were only twelve. I finally realized I was only going on what that idiot André had told me."

"So he *wasn't* tried at Nuremberg?"

"No, he was—along with hundreds of others—*and* he was convicted *and* he died so I can see how André got it wrong. But Bauer was sentenced to two years at hard labor."

"How do you know all this?" Laurent stepped away from the

window and lit a cigarette, its end glowing harshly red in the dim light. "You reached out to your German friend again?"

"I sent him one little email and promised him it was the absolute last time I'd bother him but I really needed to know."

"You mean you really *wanted* to know."

Maggie ignored the comment. "Dieter told me that after Bauer finished his two years a lower German court wanting to de-Nazify the country tried him and a bunch of other low-level Nazi party members again. This time he got life. And he committed suicide."

"So much for double jeopardy."

"I guess in those days a lot of the rules didn't apply."

They stood quietly for a moment, the timeless never ceasing activity of cars and taxis still coasting silently below them on the Quai St-Michel. The illuminated façade of Notre-Dame loomed in the distance.

"That helps a little," Laurent admitted. He tore his gaze from the night scene outside the window and looked at Maggie. "I mismanaged this," he said. "Badly."

"Oh, Laurent. What could you have done?"

"Ever since I was a boy, all I ever felt from my grandmother was shame," he said, slowly shaking his head. "And all along it wasn't *me* she was ashamed of. It was herself."

Maggie led him back to bed and they sat together, his arms wrapped around her.

"My grandfather was a national war hero," he said. "Did he *know* his wife had carried on with the enemy?" He ran a hand through his hair. "The decorated Resistance hero married to a *collabo*? Delphine and my grandmother must have spent their entire lives guarding this secret."

"Are you sorry you know?"

He hesitated.

"Remember, Laurent, your grandmother committed no crime. She just fell in love with the wrong man at the wrong time."

Laurent's face relaxed as he realized what Maggie was saying.

"*Delphine* was the one who committed murder," he said.

"Yes, to save her sister. And she was punished a whole life long for it."

Maggie thought of Delphine's final words. *It is just.*

Dying by an act of betrayal herself, Delphine finally paid for her crime in full.

Maggie took Laurent's large hands in hers.

"Look at me, Laurent," she said urgently. "Those two children sleeping in the next bedroom have an amazing legacy. Nothing can take away the honor and bravery of who your grandfather was. And your grandmother was the head of every possible charity in Paris. She did so much good! I will tell both Mila and Jemmy that she was an amazing woman they should be proud to be related to. She was French, so she was passionate. I wouldn't hold that against her and you of all people shouldn't either."

Laurent smiled and drew her in for a kiss. When she pulled back, she could see the lines around his eyes had relaxed.

"As far as Delphine goes," Maggie said, "I'll do whatever I can to keep her name alive for our kids. Delphine didn't think she deserved it, but she was worth loving. One action—no matter how terrible—doesn't take that away. Not with family."

As they slipped back under the covers, Maggie could tell Laurent was still thinking, still processing everything that had happened.

"Do you think the painting is real?" he murmured.

He had watched Maggie carefully wrap the canvas to bring it with them to the apartment.

"Oh, it's real," Maggie said, yawning.

"Any idea where the damn thing came from?"

Maggie turned in bed and put her hand on his arm.

"I've thought about it a lot and my best guess is that your grandmother somehow got it from Helmut Bauer and kept it hidden until she became ill at which point she gave it to Delphine."

"Why the hell did my grandmother hang onto it?"

"She could hardly return it after the war in between all the parades being given in honor of her husband, the Resistance hero."

"And after my grandfather died?"

"Delphine told me that the things in that closet were your birthright. I think she was trying to protect you and Gerard. So when she gave me the key to the room, in a way she was saying she trusted me to protect her secret after she died."

"We're giving it back."

"Yes, of course. Anonymously. But nobody ever needs to know it was in your family attic for the last seventy years. And trust me, as soon as it's in a museum somewhere, I cannot wait to take Jemmy and Mila there to see it. I feel like it's ours in a way."

Laurent kissed her and lay back down, his back to her.

"*Faites 'tentions, ma chèrie.* I think that's exactly the kind of thinking that got the Nazis in trouble," he said.

56

Maggie sat on the leather bench in Terminal 2 of Charles DeGaulle Airport. She hesitated to go through security just yet since the moment she did marked the moment when she would become a single mother for two long months. It also signaled the time when she would have to listen to seven hours of nonstop self-recrimination from Grace, her traveling companion, and begin the anticipation of whatever drama was going on with Maggie's family in Atlanta.

No, Maggie was in no hurry to get to her gate.

Laurent stood holding Jemmy in one arm and Mila in the other. She knew he was relishing his time with them and that he would miss them but she also knew he would walk away from the airport with a spring in his step at the prospect of eight weeks without all the work of being the other half of a parenting tag team.

She couldn't blame him.

Grace was sitting beside Maggie and flipping through a French fashion magazine. She was dressed in her usual impeccable style. She wore figure-hugging knit slacks with a cropped silk jacket. On her feet she wore Todd driving mocs. She was the picture of unselfconscious elegance. Next to her, Zouzou sat, her hands in her lap, her little face serious and unhappy. Grace had agreed to bring Zouzou to Atlanta where Windsor and his new wife were now living and to stay as long as necessary to qualify for equal custody of her children.

And to see Taylor and apologize.

Maggie knew both Grace and Zouzou were heartbroken—Grace for her disastrous love affair with André and Zouzou for having to say goodbye to her beloved Beatrice. Maggie could only hope that they might at some point in the long flight turn to each other for comfort.

Maggie also knew that Laurent had spoken several times with Windsor and without diminishing Grace's bad behavior had reinforced to him the importance of not letting his anger distract him from the main point which was to heal the breach between Grace and her daughters.

Laurent walked over to Maggie. "It is time," he said. "You can wait at the gate. The children will want a snack before you board."

Maggie reached for Mila and Laurent set Jemmy on his feet. Instantly the little boy grabbed Maggie's carry on and began to roll it around the waiting area.

Laurent held Maggie's chin with his fingers and looked into her eyes. "You will return soon, *chèrie*," he said. "Your mother needs you. Your brother needs you."

"I know." Maggie was no longer afraid of finding Georgia too convenient in comparison to St-Buvard. In fact she was a little amazed she'd ever been concerned about that.

Her life was with Laurent. Wherever he was.

"Before you know it you will be back in time to help with the harvest," he said.

"We can hire more people this year, right?" Maggie asked. "Now that we're rich?"

He made a face. "We are not rich," he said. "The vineyard has been running at a loss for the last five years."

"Then maybe this summer isn't a good time for me to go to Atlanta."

He grinned. "Unfortunately, I have already told Monsieur Jemmy about the monster slide at Six Flags. You cannot back out now or you will answer to him."

Maggie raised up on her tiptoes and kissed him. "I'm not worried about going to Atlanta, darling Laurent," she said. "Not a bit."

He pulled her into a hug, with Mila still between them.

"Perhaps it is Atlanta that should be worried about *you*," he said with a smile.

Then kissed her thoroughly.

RECIPE FOR POT-AU-FEU

The streets of the Latin Quarter are virtually lined with brasseries that make excellent pot-au-feu, and since Laurent is from Paris it stands to reason his version would be exceptional.

You will need:

1 pound beef tenderloin
6 cups chicken stock
2 carrots, sliced cross-wise
2 parsnips, likewise sliced cross-wise
1 leek, white part only, quartered
2 celery stalks, PEELED, and quartered
One fresh sprig each: thyme, rosemary, parsley

Brown the meat in a heavy pot over medium heat. Add all other ingredients and simmer for 30 minutes. Once the veggies are fork-tender, remove the meat to a cutting board using a slotted spoon. Arrange the veggies in four shallow soup bowls, ladle broth over them from the pot. Slice the meat and give each bowl two slices each.

Whip up mashed potatoes laced with horseradish and put a major dollop in the middle of each bowl.

ABOUT THE AUTHOR

USA TODAY Bestselling Author Susan Kiernan-Lewis is the author of *The Maggie Newberry Mysteries,* the post-apocalyptic thriller series *The Irish End Games, The Mia Kazmaroff Mysteries,* and *The Stranded in Provence Mysteries,* and *An American in Paris Mysteries.* If you enjoyed *Murder in the Latin Quarter,* please leave a review saying so on your purchase site.

Visit my website at www.susankiernanlewis.com or follow me at Author Susan Kiernan-Lewis on Facebook.

Printed in Great Britain
by Amazon